STRANDS OF TIME AND MAGIC

WEAVERS OF DESTINY

BOOK ONE

ANDREW PLATTEN

Dedication

To Darielle, my wonderful wife who supports all my crazy projects and who helped me make this one better.

Note to Reader:

This book follows British spelling and grammar conventions, reflecting the author's British heritage.

Thank you for your understanding. Happy reading!

Chapter One

The 470th Year of the Morde Dynasty–The Year of the Unravelling

The cat froze, lifted her head, and sampled the air. Her hackles spiked, her back arched, and her claws worried the ground–a predator hunted ahead.

Edging backward, she slunk deep into the darkness beneath the stone horse trough. From that vantage point, she could see that the thick shadows beside the smithy concealed a hooded man. He had no scent, made no noise, and the snowflakes drifted through his body, as if he was made from smoke.

Run or hide? Her instincts warred within. She inhaled to fuel her loudest howl. The hunter in the shadows swung his gaze her way and smiled. Calm flooded the cat, and she released the breath without a sound. She forgot her panic, confident she could continue her journey, after a short delay.

I can wait, she thought stoically. *I can be as patient as . . . well, a cat.*

Levinial resumed his vigil. He gripped the amulet and its chain, ready to depart, yet his instincts made him pause.

Back away, or risk more?

The cat had spotted his bodiless form, and he had reacted quickly enough to still her fear. If any humans saw him in this form, it could cause the chaos he was here to prevent. People could not be controlled with such ease.

Clumsy weavers have destroyed many worlds.

The cat swivelled her ear to isolate a sound which Levinial heard over the mind-link he maintained to calm her–it was the distant scraping and low rumble of a cart's approach. Wooden wheels grinding on wet stone and the plodding steps of an ox and two tired men, she sensed. Its slow pace meant the cart was laden. As for its contents, she could only smell woodsmoke, as the breeze was blowing the wrong way to reveal what the cart was carrying.

Levinial urgently sought an escape route. The snow had thickened, but not enough to cover his retreat. If he used the amulet to open a travel portal, its unnatural glow would be seen by the approaching men and start rumours whose ripples might disturb things.

Too late, I'm trapped.

He slunk deeper into the darkness. Since his body had no substance, he left no tracks in the snow. He would wait it out, splitting his attention between the approaching danger and the eighty or so life-links on the roof top of the warehouse. A roof top tavern, he surmised.

It won't be long now.

One of the life-links had the tremor that the aggar sensed, indicating an involvement in the pending catastrophe. Another was approaching the building, but was some way off. If they interacted, he would know this is a critical moment and he would return in the flesh.

The cart emerged from the swirl, pulling his attention back to the scene before him. It was piled high with ale hops.

The desire for beer does not respect the seasons on this world. The memory of tasting real food gnawed at him.

One man was old and crooked and, like the ox, indifferent to the cut of the wind. The other man, a teenager, had a grim expression, with hands wedged into his armpits. His fluffy attempt at a beard gave no protection from the wind's bitter bite.

"You're makin' the delivery, Joff." The older man coughed as he reached under his winter coat for his pipe. "I'll have nuttin' to do w' that place."

Joff sighed. "You're daft, Old Grob. You can't catch magic from an evercold. Just help me unload, w' ya?" Joff had wasted breath on this point a hundred times before, and both men knew it was merely a protest, not an argument.

Old Grob walked away and took up a position in front of the smithy, oblivious of the ghostly shadow a mere six feet behind him as it shrank down into a crouch. He struck his flint and lit his finger of barr root, sucking quickly to help it catch. The sulphur flare illuminated Levinial's face, but no one looked his way. Grob's first puff sent a cloud into the air to challenge the snow and sent his body into a fit of coughing.

Levinial let his mind connect to Grob and Joff's to read their thoughts. A task easy in this form, but much harder when he manifested fully.

Joff shook his head at Grob's stubbornness, then turned and walked hunch shouldered to the large delivery doors, where he rang the bell. From a sack tied to his belt he sprinkled four handfuls of grain into a food trough for Dolly. Anymore and the ox would turn as intractable as Grob, refusing to pull the cart home.

"If you could catch magic from an evercold, Old Grob, no man in his right mind would work here, would he?" Joff said. "I saw a girl have her magic skriked right out of her by a full mage once. He pinned her with hardened air and consumed every drop while she screamed like a rat's nest on fire. Then he left her to die.

"I still witness it in my dreams, I do. But you ain't gonna catch magic from an evercold." He enunciated the last sentence as if talking to a child. Everyone with any smarts knew that if they developed *affinity*, they had best keep quiet about it. Either that or become strong enough to fight off the predators seeking to boost their power by taking yours.

It saddened Levinial that this world's powerful magic users preyed on the weak, but it wasn't uncommon.

Joff's grumbling was lost in the snow—Grob was puffing and looking away—so the teenager turned back to the cart, resigned.

As the cat watched the spectacle, Levinial sensed her thoughts. She sided with the old man. *You don't do any work you don't want to do*, she thought. *Just like me.*

The loading bay's heavy wooden doors opened and the night porter warily stuck out his lamp, followed by a bald, tattooed head. Spilling out with the light were a thousand complex fragrances from the warehouse's five floors of storage and processing benches.

"Cautious! Who's there?" Jake shouted. He was an Abbonite, marked by his prefacing sentences that verbalised his emotions—or suggested emotions for others—as much as his inkwork.

"Late delivery of hops, Jake," Joff said. "Dolly got wilful and refused to pull the cart for hours, Ag curse her."

"Calm! The cycling elevator's not available for deliveries at this hour. I'll help you unload just inside the door here, and the day shift will see your hops upstairs in the morning. But you'll need to get your proofer next time you come through, OK?" It was normal procedure to wait for a receipt if they delivered late. Old Grob waved his half-smoked finger in acceptance. Joff's eyeroll conveyed that Grob was work shy and hiding behind his supposed fear of the magic that maintained the evercold.

Jake snorted. "Reassuring and slightly offended! Mage Wickham made Haxley's evercold. Dangerous to question his workmanship. It won't leak and turn you into a charmer, Grob. Only a full mage like Wickham can tie off magic to leave a thing so it stays warm or cold or light or dark or floating with no wires. And they do it so they never leak! Ever."

Another bell rang, summoning Jake to a door on the city side of the warehouse where patrons of the Crow's Nest Tavern entered after deliveries had concluded for the day. The city side doorman signalled that the three men and a woman who were removing their heavy coats had paid their door fee, so Jake walked them over to the cycling elevator.

Levinial cursed himself; one of the arrivals had the tremoring link he sought but he was trapped too far to observe her likeness or touch her mind. He drew what information he could from the others, but Joff was thinking more about the building than the woman as he lugged sacks in through the doorway.

As one of the twelve large loading platforms rotated up from the shaft below, three of the patrons stepped aboard as it passed floor level. The fourth shied, his eyes wide. The man had rushed in and hung one leg out over the platform, then lost his nerve and pivoted, crossing himself and huffing as he stepped back with a curse on his lips.

Jake knew what to say, as he said it to most people who rode the paternoster for the first time. He calmed the man down and stepped onto the next platform with him. He rode it for a floor and a half then hopped across to a descending platform and rode back to ground level.

The first three patrons, including the woman with the tremor, had ascended past openings on each floor, peering at the vast array of goods that awaited sorting and shipment before stepping off at the rooftop tavern to await their friend. Their platform looped over the top and began its rumbling descent.

Levinial touched Jake's mind next, but he was thinking of the tavern, not the patrons. Jake knew that the paternoster's ability to move goods quickly had revolutionised trade and made the recently deceased Jin Barrow his fortune and elevated him (a frequent pun) to the Haxley Council of Aldermen. He gave the donkey powering the paternoster a carrot and then returned to help Joff, who already had half the cart unloaded and stacked inside the doors.

The Crow's Nest attracted locals and travellers alike; even the occasional member of the gentry came to enjoy it. Raegan Fenn had created and operated the one-of-a-kind rooftop pub in a space rented from Modwyn Barrow, the late Alderman Barrow's daughter and heir. The unparalleled views, keenly priced and excellent fare, along with entertainment as good as anything in Haxley, were a draw in themselves.

Another alluring feature in the winter was that the heat created as a by-product from the evercold was diverted up through vents to warm the rooftop patrons when the chill set in. Jake warmed himself on the vents, too. In the summer it could be used to warm the kitchen's water. The two log fires set among the pub's tables burned primarily for atmosphere, most of their heat escaping into the night from under the canvas awnings.

Interesting information, but not helpful, thought Levinial.

After a sweaty half-bell of two men doing the work of three, the hops were unloaded. Dolly was fed and well-watered and showing signs of wanting to be off to her next feed. Joff got to ride on the cart while Grob led the ox.

"The least I could do," Old Grob said. Throughout it all the snow had thickened, the cat had dozed, and the shadowed figure remained motionless.

Grob led Dolly just one building north before stopping against the stonework of the monastery. He banged on a one-foot-square solid wood panel set deep into the wall. After a moment the panel opened, and a pink, bearded face peered out. No words were exchanged, the ritual common and the night cold. Old Grob pushed a grubby coin into the monk's hand and received a growler of ale in return. The panel snapped shut, protection from the weather and any potential muggers, and the cart rolled onwards with enough lubrication on board to see out the evening.

Full dark returned as Jake closed the warehouse door. Levinial relaxed and stepped forward. His weaver-mind would sort through his observations. He had gleaned most of the conversation from the thoughts of the three men; he would learn this world's language once he manifested fully.

There!

The two life-links he had been monitoring on the rooftop interacted. Their sudden flickering was clear. Levinial's weaver-mind recorded his deductions about this location and events while he knelt and smiled at the cat. He couldn't touch it in this form though he wished he could.

Should I slip back an hour and reposition myself to see the woman? No, I've disturbed you enough. I will return and observe once I manifest.

Standing, he activated the portal and stepped back in time, following the trail that had led him to the rooftop.

Chapter Two

The 467ᵗʰ Year of the Morde Dynasty–Three Years Earlier

Lu paused and let her senses expand outwards. *Yes, this is a good place to bathe,* she thought. Lu and her companion cat, Shanna, had travelled fast, running for two days, and their destination was just over a mile ahead. They had followed the Cray River since dawn, through canyons and marshes, and for the past six hours, through groves of spanion trees. The marsh mud had stained Lu's clothing, and the spanion's barbed spores were hooked in that mud. It would not do for a Mobi'dern to arrive in such a dishevelled state. Her cat groomed herself as they travelled, so she had no need to bathe. She didn't love fast-moving water either, so Lu offered a thought to Shanna.

Range?

Of course, Shanna replied.

Lu and Shanna always offered ideas to each other rather than give commands. How a Mobi'dern communicated with their prida, their partner animal, varied, their style highly influenced by how their communion had fared. At a communion a fledgling warrior was introduced to the gathering of beasts that were mature enough to partner. Many factors contributed to who, if any, made a mental connection. A warrior might stride boldly into the group or approach cautiously and sit quietly. The warrior's mind might be calm or anxious or have an affinity for cats, dogs, birds, and so on. This blend of conditions might cause one of the animals to claim their Mobi'dern—for the animal was always the initiator—and the communion, a literal meeting of minds, would be achieved.

The fiercely independent prida was expected to contribute to decisions in the symbiotic pairing, and this extended to the nature of their communication style. In some cases, the animal was responsive to direct commands, and in others it was more of a negotiation. Lu and Shanna both felt their offering style suited them best.

The river was some thirty feet wide, its surface deceptively calm in the centre where the current was strongest. At the edges the water splashed where it gushed across rapids, creating shallow, swirling pools. On the far bank the trees hung over the water, forming dark pockets, but the toing-and-froing of hummingbirds and the fluttering of butterflies felt benign, not sinister. Through their connection Lu sensed Shanna was at ease, so she felt confident no danger lurked in that darkness.

They were at an elbow in the river, on its inside bank, following a well-used deer trail, so close to the place they had called home for the past year that this was territory she knew well. With the river curving away on either side of her, Lu could disrobe without being observed. In the unlikely event someone approached, Shanna or Lu's own highly developed senses would give her ample warning.

Naked, Lu took her dirty garments into the water and sat in a small side pool to scrub them clean. When she was satisfied, she hung them to dry on a branch just over the broad red stone on which she had reverently laid out her weapons. *Just time for a swim*, she thought. A brief connection to Shanna confirmed the cat was loosely following the scent of a hare.

When she had been offered the chance to range, Shanna felt released from the previous offer to escort. To escort, Shanna would remain close to Lu, perhaps six or seven quick bounds away, and follow her lead. She had been escorting all day, and despite Lu sharing some beef jerky as they travelled, she was ravenous. But "range" didn't mean "hunt." It meant searching covertly around the area, up to a mile or so at times, and reporting anything unusual. But should she happen upon a meal she could take down without its cries giving away her presence, she would satisfy her hunger.

After twenty minutes Shanna was almost a mile ahead and hunched behind a fallen log at the edge of a circular clearing. In the centre of the clearing was a hare. It was unaware of her, and upwind, although the breeze was light and its direction varied. Shanna's mouth watered, but she would wait until the hare turned away before pouncing to maximise the chance of a silent kill.

On the far side of the clearing, the trees were sparse, and Shanna could glimpse their destination, their temporary home, perhaps another quarter of a mile beyond the treeline. It was a complex of buildings from which the familiar scent of many people and animals poured. Close by, around the clearing, she sensed many birds and a large deer, which was too big to take silently, but no people. The hare took a couple of steps towards her and then turned sideways.

Patience.

The sun would sink below the trees in another hour or so, and Shanna felt that as the temperature dropped, clouds would form to bring rain. The hare was almost finished munching the small yellow plant that held its attention. Then it would move, but which way? Shanna sensed Lu swimming in the distance, relaxed but enjoying challenging herself against the stream.

Why be in the water? The cat thought. *Yuck.*

The hare turned and stepped away. Now was the moment, as it was already past time for Shanna to begin circling back behind Lu to confirm no danger was approaching from their flank or their rear. Shanna sank lower, rehearsing her leap in her mind and confirming where she would land before falling on her prey. If she were hunting rather than ranging, Shanna would have also spied out the hare's escape routes and planned ways to cut it off. But there would be no chasing, as she was ranging.

In the fraction of a second before her leap, Shanna froze at the urgent behest of a deep part of her mind that sensed a danger her physical senses had missed and couldn't pinpoint. Even as her hackles rose in response to the sensation, a doorway of green light appeared on the far side of the clearing. It flexed, and a man stepped out of the light, his back to Shanna and her prey. The man had not been in the woods a second before, of this Shanna was certain. The doorway shrank to a pinprick and then vanished, and the man stood observing the distant buildings. His arrival had been so soundless that it had gone unnoticed by the hare, who munched on a root. If the intruder was aware of Shanna's presence, he did not show it.

Alarm? Shanna urgently offered to Lu, who stopped mid-stroke and looked back towards her distant cat. Shanna sent a mental image of the man.

I see a man watching the settlement, Lu replied. *Where is the danger?*

Shanna was confused by her response. *It's that he's not here.*

Shanna backed away from the clearing and was soon sprinting back to Lu, terrified for herself but also desperate to protect Lu, though from what she wasn't sure.

Lu received a jumble of confusing offerings: *no scent, ghost man, extreme danger, his cape doesn't move with the breeze, appeared from nowhere through a door that was no door . . .*

By the time Shanna reached the bend in the river, Lu had dressed in her spare outfit and packed her damp clothing. Shanna found her crouched with weapons drawn, surveying the woods. Nothing seemed to have followed Shanna, who slid to a halt and turned to challenge the trees through which she had just fled, panting to dispel heat and recapture her breath. They stood side by side, tense, their senses stretched around them, for ten full minutes. Lu tried to interpret what Shanna had seen, but the cat's mind remained jumbled and disturbed. In the end they both offered the same thought. *Let's press on to the settlement but circle well to the south and give the clearing a wide berth.*

Chapter Three

Levinial could feel the twist in the timeline start here.

Yes, this is the nexus. This day would see something crucial happen within the dwellings a short walk from this clearing. It would start the chain of events that would eventually cause the Unravelling he was here to prevent. He'd known chaos to start with something as innocent as someone pausing to look at a frolicking horse and by doing so, disrupt the future. Yet this nexus felt different. Darker. Complex.

If he wanted to witness this day's events, he would travel back several moons and manifest in physical form and acclimatise to this world's languages and customs. Then, seek a disguise and excuse for being here that would raise no attention from those ensnared in events to come. Experience from countless missions for the gods' railed against that thought, and he would listen to his intuition. His mere presence could cause the nexus to move elsewhere.

Levinial activated the amulet, stepped into the flow of time and examined the hundred or so life-links of people in the settlement. As he observed for the next few hours, he saw the chaos start and one of the links begin its telltale tremor that unsettled the whole timeline going forward. He would hunt earlier in the timeline for the optimal moment to become involved.

Chapter Four

In view of the clearing recently vacated by Levinial lay the Health Advocate's Campus, known as the HAC. Ostensibly a school funded by the Council of Magical Law, the campus was a fortress. As twenty-two of the hundred or so HAC residents were healers-in-training—charmers licenced and protected by the state—the campus was a target for two groups: predatory mages desperate to skrike to consolidate their magical power, and Wigs, militant conservatives whose avid beliefs demanded that charmers be eradicated for the good of society.

Four hundred years ago, Raile was an independent country which had been dominated for centuries by the Karron Dynasty. They were mages of lacklustre power, so the Karrons jealously maintained magic as a power exclusive to the family. They achieved this by ruthlessly hunting down and killing lesser mages and charmers. They employed agents authorised to have suspects arrested and taken for testing and subsequent execution if found to have "affinity," as their magical ability was called. These agents wore blue wigs, constructed from the dyed hair of the charmers they had captured. The length of their wigs was a point of pride and a gruesome symbol to all.

Even after the Karron Dynasty ended, the Wig mentality they ingrained in the population persisted in many of Raile's citizens. Mages of great power were revered in Raile, but "crafty, dirty charmers with an advantage over normal folk" remained highly stigmatised with a viciousness unseen elsewhere in the nation. Wigs, as the ultra-conservatives were known, were rare in the progressive regions of Mordeland, but in the backward region hosting the HAC, they were both common and bold, despite the outlawing of the blue hair custom.

This antipathy was why, in their wisdom, the Council of Magical Law had chosen Raile for their grand experiment. If charmers could be trained to be effective healers and then sent out into the community to do good—assuming a way could be found to keep them alive—eventually all communities would embrace the model. This would have several benefits, such as giving charmers a valid station in society, supplementing non-magical healers, of which there were few, and relieving full mages from the burden of healing, which they hated and did predominantly for the wealthy. Convincing charmers they were safe to practise openly without fear would be a challenge too.

The twelve-foot-tall walls surrounding the campus and the solid, guarded gates were a physical manifestation of the site's defences, but its real strength came from the full division of Mobi'dern and their prida billeted at the site. The eighteen warriors and their beasts patrolling the property and surrounding area, complemented by thirty city guards from Nuulan—Mordeland's distant capital—had proven a sufficient deterrent. There had never been an attack on the campus throughout its five-year history.

"But this is precisely why I must try, Tuli," Gideon argued. "Lord Arkly's wife might lose the child before Mage Dion arrives from the capital. This is our chance to prove charmer healing is viable. Saving the child of Raile's ruler would surely convince many of the value of our mission, no?" Tuli's hand hovered unconsciously near her throat. Her brother was blind to the fact that Arkly was as dangerous as Gideon was rash.

"You've seen Arkly's contempt for us, Gideon. If there was anyone else nearby who could treat her, they surely would. The HAC's non-magical doctors, our teachers, are the only medics available for leagues and are doing their best, but she's beyond them. And now she's too sick to travel," Tuli explained for the third time.

"Exactly," Gideon replied, missing her point yet again. Tuli felt that Arkly's anxiety was so high that it was a dangerous moment to press their agenda. "And we could help. *I* could help. I reminded our principal of this just an hour ago. She pointed out that Lord Arkly was even having food and water brought into the HAC from outside rather than risk tainting himself by consuming ours. If the lord won't even trust our water, she said, he would never let us near his wife. She sounded scared, if you ask me. We need to be bolder, Tuli. Force the issue."

Tuli grabbed her brother's arm. His impatience terrified her. "Promise me that you won't do anything without Principal Lydd's permission, Gideon. Promise me!"

"Of course, Tuli. That would be pointless anyway. I don't have enough knowledge about her specific symptoms. I would need some guidance from one of the medics attending her before I could be useful."

Tuli knew her brother's pride was hurt. He had worked hard and learnt anatomy and the healing arts as well as any village doctor. He could leave the HAC today, and any village would welcome him, if they didn't know he was a charmer. But his pride had allowed him to be talked into becoming the HAC's celebrated example, his likeness displayed across the region despite her urgings against it. Now his notoriety was working against him, as people did not want to be treated by a charmer. He was trapped, but rather than stepping back and letting things settle, he had become arrogant and desperate. She had finally admitted this flaw to herself but was terrified of how this knowledge altered her view of him.

The gate horn sounded, signalling someone arriving at the complex. Tuli walked across their shared living space to the window. In the distance she saw a female Mobi'dern heading towards the compound using the long, loping run that allowed them to travel great distances with little rest while her cat bounded along beside her. She recognised the pair; she had become good friends with them both over the past year while they had been assigned to the HAC.

"Lu is back, Gideon. Mage Dion won't be far behind, and this will soon be over. We can get back to studying." The relief in her voice annoyed her brother.

"What's the point of studying if all we're allowed to do is heal ourselves? I'm wasting the life Ag gave me, and so are you, Tuli. You have more magic than I do—more than anyone here—and you're the better medic too. But for what?" Gideon's voice rose to a shout with frustration, and Tuli glanced at the window, wondering how far it carried. Gideon marched over to the door and pulled it open. He stepped into the courtyard, then slammed the door behind him. Tuli poured herself a cup of cold water, added a calming herb, then downed it and followed him outside.

Jeef, the leader of the Mobi'dern division, stood in a battlement atop the gate, trading hand signals with the approaching warrior. The two dozen or so guards, healers, and servants who were in the courtyard busy with activities wondered about the news.

There was a commotion on the far side of the courtyard as the doors to the quarters that Lord Arkly had commandeered were flung open. The region's leader marched out into the sunlight, followed by two of his personal guard. Arkly wasn't a tall man, and he compensated for his lack of stature with aggression. His silver robe's shoulders were tailored an inch wider and two inches taller than needed, and the gold stripes in the cloth ran vertically to make the most of his height. Even his hair was swept backwards and upwards, held by stiffening oils, adding two more inches to his stature, and his beard was shaped to widen his face, maintaining a semblance of proportion to his look.

A man dressed in the long purple robes of a Bredden cleric followed at a more dignified pace. He paused and considered the mood of the quickly increasing crowd. His own face was unreadable, but several people around him averted their eyes from him. Arkly's abrupt appearance and aggressive movement brought Jeef's hawk down from its rooftop perch to settle on the gate, protecting his mistress's back. Jeef calmed him with a thought, but he remained watchful.

"What's the news, Da-Jeef?" Lord Arkly asked, his tone impatient though he respected Jeef's honorific title. That Arkly's manners were impeccable with non-charmers further rankled Gideon. Jeef took her time, passing a final signal to Lu, who was approaching quickly, then turned and swung down from the tower, landing in front of the lord. She stood at ease and adjusted her sword belt, paying no attention to the two guards who had positioned themselves on either side of Arkly, both of whom were bristling at her lack of urgency and respect in answering their lord's question.

"Not good, Lord Arkly, not good. It seems Mage Dion fell off his horse partway here. His back is broken, he needs a healer himself. His apprentices have been sent for, the senior to come directly here and the junior to attend to Dion himself. Lu came ahead with the news. I doubt we will see the apprentice for three days, and that's assuming nothing else goes wrong."

Arkly put his hands to his head, then turned and paced. The growing gathering parted, and the cleric stepped up to stand next to Arkly. Jeef adjusted her stance, turning to face the priest as her hawk dropped off the gate and glided down to settle on her partner's shoulder. The cleric didn't flinch as the hawk's intense eyes stared into his. Instead, he spoke in a hiss, disdain dripping from his mouth. "Your warrior's incompetence at letting harm come to the healer could be considered by some as criminal, Da-Jeff. Don't you agree?"

"My warriors accompanied the group to protect them from bandits, not themselves, nor to give riding lessons, Cleric Oliver." The warrior's lips flattened slightly, but her voice remained steady.

Principal Lydd pushed her way through the crowd. "Sire, this is terrible news. I don't think Lady Arkly has that much time. We need to do something to relieve the pressure on her heart."

Arkly spun on the unfortunate woman, his rage spilling over. "But as you yourself explained, Lydd, without a mage her worsening condition means you might lose my wife and child, but to save either one, you must risk the other. Are you certain she can't travel? Even lying flat in a cart?"

"Sire, I wish she could, but her blood pressure is so high, I would worry about moving her from her bed to the cart, let alone further. I can't stress how delicate things are at present."

Tuli had moved in front of her brother, to intercept him should he be stupid enough to try to join the conversation, but as Lu and Shanna loped into the compound, the cat slowed and dropped at Tuli's feet, rolling over, expecting to be petted like a kitten. The timing of the distraction was unfortunate, as Gideon could contain himself no longer. He stepped past his sister, over the cat, and strode over to confront Arkly.

"But sire, there *is* another option," Gideon pleaded. All heads swivelled his way. "If high pressure of the blood is the issue, many of us here can help your wife." Arkly's personal guard reacted to Gideon's outburst by stepping between him and their lord and drawing their swords.

"You'll not even be in the same room as my wife, you filthy charmer," Arkly said. "I'll see you hang first." He took two steps towards Gideon, and the guard nearest the healer pushed Gideon to the ground.

"Gideon, shut up and go back to your room," Lydd warned. Tuli rushed over and knelt by her brother, but he pushed her away and struggled to his feet.

"Arkly, your stupid pride and outdated ways will literally be the death of your family," Gideon said. "Please see reason. This isn't a difficult medical problem requiring a full mage."

The crowd went quiet. Even Arkly's guards froze, caught between Gideon's logic and his disrespectful tone. Arkly appeared to withdraw into himself for a moment before stepping forward to stand between his guards. Gideon mistook Arkly's mood, assuming his offer was being considered, and completely missed the malevolence that had surfaced in the lord's eyes.

"That's it, Lord Arkly," Gideon said, softening his tone. "Please accept my help. We can do good work here."

Arkly grabbed the sword from his guard and thrust it into Tuli's side as she attempted to drag her brother back.

"Heal that tainted bitch, healer. If you can, then perhaps we can talk."

Gideon turned to his sister as she coughed blood into his face, her arms clutching at him for support and her eyes wide with shock.

Gideon pressed his hand over the wound and flung his magic into it, but he already knew such an injury was beyond him.

"But this is different—"

"Filthy blight!" Arkly yelled, cutting Gideon off as he turned to go back to his room, but he managed only two steps, the last of his life.

"No!" Lu yelled both mentally and out loud as Shanna tore into the lord, severing his neck with one bite of her powerful jaws.

Vengeance! Shanna thought to Lu.

After a few moments of shock, every warrior in the courtyard exploded into action. Swords were pulled, Mobi'dern faced off with Arkly's men, and the city watch spun in confusion, not knowing whom their loyalties belonged to but aware that the Mobi'dern were the biggest threat to their lives.

"Kill that cat!" the cleric yelled. One of Lord Arkly's personal guards shook himself from his stupor and lunged for Shanna, sword held high, but Jeef stepped into him, grabbed his wrist, and tossed him to the floor. Shanna dropped low and spun around to face the approaching threats, her teeth bared.

What have you done? Lu asked.

Why do they attack? Shanna replied.

You've killed a lord, Lu said.

But he killed our friend, and we defend our friends, don't we?

Lu felt chastened but also understood that in the world of clan politics, it might not be that simple.

Run to the woods. Forage and avoid people. I will come for you. It was a rare command, not an offer. Reluctantly at first, the cat loped away, but within a few strides of the gate, she was at full speed and, before anyone else could react, out of arrow range.

Cleric Oliver scowled at Jeef, hatred pouring from him. The courtyard came to a tense standoff, everyone waiting for instruction on what to do next. The cleric's sharp nose for politics helped him react first.

"Da-Jeef, arrest that woman. She killed Lord Arkly. Do it, or I'll have the Nuulan guard do it."

Jeef didn't want to accept instruction from the cleric, but she didn't want him to take the initiative either. Glaring at Lu, she gave a curt series of hand signals. Lu held Da-Jeef's eye, wondering if protecting a friend would extend to her, but after a long moment the warrior swallowed her anger and unclipped her sword belt. At another signal, two more Mobi'dern stepped forward. One accepted Lu's sword, treating it with deference, before they escorted her to the barracks.

"Principal Lydd, detain all the charmers until we decide what to do here," the priest instructed. The flustered HAC leader didn't hesitate. Although her tone softened his words, she echoed his command.

"Have all the trainees wait in the main hall, please," she told the captain of the Nuulan guard. "And Da-Jeef, please have your group return to the barracks for now." The leader of the Mobi'dern didn't want to leave Lydd alone with the fanatical cleric and was about to say so when one of Arkly's guards grabbed Gideon, attempting to pull him away from his failing attempt to save his sister.

"You heard the cleric. Either leave that witch or pick her up and take her with—" He didn't finish his sentence because Jeef grabbed the thumb of the hand that was pulling at Gideon's shoulder. The snap was clearly audible, followed by the man's cry of agony. The other member of Arkly's personal guard looked like he was about to go to his colleague's aid, but Jeef's hawk let out a cold, piercing screech that stopped him in his tracks.

"Enough of this. Stop it!" Lydd yelled. "Da-Jeef, help Gideon get his sister to the infirmary. The rest of the trainees to the hall, warriors to their barracks." It was the reminder of poor Tuli's undignified and desperate situation that made up Jeef's mind. A flurry of hand signals spurred the warriors into action. They sheathed their swords and left the courtyard, two of them helping Gideon carry his sister to their quarters under the smiling gaze of the Bredden cleric.

Chapter Five

The 470th Year of the Morde Dynasty

City folk regarded Rostal as the jewel of the region of Lanthe, and few dared argue with city folk, at least within earshot, as the customer was always right. But the lack of a good argument did not amount to agreement. Most townies, even those from other townships, asserted that the jewel of Lanthe was Haxley. It was bigger than other towns, more affluent, had a cathedral, and boasted several establishments otherwise found only in the city: a glassblower, a bookseller, a dentist, and a locksmith. And if one still harboured doubts, some would point to Haxley's small, tidy garrison as proof of something worth protecting. But the down-to-earth farmers know Lanthe's true gem was Plainhand Estate.

Rambling over the most fertile one-fifteenth of Lanthe's landmass, the roughly rectangular estate was 80 percent arable, growing barr root mainly except for a sliver used for crops to feed the estate's 800-strong workforce. The remaining 20 percent was grassland and buildings for the horse stock. With stables and barns aplenty, as well as farriers, coopers, smithies, and all the skills required to maintain horses and farming, including growing their own hay and grain, Plainhand's core business was independent of most suppliers.

Plainhand had invested in quality accommodations, not just bunkhouses but also a general store for the staff and a small stage that troupers and entertainers could use as they passed through. They even brewed a good ale, lovingly called Plainhand Sludge, due to its heavy, hazy nature.

If one was to walk the length of the estate, it would take two full days, and they would encounter folk who kept their spaces tidy and productive, who would welcome visitors to their hearth and table in exchange for news, a story, or some simple chores.

At the northern end of the estate was the transportation compound, owners' and management accommodations (which were no grander than those of the workers), and central kitchen, which ran from early to late, turning out hot meals for those within easy distance, perhaps half of the estate's population.

That particular morning saw a quarter moon winking through thinning grey clouds, which were drifting south on a wind that seemed exhausted from blowing through the past week and was ebbing at last.

Heavy overnight snowfall meant a few would start work at fourth bell, an hour earlier than most of the community. The road to Haxley needed to be cleared ahead of the daily procession of wagons and carts. The market town lived and died by its reputation, and the Plainhand family's Wispy Weed brand was pivotal to Haxley's success. It would not be late.

Leaving first, with reheated stew and yesterday's bread in their bellies, were two men driving four plough horses of a breed known for their strength, reliable nature, and most of all, their keenness to work. Unlike oxen, which were stronger but often uncooperative, the horses were ideal snow pushers.

Pushing rather than pulling a plough was a skill in itself, and they were an experienced team. They were well out of sight before the fifth bell roused the Plainhand workforce en masse, and soon all the kitchen stoves and ovens were hot and productive. A similar plough team would have left Haxley heading south to the farm, leading the empty carts back to refill, and everyone wagered on where on the road the two processions would meet.

Since war was looming between Lanthe and its southern neighbour, Backalar, all the main roads had seen a sharp increase in banditry. In hard times, when the guard—Lanthe's rangers who policed the rural areas—were thinned to support the army, the dross slipped out from the rocks they'd hidden under to prey on honest folk. Losses had been high for some, but the Plainhands had invested early and retained the Mobi'dern. They were expensive, assuming one could hire them at all, but they offered the best security. As a result, Plainhand Estate was the only business not raided by bandits. In fact, there had been few attempts, as the reputation of the Mobi'dern was fierce.

Although the plough team had no carts to hijack, one of the Mobi'dern walked with them anyway, her large cat scouting unseen along the trail ahead, unworried by the weather in its thick grey coat.

The road to Haxley followed the snowmelt-bloated Hax river through farmland that seemed to have been pressed into many gentle undulations that rarely amounted to a significant hill. Millers and other business owners lining the Hax relied on its current to power their waterwheels. They were already up and adjusting the rake of their paddles and digging their own paths out to the road so they could fall in behind the Plainhand's wagons and take their own products to market.

Midway between the wagon train and the plough, two women rode alone, their argument warming the morning air. Raegan raised her voice in exasperation, causing the pony beneath her to skitter nervously.

"Brylee Plainhand, you didn't even like him, for Ag's sake. You let Jacon Dees take you to bed, just because he dared you. All he had to do was imply you were too scared to do the night dance, and you pretty much threw him over your big shoulder and dragged him into the sack! Admit it."

"That's nonsense, Rae," Brylee replied, although her blush spoke otherwise. "We never *did it*. And it wasn't a bed. We just groped in the dark. And besides, I liked him a little bit." It was like they were twelve instead of their mid-twenties, still arguing about boys.

"You only stopped because you heard your pa come into the stables while you hid in the loft. If Daddy hadn't broken the mood, how far would you have gone, eh? Would your pride sell your virtue to prove yourself braver than stupid Jacon?" But Brylee didn't look chastened; she looked angry. Raegan reminded herself that honey worked better than pepper with her best friend and changed tack, softening her voice.

"Look, my point is, your parents *are* overcompensating for Nalik's death. He was their firstborn and heir to the business, their pride and joy. So they swaddle you in sacking and try to stop you from growing up. You're a talented force of nature with something to prove, and you rail against them. Especially when they credit your brilliant ideas to Nalik or ignore them completely. You have single-handedly doubled Plainhand's profit but get no recognition, and that's unfair.

"But it's become more than that, Brylee. Anyone has only to hint you're not up to a challenge and you go cods to the wall to prove them false. I'm right, aren't I?"

Brylee yanked Summer to a halt and threw off her hood, bristling. She stood tall in the saddle and huffed as she searched for the words that would convince Raegan—and herself—that the accusation was false. To add insult to injury, the subject of Brylee's immediate anger had kicked her pony into a trot and was moving away with . . . with . . . what was that? The faintest of smirks tugging at her cold, rosy cheeks?

"And when you toss your head, flare your nostrils, and create clouds of steam in the cold morning air, you remind me of Summer!" Raegan shouted without looking back. Was that laughter, too? Brylee bit back the retort forming in her mouth. Her eyebrows were wrenched together, and her lips were a tight, flat line. She massaged her temples, shaking her head and taking stock.

The penny suddenly dropped that Raegan was pulling her leg, and Brylee's tantrum evaporated despite her desire to keep it stoked to defend her point.

"You cow!" she yelled at her friend, squeezing her thighs to prompt Summer to catch up. Raegan's new tavern had kept her busy of late, but she'd used her first night off to make the round trip to the estate, and Brylee realised just how much she had missed her best friend's company.

Chapter Six

Brylee and Raegan rode in companionable silence for a measure, both enjoying the waking of the fallow fields in the frosty dawn. Bullrushes so stiff they refused to sway with the breeze. Frozen spider webs. The land was swathed in black, then transformed to ash grey before being tickled into shades of pink and orange as the sun crested the horizon.

As they passed the gateway to Lodeberry Farm, a small man stepped out of the shadows, causing Brylee to put her hand on her short sword and Raegan to reach over her shoulder for her crossbow. They relaxed when they realised it was just Ben Hepper, Lodeberry's owner.

"Forgive me, young ladies," Ben said with a chuckle, although he didn't show much remorse.

"Sunny crops, Ben," Brylee replied, biting her tongue.

"Can I have a quick word w'yer?" Ben asked, not waiting for her answer. "I may have an interest in taking advantage of y' transportation services, but they sound a bit rich for the likes of me. I would be interested to hear your offering, though."

Brylee kept her face straight, her eyes locked on Ben so she wouldn't be tempted to trigger the eyeroll she knew Raegan was keen to share. She let a few seconds slip by before responding. From hard-won experience in dealing with close-fisted farmers, she knew silence conveyed her distaste better than sarcasm or rhetoric.

"Of course, Mr. Hepper. You will have heard that I split off our secure shipping from Wispy Weed in the summer, and most see the value once they try it." She dropped out of her saddle as she spoke and handed the reins to Raegan before striding through the snow toward the farmer. She took a short step back once she realised she was too close and towering over him. Her intention had not been to intimidate.

"We always use our own wagons, horses, feed, and employees," she continued, no longer having to raise her voice, "which saves you a lot of headaches and cost. We drop off wagons, and you load them and tell us when to pick them up. Plainhand employees haul your products to the Barrow Building and we unload them, after which you're responsible for them again. And on top of that, I guarantee the delivery. We will refund you for any product lost to bandits or mishaps along the road."

"That sure would be a relief, what with this weather and my sons, Bob and Ben Junior, off fighting in the south. But what does it cost? It's sure to be a tough winter and a short growing season by the looks of things," he grumbled, not quite meeting her eye. From what Brylee had heard about Hepper's profits, she wasn't going to be taken in by his tactic.

"It will be a tougher year if you have to ship things yourself, Ben," Brylee replied. "The fee is less than it will cost you to do it yourself, and we take all the risk. It's fifteen punts and fifty pennies a cube sharing a wagon load if the logistics allow or sixty punts for a full wagon if they don't."

"Would y' consider fifty punts a cart, and I'll throw in a half sack o' feed per load?" Ben countered. "Considerin' my boys are fighting for all of us, you know."

"A half sack of feed is thirty pennies, Ben. I think your boys are brave, and I'm grateful for their service, but nine and seventy is a hell of a lot of respectin'. And most folks who pay the full price have kin in the wars too. The price is fair, so it'll be sixty a cart." She let that hang in the air.

"I guess I can stretch to it," Ben said. "I've got four ponies down with hoofblight, and the veterinarian thinks two weeks at least till they can haul again. My crop needs to go today. Can y' help?"

"Oh, Ben, hoofblight is hard to deal with. Yes, we can help. When we pass the team bringing the empty wagons back to my farm, I'll tell them to drop two carts off for you to load and arrange for them to be picked up with the afternoon run. Will you have one hundred and twenty punts ready, or will you need to give me a note?"

"If I'm going to do this," Ben said, "I need to go all in. I'll sell all my horses except one pair and use the stable space for crops. Could you provide six wagons and take a note until I get paid for the horses?"

Brylee spat on her hand and held it out. Ben did likewise, and the two pressed their palms together to seal the deal.

"I'll have my horse-wright come by, and if you can agree on a price with him, I'll buy your stock, hoofblight and all."

After Brylee and Raegan had put some distance between themselves and the Hepper farm, Raegan aired her views on Ben's sad attempts to cheapen the deal.

Brylee laughed. "Oh, I don't mind, really. It's a good deal, and he knows it, but I'll get my own back in the summer. Just you watch."

"What do you mean?"

"Secure transport makes small coin, but the real magic is that most farmers don't maintain their relationship with distributors. Ben's one of the lazy ones. In times of shortage, I can be relied upon, and most distributors stay with me in good times to secure my supply in bad, even if I'm a little more expensive than the competition. I'm becoming the market maker in several sectors. I set the price, and that gives me options other suppliers don't have."

"Don't your competitors give you a hard time?"

"Some do at first. Then I show them that distributors now favour Haxley suppliers over Basham or Mapleton's. A farmer might not make quite as much as me, but they're earning more than farmers in other towns and more than they would if it were a fragmented system. Share the pie, keep people happy and at my table."

They came to a turn in the road with a small hill, down which a mini avalanche of snow had tumbled, half filling the freshly ploughed tracks. Without a word, the women dismounted, took shovels from their saddles, and set to work clearing the small blockage. Brylee was a head and a half taller and significantly wider and more powerfully built than Raegan, who would be considered average for a Haxley lass.

"I hadn't realised how clever you'd been with shipping, Bry. Congratulations. Have you explained this to your parents?"

"Ag, they drive me nuts. They're more focussed on marrying me off. They expect me to produce the next heir." Brylee began impersonating each of her parents in turn. "Lifting bails and working the farm . . . Your face is pretty and your waist is narrow, but your shoulders are too wide, and your legs are like tree trunks. What man would want a wife who has more muscular arms than him and doesn't know how to keep a house? Who wants a lass who is always interfering in men's business?" They both laughed, but it wasn't really funny.

Brylee glanced at Raegan and marvelled at how lucky she was to have such a friend. Then as too often happened when she appreciated her luck, her shameful secret clawed its way out of the shadows of her psyche, causing her breath to hitch as she looked away, her cheeks aflame. Brylee lived with the shame of not just being a charmer but also benefiting from it.

If anyone learned that I'm a charmer, I'd be dead, she thought. *Maybe I deserve that for cheating.*

Each fall after the final harvest, barr root farmers sowed daighberries. It restored the soil and improved the next year's yield. Brylee's parents and her brother bought daighberries from the Foresters of Roe, as did most farmers. It was a well-known technique, and the Foresters had a solid reputation for quality and saving the farmers' time. But Brylee planted her own daighberries, drawing snickers from the old hands. "There she goes again, always breaking with tradition, to her peril" was the whisper as she spent much of each autumn preparing her own crop.

What they could never know, a secret she could never share, even with Raegan—especially with Raegan—was that she used her magic to enhance her daighberry crop. Her berries looked the same, but they were far more potent than those imported and gave Plainhand barr root a toastier flavour and a little more bite when smoked.

When she took the reins of the family business, desperate to be taken seriously and establish her place in the company, she felt she had little choice. But her natural business acumen soon cemented the respect of most people, if not her father, and she realised using her abilities had been a mistake. Suddenly stopping her magical enhancements would be noticed, so she had committed to weaning the crop back to normal over the next three harvests. And she donated some of their profits to the monks of Oster Chapel, who helped the needy, to atone for her actions. But she would always live with the knowledge of the advantage she had gained through her unnatural abilities, and she hated herself for being so weak.

Chapter Seven

It took longer than expected to clear the mini avalanche. As they shovelled, more snow tumbled down the slope, but eventually the path was clear. The work was hard, but they set to it with alacrity. Both women had removed their thick cloaks and loosened several layers despite the deep chill.

Though dressed similarly, they looked quite different. Both wore common thick grey leather riding breeches, seamed down the front and back to avoid ridges that would chafe from long periods on horseback. On top of these went padded trousers, laced close to their legs with leather thongs. Brylee's laces matched her outfit's colour, whereas Raegan's were a sharp red. Brylee's boots were flat—she was tall enough already—but Raegan's had sturdy one-and-a-half-inch heels.

They both wore Plainhand-issue uniform jackets. Raegan's was subtly tailored to more than hint at her curves and sized for a petite teen. Brylee's was a large man's size, which her muscular frame filled completely. The fleece-lined jackets were heavy canvas with pockets on the inside, so they would not fill with dirt or barr root flakes while working in the fields.

Although clothed similarly, the difference was in the wearing, not the cloth. Brylee's clothes were fitted for utility and function, and her feline grace, although feminine, suggested a rugged demeanour. Both women turned heads—one powerful, lithe, and striking, the other compact, sensual, and bright.

They repacked their shovels and shared some meat, cheese, and water as they cooled off. Brylee buttoned up and pulled her cloak back over her broad shoulders. Her thoughts turned to Jacon Dees. She warmed quicker than usual as she remembered the aforementioned rough and tumble and the few others that followed. It would go nowhere, and she would die before admitting it to Raegan, but she did have a soft spot for the rough stable hand.

After they remounted, Brylee picked up her teasing of Raegan and the bad habits she'd collected since escaping the clutches of Gunnar, her mean-assed ex-husband.

"Where were you last night, eh? I know you lied about being in your own room."

Raegan laughed. "A girl needs her secrets." Then a shadow crossed her face. "Besides, I wasn't being depraved. I was having therapy. My skanky ex-husband made me *really* doubt myself. I'm a free woman who is a new but successful bar owner. I have a diva reputation to create. The Crow's Nest will soon be the talk of Rostal, and I need to be a legend before similar taverns spring up in the big city." Raegan did a mock eyeroll for effect.

"As much as I love you rubbing Gunnar's nose in your kack, you might take a little care. He *is* the market warden," Brylee said. "He can cause trouble for you. Antagonising him by being so brazen may be enjoyable, but it isn't wise. A respectful truce might be smarter."

A sharp laugh burst from Raegan's lips, but her tone was angry rather than funny. "You know that pig doesn't work that way. I certainly do after three years of him crushing me on any topic he felt threatened by, just to make sure his ego was top of the pile."

Brylee nodded. "He's a piece of horseshit. I wanted to take gelding shears to him for the way he treated you."

"But you feeling sorry for me was the worst part for me, you know?" Raegan's voice was quiet and tight, and she had shrunk down into her saddle, her eyes locked onto her pony's ears. This was something she hadn't been ready to share before. Raegan slipped into silence, her mind going somewhere that her words had never been able to follow.

*

18 moons earlier . . .

It had been the worst moon of their three-year marriage, and today was Gunnar and Raegan's anniversary. *Perhaps I'll find a better way to support him and turn things around,* she thought. At her wits' end, Raegan had the idea of making Gunnar a special lunch and take it to him at work. He had been staying out later and looked so tired. Work was tough on him already without worrying about a wife he couldn't rely on, as he often reminded her.

Raegan wrapped his favourite meats and cheese in a cloth, put on the shorter dress he always admired, and with hope putting a

35

bounce in her step, set off to surprise him. He was auditing at the Barrow Building, a practice that some equated with soliciting bribes. Raegan had asked him about such whispers once, only to gain a sharp rebuke, then listened as he explained, as one would to a child, that "oiling the wheels" was expected in his role as market warden, as everyone agreed he was undervalued. "Think of it as a gratuity for faster service," he said, laughing at his own joke.

Raegan detoured to walk down Stock Row, a street known for several stores that sold the rarer and more expensive food. At the end of the street by the river stood the Haymaker Tavern. It straddled the street corner so that the main entrance was on the crossing street, but on Stock Row was a small serving window. From that window she purchased a small growler of ale, leaving an iron penny as security for the capped jar, which she would return later. Then, backtracking up Stock Row, Raegen picked her way across to the warehouse district.

Raegan rode the paternoster up to the rooftop, where Modwyn Barrow worked out of her late father's offices, overseeing the massive warehouse. Raegan knew better than to barge in unannounced if Gunnar was working. She had embarrassed him once before and received a backhander for being so dumb and disrespectful.

Raised voices drew her deeper into the offices, and as she passed an open doorway, she looked inside. Her eyes went wide as she witnessed Gunnar forcing himself on Modwyn. He was threatening to take away her business licence if she didn't kneel before him, in both senses of the word. Modwyn was red faced, trying to bite Gunnar. She had been pinned back against her desk with Gunnar looming over her, gripping both of her wrists in one of his big hands and holding them high above her head. Looking under Gunnar's shoulder, Modwyn saw Raegan and gave her a look of desperation. As eyes locked, Raegan grew dizzy, and darkness clouded around her.

She shrank back out of the room, her heart racing and her hand clamped over her mouth and nose to muffle her breathy sobs. Her mind full of self-doubt at what she had seen, she was both appalled and scared. She took another step, picturing herself at home trying to conceal her discovery from Gunnar when he walked in but failing. She hunched over, her eyes darting about.

Then she thought of Modwyn, the fire in her eyes, her fight, and her spirit despite her desperation. For a moment she felt the woman would survive the assault better than Raegan would survive the backlash if she interfered. Then the shame of not acting gripped her, and she succumbed to the notion that Gunnar should not be allowed to snuff out Modwyn's spirit as he had her own. But what could she do? He was so strong.

Raegan dragged herself back to the doorway. Collecting what threads of courage she could, she put down her basket. Clenching her fists, she yelled for Gunnar to stop. She had to repeat it twice, before she broke through the fit that was on him. He looked over his shoulder, initially with the expression of a schoolboy who had been caught, but when he saw it was only Raegan, he laughed with disdain. Then he threw Modwyn back and stepped away from her, panting.

Gunnar hadn't shown a shred of remorse. In fact, he went on the offensive instead. First, he blamed Modwyn, "The whore made advances," then berated Raegan for "bothering him at work." Then he asserted Raegan had misread the situation and was an embarrassment to him, saying she was too stupid to understand what she had seen. Then, getting as close to an admission of guilt as he would get, he implied he felt entitled, accusing Raegan of sleeping with their stable boy. She was stunned and denied it. He glared back, slobber flying from his lips. "I'm sick of the way the stable hands look at you. It's clear you've been bedding them behind my back. You won't make me a laughingstock. I've fired three and sent them and their families away, destitute. And their suffering is your fault because you can't keep your legs closed or aren't bright enough to at least be discreet. You're disgusting!"

Raegan was so broken down that Gunnar's narcissistic rant cowed her. Her eyes were on the floor, her head down. He might have convinced her that she was in the wrong if he had gotten a chance to finish. Before he could, though, Modwyn kicked him so hard in the balls that he crumpled to the floor. She spat on him as he lay gasping at her feet.

"If you still want him, I can get some loaders to help you carry his scraggy ass home!" Modwyn said, her chest heaving and her lips pressed together as she glared down her nose at her assailant.

Sometimes it takes just one act of defiance, perfectly timed, to turn the course of a life. Seeing Gunnar down and vulnerable, put on his back by a woman, no less, snapped something in Raegan's psyche. Her fear of Gunnar turned to anger. Shaking, she rushed over to him, mixed her spittle atop of Modwyn's, and kicked him in his side, winning a satisfying grunt.

Gunnar dragged himself to his feet, cursing. Pain gave way to rage, but when he found himself facing two equally angry and determined women—Modwyn armed with a knife and his wife with a wooden rod used to lock down a crate—his ire ebbed into cowardice. He stumbled out, ostensibly to call the guard to report the assault, but they knew he would soon realise that forcing himself on Modwyn, which his wife had witnessed, was the bigger crime. And in his eyes, admitting to being bested by anyone, let alone two women, was shameful. No, instead he would sulk in a dangerous silence.

Over the next ten minutes, the women comforted each other and raged about Gunnar, but their lack of familiarity soon led to an awkward silence. At that moment, Raegan realised she could not go home. Panic surged within her. She could return to her parents, as they had long wanted her to do, but it felt like such an admission of failure.

Modwyn sensed it was the wrong moment to let the stranger wander off to her fate. She looked at the lunch basket, which Raegan had set down in haste by the doorway. "It would be a shame to waste that," she had said, nodding at the food, her expression deadpan aside from a raised eyebrow. The joke planted the seedling of a friendship that was watered with tears throughout the day, then drowned with wine that evening.

Modwyn's rooms atop the Barrow Building were too big for her own needs, and she invited Raegan to move in until things were sorted out. Though the arrangement was supposed to be temporary at first, days turned to weeks and moons and eventually into a successful business partnership and friendship. Raegan's scars, however, were not mended as quickly.

Over the subsequent eighteen moons, Raegan recovered somewhat. Modwyn's wisdom and intuition helped her heal, and her effervescent attitude toward life, so different from Raegan's own upbringing, nudged the younger woman's mood in a new direction. With Gunnar pushed away, Brylee and a few other close friends gathered around Raegan in support and protection. They ensured Raegan got up each day, was busy, and felt loved. They also ensured that Gunnar would not intrude on Raegan's life in any way. Although fragile and still quite splintered, Raegan rarely found it hard to leave her bed, and sassy, strong days became the norm, her panic attacks fewer.

Brylee no longer apologised for what she had deemed was her failure to act on her friend's behalf, as it only opened the scars once more, but she harboured the shame of it, burying it deep. "I begged you to stay out of my business," Raegan argued. "You were merely respecting my wishes." It was an old argument now, no longer raised, a tacit agreement to disagree.

*

A few tears froze unnoticed on Raegan's cheeks as she began to release her thoughts into words. They hung like vapour in the cold air, just as they had in her mind for years.

"I can see, looking backwards, that Gunnar had a knack for constantly pointing out my flaws in a way that got deep under my skin. It was relentless. Sometimes it was obvious, but many times it was subtle. If I mentioned that others supported my view on something, he would convince me that they were crazy, and I was foolish to side with such idiots. He said things could get dangerous for me if I didn't smarten up. Then he would about face and claim my ideas as his own and chastise me for copying him. My head spun, tangling my thoughts up.

"If I agreed with him, he praised me but in a tainted way, as if he was surprised that I understood properly at last. He was full of grand gestures and easy charm one moment and angry and threatening the next. When I began to have serious doubts about myself, I felt I had few places to turn. I know that wasn't the case, that you were ready to help me, but he had all but convinced me that my family and friends were useless, immoral, crooked, or cheating on their husbands or worse.

"I never fully believed his version of anything, but it made it increasingly difficult to open up to those I loved most. I felt more and more alone and ashamed."

"But we knew none of his lies were true, Rae," Brylee reassured her. "There was nothing to be ashamed about."

"Oh, I'm not ashamed of what he said I failed at because deep down I knew it was a lie. I'm ashamed because I couldn't stand up to him. I even stopped denying his accusations about people I cared about, people like you. I hated myself for staying quiet when he slandered you, and I despised myself for the times I let myself believe some of the lies he spun about you."

Raegan fell silent for a moment, working up the bravery to choke out the next part. "Yet when you saw him treating me badly, you were fired up and ready to fight him for me. I was failing you, and you were ready to take him on for me. I felt I was so unworthy of you. I didn't deserve your fire and your loyalty. I disconnected myself from you, and I isolated myself even further because of my shame and guilt. And that was when he really took me down."

A horn blast snapped Raegan out of her gloomy reverie. Without thinking, the women kicked their mounts into a fast canter towards the sound of the alarm, not wanting to risk a full gallop in the icy conditions.

Chapter Eight

"One blast. Not bandits. That would have been three!" Brylee called out over the wind and the sound of their horses' beating hooves. "Some sort of accident?"

It took twenty minutes to close the gap on the snowplough. As they reined their mounts to a halt, they saw only one wrangler with the horse team. At their unspoken question, he pointed to his teammate and the escorting Mobi'dern, kneeling over a body under a tree next to a ramshackle cabin some fifty yards off the main trail.

"Her cat found 'im," he said, but whether he was screwing his face up at the injury or the cat, Brylee couldn't tell.

Hitching their mounts to the plough, the women made their way through the snow to investigate. As they approached, the cat, whose head was nearly as high as Brylee's hip, stepped out of the bushes to challenge them. He retreated as he recognised Brylee, allowing them to approach his mistress while her back was turned to attend to the injured man. Brylee wondered as she always did, when she saw these mercenary fighters interact with their beasts, if they could communicate with thought. The Mobi'dern remain notoriously silent when questioned about such matters.

It didn't take a scholar to see what had happened. The woodsman had been standing on a fallen tree, lopping off thick branches. He had evidently slipped, and either his own axe or a broken branch had torn through his thigh as he fell. The ugly gash had penetrated a major artery, and blood had spurted out, covering him and the surrounding snow in red. The man had fashioned a makeshift tourniquet that stemmed the flow before he fainted.

"He's lost too much blood," the teamster said, shaking his head. His breathing was elevated, his face almost as white as the victim's. He had made the man as comfortable as possible. "He's a goner, I'm afraid, Miss Plainhand. Doesn't seem to be anyone else in the cabin."

Brylee looked at the Mobi'dern and raised an eyebrow. The woman shook her head and slid her index finger across her own throat, signalling agreement. The Mobi'dern were exceptional warriors, and she would have seen many injuries and been an expert in the signs of certain death. Brylee nodded and then took charge.

"Yaris, isn't it?" Brylee said to the wrangler. "You carry on and get the road cleared. We'll stay here." She looked at the Mobi'dern and used the hand signals for "doctor" and "farm," then pointed back down the cleared trail. Nodding, the warrior stood and sprinted down the track, her cat loping after her. They would make the trip on foot almost as fast as someone on horseback, especially with the icy conditions.

"Raegan, can you bring our horses here, then go into the cabin and fetch blankets or anything else to keep him warm?" Raegan and Yaris shared a look that translated to it being better to let the fellow slip away quickly in the cold rather than prolong the inevitable.

"I know it's a long shot, but let's get to it. Now, please!" Brylee pressed. Raegan and the wrangler hurried off to do as she had ordered, giving Brylee the opportunity she had secretly been working towards.

Brylee pushed her fingers into the wound. The man was unconscious and didn't react. She cleared her mind and focussed on the artery's damaged wall. It was a small nick, but it didn't take much of a hole to drain a man. She steadied her breathing and poured her magic into the tear. *At least I can put this taint in my blood to good use here,* she thought.

As a charmer, she would be shunned if she sought knowledge from a mage on how to heal properly. To do so would be like signing her own death warrant anyway. While using her talents to encourage plant growth, she discovered she had an affinity that could make organic things, including skin, grow extraordinarily fast. She couldn't grow a hand from a foot, but if the body part itself knew how to grow or repair, she could speed things up dramatically.

She had discovered that she could only influence certain aspects, though. She had some success at making her own muscles more defined and certainly stronger. She had also subtly altered her own hair colour and even controlled the growth of unwanted body hair. Once, as a young teen, she had been teased for being too tanned. A week later she was several shades lighter. It was exhausting work, but the teasing stopped, though she'd felt dirty, like when her maid had caught her touching herself experimentally during her eleventh summer.

Brylee paused and caught her breath while Raegan tied the horses to a nearby tree and then went to search the cabin. Using magic always drained Brylee and using so much so quickly was taking a toll. When the coast was clear, she examined the artery and decided her quick patch would hold. But the man needed to replace the blood he'd lost or he would die despite her having plugged the leak.

Her uncle had been sick years ago. His skin went pale and yellowish, his heart faltered, he was endlessly weak and achy, and his hands and feet were always cold. He had been senior cook to Lord Lessinger's sister-in-law, and as a favour to her, Mage Wickham himself had attended. The uncle recovered and shared around the dinner table that the mage had explained that his blood was tainted. It lacked the part that makes blood red in colour. The mage had reached inside her uncle's bones and repaired the sickness. Recalling this, Brylee focussed inside the injured woodsman's hips and thigh bones, the biggest and most productive blood sources. She pressed energy into them, not knowing what else to do, hoping the bones wouldn't grow.

She was so deep in concentration that she almost missed Raegan's approach. Had it been seconds or minutes? All Brylee knew was that she felt dizzy.

"Are you OK?" Raegan asked, seeing her friend's apparent distress.

"Yes . . . I . . . it's all this blood. I felt nauseous," Brylee said. "Cover him, and I'll force some water into his mouth. That's about all we can do for him. I suspect he won't make it, but let's see if we can at least keep him alive until the doctor comes."

It was over two hours before they heard horses hammering up the track. Raegan went to the road and directed the doctor to the injured man. Then the women backed away, giving him room to work. After examining the man and applying a dressing, the doctor came over to update them.

"He's a lucky fellow. If the cut had been a hair's width deeper, he would have bled out. He lost a lot of blood anyway, and there might be complications, but at the moment he seems stable. I'll get him onto a wagon when they roll through. I passed them just a mile or so back."

"Thanks for coming so quickly, doctor," Brylee said. After saying their goodbyes, the two women returned to their horses. It was all Brylee could do to haul herself up into the saddle.

"It's a shame we don't all have the power of a mage," Raegan said. "The good we could do in emergencies like these."

Her comment hit so close to home it almost made Brylee throw up.

Chapter Nine

Jacub Morde, the Elect of the 470-year-old Morde Dynasty, rarely interacted with the citizens of Mordeland. Instead, he explained that he needed—most whispered it was more of a preference than a need—to focus on international matters of state, courting alliances to fend off the threat at the southern border and such. For home rule, he relied wholly upon a three-headed bureaucracy called the Trilogy to govern his nation.

The Office of the Land, the Office of Military and Enforcement, and the Office of Trade were the three pillars from which the name of Mordeland's government had spawned. Over time, several lesser councils had evolved to support matters not well attended to by the big three, namely the councils of Science, Education, People, and Magical Law. No one sought to update the government's name.

The Trilogy was governed by the Council of Morde. The duty of chairman rotated annually to one of the leaders of each of the three main pillars. The Elect would meet with the sitting chair weekly and with other council members much less frequently. The Office of Military and Enforcement currently held the title of chair, which was timely given how matters were deteriorating in the south. As a result, agriculture and internal trade were far from Jacub's mind. Unless it was to feed the campaign or trade for goods of war, he showed little interest.

The Trilogy demanded a census every five years for the primary purpose of assessing taxes across Mordeland's five regions. According to the Council of People's Counting, the Region of Lanthe—Lord Lessinger's fief—had over 250,000 residents, almost half of which resided in the city of Rostal. Including transients, visiting traders, students, and unregistered peoples, Rostal itself had to feed, clothe, and provide shelter to roughly 150,000 souls every day.

The town of Haxley was a significant cog in a vast logistical machine that ensured the gentry in Rostal wanted for nothing and the city's lesser citizens had at least what it needed, and often much more. Rostal was an affluent jewel, the envy of many.

Haxley was Rostal's leading market town in part because of the rich farmlands to its south and easy access to trouble-free ocean trade to the west. But more credit rested with its progressive ruling body, rather modestly named the Haxley Council, and its efficiency-minded aldermen and alderwomen.

With the recent passing of Modwyn's father, Alderman Barrow, a seat was open for election, and Brylee had her eye on it. She wasn't alone, nor was she the lead contender. Her business acumen had been noted by the more observant members of the council, but that her fiery spirit needed much tempering was clear to all. Still, Brylee wanted to be considered, knowing that losing with grace in that round would help position her for the next time such an opportunity arose. As a member of the council, she would be well placed to promote her family's agenda, which was her top concern.

The west of Haxley was dominated by stables for nearly 1,500 horses involved in the town's vast logistics operations. The stables were laid out in rows that fit into the cartarium like fingers into a glove. The cartarium stored and maintained all the carts and trade wagons of the extensive supply chain and spanned an area so large it took thirty minutes to cross on foot. The cartarium complex had several carpenters, coopers, and smithies at strategic locations. It was covered in canvas awnings and had drainage ditches to carry off the water to prevent it becoming an impassable bog.

Each day an intricate dance played out as each horse team collected the correct cart and arrived at the Barrow Building or smaller warehouses at the correct time for its specific load. Then the teams would set off for Rostal. Traffic returning from the capital carrying waste and reusable containers, as well as other traffic returning to the farms, was part of the weave of the city's paths and politics. Planners came from across Mordeland to study the supply chain that had taken Haxley over fifty years to perfect.

Along the southern flank of the cartarium were vendors for everything a busy carter might need, from food for horses and men to clothing, tack, and light weaponry. The unemployed also gathered there, hoping for a day's work, as did prostitutes, hoping for shorter shifts. It was a hive of activity where one could get news from all over Mordeland and beyond from carters, troupers, and tinkers alike.

Plainhand Estate's offices occupied a cottage on the west bank of the Hax, adjacent to the town's transportation hub, two streets south of the food vendors. The wind prevailed from the south, so the offices were upwind of the food smells, which Brylee regretted, but also the stables, which was a blessing. That the tannery was on the northern side of it all, which meant its stench bled away into the countryside, was a godsend that she thanked Ag for often.

Brylee and Raegan stabled their mounts, fed them, brushed them down, and then set off on their respective errands, agreeing to meet at the Crow's Nest for dinner. Brylee purchased a hot pork roll from Tessa's Meat Stand and all but inhaled it. She was always ravenous after using her magic in any significant way. She bought a second one to eat once she changed out of her road clothes.

She climbed the stairs to her small suite in the loft above the offices, which she had commandeered to escape her parents' suffocating oversight. She found a note under her door from her father summoning her for lunch, for which she was already late due to the delay on the road. With a sigh, she collected a clean set of clothes and then jogged a block to the bathhouses. She paid the tuppeny fee and then took a towel and strode into the women's section.

She took a private stall, which was included in the cost, stripped off her clothes and folded them meticulously—a habit that surprised the rare observer as she was thought of as reckless and untidy—and sank into the room's tin bath. The water wasn't hot—probably to discourage patrons from lingering—so she made quick work with the soap provided. She stepped out, rinsed down with the jug of clean water on hand, then walked through to the hot pool.

Less than a dozen women were in a pool that could accommodate three times that, so it was easy to find a quiet spot to relax for a few moments before meeting her parents. She lowered herself into the hot, salted water, her skin itchy and prickly as it adjusted to the heat. In no time she was revelling in it, her muscles unknotting, and the last of the bitter morning's cold leaving her fingertips. She sank so the tips of her ears were warmed too.

Her pleasure was interrupted by someone splashing in beside her. She scrunched her face and opened one eye to see Mella harrumph with discomfort, her lips pursed and her thin eyebrows pulled down.

"I don't like how hot they keep it here," the elderly alderwoman groused. "In Bain we always had three pools of differing temperatures so you could choose the one that matched your taste. I've tried to convince the council to invest in such a system here, but apparently schooling and the hospital are higher priorities." Brylee smiled at her mentor's deadpan expression, knowing this laughable prioritisation to be part of Mella's witty yet always grouchy persona.

"Sunny crops, Mella," Brylee said, employing the common greeting of the farming community. "I'm not sure why you come at all seeing as you have a private pool at home."

"Yes, but then I would have the cost of running it." Mella was famous for her grousing and her stinginess. "But more importantly, here I have the benefit of being able to ambush people in pursuit of my agenda. My victims find it hard to argue they're running off on an errand, and their nakedness leaves them feeling vulnerable. I aim to take full advantage. And there are no men preening and cocking about, so work is more productive. You'll do well to remember this when you get into politics, which brings me to my point."

Mella didn't get right to the point. Uncharacteristically, she paused to consider her words, apparently not quite set on her approach. She was fond of Brylee and wished for a way to accelerate the youngster's tempering as her lack of control was a hindrance in the pursuit of the art of politics. It would have been instructive to let Brylee fall foul of the plot rising against her—Brylee would have been angry but eventually soaked up insight from it—but Mella worried that the girl's pride would lead her to disaster. Perhaps there was a middle ground though.

"Trouble on the road?" the older woman asked as she organised her thoughts. Brylee wondered yet again how Mella could be so well informed. She provided the highlights of the accident—careful to conceal the role of her magic, of course—and gave an account of the conditions of the road. Before Brylee could go further, Mella reached her decision on how to play her cards.

"Brylee, I'm not one to interfere in people's lives," Mella began, holding up a finger to shush the younger woman, as they both knew that statement was far from the truth, "but a confidential source indicates that you may have a trying afternoon. No, I won't go further, other than to stress that your reactions today could shape the rest of your life. Your fire reminds me of my own youth, but it will only harm you today with your family. You would do well to quench it here in the pool. I should know; I admit to the odd brash misstep in my younger days."

Brylee flushed, and not from the water's heat. She was filled with as many questions as emotions, but she bit her tongue.

Mella chuckled. "Well, that's a good start at least. Now, on a completely different matter, are you attending the council meeting today?" Brylee nodded, and Mella continued. "I have two pieces of information that did not come from me . . ."

Fifteen minutes later, Brylee was dried and dressed and across Westbridge, halfway to her parents' apartments in the south of Haxley's higher-class residential district, Silverside. It was on Mella's route, so she accompanied Brylee, leaning on her arm at times when the pace was too fast and refusing to allow the younger woman to slow down except to return the many "Good days" and "Sunny crops" from almost everyone they passed. In her other hand Mella held a finger of barr root, which she pulled on occasionally, its smoke trailing behind them. Brylee noted it was one of the special brands her family's estate produced.

Seeing Brylee's eyes on her smoke reminded Mella of a question. "There must be a good story behind Barr Royal. Care to share while we walk?" Mella asked.

"OK, but only between us businesswomen," Brylee replied with a conspiratorial wink. "While delivering Wispy Weed fingers to Rostal, I was reminded how gentry frequently seek to show off their status with exclusivity in clothing and whisky, so why not with barr root, too? A finger is flaked or crushed barr root wrapped in wan leaf and shaped into a tube that can be smoked. One finger looks much like another, although some farmers pack them longer or fatter or add a fragrance for variety, of course.

"I came up with the notion of purchasing wangen leaves, a cousin to wan leaf stock. It's cheaper because I pick it up from traders at the western seaport. They use wangen to keep fruit fresh through its voyage up from N'Tassi. They would normally dump the old leaves into the sea on the journey home, but a small payment keeps my source exclusive and secret, and the boat has space for additional cargo, so we all win."

"What's so special about wangen leaves?" Mella asked, tilting her head to indicate her interest.

"Wangen is sweeter and finer than wan, and it's white where wan leaf is brown. Being white means it's easier to colour. I've rented space in the Mellee Hills where a trusted few employees combine the leaves with late-harvest barr root. With a little dye and artwork using gold honey pens, they churn out short, dainty lilac-coloured fingers for ladies and stubby black thumbs for gentlemen. As you know, lilac is associated with luxury and black with toughness. On holidays, and/or just to create a rare edition, a different colour or pattern is produced. Same content as a regular finger but with different wrappings, selling for five times more than standard product—and even more if I deliberately short supply to create a scarcity. All because we found a more malleable leaf. And Plainhand Barr Royal enhances the original Plainhand Wispy Weed brand enormously."

As the conversation continued, Mella wished Brylee's ascent to the council could be accelerated.

They cut through Baylan's Courtyard, where their eyes were drawn to a sign in the window of a small cottage with a red door, signifying that the house was for rent, having stood empty since Markus Brent, its previous owner, was killed.

"Good luck finding a renter," Mella mumbled, her lips curling. Nothing had been proven, but gossip asserted that Brent had been a charmer, skriked by a predatory mage. Most of Haxley's residents avoided walking through the courtyard, and when they did they averted their eyes.

"Don't you find these old ways so conservative?" Brylee asked, surprised her thoughts had found a voice. Committed now, however, she continued. "It's just that sometimes I think distrust of charmers is questionable. We don't assume all mages are sneaky and treacherous because they have power. In fact, they're the ones murdering charmers, but no one seems to care about that as much. Anyway, I don't understand why we stigmatise people we could put to use to help society. There are apparently way more charmers than mages, and mages are loath to help the poorer folk."

"You foster some fascinating ideas, Brylee, but . . . well, some ideas are dangerous." She gripped the younger woman's arm, sad that Brylee's rise to the council might be further away than she had hoped.

Although Brylee felt bile rise to the back of her throat, she agreed with her mentor that she needed to keep her mouth shut on the topic.

At least for now.

Chapter Ten

Silverside boasted almost 200 homes that reflected the proud but no-nonsense attitude of the self-made business folk who made up 80 percent of its occupants, wealthy but not lavish. Two huge manor houses containing many sprawling apartments nestled among the 170 or so other buildings ranging from large cottages to small mansions. Each manor house was replete with concierges, gardeners, and maintenance staff for all the common spaces and boasted ten to fifteen multi-room dwellings with living space for their owners and private staff. There was even a central kitchen and dining room for those who desired such amenities.

The Plainhands owned one of the nicest apartments on the upper floor of Dalebrook Manor at the west end of the building. It spanned the southeast and southwest corners, providing 270-degree views, and overlooked the parkland between the manor and the city's south gate. Looking west on a clear day, one could see the Mellee Hills in the distance. If not for them, the seaport beyond might have been visible.

Brylee trotted up the manor's front steps, trying to inject some energy into herself to fend off the foreboding in her belly as her mind worked to decrypt Mella's vague warning. She nodded to the concierge, then checked in on his back condition, the health of his failing mother, and his luck with the dog races. Poor, poorer, and poorest was his usual accounting.

Once inside she jogged up the ornate central staircase, enjoying new artwork hung since her last visit, the odour of polished wood, and the expansive daylight allowed in by the large windows. At the top she turned left to walk along the corridor, resigned to meet whatever her parents had cooked up. She hoped they had given up on their idea of expanding Barr Royal. More production only diluted the market and the profit. They didn't grasp that its scarcity was what created its value.

As she let herself in through the double front door, she was assailed by the wonderful smells of Fifi's kitchen. In all of Brylee's twenty-three years, the family cook had been her "safe place." In contrast to her parents' mercurial conservatism, Fifi's manner was consistently upbeat, and she always presented the best food for a given moment, be it a six-course dinner or a midnight plate of cookies accompanied by a personalised note. Fifi had a softness that Brylee's parents lacked and held court in her kitchen with outrageous stories that Brylee still struggled to believe.

Instead of walking straight into the main rooms, Brylee darted right, through the mudroom and into Fifi's domain. She snuck up on the cook, who was putting lunch leftovers into a storage jar, and stole a chicken leg.

"Hoy, young lady. Manners!" Fifi laughed, her round pink face lighting up before a flicker of concern was followed by a glance towards the door. Brylee shrugged, raised an eyebrow, gulped down a mouthful of chicken, then licked her fingers as she walked through to the grand sitting room.

"We were starting to doubt you'd bless us with your company." Her father, Luka, never wasted time making his point, often doing so with sarcasm.

"No, Pa," Brylee replied with the patience Mella advised, though she didn't feel it. "Seeing that it would snow overnight, I rode down to the farm last evening to see that the roads were cleared early today. On the ride back we came across an accident, so it took longer than expected."

"We've got people for that now, Lee," her mother, Celeste, said. No thanks was given, nor did she ask if anyone was hurt. "Anyway, you're here now, and we have a visitor." She smiled towards a figure Brylee hadn't noticed, who was propping up the fireplace drinking from a wine flute. Judd Brown.

Ag, give me strength, Brylee thought.

For his part, Judd was enjoying the scene, especially the elder Plainhands fawning over him. Judd had recently suggested to Luka Plainhand, the supposed patriarch, that he buy the Plainhands' business outright, or if not, that an alliance between the Brown Estates and the Plainhands would be advantageous to both families. Luka was leaning towards the latter and had suggested marriage—heavily influenced, Judd suspected, by his wife, who was clearly concerned that Brylee had yet to find herself a husband. Grandchildren had been mentioned more than once.

Judd had indicated earlier that he would consider marriage, for the good of the families of course, but his internal voice questioned once again if he could really see himself with such a headstrong firebrand some twelve years his junior. As an asset to his business interests, possibly. Brylee did have a raw, if overly moralistic, business talent. As long as he had the controlling interest and last word, perhaps. But physically, he wasn't drawn to her.

As he watched Brylee stand tall to challenge her father, he was reminded that she was an inch taller than his own five feet nine inches and several inches wider at the shoulders too. She was muscular, though not overbuilt or sinewy and not masculine either. A life spent farming and competing with the male workers, be it hauling bales by day or arm wrestling for drinks at night, had given her formidable strength and stamina. And although her shoulders were broader than any woman's should have been, their squareness and the way her torso flowed down to her taut waist was more feline than anything. She turned heads, to be sure, although he had heard several men whisper that one so big would benefit from more bosom. In that regard, however, Judd felt she was sufficient, if only she would wear something to show it to her advantage.

Her face was unpredictable, almost pretty when she laughed, especially if a dimple emerged, but fierce if she were wrangling crops onto a cart or menfolk's arms or wallets across the table. Her sandy-coloured hair was cut functionally tight, just below her ears in a light bob, and her m-shaped hairline was echoed by dark eyebrows. Her face was more round than long, her mouth small but her lips full. When she did smile, her teeth were white and even. Her tawny skin hinted at blood from the south, masking the weathering of her lifestyle, and he would have preferred she looked less like she had just been plucked from the farm when she was on his arm at elite functions.

Yes, he concluded, if he could bring Brylee to heel, especially in polite society, he could make room for her in his life, since absorbing the Plainhand business into his own would seal his place as Lanthe's trade powerhouse. He already had a seat on Haxley Council, but his eyes were set on the deputyship of the Office of Land in the Trilogy. Five or so years understudying its current leader until their retirement would leave him well placed to join the Council of Mordeland proper and have the ear of the Elect.

Judd's mind was forced back to the present as he felt the piercing gaze of his potential new mate. He coughed and then tipped his glass of rather average wine to her, followed by a courteous bow.

"Miss Plainhand, I've just enjoyed a wonderful meal with your parents, and you were all they talked about. Their pride and joy, no doubt. I feel an opportunity to know you better was missed due to whatever befell you on the road. I hope all is well now, and no one was seriously hurt. I also hope to put this missed opportunity right and would be honoured if you would consider dinner with me tonight."

Brylee was silent, her lips pressed between her teeth. Her first response was to cross her arms, but as she looked back and forth between Judd and her parents, her hands shifted to her hips, her nostrils flared, and she opened her mouth as if to speak, then clamped it shut once more. A small voice in the back of her head warned her that the earlier expenditure of magic was to blame for the lack of filter on the spectrum of emotions that were whipping through her.

"It wasn't all about Lee and Judd," Luka said, realising Brylee had correctly guessed that nuptials had been the topic. "We've been exploring the benefits of merging Plainhand and Brown businesses." Judd turned and placed his glass on the fireplace, allowing him to mask his eyeroll at Luka pouring oil onto the barely contained blaze that was his daughter.

"What would you know about our business, Pa?" spat Brylee. "When was the last time you visited the offices, let alone went to the farm? Expensive lunches with your old cronies aren't really business meetings, you know!"

"Don't be cheeky with your father, Lee," Celeste chided. "At least we know when to ease back a little and enjoy the fruits of a life of hard work."

"Come off it, Ma. I'll never forget that you gave us our start, and I'm grateful. And I'll concede Nalik was a hard worker. But could you afford to live in Silverside before I took over the reins? Could you afford trips to the theatre in Rostal?"

Celeste flushed. "If you've helped us along the way, then some of your father has rubbed off on you, but you're merely making my point. When you start to have babies, who's going to run the business then? Have you considered that?"

"Have you?" Brylee replied.

Judd closed his eyes, silently agreeing with Brylee that despite her naivety, she had made more of the business in a few years than her parents had in the previous two decades.

If Brylee had felt contempt for her parents lollygagging and discussing her marital future, discovering they were dabbling in a business they hardly understood ensured that a full-on fit of anger threatened to take over.

"Am I to understand this lunch was arranged to discuss . . . what?" It seemed even Brylee sensed that saying out loud they planned to marry her off would unleash the tsunami that was building. Mella's warning screamed in the back of her mind. It was nearly strangled by her rage, but somehow she contained the worst of it. She took a breath, then a second, before continuing in a quiet, stiff voice that conveyed more menace than anger. "I don't appreciate your discussing selling our business with others before having the good grace to talk to me first. And I have no plans to settle into the role of housewife anytime soon. And Mr. Brown, please don't take offence, but I don't believe you and I would be in the least bit compatible."

Recalling another lesson from Mella about burning bridges, her tone became a bit more conciliatory. "I think I'm the expert on both our business and my life, and I suppose I don't know you well, Mr. Brown. I have a previous engagement tonight, but I'm free for lunch tomorrow. If I've calmed down by then, I would be open to discussing any area of business in which you feel we might have a joint interest, but marriage is *certainly* not on the table."

Before anyone could say anything that would cause her to lose control, she stomped out of the room, punctuating her exit by slamming the front door.

Instead of leaving the way she had come, she ducked down the servants' staircase and out through the delivery bay. She cut through the garden, all but running, her face red and lips holding in a scream.

Brylee marched across the road and into the parkland, then beelined for a small corner of bushes planted beside an ornamental pond. Inside the carefully arranged shrubs was a quiet place not obvious from the path. It contained a bench that offered a favourable view of the water and the land beyond. It had been her bolt hole, her escape from family frustrations since before she was allowed out of the house unescorted, a rule she broke many times.

Her desire to fling herself onto the bench and yell at the sky was thwarted when she realised someone already occupied the seat. She was stuck between choosing another destination and demanding the occupant relinquish the spot when she realised the intruder was Fifi. The cook gave her a sympathetic look before removing a small basket from the seat next to her, which had been saving a place for the angry young woman.

Much of Brylee's rage seeped out of her with a huge sigh, deflating her "ready to take on all comers" stance and leaving her feeling old and slouched as she plunked down on the bench.

"How did you know I'd come here?" she grumbled.

"I used to follow you here when you were no more than this tall," the cook replied, holding her hand about the height of a toddler. "Watched you act out. I think I stood in these bushes when you cussed the first time because Nalik was allowed to go to the estate to choose a new horse for his birthday, and you were held back for sewing lessons. They couldn't find you for hours, and I let them search, but I knew you were safe."

Brylee turned to her, shocked. "Really? I never knew. Why didn't you tell me or take me home?"

"And miss watching you grow up to be independent and successful? Nah, I like your flair for drama too much." As Fifi chuckled, Brylee's eyes were drawn to the basket.

"Raspberry cream scones?" she ventured. Fifi opened the lid, and the rich raspberry scent filled the air. A huge lump formed in Brylee's throat, and her eyes burned. Fifi drew Brylee into a hug, ignoring her shaking shoulders.

When emotional order was sufficiently restored, they tucked into the scones. Fifi also produced a flask with two cups, and they each consumed a half glass of wine. Brylee looked at the sun and realised it would soon be time for the council meeting.

"Thank you, Fifi. You've always known what I needed." Brylee smiled, placing a hand on top of the cook's.

"Well, maybe," Fifi said. "But before you rush off, I need to tell you something. And mark me, I'm not telling you this to change your path. Be as independent and dramatic as you like, but you should know that your pa's sick. Very sick."

"I know he has a growth in his side. The healer said it might eventually take him but that he would have many years yet."

"She did, but it seems the growth has spread. He pees blood some days, and others his back hurts so fierce that he won't leave his bed. I mix cariseed into his breakfast to relieve his pain."

"Why haven't they told me?" Brylee asked. "Is that why they're so keen to marry me off? He wants to see grandchildren before he dies? Is that why he smothers me so?" Brylee detested guilt, so she often reacted to it with rage. Fifi shook her head.

"No. For one so smart at business you don't know people very well, do you? He's extremely proud of you, although he feels too disloyal to Nalik to voice it much. He sees you striding off as confident as he used to be with business acumen aplenty but little wisdom. You remind him of himself, actually. He's a little envious of your youth and confidence, to be sure. An affliction of the old everywhere. But he's acting the way he is because he feels *useless*. He can no longer keep up with you, and he knows he won't be here to guide you. I also think he's sad that you won't listen to him anymore, even when he's right."

"Of course, I . . . well . . . but marrying Judd? Merging our business with that unethical conniver? Those aren't good ideas, so why should I listen?" Both women were aware that Brylee's last statement was a placeholder, her mouth pushing ahead while her brain processed Fifi's revelation. They let her words drift away on the breeze.

Fifi laid a hand atop Brylee's. "He isn't trying to be controlling. He's an old, dying man trying to be useful one last time. Your mother would love grandchildren. She's already yearning for the company to fill the space your pa will leave." She let the silence settle before continuing. "So, go be independent. Truly. We all want that for you, including your parents despite their words and actions. Don't stop doing what's best for you and the business. But know that your father loves you and is trying to find a way to show it."

Brylee stood. "I should go back up there."

"Ag, no, and embarrass him in front of that ass, Judd? Get to the council meeting and make him proud. Again. And stop being so reactive. Think about what I've said, then decide how to circle back to him, eh? Now, take the last scone and be on your way."

Chapter Eleven

Despite her fear of running late, Brylee entered the council chambers ahead of all the elected members. She greeted the staffers who were setting up for the meeting and then slipped into her favourite seat.

Brylee's father had brought her to the council chamber ever since she was old enough to sit through meetings without interrupting. "A wife with a nose for politics is an asset to any family" was a mantra he espoused often as he sat her at the back of the room and bade her to be quiet. Brylee would never trade a day in the fields for that place, but she was fond of it.

The room was round, smelled of the oak it was made from, and boasted fifty seats that tiered downward from the walls so the central table could be seen by everyone in attendance. The circular table had a plain white ring around its edge where notes and papers could be placed by the seven elected aldermen and women. Within that circle, a space twelve feet in diameter bore a detailed map of Haxley, including roughly a mile of its perimeter. The town's important features were depicted, including the cartarium, warehouses, and rivers. This was overlaid with a detailed web of roads and trade routes. If discussion needed to be geographically broader, staffers would bring in boards that were painted with a map of the region or even the entire country, showing the terrain, major towns, farms, ports, and the capitals. Wooden markers and models could be placed on the maps and moved around using sticks to aid the discussion.

Brylee had always been fascinated with the charts. They had captured her attention as a child until she became interested in the topics discussed. She loved the way the Hax River swept up from the south and then darted to the right to enter Haxley from the west. At the town centre, it bent due north again, flowing away to Rostal. The Chandler River ran into Haxley from the east to intercept the Hax at this crook. But this joining was too simple for Mother Nature, and over the aeons erosion had formed a triangular island created by a short secondary channel linking the northern arm of the Hax back to the Chandler a mile from the main junction. The island was named the Eye of Haxley, thought to be a corruption of the "Isle of Haxley," but as the Council of

Haxley chambers were located on it, calling it the Eye seemed fitting. If one followed the Chandler east, it eventually looped north towards Rostal, but the two rivers never met again as they found their way into the mountains north of the capital.

Aside from the good view of the map, Brylee favoured a particular seat because it was directly opposite Mella Stonebrook's chair, and Brylee found it instructive to watch her mentor's expressions and movements during the course of debate.

Mayor "Windy" Hollowhill sat on Mella's right in a slightly raised seat denoting her status as chairwoman of the council. The nickname Windy—her given name was Darbi—stemmed from her unruly hairstyle, which, from a young age, persisted with a mind of its own despite her mother's best efforts. The ironic appropriateness of her sobriquet in politics was something she played on often. The family name Hollowhill stemmed from the large family farm being set deep amongst a semicircle of hills shaped like the inside of a bowl and not, as some wags would have it, her abundant cleavage.

The remaining seats were occupied by Judd Brown, Ashli Buttonmeadow, and Deek Cherrywood, predominant farmers in Lanthe; Caelee Star of Star Ranch and stable master and owner of the cartarium's stable complex; and the two largest distributors of goods to Rostal, Erich Bane and Mella Stonebrook. All of them were elected by the council except Caelee Star, who was temporarily sitting in the deceased Alderman Barrow's seat by common agreement until the upcoming election to replace him permanently.

As the fifteenth bell neared, over half of the secondary seating in the chamber was occupied. The bell sounded, the arched doors from the antechamber opened, and the mayor and other council members trouped in. Mella didn't make eye contact with Brylee, perhaps because she didn't want to offer a hint of the plans they had concocted in the baths earlier. Judd, by contrast, seemed determined to catch her eye, a sober grin on his face, clearly still enjoying her discomfort over her embarrassing loss of control at her parents' apartment. Brylee tried to give him the benefit of the doubt, that he was trying to make her feel at ease by making light of it, but she wasn't wholly convinced.

The hubbub faded as Mayor Hollowhill called the room to order. The short agenda contained but three items: agreement on the minutes from the previous meeting, formal acceptance of the shortlist of candidates to replace Alderman Barrow, and the need to make a final decision on the damming of either the Hax or the Chandler rivers.

As the six candidates' names were read aloud, there was a motion, a seconding, and an accepting of each. Aldermen or alderwomen are elected by the council—as distinct from councillors, who would be elected by the public—and each of the six candidates had been vetted and discussed ahead of the meeting by all seven officials. Brylee breathed a small sigh of relief when her name was read and there were no objections.

"Be it noted that the council has its final list of candidates, and the list is now closed," Mayor Hollowhill said. "Congratulations to all of you who were successful, and for the five who were not, we extend our thanks and appreciation for your interest. Staff will arrange interviews for the successful candidates with council members ahead of the final vote next moon. Now, let's discuss the damned dam." Everyone laughed at her joke, for the proposal had indeed caused passionate debate. During the laughter, several observers whose only interest was the candidate list seized the opportunity to slip out.

At a prior meeting, the decision to create a dam to increase the depth of one of the rivers to allow goods to be transported by water to and from Rostal had been confirmed. Which of the two rivers, the Hax or the Chandler, was the current topic of debate. It was an expensive and disruptive endeavour, so everyone agreed that only one river would be chosen, at least for now.

It was a complex decision. The Chandler route was longer and slower for barges, but it would cost less to build because it passed through the Brown Estates, and Judd had agreed to bear the cost of that section himself, as he would benefit from a more direct path into Rostal. Both routes had communities that were against the flooding and land repurposing, and so it went.

After an hour of discussion, Mayor Hollowhill took the usual step of opening debate to those seated outside of the council table. Several people spoke, including the cathedral's deacon. He didn't seem to have a valid point, but he never missed an opportunity to remind everyone of the church's agenda.

As agreed with Mella, Brylee stood, indicating she would like to contribute. She had spent the session going over how she would speak, as the issue she planned to raise was a sensitive topic. Whichever way she approached it she would cause an uproar, but how tactfully she positioned the contentious information Mella had provided would be noted as part of her application to become an alderwoman. She hated that everyone saw her as impulsive; she was determined to show a more mature side of herself.

"The council recognises Miss Plainhand," Mayor Hollowhill intoned.

"First," Brylee began, sounding more confident than she felt, "I must apologise for the unfortunate timing. I only came by this information in the last twenty-four hours and have not had the opportunity to speak to the individual it most concerns ahead of this meeting. I believe the information might be pertinent to the council's decision today, but I have not had time to verify what I heard. As such, the council might consider hearing what I have to say in a closed session, as I cannot confirm the information's veracity."

"Could you be more specific, Miss Plainhand?" Alderman Cherrywood asked, not at all pleased that his long journey home would be delayed.

"Well, the information inferred that a large quantity of damming materials purchased in anticipation of today's decision might not meet the standard required. If this information turns out to be correct, the purchaser is likely unaware of the issue. However, some might imply it could be a deliberate effort by the purchaser to lower their costs. Rather than allow such a rumour to fester, a closed session would allow the council to decide if it wanted to delay today's decision to allow time to check the facts."

Out of the corner of her eye, she noted Mella's brief nod of satisfaction at her sensitive handling of the topic. She also saw Judd's face flush a bright red. Judging from his reaction, Brylee suspected Mella's information was accurate.

"OK, but let's make this quick," the mayor said. "We must reach a decision, and I don't want any more delays. This is Haxley. We don't do delays. We will adjourn to the antechamber—briefly."

Brylee's stomach turned over in response to the mayor's disapproving tone.

Minutes later, when the seven officials, Brylee, and the scribe were all seated in the antechamber and the doors closed, Mayor Hollowhill asked Brylee to explain herself.

"Well, again, let me apologise—"

"Let's not repeat ourselves, please!" Alderman Cherrywood grumbled.

"Give her a moment, Deek," Mella chided. "She's not known for wasting time, and this forum is new to her. Carry on, dear. But keep it short."

Brylee nodded before continuing. "Yesterday evening a train of carts came south through my family's estate. They were loaded with manure from town, but their previous load had been ironwood for the Brown Estate. The ironwood had been collected three weeks prior from Mage Kahn in Yarrow. The carters understood the ironwood to be intended to raise the banks of the Chandler where it flows through the Brown Estate, should the location of the dam favour the Chandler route."

"Well, what of it?" Judd asked. "I wanted to get my supply ahead of the price increase that would come from us deciding on the route. There's nothing wrong with that. If the decision goes against me, I will simply sell it at cost to supply the needs for the Hax route. That's just good business, girl."

Anger flared inside Brylee at his condescending tone, but she was determined to keep a clear head. "Of course, Alderman Brown, but that's not the point. The carters claimed that when unloading, they saw that the ironwood was 'braded.'"

Everyone turned to Judd, whose face was turning from red to purple.

"That's preposterous! Are you implying I would use inferior product for something as important as shoring up the banks of my own estate? Are you mad?"

"Er . . . excuse me," the scribe said. "Am I capturing this correctly? What is braded?"

Brylee was hoping that, having delivered Mella's revelation, she could withdraw from the dramatics and was glad when Ashli Buttonmeadow stepped in with an answer. "'Braded' is carter slang for goods that get scratched or abraded from sitting on the bed of a cart over a long distance. It can happen, for instance, if the load isn't properly padded and secured."

"Got it," the scribe replied. He wasn't supposed to participate but he couldn't help himself and continued. "So the wood is scratched? Does that matter? It's going to be buried anyway if it will be used to shore up the riverbank."

"Actually, it does, *scribe*," Judd said, seizing the opportunity to put the man in his place and to position himself as the innocent party. "Ironwood was specified by the council because it can never rot or fail. It's a hardwood, shaped for purpose, then a mage transforms it so it is harder than iron. You could swing at it with an axe all day and you still wouldn't scratch it. Carters don't bother with packing when they ship it because it will never be abraded."

"Alderman Brown, are you implying Mage Kahn has cheated you?" Mella asked. Her expression was deadpan except for the cheeky twinkle she couldn't keep from her eyes.

"He is probably the most powerful mage in the five regions, and I wouldn't imply anything of the sort," Judd said. "It's likely Brylee's carter has led her on a dance—or stolen my order and replaced it with untreated wood. Let's get him in here and ask him!"

"If we can locate him," Brylee said. "This was why I was so cautious in raising the matter. My foreman heard the information from one of our workers who unloaded the carts before they continued south. Both are reliable men, but I didn't have the chance to talk to the carter myself." That was the story Mella had suggested would cover such a question. "We would need to inspect the ironwood to check if there's anything to be concerned about."

"Perhaps there was a mistake at the mage's end and Judd's load was missed," the scribe said, forgetting his place again. "Just get Mage Wickham to harden it, or whatever it's called."

"It's not that easy," Erich Bane cut in, seeing an opportunity to hold forth on one of his favourite topics, magic. "Mage Meddison in Lanthe is my uncle, so I know a bit about this. Mages are powerful, to be sure, but they have limited endurance. It drains them to use their magic, you see. Some say it shortens their lives, but that's an old wives' tale. Uncle Meddison explains it like barrels of water. You can let your magic flow out fast or slow, and the barrel empties accordingly. The phrase 'as miserly as a mage with his magic' reflects why they are cautious not to use too much in one go, as they become vulnerable to attack."

"Is that why a powerful mage skrikes magic out of lesser mages or charmers?" Ashli asked, drawn into the discussion.

"No. When a mage skrikes, it's like they make their barrel bigger. Then they can fill it up with more magic and use greater quantities before it gets low. But the bigger barrel takes longer to refill. The amount of magic we're talking about to harden wagon loads of ironwood is enormous. That's why ironwood can't be widely used. A mage will spend weeks or moons hardening a little at a time, so as not to deplete their reserves. Mage Wickham would probably suggest you ask Mage Kahn to take care of it or charge you a fortune. There's no love lost between those two, I hear."

"Look, this all needs to be sorted out, but I have a long ride home tonight," Alderman Cherrywood complained. "Alderman Brown, if the decision goes your way and there turns out to be a problem with your ironwood—not that I'm not accusing you of anything—but if it was stolen, for example, can the council assume it's your problem either way and that you will cover any associated costs? Will you stand by your agreement to fund that section with ironwood regardless? Because if so, this is a side matter and we should move on, conditional on Judd's written assurances." All heads turned to Judd.

"Probably," Judd replied. "But before I give such assurances, give me a week to get to the bottom of this . . . helpful intelligence Miss Plainhand has brought us." Everyone noted his tone didn't live up to the gratitude expressed by his words.

"Do I have a motion for a week's deferral of the decision?" Mayor Hollowhill asked.

"I so move," Mella said. Cherrywood seconded it without delay.

Brylee was relieved. She was just allowing herself to relax when she caught a glance between Mella and Ashli Buttonmeadow.

"And one more thing," Buttermeadow said. "Miss Plainhand clearly has no vested interest, as her farm and business is all south of Haxley. While we, of course, completely trust Alderman Brown, would it not be wise to ask Miss Plainhand to accompany the good alderman to his estate to inspect the material? Her independent report of the issue, especially as she was the one who raised the concern, would stand up better under public scrutiny. If the alderman has no objections, of course."

Judd's face flushed again, but he raised no objection.

"Miss Plainhand, can we rely on you here?" Mayor Hollowhill asked. Brylee had no interest in becoming further embroiled in Mella's web, but she didn't see many options.

"I will do what the council requires, as always, as long as you all believe it's appropriate, given that I'm a candidate for election." Brylee was sure she had just burned Judd's vote, but a majority was not required. Everyone looked around the table, and there was no dissent.

"So ordered. Meeting adjourned," Mayor Hollowhill said, punctuating her decree with a bang of her gavel.

Chapter Twelve

Brylee was attempting to flush away her concerns about being sucked into Mella's game by taking the first sip of her second Broken Down Cart. The fruity liquor was a speciality cocktail of the Crow's Nest's spirit witch, a term of admiration for a barkeep who worked magic by blending strong liquor. She had consumed her first drink slowly while venting to Raegan about her parents' antics, Judd's stalking of the Plainwood business as well as her hand, and finally, that she now had to visit the Brown farm in accordance with the council's wishes. The latter would disrupt her plans to meet with a delegation of traders from the Northern Region of Mordeland who were meeting with barr root farmers to secure stock for the next quarter. It chafed at both women that Brylee could not disclose the purpose of the trip, as it was confidential business on behalf of the council.

Brylee sat alone at the end of the bar and stared into the distance, watching the wind push rolls of clouds into the rough shape of a donkey. The onset of sunset had coloured the clouds pink against the azure sky. Raegan had stepped away to make a circuit of the rooftop tables and engage with her patrons. She was a natural at such socializing.

Many a tavern made a living with average food, ale, and entertainment, relying heavily on overly friendly servers with deep cleavage. Raegen's staff, in contrast, were groomed, pleasant, and sharp, and like Raegan they had learned from Modwyn how to politely turn back inappropriate propositions or touches and how to settle a rowdy customer. The Crow's Nest staff communicated well, so together they were able to manage the worst clients. Jag and Jig, huge twins from Yarrow, took alternating shifts at the front door and could be called up to eject unruly patrons. At the moment, Jig was downstairs, checking people through to the paternoster. He had a nose for troublemakers.

Stacii Willow was working the bar alone, filling drink trays for the staff who conveyed them to the fifty busy tables and collected payment. Other shifts required two bartenders, but Stacii's speed, efficiency, and insistence that no one enter "the hot zone"—as she called the space behind the counter—allowed her to be a solo act. She was amazing to watch, and her non-stop, pithy, but quiet commentary about the customers' antics was hilarious, as long as one wasn't the focus of her sharp wit. Brylee saw that Stacii was struggling to drag a pallet of empty ale kegs to the slooper, so she hopped off her stool, stepped around the bar, and helped. Brylee's strength easily propelled the pallet to the edge of the slooper's twelve-foot-wide circular hole, which led to the loading dock a dozen floors below.

The slooper was a shaft used to return sturdier goods from all floors down to ground level. It relieved the busy paternoster at peak times. The vertical shaft had an opening to each of the higher eight floors. Toward the bottom, it curved until it was horizontal some twenty feet underground. Then it rose up as it circled back on itself to the loading dock on the city side. The gradual change of angle and the nature of the mage-treated surface ensured that objects dropped down the shaft were rarely damaged.

Brylee was one of the few who saw "riding the dragon" or "shooting the slooper" as a rite of passage for the foolhardy and the brave alike. She smiled as she recalled her first time—and the seven further drops she had made since. Each time she completed the challenge, she received a small dot tattooed on the underside of her left wrist. She frowned, recalling Raegan's assertion that she often did stupid things if someone dared her, especially if someone suggested she was too scared to do them. She had to admit, most of her dragon rides bore some element of that truth. *Ag, Raegan's right. Could this day get any worse?* she lamented. She returned to her seat and gulped back the rest of her drink, determined to end the day on a better note. She signalled Stacii for a refill.

Brylee went back to admiring her friend working the tavern. Raegan had made the tavern her own and stalked about it with confidence, showing none of the fragility she had displayed earlier that day. She slipped from table to table, a word here, a story there. It was lovely to watch, and Brylee lost track of time. She was just noticing her third Broken Down Cart was nearing its end when a trader, who had been eyeing her all evening, rose from his seat and approached. Her glare dissuaded him, so he veered towards the paternoster, which would take him down to the privies. *Or further,* she hoped.

Modwyn plunked down next to Brylee and asked Stacii for a Broken Down Cart for them both. Brylee caught Stacii's brief expression, which questioned if Brylee needed another.

"What, are we twelve years old now?" Brylee grumped.

"Sunny crops, Brylee," Modwyn said, clinking mugs with her.

"My crops have taken a bit of a rain lashing today, if I'm honest," Brylee said, noting her voice sounded both slurred and churlish. She shook her head. "Ag, I'm sorry, Modwyn. I'm frustrated is all, and I already vented to Raegan. Stop me from getting a reputation as a bore and a grouch and tell me about your day."

It seemed that Modwyn, by contrast, had had a wonderful day. First, she had slept late, while Brylee had been out in the cold at fourth bell. Then she had secured favourable terms with the Northern Region traders for storage of whoever's product the traders bought. Brylee's trip to the Brown Estate at the behest of the council meant she had to forgo her own meetings with them and would have to delegate to her lead grower. She was good, but Brylee feared the Northern traders might take her absence as a slight. A gown that Modwyn had ordered from Rostal had arrived and fit her perfectly. Brylee never suited such finery due to her physique; standard sizes did not fit her well. Modwyn's accountant had advised her that his review of her business confirmed that the additional revenue from her share in the Crow's Nest had taken profits higher than her father's best year. She was quick to add that she was only able to do so standing on her father's shoulders and through Raegan's good business.

While Brylee was pleased for Modwyn, sometimes the good news of others drove her further into a sour mood rather than lifted her from it, and this was such an occasion. Brylee was sober enough to realise she was in her cups, and it was time to leave.

"Kack," Modwyn groaned, "what's that ass doing here?"

Brylee glanced up to see Gunnar swagger onto the deck. She noted he seemed to sway a little from ale. He saw someone at the far side of the tavern, waved, and made his way over to their table. Raegan had commented on the table earlier. They were a rough lot, and the staff were being careful with them already.

Gunnar stumbled into a woman sitting at a table, causing her to tip her flagon.

"Watch what you're doing," Gunnar growled. The woman's companion shoved his chair back and stood, but Raegan appeared at his shoulder and pushed him gently back into his seat. She signalled to a server to replace the drink Gunnar had spilt, then stepped between Gunnar and his destination.

"You're banned from here," she said, her voice level although bitterness tinged her tone. "You know that."

"I'm the warden," Gunnar retorted, his voice overly loud. "I drink where I want."

"Nope. The council designated the Crow's Nest as a tavern. Therefore it's not part of the market bylaws. Here you're just an ass who has upset other customers before you've even sat down. Get out before I call Jig up here." Raegan's words were strong, but her arms were crossed and she was hunched over, almost cowering.

Gunnar bristled at the insult, especially as many onlookers were from the market. He decided to just ignore her, sure she would give in as she always had. He tried to bypass Raegan, but she stepped into his path once more.

Later, some would say that Gunnar had meant to push Raegan. Others argued he was shocked she had blocked him and he had raised his hands to stop his advance, inadvertently pushing her down. But in that moment, neither reason mattered much to Brylee. She leapt out of her seat and spun Gunnar around, going nose to nose with him, having to crane her neck downwards to do so.

"Back away, you bully," she said, her voice full of menace.

Gunnar laughed. "This whore isn't strong enough to make me look bad, and I'm not scared of her ape either." He cuffed Brylee around the ear. His backhand looked practised, and Brylee knew her friend had felt it many times before.

Her earlier magic expenditure and the cocktails had combined to undermine Brylee's judgement. The bloody accident, her parents' and Judd's antics, as well as her embarrassment at her lack of self-control were fuel that now ignited. The drinks and her guilt over her own churlish behaviour all added to the moment too, but it was the shame from the earlier conversation about how Brylee had not acted to protect Raegan from Gunnar that ignited the rage within Brylee and fanned it into a firestorm.

She grabbed Gunnar by the throat in one hand and snatched his belt with the other. The perfect technique used to load hay bales worked equally as well with this lump of man manure, she noted. She hefted him up to shoulder height and, with two steps, threw him into the slooper. Seeing his shocked expression disappear into the shaft was a hoot and she burst out laughing. With a happy sigh, she turned to help her friend back to her feet, but she froze when she saw the silent tavern. Every face, including Raegan's, was punctuated with an open mouth, and every eye was wide. They didn't bear a pleasing look of shock and awe either. It was true shock and concern. It dawned on her what she had done. She looked from Raegan to the hole and back again.

"Ag . . . Kack . . . Kack . . . Kack!" She sighed, rolling her eyes. Then she turned back to the slooper and leapt after Gunnar.

Chapter Thirteen

Levinial sat alone at a table and watched the magnificent woman haul the drunk off his feet, throw him into the goods chute, and fearlessly follow him down. The man's link to the timeline persisted, so the fall hadn't killed him, and it had started to tremble. Another piece of the puzzle acquired.

He kept his cloak's hood raised–to ensure his face would not become familiar to those he observed–but secretly wished it was time to confront the woman. Her strength, confidence, and openness were captivating, but he knew it was best to wait.

And there is something more. Something new. Deep down he accepted whatever thought eluded him was a warning sign, but his recently formed body flooded him with emotions that encouraged him to ignore it.

It wasn't uncommon for weavers to be attracted to those they hunted–people come in all shapes and sizes–but he was a being of duty and took his work seriously; worlds were at stake.

Why had she reacted to the man so aggressively? An ex-lover? He felt a wave of emotion he identified as jealousy and chided himself.

Perhaps it was that liquor she'd nursed through the evening. He called one of the staff and ordered the same drink out of curiosity.

Chapter Fourteen

Being a charmer, albeit a secret one, meant Brylee never suffered from hangovers. Well, only for as long as it took her to focus and fix her head. She wasn't sure how she cured them, but a half dozen years of drinking games with drovers, wranglers, and labourers had provided her with plenty of practice.

As her head cleared, her nose told her dawn was nearing. The first half an hour of the day held a unique combination of smoke from a fire recently lit, mingling with bacon, eggs, and warm bread.

She was enjoying the last moments of warmth snuggled in her bed, contemplating her breakfast decisions, when the horror of last night surfaced in her memory. She had taken the curve of the dragon on her back, flipping onto her feet as she slid up to the loading bay, to find Gunnar lying still. He was surrounded by onlookers. She pushed through the crowd and asked if he was dead.

"Soothe!" Jake the Abbonite said. "There are no injuries. He sleeps."

"And he's soiled himself," Jig said, laughing. "I would have bet my twin against that one having a pair big enough to ride the dragon. I expect he's just fainted." Karma's wicked humour caused Gunnar to open his eyes just as everyone was laughing at Jig's joke. It took Gunnar no time at all to realise his pants were wet and the crowd was laughing at him.

If a look could kill, Brylee would have been shaking hands with Ag at that moment. Gunnar's hatred of her was clear on his face. Brylee considered an apology but couldn't bring herself to do it. She settled for a half-hearted comment, welcoming him to the club of the dragon riders. That only enraged Gunnar further. Stumbling to his feet, he took a step towards Brylee, only to find Jig blocking his path.

"I think you'll want to get clean britches before you take on Miss Plainhand, Warden. And maybe bigger shoes while you're at it." The insult didn't help matters, but Brylee appreciated Jig's support.

Should I go to Gunnar this morning and apologise? she wondered as she pulled herself out of bed. She poured water into a large tin bowl and washed. The town watch hadn't come for her in the night. That was something, at least. No, she decided. She was headed out of town to the Brown Estate, then she planned to head up to Rostal on that other matter Mella had shared with her in the baths. She would be gone for at least a week. Hopefully everything would cool down by her return. If not, a few weeks down at Plainhand Estate might be needed.

Within thirty minutes she had eaten and reached the stables. Summer was pleased to see her and the apple in her hand, but she had little interest in leaving her warm stall. A quick brush down and some fresh hay made her more pliant. By the time Judd pulled up on his white stallion, Summer was saddled and ready for the road.

"He's a brute," Brylee said, admiring Judd's mount. She noted Judd had set the bit too tight, but she didn't comment. He was no doubt still cross about her challenge at the council, and she preferred not to make matters worse. She had enough problems with throwing Gunnar down the slooper.

"Blazer is one of my favourite rides," Judd replied, giving no sign of unfriendliness. "Fiery but compliant when I put the spurs to him."

Is that a reference to marriage? Brylee wondered. *We're playing that game, are we?* She ignored him and pulled herself into the saddle.

They ambled to the east edge of town to warm their horses. Not much was said, both riders choosing to brood while they navigated the growing throngs as Haxley awoke. Four large men joined them as they took the road out of town and into the countryside. A four-hour ride would see them to the Brown Estate.

"I thought it safer to travel home with my guard," Judd explained. "There have been several attacks on this road recently. The Ag-cursed bandits are getting bolder." Brylee hadn't heard of any issues that should trouble two riders with nothing much to steal, but she said nothing. The four men led off in two pairs, and Judd and Brylee followed.

Brylee's brow creased as the group rolled into a canter, and she took stock of the array of weaponry the group displayed. They looked more like mercenaries, although they didn't move with the easy confidence that such men typically displayed. In fact, they seemed nervous and guarded.

On closer inspection, she observed the pair of riders in the centre of the group had heavily laden saddlebags. Their horses were struggling under the weight. *Kack, Judd's running his profits home,* she deduced. It was more common to leave money in the Haxley bank, but some preferred to convert their coin into ingots of gold or silver and ferry them home. No wonder Judd wanted additional security.

In an attempt to improve on yesterday's churlish mood, Brylee struck up a conversation with Judd. Romance and marriage were shunned by both as a topic, but they ranged through many related business matters, and Brylee found Judd knowledgeable about grapes and wine production, the staples of the Brown Estate. After an hour, Brylee had to admit Judd had some charm, at least when he wasn't trying to be charming.

Alternating between a walk and a canter, the group of six riders overtook several caravans and cart trains as they followed the River Chandler until it wandered south and parted from the road for a spell. Later it would begin its sweep north and curve back to meet them again, so they would cross it at the Ford Inn. A millennium of traffic had forged a straighter trail to the inn, up and over a hilly section known as the Crags, around which the Chandler deviated. Far from mountainous—the peak only equalled the height of the Barrow Building—the Crags were squat and blocky. Some had nicknamed them the Giant's Table, for it looked like a place such a creature might sit to eat. Up close, one saw that the Crags were made of jagged boulders, each the size of a small cottage.

As the path rose into the Crags, rocks and shadows loomed around the party, and the conversation, which had felt more amiable than the temporary truce it probably was, petered out. The empty road and uneasy landscape created and then fanned a sense of foreboding. Caught up in their conversation, Brylee and Judd had drifted well back from the four guards. Now, with unspoken agreement, they nudged their mounts into a trot to close the gap.

The guards were still well ahead and passing a small shelter, one of several set within the Crags for travellers in the event of bad weather. It was large enough for perhaps six people crammed together but not tall enough for a horse.

From Brylee and Judd's distant viewpoint, it appeared that the two lead guards simply fell off their horses. Both hit the ground, and neither moved.

An attack, Brylee realised.

The other two riders swirled and circled, looking for the bandits that were raining arrows down on them, then looked back at Judd for instruction.

"Ride, you fools!" he yelled. They responded by kicking their mounts into action. The rider on the south side of the road was doubly unfortunate, as their surge resulted in him taking the arrow meant for his colleague while the shaft meant for him took his horse in the neck. Horse and man went down in a heap while the other guard bounded off with more arrows bouncing off the rocks behind him.

Brylee had Summer half-turned to flee back down the road when she saw two men detach themselves from the boulders behind them. They were advancing with crossbows pointed. Brylee kicked Summer forward, hoping to bolt after Judd's escaping guard. Judd was already galloping that way, he and his man bent low in the saddle and hugging their horses' necks.

Three men jumped into their path some one hundred yards ahead, blocking their escape. Charging them was an option, but the bandit's crossbows would certainly score. Brylee considered attempting to turn Summer up into the rocks, but there wasn't even room for a person on foot, never mind a horse. The location of the ambush had been well chosen. She was proficient with the short sword and long knife she carried on her belt, but they were useless against such firepower.

"Into the shelter!" she yelled, indicating the building midway between the attackers.

Brylee leapt from Summer, then smacked the horse's hindquarters and yelled at her to go. She was almost surprised when Summer obeyed, although she put it down more to panic from the attack than obedience.

Brylee darted into the shelter. She looked for weapons but found nothing but warm clothing and rations. Judd had likewise released his horse but had stopped to check on his guard, or so

Brylee supposed. When she turned to work out how to bar the thick door, she was dismayed to see Judd duck inside, clutching the weighty saddlebags full of gold.

"Leave that out there for them," she said. "They won't leave empty handed."

"They'll want to kill us either way," Judd replied. That made no sense, but there was no time for debate. Crossbow bolts were already thudding into the walls of the shelter.

Brylee slammed the heavy door. It was a substantial piece of oak designed to withstand the worst weather. She unsheathed her long knife and slotted it through the iron ring that held the door closed, then wedged it between the dense wood planking.

It seemed only a second before the men outside were yanking on the door, which barely held. She slid her sword in beside the knife, further strengthening the makeshift arrangement.

"Help me!" she yelled, bracing the door. When Judd didn't reply, she glanced over her shoulder and saw a crossbow bolt protruding from his back. It was at a shallow angle, lodged between his left shoulder and his spine. Judd was face down, sprawled across his gold, and not moving. Had a lucky shot come through the door and caught him, or had they shot him outside? Torn between bracing the door and seeing if she could aid Judd, she chose the former. If they got through the door, they would both be dead anyway.

There was a brief respite, and she heard a muffled argument outside. It was followed by a period of banging all about the shelter, including on the roof, as the bandits probed for a weakness. Then there was silence for a spell. It was followed by the sounds of what could only be a horse being backed up to the door and tied to the handle. The door strained a few times, only to snap back as the horse broke whatever tether the men had employed. They clearly didn't have rope. She assumed they were using leather from the tack of Judd's guard's horse.

"Throw the gold out if you want to walk away from this." The gruff voice carried a tone used to command. "If not, we'll burn you out." Brylee caught her breath and thought about it. She crept away from the door and risked a quick inspection of Judd's injury. He was barely conscious. The bolt hadn't gone deep, and she was sure he was not fatally injured, but he was in excruciating pain. He screamed as she probed, then the bolt came free. A barb had caught on one side, but the other had not penetrated deep enough to set. Judd's cries subsided as soon as the pressure was relieved and he passed out.

"If I open the door, you'll kill us anyway!" Brylee yelled. "And no, I won't take the word of a bandit if you say otherwise."

"You're to burn then?" the voice asked. "Tell Ag 'sunny crops' from us, will you?" She heard muffled laughter from outside.

Brylee considered pointing out that the shed was saturated from a winter of rain and snow, and its wood would never take, but she held her tongue. The more time they wasted on such tricks, the more likely other travellers would come along. In fact, she recalled, the last caravan they passed had several heavily armed mercenaries. How long had it been? She couldn't remember. She decided to stay quiet and make Judd as comfortable as possible.

Perhaps a whole bell of time passed while the men outside fumbled about trying to break through by various means before their tone became more urgent. She guessed a lookout had spotted the approaching caravan, though it would still be a distance away.

"Last chance. I hear burning is a grisly death."

She stayed silent. After a time, she heard the men mount, curse her in several imaginative ways, then gallop away. Brylee decided she would not unbar the door in case someone had stayed behind, lurking in wait. She would sit it out until she heard the caravan stop and investigate the three bodies and the dead horse.

That decision lasted only until she detected the first hint of smoke. The bandits had either found a way to light the damp wood or, more likely, had piled debris around the shelter, intending not to burn them out but to suffocate them. She grabbed a blanket, wet it from the emergency water barrel, then wedged it into the crack under the door.

The blanket made little difference, however, and in no time she and Judd were coughing. She had to risk opening the door, hoping the bandits had fled. She pulled both blades free and dropped them to the side, then leaned into the door to open it a crack. It wouldn't budge. With nothing obstructing it on her side, she realised they must have wedged something against the outside.

Frantic pushing and banging had no effect, and she realised she was quickly succumbing to the smoke. The shelter was solid, as the bandits had discovered. The only way out was the door. She examined the hinges, or what of them were visible from inside. She could only tell where they were mounted but could discern no detail of their construction. She hammered on them with the hilt of her sword and dug at them with her knife. Nothing. Her breathing was becoming laboured, and she was constantly coughing. She was becoming desperate.

In her mind, she pictured how the hinges were set. Plates of iron pegged into the wood. There was little she could do about the iron, but was there a way she could charm the wood? It would be dry, protected from the elements by the door frame. She had experimented with setting things alight. She could light a wick from a distance of about a yard, and she had lit kindling twice from a foot away. Could she use that skill now? Her mind was becoming clouded. She was weak from using her magic to save the woodsman the previous morning, but she had to try.

The door opened outwards, and it felt that it was secured firmest near the handle on the opposite side from the hinges. A stake braced from handle to the ground would be simple and effective. She knelt and put her hand to the wood around the lower hinge. She didn't need to burn it all, just a small section on the outside so the hinge would slip through the gap. She pictured that situation and put her mind to it, pouring everything she had into the bond she created with the wood fibres. It took more magic at once than she had ever tried to flow. Brylee held nothing back, knowing she would be dead if it didn't work. She felt heat on her hand, but was it enough? Was it from her efforts or the bandit's blaze?

As the last of her magic drained out, she felt dizzy. She stood back and kicked the hinge. Nothing. She kept at it. On the fifth kick, it budged a fraction. With renewed hope, she thumped on it twice more. The hinge broke free and the door shifted outwards. Whatever was barring the door fell away, and the door swung wide open on the remaining top hinge. Gasping, she grabbed Judd by the ankles and dragged him towards the sunlight, turning him on his side as he slid through the bandit's fire, which was blazing in the doorway. When they were clear of it, she collapsed into darkness.

Chapter Fifteen

The 467th Year of the Morde Dynasty—Three Years Earlier

What a mess, Cleric Oliver thought. A week ago, his long-wrought plans had been progressing nicely. The Order of Bredden Clerics had manoeuvred for decades for influence in Raile, and their more militant sect of the Church of Ag had floundered until Cleric Oliver's appointment as its leader eight years ago. Under his figurative, and on occasion literal, whip they had become the true power behind the throne. But a week ago, that idiot Arkly had conceded to his feeble bride's whim to birth the heir at her parents' castle in the south of the region instead of the seat of power in the region's capital. The ill-conceived trip had turned into a disaster. *But what to do?*

Rea, Arkly's wife and now the de facto ruler of Raile, was at death's door but could probably be saved at the heir's expense. She hated Oliver with a passion, believing his methods cruel rather than necessary. But if she died and the heir survived, it was highly likely Arkly's brother, Thom, would be confirmed by the Elect of Morde as Raile's regent until the child reached the age of majority. Thom was weak willed and easily managed, and the Breddens were well placed to groom the heir, thus solidifying his grip on the region. The more he thought about things, the more Cleric Oliver determined that rather than the trip bringing complete disaster, blessings could still be harvested if he acted boldly.

He turned his calculating mind to what to do with the HAC. Outwardly, the Bredden Order neither promoted nor opposed the Wig mentality, but behind closed doors, Oliver had presented himself as an ardent Wig to assuage powerful idiots like Arkly. Secretly, he thought the whole magical healer thing was ludicrous and dangerous. Such progressiveness could eventually undermine the Bredden Order's political power. The church benefitted from an ignorant populace respecting Ag's will, as interpreted and espoused by his brethren. Hundreds of magical healers with increased education, stumbling around healing people and gaining influence, had to be discouraged.

In the few minutes it took to walk back from the courtyard into the lord's quarters, he made a series of quick calculations and roughed out a strategy to grab power. The heir had to survive and the mother perish *bravely* during childbirth. Lydd and the charmers had to die at the hands of a distraught Gideon Strangelore, who would then follow his sister into oblivion. Jeef and her Mobi'dern would return to their home in the south, and the Nuulan guard would be released back to the capital.

Oliver whispered instructions to two of his trusted aides. One went to the HAC healer who was tending Rea to ensure that Lord Arkly's fabricated dying wish, that his heir survive, even at the expense of the mother, was communicated clearly. The other aide had Principal Lydd and her senior staff assemble in the hall with the charmers. The aide also prepared a chalice of wine for Oliver and a chalice for Lydd and each of her staff and the charmers. To all but Oliver's he added enough Devil's Kiss to poison the largest horse. The scentless strangler powder was cruel and fast acting. The aide was grateful he would not be present at the end.

As instructed by Cleric Oliver, the aide and three servants carried the goblets into the hall and handed them out with a stern admonishment to wait for the toast, which Oliver was about to give, to mark the tragic passing of their lord. Then the aide led the servants from the room and pulled the door closed.

Chapter Sixteen

Gideon raced ahead into the quarters he shared with Tuli. He swept the dining table's contents to the floor, then rushed into his bedroom for his personal medical kit.

The Mobi'dern lowered Tuli onto the table, and Gideon pushed past them as he ripped gauze pads from his pack. He had already exhausted his magical reserves, and she was fading fast. He asked one warrior to put pressure on the pads, but even as he did, Gideon acknowledged there was little blood left in his sister to save. Tuli whispered something, but it was too faint to hear.

"What is it?" Gideon asked, leaning in close to listen and to hug his sister.

"Send them away," she said, her voice faint. Gideon assumed her request related to allowing her some privacy for the inevitable and could think of no reason to keep the warriors there. He asked them to leave, and they slipped out, having seen enough of such wounds to know her fate.

Gideon abandoned his attempt to save Tuli. It was too late. They had just a few moments left, and he would try to make them as peaceful as possible for her.

"I'll miss you," he began, but she slapped weakly at him to silence him.

"Take my magic," Tuli murmured.

"What? How?"

"Skrike me."

"No!" he said, horrified.

"Listen, brother. I have much more power than you . . . and it would be a sin to waste it. You said it yourself, we need to take risks . . . you will be able to do more if you increase your magical reserves."

Her words made him nauseous, but he was also ashamed to admit he felt a rush of excitement.

"But I wouldn't know how," he protested.

"I'll show you. Mother knew. When she died . . . why do you think I have so much more magic than you?"

"Mother?" His mind was spinning. Tuli took Gideon's hand.

"Open your mind and relax," she said. He struggled to do so, but panic overwhelmed him. She squeezed harder. Then through his magic senses, he felt her in a way he had never felt anyone. In his mind's eye he saw a glow inside her and a thin line leading away from it, vanishing into nothingness.

"That's it . . . you see it? Take that link and pull it to yourself."

Gideon tried to imagine pulling the thread. The line wavered, then moved towards him. He knew Tuli was pushing it to him as much as he was pulling. As the glow followed the thread to him, he gained control. He felt her thread slide into his mind, where it found another line, which he recognised as his own. He had never looked inside himself in this way, and he was astonished to see the line or cord or whatever it was. It vanished into the distance, just like Tuli's. He felt a rush of euphoria as the two cords wrapped around each other, and he sensed his world expanding. Starving for more, he suddenly remembered at what cost he was receiving this gift.

Gideon looked down at Tuli. She appeared to be at peace. He even thought that she smiled briefly. Then the light left her eyes as they lost focus. Did he imagine it, or was there a flash of blame and disgust in her expression before her face went slack?

He felt a terrible sense of loss—and something else. He floundered about mentally to identify the sensation. He saw a third line vanishing away, followed by a fourth and a fifth, then a dozen, then over twenty. He grabbed them all with his mind with a desperate fervour. Taking each one in, he bound them to his and Tuli's, wondering where they were coming from.

In the main hall nearby, Cleric Oliver walked away from twenty charmer corpses with a smile on his face and a spring in his step.

Chapter Seventeen

Lu stood at attention four feet in front of Da-Jeef. Her head was high, but her spirits were low. Five Mobi'dern stood in a straight line behind their leader, five flanked Lu to her left, and five more were to her right. They formed a three-sided box with Jeef and Lu in their centre. The remaining member of the eighteen-woman division was not present. Instead, she watched the guards posted outside of Gideon and Tuli's room from a dark corner in the eves of the building across the courtyard, where she had slipped as ordered by her leader's hand gestures.

The severing ceremony was typically reserved for deserters, of which there were few, and for the even fewer occasions of gross breaches of discipline in the Mobi'dern ranks. Lu had attended such rites twice, and in each case the crimes were deliberate and the subjects reviled. By contrast no one in the room blamed Lu for Shanna's actions, and she was esteemed and even loved by her peers as well as a favourite of Jeef's. But no one present questioned the blame or the shame that would fall on the Mobi'dern following the tragedy for which they each silently blamed Lord Arkly.

"Lu, duty tears my heart in two," Da-Jeef said. "There are those in our clan who will use this tragedy to argue we should withdraw from the world and return to our insular roots."

"Aren't we here to protect the HAC's charmers?" Lu asked, her voice choked with emotion. Everyone present understood their leader's quandary and the need to limit the fallout by removing Lu from their ranks. Even Lu understood. She sent a constant stream of reassurance to Shanna, who continued to offer to defend Lu from whatever was troubling her.

No, you will put me in more danger by coming, Lu said. *Rest. I'll come to you soon.*

Unable to speak anymore, Da-Jeef bit her lip and hardened herself to what she must do. She shook her head as she gave the hand signal to commence the ceremony.

Lu's weapons had already been taken, so she removed her distinctive uniform, folding each piece and placing it on a stool at her side. Civilian clothing had been provided, which she slipped

into, struggling with buttons and ties she had never worn before. She felt naked in the new garments.

She looked up to see tears streaming down Jeef's face. Unable to hold back her own any longer, she felt them burn lines down her hot cheeks. Most of her fifteen peers were likewise afflicted. They would take her clothes and weapons, but her link to Shanna was for life, so she would have that at least.

"Thank you for your service," Da-Jeef said, both in words and in signs, contrary to the norm for the severing custom, which was typically conducted in total silence. Not wanting to prolong the pain, Da-Jeef made a cutting motion with her left hand, and closed both fists before turning them over so their backs faced the floor. As her fists slowly rotated, all the warriors except for Lu turned and presented their backs to Lu as they stared at the cold walls.

It was done, and Lu was terrified. Her hands shook, and the room seemed to close around her. She stood there for a moment, knowing no one would turn back to her yet hoping they would. Eventually, with a deep sigh she picked up her small pack of personal belongings and walked to the exit.

Lu opened the door and was surprised to find Cleric Oliver outside, his hand reaching for the latch to let himself into their barracks. He didn't recognise Lu in her civilian clothes, and he brushed past her as the sixteen warriors turned back to face the room.

"Da-Jeef, there you are. There's been another tragedy. Gideon Strangelore has lost his mind. What Arkly did to his sister must have broken him. He's poisoned Lydd and all the other charmers. He was caught red-handed with the poison. We tried to restrain him, but he stabbed himself. It's terrible."

"Really?" Jeef said. She had instructed her watcher to report if Gideon left his rooms or if anyone went inside, and she had received no such report.

"Yes, and that's not all. Lady Arkly died in childbirth. There was nothing anyone could have done, I'm afraid. It's a tragic day. Utterly tragic."

It seemed like Oliver was trying to sound upset—perhaps even practicing a script he had rehearsed—and Jeef remained sceptical.

"That's terrible news, Cleric. I'll send Mobi'dern to guard the heir and to secure Gideon's body too. There will be an enquiry, of course."

A surprised look flitted across the cleric's face before it dissolved back into the shocked pretence. "That won't be necessary, Da-Jeef. The Nuulan guard are doing both already and preparing to depart for the capital within the hour. The HAC has been closed, at least for now. Your new orders are to return to your home straight away. Of course, you must report to your superiors on arrival, but you and your division are not to talk about today's events otherwise. Is that clear?"

It was amazing to Jeef how quickly he flipped from upset to menacing. She didn't recognise Cleric Oliver's authority, and she was highly sceptical of his story, but she didn't see a point in confronting him here. More people would die needlessly, and to what end? The Nuulan guard would protect the heir; that was true.

"What did you do with the warrior who killed Lord Arkly?" Oliver asked, scanning the room.

"She's been severed from the Mobi'dern and banished," Jeef replied. "We will return home to report immediately." In what appeared to the cleric as a nervous tick, Jeef's fingers flicked towards Lu, who was still in the doorway dressed as a civilian. *Find and protect Gideon*, the signal said. *Go with the Warrior's Grace.*

If Oliver had been more observant and less smug, he would have witnessed the right hand of each Mobi'dern echo their leader's ritual salutation.

Filled with a renewed and unexpected sense of purpose, Lu slipped away. She climbed out through a back window and up onto the roof, invisible against the late-dusk sky. By the time Oliver pulled himself away from Jeef's onslaught of delay tactics and arrived at Gideon's quarters, he found the guards he had assigned to detain Gideon dead and his rooms empty.

As Lu and Gideon completed the short dash across the open ground to the clearing where Shanna had stalked the hare, they found the big cat waiting for them. Shanna stood on her rear legs and placed her paws on Lu's shoulders to nuzzle her face.

New adventure? Lu offered. Her eyes were dry but bloodshot from tears not felt since the early days of her training.

What happened?

Lu was too raw at that moment to explain. She wanted to blame Arkly, Gideon, and Shanna for how her life had exploded in seconds, but deep down a barbed shard of self-blame was hooked into her psyche. *I'll explain on the way, my friend. Range ahead and ensure the way is clear. We go towards the sun.*

Chapter Eighteen

The 470th Year of the Morde Dynasty

The familiar rumble of the cart and the lazy clopping of horses' hooves sounded distant. It was reminiscent of dozing as her pa steered the cart home during childhood and later in life from all-too-drunk wagon rides home from the tavern. Each time Brylee pulled herself close to consciousness, the noise lulled her back into oblivion. Hours passed.

"Summer!" It started as a shout, but the dryness of her throat and the weakness of her body reduced it to a whisper. Brylee had been dozing when the memory of her horse galloping away reared in her mind. Her eyes flew open, but her attempt to rise was thwarted by a coughing fit.

Firm hands helped her forward as cushions were bolstered at her back. Someone pressed a cup of water to her lips.

"Your horse is fine. She's in the stables in a lot better shape than you," a kindly voice said. Assaulted by a strong smell of sweetmint, Brylee turned her head away from the cloth being held near her face.

"Easy now. Breathe it in. Sweetmint will help clear any vestige of smoke from your lungs." Slowly, her memories returned to her. The attack, the smoke . . .

"OK, OK." She coughed, taking the cloth in one hand and the cup in the other. "I'll do it. Just give me some space."

The speaker was right. The fumes quickly softened her cough, and soon Brylee felt that she could breathe easier. She went to wipe her eyes on her sleeve, but there was no sleeve. Her arms were bare. Brylee looked around for the first time and found she was in a large bed in a small, tidy room. She saw her clothes—they looked clean too—draped over a chair by the door. Checking under the covers, she realised all she was wearing was a slip. She owned a slip, but she hadn't travelled with it.

"Don't worry," the voice said, guessing at Brylee's discomfort. "My wife and the maid changed your clothes so I could examine you properly. I'm the Brown Estate's healer. My friends call me Niff."

Brylee focussed on the tiny man for the first time as she sat up straighter, moving the cloth to her other hand as she pulled the coverings up for modesty. He had a pleasant face, his eyes peeking over a neat, thick black beard. His hair was cut close, in the healer style. His eyes were kind, although she wasn't quite sure if they were both pointed precisely at her.

"It's the left one," Niff said. When she looked puzzled, he continued. "People take a while to work out which one is fake. It was defective at birth, and that was my inspiration to follow the healing arts. We will all feel more comfortable if you look at my right eye when we talk." He touched the right side of his face so there was no confusion regarding whose left and right side he was referring to. His smile was warm and genuine, and he was clearly practised at this explanation.

"It looks real," Brylee said, referring to the false eye and feeling a little dumb as she heard her own voice. His smile grew, lighting up his face.

"Thank you. It's my own design, actually. I call it 142. It was my one hundred and forty-second attempt at it. I studied healing at the Pope School in Raile for four years. As you know, Raile glass is considered the finest of the five regions, and the Pope School sits adjacent to Raile's best school for apprenticing glass formers. That's where I met my wife. She taught me the basics of glass forming, and . . . sorry, I'm blathering. How are you feeling? I was quite worried about you."

Brylee spent a few moments taking stock. Her cough was easing quickly. Her body ached, and she was tired. Her magic was low but seemed to be replenishing itself. She was also ravenous. She conveyed all but her magical status to Niff.

With her permission, Niff listened to her chest, checked her eyes, and poked at her for a few minutes. His technique was unobtrusive and easy to tolerate, but Brylee was relieved when the examination was over.

"Do you feel strong enough to dress yourself?" he asked. When she nodded, he did the same. "There's hot food in the kitchen. Follow the smell down the hallway. Come through when you're ready, and we'll see how you feel after a meal."

Niff left Brylee to wash and dress. Her clothes were as clean as they appeared, and she found her weapons leaning in the corner with her saddlebags. Nothing seemed to have been disturbed. It didn't seem appropriate to wear her blades in the house, so she left them where they were.

It was a short hallway, and the kitchen was easy to find. Niff's wife was as petite as he was, so they were well matched in height, although her arms showed the muscles of someone who used them often. The kitchen was clearly the centre of the home and was festooned with glassware, including vases, containers, and ornaments galore. They were craftily placed, making the room cosy rather than cluttered.

"Come through, dear," Niff's wife said as she piled some steaming stew onto a plate and set it on the table. "I'm Zally, Niff's wife. I'm also Mr. Brown's head bottle maker, but as you can see, I dabble in other glass forming too." Brylee made a show of examining some. They were worthy of the best stores in Haxley, Rostal too probably, and she said so.

She sat and tasted the stew, intending to ask how long she had slept, but she was halfway through the bowl and the thick slice of salt bread before she came up for air.

"I'm so sorry," she said. "I had no idea how hungry I was, and this food is delicious."

"You've slept for almost two days straight," Niff said. "The caravan brought you and Mr. Brown in the day before yesterday. We got some water into you but that's all. It's a wonder you're not eating the plate too, tall girl like you."

"How is Judd?" Brylee felt a flicker of shame that she had asked about her horse before her travel companion.

"Grumpy as hell, but that's not unusual." Niff laughed as he sat down with his own bowl. Then his face grew serious. "Terrible about the guards, though. Two died, and the third still might. I worked on him for four hours when they brought him in. Mr. Brown needed stitches and will be bruised for weeks. The arrow hit a bone but must have ricocheted off something first. The bone would have been smashed otherwise. He was up and about yesterday, although moving tenderly."

By then Brylee was mopping her bowl with bread. Zally offered her a second helping of stew, which Brylee refused, only to let herself be persuaded.

Niff laughed. "Healer's orders! Just slow this one down. Do you feel sick at all?"

"Just tired," Brylee replied, counting to twenty before diving into the bowl again.

"We couldn't find any real injury, other than scrapes. It's not unusual for folks who have such a fright to be tired, but sleeping so long indicates something else might be wrong. I wondered if the smoke might have stifled your breathing to the point your mind was damaged. That can happen with people who nearly drown too. But you seem fine now that you're awake." He stared at her as if he could solve the puzzle that way. It clearly niggled at him.

"The past week has been hard," she improvised, concealing the real cause of her weariness. "I recently found out my pa is a lot sicker than we thought. I had to clear the roads of snow and help load many bales at the farm too. I was feeling exhausted before the attack. Could it just be that?"

"Yes, it could." Niff's body relaxed, but Brylee could tell he wasn't quite convinced. "I'm glad it wasn't anything more serious," he continued. "I'm skilled, but if you had needed healing from a full mage, I think they are all in the south, and they'll be gone for another week at least. The Council for Magical Law has them all helping with the war effort." Brylee was shocked that Judd had the ability to call upon a mage at all. Plainhand Estate certainly couldn't. Niff explained there was a family connection.

Brylee insisted on helping wash the dishes. She thanked Niff and Zally profusely, then made her way up to the main house. The walk through the rows of vines was interesting, even though there was no fruit at that time of year. She studied how the plants were strung and irrigated, making some mental notes to share with her own growers.

The Brown residence was a small mansion. She hadn't visited all the local estates, but she would have bet the house was one of the most prestigious. It was made of a cream-coloured stone and had a black slate roof. Ivy clung to the south side of the house, softening its appearance. Huge, curved windows dominated the front of the house, bracketing a double front door, which was painted bright red. The door frame and the window frames were stained to match the slate. Through the window above the door, Brylee saw a chandelier, and she wondered if Zally had sculpted it.

The door opened before she got to it, and Judd stepped out, closing it behind him. He steered her away from the house.

"Glad you're looking so well. I'm told I have you to thank for saving my life." He laughed. "But look, do you feel up to inspecting the ironwood? I know it's a bit rushed, but the council will be waiting for my answer. You know how it is."

Although his request verged on being rude, Brylee was secretly relieved. She had no desire to be there. As Judd walked her to a storage area behind the main stables, they talked about their experience with the bandits. His horse hadn't been located, but he was relieved not to have lost his gold. If he thought about the dead guards at all, he didn't mention them.

The wood had been sorted into two piles. Roughly 40 percent of it was ironwood, and the remainder had not been mage treated. Judd insisted Brylee walk along each large stack and test it randomly with an axe he supplied.

"Assuming you still plan to ride on to Rostal, I took the liberty of drafting a letter to the council for you to sign, which I will take back today," Judd explained. "Or you could write your own, of course. Just trying to save time. My draft explains you've had the opportunity to test the wood to your satisfaction, and I've clearly been swindled, you see. I'm heading back this afternoon, and if you feel you have time, it would be helpful if you would confirm the facts. I've been bilked, and I'm glad you brought it to my attention."

"I'm sure your draft is accurate, Judd. But for formality's sake, I'll write my own. However, I expect it will say much the same." Brylee had no intention of including wording explaining how Judd came to have less than 100 percent ironwood but would confirm that 40 percent of it was hardened. He could explain the rest.

Judd walked her back to the healer's house. He said she was welcome to stay until she felt well enough to travel. In fact, he seemed genuinely keen for her to stay, despite not accommodating her in the main house. Brylee offered to pay for the healer's costs and Summer's stabling, but Judd wouldn't hear of it.

By the time Brylee had sealed her letter to the mayor with the crest on her ring, Judd was back at the healer's door, mounted and ready to ride back to Haxley. In the distance Brylee saw a gathering of riders who seemed to be set to accompany him.

It would take Brylee five hours to reach Rostal from the Brown Estate, and she worried the meeting that Mella had arranged for her would spoil were she late. She collected her things, thanked Zally and Niff for their skill and hospitality, then allowed Zally to press a food package into her hand as she walked out to find Summer. Twenty minutes later she was on the road to Rostal.

Chapter Nineteen

Judd kept two homes in Haxley, although most of his circle of acquaintances only knew about one: his three-storey home in one of the wealthiest streets in the northwest part of town. More exclusive than Silverside, most homes in Bishop's Mews were attached, and as was common to houses of great wealth, they had the kitchen and washer room in the basement and sleeping quarters for staff in the attic. The ground floor rooms were raised and were reached from the street by an elegant stone staircase, so that passers-by could not gawk inside. It was the familiar design that formal and entertainment rooms occupied that level. Bedrooms and guest parlours sat above on the second floor.

Known only to those whom Judd wished to have a more private assignation with was an address in Willow Tree, the sister complex to Brylee's parents' Dalebook Apartments in Silverside. There Judd maintained a small one-bedroom unit with a private entrance under the name of Mr. Black. It was from there that Judd slipped out into the dark night, dressed in tradesmen's clothing, foregoing his usual finery. A hooded cloak hid his face from casual observation, as it did whenever "Mr. Black" came and went.

Judd hurried north, winding through neighbourhoods displaying signs of decreasing wealth with each mile. He crossed the Hax into the northwestern sector at the Tanner Bridge and then turned right to follow the river north.

Drover Lane boasted at least eight taverns, each enjoying a lively trade while serving the large number of inns and hostelries used by transient carters, teamsters, and traders. Each evening, perhaps a quarter of the town watch would patrol a three-street radius around Drover Lane to manage perhaps half of Haxley's daily crimes. It was not the safest area.

The Olde Sod had started life as the Fertile Sod, but its name was misused so often the proprietor accepted the will of the neighbourhood and renamed it. In recent years, Judd had covertly acquired it and two other taverns. They made fair coin, but more importantly, they provided a never-ending stream of information from a network of employees controlled by a woman he trusted, be it business intelligence or gossip that could be leveraged, as well as a place he could conduct business anonymously. Judd slipped through a delivery alley to the back of the tavern and let himself in with a key.

Emerging from the storeroom, Judd ghosted past the kitchen door and into a private room. As instructed, Gunnar Fenn was already there, helping himself to the daily special of chicken pie, potatoes, and ale that he had collected from the barman. Judd withdrew another key, which fit a small cupboard built into the wall at the rear of the room. From there he chose a glass, from a collection made by Zally, and a bottle of Brown Prime, his estate's best vintage. He had eaten earlier. Although the fare at the Olde Sod smelled wholesome, he knew it was not.

As happened every two weeks, Gunnar updated Judd on activities in the markets and answered numerous questions. Nothing was said of Gunnar's induction into the Dragon Rider's Club, but both knew of it. Over another ale, Gunnar listed the bribes he had accepted from various vendors for favourable spots for themselves or restrictions imposed on their competitors. No coin would be passed to Judd that night for his share, but Gunnar would ensure an ingot of the correct weight and quality was left at an agreed-upon place in due course.

When their regular business was concluded, Judd broached another topic.

"Gunnar, without raking over the recent foolishness at the Crow's Nest, what is your opinion of Brylee Plainhand?"

"She's an arrogant bitch. A big oafish bitch, to be sure. It's a shame those bandits didn't do us all a favour, although I'm glad you safely fended them off, sir."

"Yes, she's become full of herself. I agree," Judd replied, pretending to be thoughtful.

"I've a mind to catch her in a dark alley and finish her, I have. Perhaps have some fun with her first, if you catch my meaning."

"I wouldn't want that, Gunner. Your involvement, I mean. You and I have too much going well for us to chance anyone catching you or something going wrong." In truth, Judd was confident Gunnar would find a way to fumble such an attempt. "But as to her sticky end, we need to ensure she has one. And I have a better idea than an alley."

Judd went on to explain how Brylee had managed their escape from the shelter. Judd thought it strange at the time but put it down to the confusion of the smoke and his injury. But it niggled at him so much that he stopped at the shelter on his way back to Haxley and inspected the door frame. The bandit's fire had scorched the side and bottom of the door opposite the hinges. That made some sense. On the hinge side of the door, there was a neat burn around the hinge itself and a few splinters from being kicked out. He explained his observations to Gunnar.

"So what?" Gunnar asked, not getting it.

"She's a charmer, man. Brylee Plainhand used magic. Don't you see?" It took a while, but Gunnar's ale-addled cogs eventually spun Judd's meaning into place. His face lit up like a young boy who had just been granted two birthdays.

"I'll tell everyone tomorrow," he said, laughing with glee. "Ruin her business in no time. I can paint Raegan as a charmer too." His imagination was galloping away, and Judd had to rein him back in.

"That's the last thing I want, Gunnar. I want to acquire her business, not ruin it, you idiot. Here's what you need to do."

Judd gave Gunnar the name of two contacts in Rostal. The first was a sergeant in the Rostal city watch, who was open to bribes. The second was Judd's second cousin, Vekki Brown. Gunnar would leave for Rostal at first light, and using funds Judd pushed across the table, secure their help with a trap. They should know of Brylee's affinity but nothing of Judd's involvement. Even with his own relative, he had to remain completely unconnected.

Vekki was apprentice to Mage Wickham. She was no threat to the mage, and she was able to carry much of the burden Lord Lessinger expected of his mage. She was also under the protection of the Council of Magical Law. She would appreciate the opportunity to skrike a charmer to build up her own magical power while not being concerned when Brylee died from it. Gunnar was not to be present. In fact, he should be back in Haxley at the time of Brylee's death. Gunnar's role was to introduce the players, point out Brylee so there was no mistake, pay, then leave them to their work.

Judd went over the plan several times to be sure Gunnar was clear on his part. Then he paid Gunnar with an ingot of silver, promising him a gold ingot when the deed was done. Then he sent Gunnar home to catch what sleep the remainder of the night would provide.

On the walk back from Silverside, Judd considered all the tasks he needed to complete to position himself with Luka Plainhand so that the Plainhand business empire would drop into his lap at a favourable price.

Chapter Twenty

Rostal was harder to navigate than Haxley, not solely because it was over twenty times larger but also because the city had embraced chaos a thousand years ago. Haxley was laid out in a disciplined fashion and had two straight rivers as well as the Barrow Building and cathedral providing landmarks by towering above mostly two-storey buildings. Rostal's streets, by contrast, were higgledy-piggledy, as if the city's architects had ripped up their plans, tossed them skyward, and then brought them to life as they had landed.

Adding to the chaos of Rostal's streets were architectural features made possible only with the use of magic. First, oxen and private horse traffic were banned from most streets to ensure cleanliness. Large, wide tunnels lit with neverdark lanterns connected a series of cartariums beneath the city streets.

There were many collections of tall buildings, some connected with lengthy footbridges or skyways at seemingly random heights. Around both the lord's House—Lord Lessinger's palace—and Government House, the pavement extended out from the fourth and fifth floors respectively, creating aerial parks and walkways. These had the added benefit of making them unassailable from the ground. And whether constructed of ironwood, steel, or stone, most surfaces were covered with blue-white cement, mage-hardened against the elements, so that shape, not colour, was the cityscape's only differentiator.

Because horses were banned, with few exceptions, the only way to travel through Rostal, other than on foot, was the public carriage system. Four- and six-seat carriages drawn by one or two Hubban ponies, a desert breed that flourished on little sustenance, thus minimising the need for street sanitation, transported passengers wherever they wished to go. Coin was not used for fear of muggings. Instead, passengers bought small ticket books from the markets and gave tickets to the carriage drivers as a fare. The wealthy carried a red coin, which they paid for annually.

The time from Rostal emerging over the horizon to Brylee reaching the city gate seemed like an age, but she enjoyed seeing the city's spires rise from an angle she had not arrived by before.

The term "gate" was a carry-over from the days the city had a wall. The city had long since sprawled past that boundary, but the gate was the demarcation line beyond where private horses were not welcome on the surface. One could give their reins to a city stable hand who would take horses to the cartarium and leaving people to travel by foot or carriage. Alternatively, one could ride their mount down into the tunnel system to a stable. Brylee chose the latter.

Brylee recalled the first time she had visited Rostal and her nervousness at proceeding so far underground. She'd long since lost count of her trips to the capital, yet she still wasn't comfortable saying goodbye to the sky.

That said, navigating beneath the surface was much easier than above ground. The decision to create the tunnel complex had come long after the city was established in its chaotic fashion and by people who appreciated order. In the main, tunnels were straight and the signage plentiful. Still, it took thirty minutes at a full trot to reach the Mason's Market Stables and another thirty minutes to see Summer fed, brushed, and settled into a premium stall.

Brylee chose Mason's Market partly because her name was known there, as much of her product entered the city from the south and used that facility, but also because she knew the market well. She spent an enjoyable time perusing the stalls, picking out food and wine that was rare in Haxley to stock her room at the inn. She planned to stop there again on the way home and stock up with gifts for Raegan and her other friends. She purchased a book of twenty carriage fares and then joined the short line for a ride.

The trip from Mason's Market to the Wizard's Mark Inn was a lengthy one, so the driver took two tickets. The carriage rode the main underground trunk for over half the distance before trundling up a ramp to the surface. They emerged near Government House, which contained the seats of both regional and city bureaucracy as well as representatives of the various councils of the Trilogy. Soon she was gawking at the mystifying architecture, as she always did.

From Government House the carriage zigzagged through the banking sector with its more formal buildings before crossing the

Stonebank Canal into the entertainment district known as Follyton. Museums, theatres, and restaurants all clamoured for attention with their unique facades. Brylee noted several collections exploring the history of agriculture were being hosted at the Mordeland National Museum's Rostal Annex. She would have time to kill if negotiations went well, so she committed to visit as her schedule allowed. She had never been to a theatre before, and she wondered if she would enjoy it.

The entertainment district bled into the Artisans' Creative. The lower-cost housing was barely noticeable, as the eye was distracted by the stunning array of sculptures and artwork.

The Wizard's Mark Inn was nestled between Follyton and the Creative on a heavily treed lane. It was only a short walk to meet with Jyan Harding, the farmer Mella had arranged for her to see the following day.

Brylee paid six punts for two nights, with the option of a third. It was an exorbitant fee, she thought, but it was worth it as a treat on her rare forays into Rostal.

She hefted her saddlebags over her shoulder and followed her host to her room. It was tastefully decorated in mushroom-cream shades and had two narrow beds, a table with two chairs, an armoire, and doors that led out to a small balcony.

Brylee pulled a change of clothes from her luggage as well as two apples to stave off her hunger until dinner. She left her bags on the bed farthest from the window and then set off to the public baths to relax and rid herself of the build-up of road dust acquired during her journey. Thirty minutes later, she was immersed in hot water, going over the arguments she would present to Jyan the following day.

Chapter Twenty-One

Brylee woke to the sound of the sixth bell and the muffled hubbub of the stallholders setting up the market. The last log she had put in the fireplace had burned down, but its remnants held enough heat to keep the chill from the room. She went through her morning routine and took down her church clothes from where she had hung them out to drop their wrinkles. Brylee had been raised church-wise, but belief was not as strong with her as it was with her parents. She would admit to a quiet prayer each evening for the health of those she loved just in case Ag existed and did hear all, but otherwise she rarely thought about religion.

The brown outfit was tailored for her muscular frame and could be dressed up for weddings and dressed down for more sombre occasions. The scoop-necked, wide-shouldered, narrow-waisted top flowed into four overlapping layers of skirt that reached down to cover the tops of the short, lightweight boots she pulled from her saddlebag. The outfit always felt alien and impractical compared to her typical working attire. She tied thick blue scarves around her waist, as was the fashion, but in her case she did so because they had hidden pockets and did away with the need to carry a purse.

Her chores completed—for that's how she felt about dressing up—Brylee pulled her cape around her shoulders and relaxed on the small balcony to sip juice and eat the fruit and herb bread with honey that she had acquired from Mason's Market. She spent an hour watching the street come fully awake. As eighth bell approached, she washed her hands, locked her room, and pushed the key into a scarf pocket.

There was only one Grinders in Rostal, but in Nuulan in the region of Yarrow, Mordeland's capital, there were said to be dozens. The stores sold grou't, the universally adopted shortening of "ground t'Yuk beans." Jyan Harding, a preeminent Yarrow farmer of ale hops, had a passion for importing and experimenting with rare plants. He had brought t'Yuk beans back from across the Green Sea and was successful at growing them at home. When hot water seeped through the ground black beans, it took on a rich flavour. A mug of grou't with breakfast was said to wash away night fug and leave one feeling fresh for the day.

As the climate at the Harding Farm was like that at Plainhand Estate, Mella had put the notion in Brylee's head that she should approach Jyan to explore a potential partnership. Plainhand could be a local grower and help establish Grinder stores and private supplies to Rostal and to buyers in southern Lanthe, cutting Jyan's distribution costs. Mella had once travelled with Jyan—it was rumoured they enjoyed a short, fervent tryst—and she wrote to him to broach the idea. He had agreed to hear Brylee out, and Mella had arranged the introductions. Brylee had never tasted grou't. She was excited to see what all the fuss was about.

Grinders was a small storefront with a large patio that was covered with breezy green canvas. It had ample fires and two types of tables for patrons: narrow but tall stations where people could stand if in a hurry and, for those who wished to tarry, squat, circular trestles ringed with benches. The storefront had two sections open to the air. The left side had a wide doorway for the serving staff, and the right had a low, curved counter where one could buy pre-ground t'Yuk beans to take home.

Brylee sat on one of the few empty benches. A cheery teenaged boy brought her a short menu that listed a few variations of grou't, a selection of milks, creams, and honeys that could be added, and four types of pastries that changed daily. She read down the list, wide eyed and open mouthed.

"If this is your first time to Grinders, you might find raw grou't a little bitter," her server said. "Many find it pleasing to take a small mug and a slop of cream." Brylee took his recommendation gladly and asked him to tell Mr. Harding she had arrived for their meeting.

In less time than it took for Brylee to wonder at the lively breakfast crowd, a short, wizened, white-haired man arrived balancing two mugs of grou't and a plate of lemon scones in his left hand while leaning on a black cane with his right. Brylee stood and helped him set down his load. He had been intent on balancing things while negotiating the busy patio, but now as he raised his eyes to greet Brylee's, his eyebrows shot up and his jaw dropped.

"Ag, Senna, it's you!" he exclaimed, stepping forward as if to hug her. He caught himself as she backed away a pace as if they were performing an obscure dance. Jyan pulled a pair of reading lenses from a pocket, wiggled them onto his face, and studied Brylee's face.

"I'm sorry, my dear. Well, I'll be . . . you just look so much like her. Sit, sit," he implored, his face flushing from his mistake. "Forgive an old man's foolishness," he continued. "Do you have an older sister or cousin you greatly resemble, Miss Plainhand?"

"Not that I'm aware of, Mr. Harding. Someone in Yarrow?"

"Someone who stayed with us for a short while but of whom I became quite fond. Like the daughter I never had, or so it seemed. I haven't seen Senna for a few years now, and I wonder what became of her. When I saw you, well, let's not start that again. Tell me what you think of my grou't."

Brylee welcomed the change of subject and took a sip of the beige liquid. Jyan perched on the edge of the bench, pinning her with his glistening eyes as he anticipated her reaction.

"I've never tasted the like." Brylee took a second sip, unaware of the astonished look on her face. "Words like 'spicy' and 'pungent' spring to mind, but they sound negative, whereas this tastes wonderful. Is it addictive?" she inquired, then felt impolite for asking.

"Try it with a scone," Jyan urged, his face beaming. "Bite a piece off, then wash the grou't through it." He reached for a pastry himself and demonstrated. "Some young folks have started dunking ginger rock cakes into the grou't, but I'm not one for that, I'm afraid."

"It changes the taste entirely," Brylee said. "I can see why Grinders is so busy, Mr. Harding."

"Please, call me Jyan."

Over the next three hours Brylee laid out her concept to be a local grower for his product. She explained the strengths and weaknesses of Plainhand Estate, her transportation business, and the area's seasons. A deep discussion emerged on what it might take to germinate t'Yuk plants in the slightly more acidic soil of Lanthe. Jyan repeatedly complimented her on her knowledge and passion.

While they talked, Jyan paraded variation upon variation of tiny sipping cups of grou't blends and a range of pastries, some being tested for the menus set for later in the week. He insisted on fetching from the kitchen and serving Brylee himself. Then he gave her a detailed tour of the store.

Soon it was thirteenth bell, and they were interrupted by Grinders' manager, who informed Jyan that another party of people had arrived to see him.

"Already? Where did the time go?" Sitting back, he looked at Brylee, his lips slightly pursed and his white bushy eyebrows lowered. "You've given me much to think about. Can we talk again tomorrow? I leave the following day for Yarrow."

"Of course, Jyan. I'd be delighted. I have no other business here, so whenever it's convenient for you."

"Let's meet at sixteenth bell then. I've been attempting to blend brandies and cream in with concentrated grou't but haven't perfected it. I'd value your opinion." He laughed, a mischievous twinkle in his eyes.

"In the name of research, of course," she replied, mirroring his smile. "And it gives me time to explore the Creative and visit the museums. I never leave time for such things. It'll be a treat."

"The King's Curse will be performed by the Rostal City Troupers tonight," Jyan said. "I would offer to take you, but I have other business, I'm afraid. It's a witty take on the blights that plagued King Carrod's beloved vineyards. I think you would rather enjoy it."

"If today's tasting experience is a measure, I must take all your suggestions seriously, Jyan. Can I buy a ticket at the door?"

"Yes, but go early," he said, standing to go.

It didn't seem strange that Jyan hugged Brylee like an uncle would a favoured niece considering what they had shared throughout the day. But the amount of attention two men at the adjacent table had covertly paid to their discussion, and that they took turns trailing Brylee back to the Wizard's Mark, would have been a grave concern had she been open eyed enough to observe it.

Chapter Twenty-Two

As sad as she was to part from Jyan's bright and fascinating company, Brylee was glad of the opportunity to walk off all the pastries she had consumed. The many small bites had each seemed delicious, but as she strolled through the Creative, immersed in the possibilities of a new business venture, she felt bloated.

The many works of art were dazzling and revealed how much more progressive Rostal was than Haxley. Many of the sculptures captured a sensuality that excited her and made her blush, but others were far more explicit and caused her to quicken her pace. She spent thirty minutes at a complex machination of wheels, chains, slides, swings, drops, and windmills that used gravity to propel coloured balls endlessly around a cunning maze.

Brylee stopped to watch a woman ignite a pan of phosphor crystals. It spat out a light so bright it hurt her eyes until the woman placed it in a box and closed the lid. The box had a glass lens on the side that magnified the light up and through a pane of flat glass onto a large sailcloth mounted above the audience. The woman sprinkled sand on the glass, which created shadows on the cloth. With deft fingers she teased the sand and enacted a shadow play as captivating as any trouper's as she intoned words and songs that brought the shadows to life.

The museum seemed dry and stuffy at first, so she considered cutting her exploration short to go relax at the baths and play with ideas from the morning's meeting. Then she lost herself in the artefacts and was shocked to realise two bells had flown by, and she was hungry. There was still more she wanted to see, but as she had the entire following morning to fill, she decided to return to her room at the Wizard's Mark, change into something less formal, and find an evening meal.

Dressed in plain brown breeches, her comfy everyday boots, a padded buttonless shirt, and a leather over jerkin, Brylee struck out to find a tavern. She ambled past a half-dozen quieter places until she found one abuzz with a lively crowd who were cheering along an energetic fiddler. The ale was stronger than expected, so she limited herself to one tankard, which washed down a spicy lamb and potato stew. Her head full of the fiddler's tunes, she set out to the theatre.

Brylee was perhaps fifty yards from the ticket window when a commotion in front of her stopped her short. A grim-looking man, as wide as he was tall, was arguing with a slight red-haired woman. Brylee watched as he backed her up against a wall, jabbing her in the chest with his meaty finger. He carried no sword, but he was imposing and angry. Unconsciously fingering the small knife concealed in her jerkin, and aware she had a good eight inches of height over him, Brylee didn't think too much before closing the distance and yelling at the man. Echoes of her encounter with Gunnar tugged on her awareness.

"Leave her be! I'll call the watch." The man half turned to see who dared interfere. He scowled and spat vulgar language, suggesting Brylee mind her own business. The small woman took full advantage of his distraction and, slipping under his arm, rushed over to stand with Brylee.

"I've told you, Buck, I'll not go out with you when you've been drinking. You promised to stay away from ale, but you stink of the stuff." The terrified woman grasped Brylee's arm, perhaps to strengthen her resolve.

"I've just had one with the lads. You can't deny me one, Vekki. Get over here, and we'll go to see this stupid theatre you've been on about all week."

"Forget it, Buck. You've had far more than one. Lying's as bad as the drinking. I'm done w'you. I'll stay with my sister tonight or until you sober up."

There were a few more exchanges but the man walked away sullenly, seemingly glad to have escaped a night at the theatre. The woman released Brylee's arm and leant against the wall, tears of anger and relief mixing on her face.

"Are you OK . . . Vekki, is it?" Brylee asked. The woman nodded, wiping her eyes.

"I will be. It's not my first let-down from Buck. He's a sweet man when the ale's not in him. And he went a moon this time without drinking. I bet his workmates were teasing him about the theatre and that led to him 'proving' himself at the tavern."

"That's hard. Are you sure he's worth the trouble?" Brylee asked, with a raised eyebrow and tentative smile to show her words were an attempt to lighten the mood rather than a serious question.

"Most days." Vekki sighed dramatically, followed up with a timid chuckle of appreciation.

"I was going to see the King's Curse, but we could get a drink instead," Brylee offered. "You're shaking. Let's find somewhere to sit."

"Buck and I were going to see that show too," Vekki said. Then she paused, her face perking up. "Can I reward you for your support by taking you with me? I have a spare ticket."

"I'd love to, but only if you let me pay for my seat," Brylee replied.

"But I didn't buy either ticket. The man I work for has a box. He's away on business and told me to use it and to take whomever I wished. I wished for Buck but not drunk Buck. Please?"

"Then your misfortune has become my good fortune, I suppose. My name's Brylee."

They exchanged pleasantries as Vekki led the way, both women happy to avoid any more mention of Buck. Brylee's impression that the theatre was new to Vekki was quickly dispelled as the woman led her past the line of people to a more exclusive door where the doorman appeared to recognise the redhead. Brylee mentioned this familiarity, and Vekki said she had accompanied her employer on occasions but had never been there without him.

Two flights of stairs and several twisting corridors took them to a wall containing several sets of elegant curtains. Vekki walked down the line to the pair of drapes at the end, held them open, and stood back to usher Brylee through.

The spectacle that greeted Brylee's eyes took her breath away. The box in which she emerged was suspended high in the air and set closest to the stage, which was dark and curtained off. Row upon row of plush tiered seating unlike anything she had seen extended up from the stage to the back of the vast space. The rows were so broad that several lines of chairs were omitted to make pathways that hundreds of patrons walked down like ants to reach their assigned seats. The walls were draped in rich cloths trimmed with silver and gold thread. The entire space was lit by a series of neverdark lanterns hung in neat rows from the roof.

The box they were in could hold perhaps eight seats, but that night it was configured with just two. There was a small candlelit side table full of meats, cheeses, and fruit along with two tall glasses and a carafe of red wine, which Vekki was busy pouring. Brylee was glad Vekki hadn't accepted her offer to pay for the seat. It would have cost a small fortune.

"Who did you say you worked for? Lord Lessinger?" Brylee was only half joking.

"Don't worry about that. My employer likes to remain anonymous at the theatre. Take a seat. And help yourself to food now, during the intermission, or whenever the mood takes you."

"I've just eaten but I will certainly try some of that cheese later. It smells fantastic," Brylee said as she sat and accepted a glass of wine.

Four sets of thick black curtains began to unfurl across the roof on cunning wires, cutting off the light from the neverdark lamps.

"Good, they're about to start," Vekki said, sitting forward in her seat. "I'm ravenous." The candles revealed a sly look on her face. Her comment struck Brylee as odd seeing as Vekki hadn't filled her plate with food, but Brylee shook off the feeling, assuming Vekki meant she was hungry for entertainment.

As the vast space grew dark, people took their seats and the noise dropped to a murmur. A single light illuminated centre stage, and a man stepped out from between the long velvet curtains. The theatre fell completely silent. Brylee attempted to lean forward to better hear the man as he started his welcome speech but found she couldn't move an inch, not even to turn her head. She couldn't breathe either. It was as if her whole body had become encased in wood. She tried to call out, but her throat was thick and solid, and no sound emerged.

Panic gripped her as she tried with all her strength to break free. Sweat burst out all over her body, some running down her brow and stinging her bulging eyes. She sensed rather than saw Vekki pull her chair up close to her side. Vekki leaned in and gripped Brylee's chin with one hand to turn her head so they faced each other. Whatever force held Brylee fast cooperated with Vekki's intent. After an eternity, a small gap appeared, allowing Brylee to breathe through one nostril.

"Now, my scared little rabbit," Vekki cooed. The eyes that now pinned Brylee with a hungry stare were much colder than her honeyed voice. "That's better. I don't want you to suffocate before I've had my fill of you. You think the cheese smells nice? All I smell is a sweet little charmer."

Brylee's stomach clenched further. When reminded she had more talents than just her physical strength, Brylee's mind clutched at ways she might use her magic. She hurled the same heat energy she had used on the shelter's wood at the Crags into Vekki's looming face, but her face lit up with delight, not flames as Brylee had hoped.

"Oh, and you're so strong for a charmer. That's a nice surprise, but it won't do you any good against a mage, little rabbit. Now, don't struggle. I'll devour your magic either way, but your fear can taint the taste, you know."

Brylee felt a pressure extend across her whole body. A tugging. A drawing of something important. Her mind began to fog up.

"That's it. Just relax, little rabbit. It will be over in no time. Oh, you do taste sweet, don't you?" There was a note of ecstasy in Vekki's whisper, and the mage lifted her head and closed her eyes as if tasting the air. The tugging became more insistent. Brylee tried to imagine how to use her affinity to contain her magic within her own body. She imagined building a wall around herself, sealing it in, all the while straining every muscle to break free. Perhaps her efforts had some effect because Vekki's face became more concentrated, and Brylee felt the tug shift to more of a wrench. And it began to hurt. Her whole body felt like it had ignited. She could feel herself fading despite the pain. She gathered herself for one last attempt and threw everything she could at Vekki, who writhed in response. But it wasn't a squirm of discomfort. Quite the opposite, it was sensual as she devoured the power Brylee directed at her.

Brylee's eyelids had all but closed as she hung limply in Vekki's magical embrace, but she thought she saw the drapes behind Vekki shift. A figure stepped out. In its right hand was a long, thin blade.

Vekki jerked, and her eyes flew open. She made as if to scream, but then she seemed trapped by the air too, and no sound emerged from her gawking mouth. Brylee felt a ripple of change.

The wrenching sensation ceased abruptly, but whatever was holding Brylee released and regripped her as if she were a ball passed from hand to hand.

Still powerless, Brylee watched Vekki squirm as the figure slipped the blade into the mage's back and pushed it through so that it surfaced from her chest. First a trickle, then a stream of blood blossomed across Vekki's dress, but still the mage was pinned, much like the butterflies in Brylee's father's study. Now it was the figure's turn to act as if it were tasting the air, but it was as if that air tasted putrid, and the skriking of Vekki was soon done.

Brylee felt some strength return, and the fog in her mind began to dissipate. She noted through the billowy black cape that the figure was stocky. She couldn't see the person's face due to how they wore their scarf around their head. Only the eyes were visible, and they were full of sorrow and dread.

As the theatre director wound down his introduction, the figure took the last of Vekki's magic and released his magical grip on both Brylee and the mage. Before the applause for the introduction could begin, the auditorium was filled with the sound of Brylee screaming. Hundreds of eyes looked up at the box to see a masked figure empty a vial of red paint over a bloodied woman's head before pushing her over the balcony rail to plunge to the floor.

"Run, you idiot," the figure said to Brylee as the person turned to the crowd and gave a theatrical bow.

He looks so familiar, Brylee thought, although as the figure's mask and cape hid their every feature, she knew it must be the person's build or mannerism that made the impression on her. When the figure urged her to run a second time, Brylee's senses returned and she didn't hesitate. She bolted from the chair and down the corridor, and in no time she was running down the street as if chased by a demon.

Chapter Twenty-Three

For the first half of her desperate run to the Wizard's Mark, Brylee's wide eyes were focussed mostly behind her. Her mind flipped between replaying her near moment of death, Vekki's hungry expression and insanely sensual actions, and blood . . . a lot of blood. Only during the second half of her flight, as the pain in her side forced her to slow and recapture her breath, did any conscious thought of where she was heading surface. Get her things. Collect Summer. Ride home. Should she leave her belongings? No, she should have her sword at least.

As her senses returned, Brylee realised that if someone was following her, they would only have to notice the many shocked faces and turned heads from the people reacting to her mad flight along the busy street. She slowed, forcing herself to walk, and took the next alley she saw. It was clearly used for deliveries to the various entertainment venues for it contained a set of steps marked by a red post signalling the staircase would lead down to the underground carriage ways. Brylee took her bearings before descending. When she reached the first subterranean level, she set off at a quick walk towards her inn.

Access to the market across from the inn was signposted, but Brylee continued to the next exit to the surface to further muddy her trail. Shock had well and truly set in, and as she emerged at street level, she began to shake and wipe away tears that spilt spontaneously down her cheeks. It took a full ten minutes for Brylee to compose herself before she walked back towards the Wizard's Mark.

The inn looked as normal as could be, and despite the many scenes of catastrophe playing out in her imagination, Brylee assessed that whatever pursuit might have been launched, it had yet to catch up to her. Reaching into the folds of her scarf, she withdrew four punts, more than enough to cover any fees at the inn in addition to her prepayment. Then she took her room key out and held it ready.

Brylee marked where the city carriages loitered and mentally rehearsed how she would inform the innkeeper she had a family emergency, pay him generously, and then pack up her saddlebags and be away.

After two deep breaths to steady her nerves, Brylee strode through the front door and up to the tavern's bar. There she waved to the innkeeper, who attended her immediately, his face grave with concern at the sight of her dishevelment.

"Miss—"

"I have to go," Brylee said, cutting off his inquiry. "Family emergency. This should cover any trouble." She threw her money onto the counter.

"But miss," he protested, but she was already halfway up the staircase to her room.

She turned left at the landing and took the three short strides to her door before her mind registered her door was open. She came to an abrupt halt on seeing two members of the city watch had packed all her possessions into her saddlebags. One seemed to recognise her. His look of shock mirrored her own.

"What are you doing here?" he asked. Brylee panicked and pulled her small knife from her jerkin but didn't brandish it. She didn't get the chance. The third city guard who had seen her enter the inn had followed her up the stairs and hit her on the back of the head with the butt of his short sword. Brylee crumpled at his feet.

"Ag, what went wrong? Shouldn't the mage have skriked her?" Brylee's assailant asked.

"Who knows?" the other replied, gathering himself back to command. "Let's take her in. Remember, she's a charmer. Fenn, gag her so she can't witch us with words. Any sign of her waking, hit her again. And you, Kepper, run down to the cart. You'll find charmer bindings in the red bag. Bring 'em quick."

Ten minutes later, the three watchmen had Brylee wrapped from head to foot in mage-treated blue leather belts, and she was gagged and hooded with the same material. They took turns hefting her over their shoulders, going out through the inn's back door and down to the cart level. The leader sent one man back for Brylee's saddlebags and weapons, which were then laid in the back of the cart next to their prisoner.

"Right, well done, boys. We'll find out what went wrong later. Remember, we don't want to be associated with all this, so hand her off to the duty sergeant as soon as you reach the garrison. Tell him a street artist reported she had witnessed her doing magic and let you know before running off into the crowd. Suggest to the sergeant he place her straight into the charmer cell before she awakes. Let Vekki or Wickham skrike her, then it's done."

When he was sure his men understood their task, he unhooked his horse from the back of their cart and headed home. He was not supposed to be on duty that night, and his real shift began the next morning. He would get a little sleep beforehand. Perhaps he would dream of the silver Judd's man had given him.

Chapter Twenty-Four

The 467th Year of the Morde Dynasty–Three Years Earlier

As they trudged through the forest to the north of the HAC, Lu's warrior's mind assessed the threats to Gideon's life and noted with irony how far down the list of dangers Cleric Oliver's soldiers scored. The pursuers had terrible tactics. They didn't—or couldn't—employ Jeef's Mobi'dern and their prida, so they were easy to avoid. They scouted in pairs, unsupported by other searchers, making them easy targets for Shanna and Lu to pick off. They were also unused to the terrain and made more noise than a train of oxen in heat. Gideon was in more danger from how much Lu wanted to strangle him than their inept pursuers.

Lu left them tied up and mostly uninjured but stripped them of anything of use, including food, coin, weapons, and blankets. During their escape, Lu had the presence of mind to have Gideon put on his sturdiest boots, grab clothing, and take any coin or items they could barter for a horse. They doubled that initial meagre purse with what they liberated from their pursuers.

For the first two days, they headed west towards the Quartt region. Of all the regions, Quartt was the most progressive and the least hostile to charmers. Therefore, it was their destination of choice. Arkly's men would correctly assume Gideon would head there, but they could not predict their route. To reach Quartt, Lu and Gideon had to cross Yarrow from east to west, circling the sprawling capital Nuulan on the way. The city would no doubt be alerted to watch for Arkly's alleged murderers. That was why Lu struck out west initially, leaving a trail that was not too obvious. When no pursuers had been spotted for half a day, they turned north. They would stay on that track until they reached Crenner Lake in the Northern Region, begin a wide detour, then follow the northern border until they were well west of Nuulan and eventually descend south into Quartt. It would triple their journey's length, but they would be in sparsely populated territory for most of the way.

For the next three days, they would stay off the main roads and hike through the forests, keeping to the barest of trails. Once the forest thinned and they began to climb up into the Brute

Peakland, a hardy mount would be essential for Gideon. It wasn't just that his body was soft and unused to arduous travel. His spirit was broken too. Gideon flip flopped between sullen silence and tears of grief. What wouldn't she give for some self-righteous anger to spur him on? She had plenty to spare, blaming Gideon for his arrogance and his naivety, both of which had provoked the confrontation that led to Tuli's death and Lu's expulsion. Lu did not blame Shanna for her part in it. Maybe the cat was impulsive, but it was a strike of honour. Now that she allowed herself room to question her leader, Lu was disappointed that Da-Jeef had so quickly put aside honour in favour of the clan's reputation and politics.

There was plenty of game to hunt, but Lu didn't want to risk a fire, not even for cooking, until they had put more distance behind them and their pursuers. She let Shanna forage for herself while she and Gideon ate confiscated jerky, bread, and cheese as well as any berries, roots, and mushrooms they found along the way.

They were grateful the weather remained dry and warm. Lu relied upon Shanna's alert senses, though she still slept lightly each night, while Gideon, exhausted from walking all day, snored soundly and woke up feeling stiff and sore.

On the evening of the fourth day of their northerly hike—six days since their escape—Shanna, who was ranging far ahead, flashed an image to Lu of the forest thinning to meadowland, which ran out to meet mountains in the distance.

Are there dwellings nearby? Lu replied. *Gideon requires a horse.*

There is smoke in the air. It's faint, but I will search.

Lu sensed Shanna surge away, intent on finding and analysing the source of the smell.

"We will reach the end of the woodland in an hour and make camp," Lu said to Gideon. "Shanna is scouting for signs of civilisation where we might acquire a horse."

"At last," the charmer grumbled. "I'm sore from sleeping on the ground, my feet ache, and it feels like it will rain soon. An inn would be welcome."

"I'm afraid it will be a while before we dare use an inn, Gideon. I was thinking of trading for a horse. With you mounted we will make better time. We can climb over the mountains and down into the Northern Region, where we will be safer." Although Lu tried to keep resentment out of her voice, her tone betrayed her.

"I'm walking as fast as I can. You don't have to nursemaid me. Why don't you just leave?" Gideon snapped, secretly glad that she hadn't.

That's a good question, Lu thought. It would have taken her less than two days to reach that point travelling alone.

Her stomach clenched as she felt the onset of the cycle of thinking that had plagued her for days. She had nowhere to go, and she had no purpose since Gideon's confrontation had resulted in her severing. As much as she resented the charmer, it was Shanna's reaction to Tuli's death that had put Da-Jeef in an untenable position. Lu also blamed herself for not anticipating the situation better, although it was Gideon's lack of accountability and gratitude that she truly resented.

Lu's chest hurt as she recalled Tuli's death. They had been friends for a year. That hurt was magnified by the flash of grief and anger the cat had imprinted on her memory at the time. Those images came with the cat's emotions, which were sharper and less balanced than her own, and it was hard to separate the two. She needed a distraction.

"Can't you use your healing powers to treat your blisters?" she asked. She knew the answer already and chastised herself for the cheap shot when she saw Gideon wince.

Gideon shut out the annoying Mobi'dern and concentrated on walking in a way that caused the least chafing from his boots. The blisters were agony. As far as he knew, no magic wielder could use their talents on their own body. He and Tuli had always taken care of each other's needs. His heart raced, and his eyes burned each time he thought of his sister's death. Why hadn't he listened to her?

To escape any uncomfortable conclusions, Gideon shifted his mind to his other concern. He couldn't seem to exercise any magic at all since he had absorbed the magic of Tuli and the other charmers. He deduced he had drawn their lifelines into himself. He was too horrified to admit he had skriked them, but there was no other explanation. Bile threatened to force him to retch, but he fought it down by focussing on his current predicament.

It wasn't that he had no magic. In fact, he could feel a reservoir of power magnitudes larger than he had before. The problem was, he couldn't access it. It was trapped within somehow, just out of reach.

The Council of Magical Law routinely employed full mages at the HAC to train charmers in how to use their magic. After all, a mage was just a charmer with more capacity and training. There were three syllabuses for the charmers: Healing, Scanning, and Other Uses. Healing covered a range of ways to kill growths, help the body expedite its own repairs, and to a limited degree have the elements of the body change their nature. Separating red blood parts from the blood's liquid, or plasma, was a common example. Scanning was the ability to look inside a body to determine what was wrong. Other Uses focussed on skills such as using magic to heat water or start a fire and similar skills that would be useful to healers. Gideon has argued for abilities such as hardening air to staunch wounds, but such skills were forbidden to charmers. Mages sought to protect their proprietary knowledge of such things, thereby elevating their social status.

As he and Lu travelled, Gideon tried to use his powers on several occasions. When cold, he attempted to heat stones with his magic, something he had been good at before. Since the "joining," as he called it, he felt he had enough power not only to make rocks glow but also perhaps to cook on them, but his attempts failed miserably. On another occasion, a cactus spine dug into Shanna's paw, and Gideon had offered to seal the wound, but he couldn't. Things that he should have been able to do in his sleep now evaded him.

Despite not being able to send magic outwards to affect things, Gideon's scanning and sensing ability seemed to be working well—even better than before, in fact. In addition to more detail in the physical dimension, he was also aware of what he had come to call the spiritual dimension, although he acknowledged that was mere speculation. The glow he had seen within Tuli resided within himself now but far larger. He could see a much smaller glow within Lu and even less within Shanna. He could also see pinpricks of it within the plant life that surrounded them.

At first, Gideon hypothesised it was a magic reservoir he could see, which made sense, as Tuli and he were charmers and had much more of it than the Mobi'dern and her prida. But he noticed its aura changed depending on the mood of its host. He could see the threads leaving each glow and fading away. His current theory was that he could see the souls of living things as well as their magic, hence his postulation that this was spiritual science. He knew he was grasping, but exploring such new ideas gave Gideon a momentary glimmer of respite from his grief and loss. It was only a few strides before he discarded these thoughts and concentrated on saving his feet from more pain.

The wind began to rise, confirming rain, as Gideon had suspected, and the temperature plunged. Lu found a group of three large stones that would shield them from the worst of the breeze, so she decided to stop for the night. Shanna had sent her some images of a village some five miles distant. Lu threw a pair of pheasants Shanna had caught down onto a rock.

"Make camp here," she told Gideon. "We've come far enough that I think it's safe for you to gather some wood and make a small fire. Make sure the wood is dry, though. There's a stream off to the north for water. Shanna has found a village, but it is distant. While you prepare supper, I'll do some reconnaissance. I'll be back in a couple of hours." Without waiting for a response, Lu loped off into the forest, relieved to be free of Gideon's depressing presence.

Chapter Twenty-Five

Lu and Shanna didn't return until well past midnight, not that Gideon noticed. He was sound asleep, his attempt at a fire having long since dwindled. He had dissected the birds like a surgeon and cooked them both. He had eaten most of one, leaving the other for Shanna and Lu to share. He had only gathered enough kindling for his brief cooking effort and none to warm them through the night. Then he removed his boots and treated his blisters, crawled under his cloak as the rain began, and fell into such a deep sleep he was oblivious of their return.

Shanna offered Lu a thought that left little doubt about how rude and selfish she thought the charmer was before disappearing into the shrubs to hunt for something fresh. Lu squatted under her cloak and ate a third of the bird, saving the remainder for breakfast.

Earlier, Lu had reached the village at dusk. It didn't feel welcoming, and her hopes of trading for a horse and supplies faded. Her instincts told her she would be rebuffed or worse. Instead, she decided to wait until it was quiet and scavenge. While the town settled in for the night, Lu enjoyed several hours of time away from Gideon with just Shanna for company. When she deemed it safe, she asked Shanna to wait and watch the perimeter—the cat's presence would set off the dogs and geese on guard duty—while she slipped between the buildings.

The settlement appeared to be a waypoint village, a stopping point for travellers but with little other purpose. It boasted three small inns and abundant stabling for such a small place, where travellers could overnight and exchange horses if required. She counted her blessings, as this meant there would be more horses than expected.

The first stable she came to contained two men playing dice. The second stable was quiet, so she let herself in via a gap in the eves and dropped into an empty stall. Once her eyes adjusted to the dark and the animals to her presence, Lu searched the place. She found a hardy pony, an old saddle, grain already bagged up, an axe, rope, and other useful supplies. She left behind a note and most of their coin, loaded the pony, and walked it away. She didn't want to add horse theft to the list of crimes that Cleric Oliver had no doubt alleged.

Gideon stirred soon after dawn to the smell of warm tea, which left him momentarily disoriented until he tried to move and his aching back reminded him of his predicament. He drew his cloak tighter around himself and shut his eyes, falling back to sleep.

"Gideon, time to move," Lu said. It was past ninth bell, she guessed, and the charmer was still asleep. He opened one eye, then closed it.

"There's no point, Lu. Just leave me here." The cold, the rain, and the aching had gotten to him.

"Come on, get up. The tea is still warm, and I've left you some meat and berries. Eat, drink, piss, then get on the horse I was up all night stealing for you. Let's go."

"No. I don't know why you're trying, but you're not helping. You're dragging me on a painful, circuitous route to Quartt, and for what? There's nothing there for me. It's futile. Leave me alone."

Lu wanted to pull him up and slap him stupid, but instead she sighed and slumped down next to him.

"Look, Gideon. Tuli's gone. Don't blame yourself. And you can't go back and kill Arkly."

"What do you mean, blame myself?" Gideon said, sitting up. "I don't blame myself. What are you implying? That I got Tuli killed?"

"No, look, I—"

"The HAC was set up expressly for such occasions, and Tuli and I were just trying to save Arkly's family—"

"*You* were trying to save his family," Lu cut in, rising to her feet. "Tuli wasn't. She was trying to save you from yourself. Everyone in that courtyard except you could see the hatred Arkly had for you and how frightened he was for his wife. How his prejudice and anger were building. *You* pushed a nasty, powerful man over the edge, Gideon. Your naivety and pride. You." Lu had been stepping closer with each pronouncement, but she grabbed a hold of her emotions and turned away, shaking her head in shame at her uncharacteristic loss of control.

In the abrupt absence of shouting, the quiet patter of rain on the leaves sounded warm and soft. The pony snorted, and Shanna stretched and raked her claws down a nearby tree. Gideon stared off into space.

"I'm sorry," Lu said. "You're not to blame for—"

"I can't use my magic," Gideon whispered.

"What? I don't understand."

"Tuli and I were committed . . . no, you're right. *I* was committed to the idea not just that charmers could help but also that they could have a purpose. We hide and we skulk, and I know some who have committed suicide because of the shame we feel. We are not normal, and we're not mages. Hated and feared by many, we even doubt ourselves. Tuli believed in me, and she gave up everything for me. Did you know she loved a man once, one who offered to take her to the altar stones? She turned him down for me and my dream."

"No, I didn't."

"And when Arkly stabbed her, do you know what she did with her dying breath?"

Lu shook her head.

"She gave me her magic. She wanted me to take it. To skrike her. To carry on."

"What?"

"I didn't want to, but she pushed her magic into me anyway. She was always the stronger one. I talked the talk, but she got things done." Gideon felt some shame that in the end he had pulled, just as she pushed, but he couldn't say that to Lu. Nor could he say that he had somehow skriked the other charmers. He knew nothing of the cleric's poison, only that in taking Tuli's magic, he had taken his fellow students' powers as well, believing he had killed them all in the process. He was horrified at himself.

"Her dying gesture has increased my magic significantly, yet I can't even heat a stone. And I can't heal a cat's paw. My pride and naivety wasted her life, and my weakness of character has wasted her gift. So there really is no point. Just take your cat and your pony and your new sense of purpose and go. Don't waste another moment. I'm not worth it."

Shanna grunted in disgust and left the clearing to hunt for more breakfast. *Accept his offer. Leave him,* she sent to Lu. But an anger had grown in Lu as his story had spilled out, fuelling her determination to complete her task. She may have been shunned, but Da-Jeef had given her a mission, and she was determined to complete it. She felt her rage burning out of control again.

"Get up, Gideon, before I drag you up by your hair. I would grab your balls if you had any. You're a spoilt brat. I'm not nursing you because I feel sorry for you, you idiot. The HAC spent years training you to be a healer, and Tuli spent her life supporting you to be a healer. The Mobi'dern guarded you for years so you could learn to heal. So now your magic, your favourite toy, is broken. Boo-hoo. You can't heal with a wave of your hand, and you're certainly charmless. You're pathetic.

"Even without your magic you're one of the best-trained healers outside of the major towns. You owe Tuli and so many other people a debt to try and be a healer. You can do that in Quartt quite nicely. Yes, your feet will hurt getting there, but there's an easy road ahead for you. Just get up and do it. Do you think Tuli would want you to just give up and die here?"

Gideon was shocked by her tirade. Guilt and shame assailed him, yet still he persisted, desperate to save a scrap of ego.

"But what about the ideal of allowing charmers, more healers..."

"Perhaps being the poster boy for the ideal meant the most to you, Gideon. Was it ever about healing, though?" With a huff, Lu softened her tone. "Look, we've just been through a tragedy. Perhaps your magic will return in time. I don't care. I need to decide what I can do now that I'm severed, but in the meantime I can at least honour my friend Tuli one last time by getting you to where you can actually do some good, with or without magic. Don't give up on me or Tuli. Now get up. Let's go."

Lu walked out of the group of stones and over to where she had hobbled the pony and dropped two handfuls of grain at his feet before loading the remainder of the stolen supplies onto his back. By the time she finished packing, she heard Gideon approach. No words were exchanged, and Lu hoped they had turned a corner and that he could move on. She loped north towards the mountains, not sure if she cared if he followed. After a few moments, she heard the pony snort in response to Gideon's heels, and she felt an unexpected sense of relief.

Chapter Twenty-Six

The route up through the mountains was a bad choice. The rain that had been warm in the forest turned icy at the higher elevations, and the bitter wind ripped through their thin cloaks. Shanna's thick fur made her impervious to the worst of it, but she was still irritable.

After three days and nights, the relentless cold caused frostbite in Lu's right fingers and toes, as they bore the brunt of the wind that whipped down from the peaks above. Pride had prevented her from swapping her thinner gloves with Gideon's thicker ones until the damage was done. Their progress was reduced to a slow stumble, as she could no longer feel her feet. For a few miles Gideon walked while she rode, his blisters mercifully numbed by the cold, but his stamina was poor.

Shanna located a shallow cave. It sheltered them from the worst of the cold, but they had no fuel to make a fire. Try as he might, Gideon couldn't push a single spark of magical heat into the pile of stones that he painstakingly built.

They removed their wettest clothing and huddled almost naked with their bodies pressed together under a thick blanket. Shanna draped herself over them both. The pony was left outside to fend for itself.

They drifted in and out of consciousness for what felt like an eternity. In reality, it only took a day for the weather to blow itself out. Then the sun broke through, and the warmth that touched them stung as they emerged from the cave, sending needles through their flesh.

When he had recovered enough to function, Gideon inspected the frost damage to Lu's hand and foot. His opinion was that unless it got infected, her foot would recover if they could keep it warm and dry. The two central fingers on her sword hand were another matter. He didn't need to scan them with his mind to know how deeply damaged they were. They would be OK for a day or two but would soon rot and have to be cut away. Neither spoke of what this would mean for her as a fighter.

With my magic, he thought, but that avenue was closed off.

The pony hadn't wandered far, and when Shanna herded him back, Gideon gave him some extra grain. Being native to the region, he seemed to have coped well with the cold. They set off while the weather held, taking turns in the saddle and making slow progress. In just a few hours, the path sloped downward, and Lu estimated their evening camp was at least four thousand feet lower than the cave. If the bad weather returned, they would survive.

The weather held, however, and another day brought them to the top of a rocky escarpment at the foot of which lay the largest body of water Gideon had ever seen. It stretched as far as his eyes could see, and he was amazed at how the strong breeze whipped up whitecaps above which white birds wheeled and twisted. Shanna had run on ahead, and from their vantage point they looked down as she approached the water, sniffed it, then walked away in apparent disgust. They followed a well-used goat trail down to the water's edge. Gideon tasted it for himself.

"This is fresh, not salty," he said. "Why doesn't your cat like it?"

"It's Genner Lake, I presume. It's said to be poisoned by the cleaning process at the Genner mines on the lake's north shore. She can smell the taint. We've now crossed into the Northern Region and should be safer. We head due west from here."

The next morning, still walking along the lakeshore, they came across a small but prosperous looking village that surrounded a bustling harbour full of small to mid-sized boats.

"Let's chance it," Gideon said. "If they have a magical healer–"

"Stop it, Gideon. You have to leave that HAC concept behind."

"No, I have. I meant a real mage. It's unlikely, but perhaps one is travelling through. It's the only thing that will save your hand, you know."

"OK, but we don't have much coin left," Lu said. "Don't be expecting to get rooms at the inn or pay for food Shanna could catch for us. We'll go in, look around, and come back here for the night. Agreed?" Gideon nodded, then led Lu and the pony onward.

Lu suggested to Shanna that she should range and explore the sandy bluffs along the lakeshore for the afternoon, and the cat was more than happy to oblige. She offered back images of hares and lizards she had seen along the trail and bounded away.

No one in the village paid the pair any attention as they walked down the main street and through the market to the docks.

Clearly, visitors were common. The store signs soon informed them they had reached Sandrick.

"I recall that Sandrick's port thrives due to shipping ore south and supplies north to and from the mine," Gideon said, almost to himself. He stopped a passer-by who directed them to the healer's house, two roads back from the main street.

"You're in luck, young lady," said the coughing, crotchety old man who answered the door. "If I were a better healer I wouldn't be in this hole of a town. But here I am, and I get plenty of practice at poison from the mine, work injuries, the itch from the brothel, and of course, frost damage. If your fingers can be saved, I can help you. Folks call me Deni."

His enthusiasm faltered once Lu removed the makeshift bandage. "Tsk, no. Sorry. The thumb I can save. That's something, seeing as the thumb is most useful, but the two fingers will have to come off before you lose your hand." Lu had been expecting that verdict, but hearing it from the healer shook her.

"Do you know if there's a mage in the village? Or nearby?" Gideon asked.

"We've not seen a mage for a year," the healer said, a cough shaking his body and causing him to pause for a moment to catch his breath. "And there are none close enough to get to and save the fingers, even if they would deign to help. I'm sorry."

Gideon opened his mind and scanned the healer's chest. He could see the lung blight growing. Without a mage, the village will soon require a new healer too.

"Can you take them now?" Lu mumbled. She held up her damaged hand, trying to remain stoic. She was surprised, therefore, when she felt a tear burn down her cheek.

"Well, ordinarily, yes, but I just used the last of my sleep syrup on a fella whose leg I had to take after a cart's wheel collapsed and dropped a rock load on him. He's sleeping in the back."

"I can take the pain. Just do what you need to do," Lu said, sitting down and bracing herself.

"You might be able to, Miss, but I won't work on you unless you're asleep or at least sedated. My stomach's not up for that. Come back first thing in the morning. I'll make a batch this evening, and it will be cooked and cooled by then."

They soon found that there was no arguing with the healer. He worked on them both and cleaned up what he could, promising to tend to other damage while she was under the effect of his medicine the following day. They paid him for his time and for the work he would do the next morning, then stood to leave.

"Do you have a place to stay?" Deni asked. "I have several rooms here for patients, but it's quiet at this time of year, and they're empty. You've paid up front without dickering on my prices, so if you like, I'll include a room tonight and tomorrow. The syrup takes a good twenty-four hours to shake off, and your hand will benefit from rest too. But I don't have any spare food, even if you have coin. There's just me, and I barely have time to cook for myself."

Touched by his offer, Lu let Shanna know about the change of plan and then let herself be shown to the room. Gideon gave her the narrow bed and said he would sleep on the floor. It would still be the most comfortable night since leaving the HAC, he thought. The healer had included a corner of his stable and some hay for the pony in exchange for thirty minutes of sweeping and cleaning the stalls, which they accepted gratefully. Gideon gave the mount a long brush down, completed the chores, and then left her to eat.

Back in the house, Gideon found the healer crushing and fusing some herbs to start his batch of sleep syrup. Gideon smelled arrowroot and just avoided mentioning that bee breeze would have been a better catalyst. He didn't want to reveal anything about Lu or himself that might identify them in the unlikely event of someone coming that far north with questions. Feeling restless, he excused himself and walked back to the main street, where he found the Iron Rock Tavern. Its faded sign boasted the best ale in Sandrick.

Probably the only ale too, Gideon thought.

Although the tavern looked tired and dull from the street, Gideon discovered it was bright and lively inside. The innkeeper kept the tables clean and refreshments flowing. The sign threatening to bar troublemakers from the only such establishment in town kept the tone friendly. Gideon took a seat in a quiet corner at the back of the room, declined the offer of a bath for three pennies to wash the smell and trail dirt away, but accepted a small mug of ale and two pastries, one of which he would take back for Lu.

There was no stage as such, but an old woman sat in the corner opposite Gideon and played a fiddle. She already had most patrons' feet tapping along to her lively rhythm. In an alcove off the main bar were two large, busy tables of card games and dice, but most folk sat alone or in small, quiet groups, chewing over the day's events and perhaps the mutton stew. Overall, it was a pleasant atmosphere that brought a lump of sadness to Gideon's throat, stirring memories of similar evenings he and Tuli had spent over the years. It struck him as odd that she had not been in his thoughts since the night in the cave, whereas before, her loss had been his only focal point.

The server dropped his meal in front of him, snapping him out of his reverie. She also topped up his mug, winked, then went back to the kitchen.

Gideon noticed a man in the corner watching him with interest. He looked like he had seen somewhere between thirty and forty summers. Although he had the hair of a young man—parted down the centre, shoulder length, and thick and black with a grey streak—his pale skin and sunken features made him look skeletal. As disconcerting as that was, the manner in which he was perched at his table was even more unusual. Rather than a relaxed, open-legged slump or a stiff upright position or anything else in the normal range between the two, it was as if the man were trying not to touch the fabric of the seat or let his hands rest on the table. Instead, they floated in front of him like rabbit paws.

Gideon ignored the man and set into his meal. When he looked up again, the man took a cloth from his pocket and used it to hold the handle of his mug as he raised it in a friendly toast. Gideon looked around, wondering if people were recognising him. He didn't see any "wanted" posters on the walls or any other people taking an interest, and the man certainly didn't have the look of a village guard. Gideon smiled back so as not to offend, then put his head down and finished the pastry so he could depart.

Gideon started as the man glided over to sit in his unique fashion in the empty chair beside him. *How did he cross the room so fast?* Gideon wondered.

"You need to be careful with that," the man said, nodding at Gideon as he spoke. His left eye trembled slightly.

"I'm sorry, what?" Gideon replied as he attempted to settle his heart rate. "I think you have me confused—"

"Your aura, man. Conceal it. You never know when there's a mage about. You would be a tasty snack, you would." He paused and looked about. "Sandrick is an unlikely place to find one, to be sure, but they don't all walk around in ceremonial robes, you know."

Gideon didn't know what to say. Denying he was a charmer was pointless at that stage, but admitting it didn't seem wise either.

"You don't know how to conceal it, do you?" his unwelcome companion said. "How did you get so much magic and have no idea how to hide it? You're acting like a charmer who has never had enough magic to worry about hiding it. Masking your aura is something you must learn if you want to survive long in this world, my friend." The man peered more intensely at Gideon, and Gideon recognised the faraway look in his eyes that the charmer healers at the HAC had when they scanned inside a person's body to sense what ailed them. The man jerked back, slack jawed.

"Well, I'll be a juggling donkey," the man said, clapping his hands together with delight. "You're a slipper. I haven't seen another one of us for over a thousand years. Where did you . . ." The man's words trailed off, and he looked around, worried. He stood and threw two coins onto the table. "It's not safe here. Leave your food and follow me."

Without looking back, the man walked to the rear of the bar and vanished around a corner. Gideon took a last mouthful of ale to relieve the lump in his throat, looked around to see if anyone had reacted to the man's hasty departure, then hesitated for a long moment before following.

They emerged from the tavern in a pitch-black alley. Gideon stuck close to the stranger who, despite the dark, seemed sure of foot and moved swiftly, reminding Gideon of a bird running across the ground. They darted in and out of the buildings, staying off the main thoroughfares. The man brushed off two of Gideon's attempts to find out who he was and where they were heading.

At the edge of the village was a stable complex for the many workhorses. The man bounded up a set of rickety stairs at the rear, taking care not to touch the handrail. Breathless and struggling with his many aches from travel, Gideon followed more slowly. Using a large key, the man unlocked the door. Then, taking another cloth from his pocket, he opened the latch and let them into the room. Once inside, he locked the door behind them.

Gideon heard the man moving across the room but could not see anything in the darkness. Then the unmistakable blue-tinged light of a neverdark lamp illuminated the small space, revealing a bed, a chair and table, and a small travel trunk. As few people could afford or even find a neverdark lamp in the capital city, the fact the man owned one marked him as someone of note. The strong smell of a cleansing agent not dissimilar to what one would use in a hospital caused Gideon to notice how clean the room was, as if it were scrubbed daily from top to bottom.

"We can talk in here if we keep our voices low. The sound won't travel down to the stables through the thick wood." The strange man peered at Gideon again, then grunted, turned, and poured water from a sealed jug into two cups on the table. He passed one to Gideon. "I boil all my water. You should make more effort to avoid germs. I'm Ostryd. Who are you? And how old are you?"

"You're a mage?" Gideon asked, not wanting to divulge his name. His age wasn't a problem, so he added that he was nearly thirty.

"Not in the sense you mean, no," Ostryd replied. "I'm a charmer like you, but I don't have anywhere near your power. But I do have a lot more sense, it seems. Or at least more skill. Why aren't you concealing your magic?"

"I didn't know such a thing was possible," Gideon replied. His instincts told him to be careful, but he would need knowledge to survive and wouldn't get too many opportunities to learn. "I was trained in medicine by mages from the council, but no one ever mentioned that our magic was even visible, let alone could be concealed."

"I'm sure they didn't. Mages like to think they're superior, but they're just charmers who can harness higher volumes of magic and who know more tricks to using it than we do. Of course, they guard most of their tricks closely to keep us from getting too much power or popularity." Talking of mages reminded Gideon of his and Lu's predicament.

"Listen, I have a friend down at Deni's, the healer's. She's injured and will have to have two fingers amputated tomorrow morning. You have magic. Can you heal her? We don't have money right now, but we will pay when we can."

"Why don't you heal her? You say you've been trained, and you certainly have more magic than I do. What's stopping you?"

"I . . . I can't. I know how, and I could have at one time." Gideon went quiet, unsure how to explain or how much to share. Was he in danger of being skriked? With his own magic blocked, he faced someone who could probably take it. He thought of Tuli, and part of him felt that being skriked might be a fitting end.

"Something happened to you recently, didn't it? And since then, you can't access your magic. Right?" He took his cloth and removed a speck of something from the edge of the table.

"I can still use it to see inside people, but I can't use it to alter things. Not since . . . Does that make any sense?"

"Can you see this?" Ostryd asked. A glow opened in the man's torso, filling the area around the top of his stomach and his heart. Thin strands of light moved up Ostryd's spine to his head. It reminded Gideon of the glow he had seen leave Tuli as she died. He focussed, and as with Tuli, Gideon saw a thread leaving the glow, drifting off into oblivion. As quickly as it appeared, the light vanished, as if Ostryd had pulled a curtain around it. Gideon was mesmerised by the man's antics.

"You can see my glow," Ostryd said, seeing the expression on Gideon's face. "Well now, if you can see that, there's hope for you yet. Maybe *I* can't heal your friend, but I should be able to teach you how to unblock your magic. The hard part will be doing it in time to help."

Chapter Twenty-Seven

Ostryd's travel trunk sat on the floor, reaching as high as Gideon's knee. It was twice as wide as it was tall, crafted from a dark heavy wood. It bore no decoration, and as far as Gideon could see, it had no opening for a key. He watched with mounting curiosity as Ostryd rubbed his finger near the front of the trunk in an odd pattern until the lock clicked and the lid rose on a hidden hinge. Noting Gideon's interest, Ostryd explained the trick.

"The catch is buried inside the wood, and there's no keyhole. The metal is stiff when cold or room temperature, but if you heat it with magic, it softens and bends, and then the bolt can slip free on its spring. It keeps out the casually curious but not a mage who knows the trick or a determined person with a hammer or a flame. It's not unlike the solution to your problem, actually."

He didn't elaborate. Instead he opened the trunk and rummaged around until he pulled out something wrapped up in a leather pouch, which he set on the table.

"This flask contains fortified wine from King Lannis's own cellar," Ostryd explained. "Only thirty small barrels were ever produced, and this is a draught from the last barrel that still exists, at least as far as I know. Pass me your glass!"

"Lannis died over two hundred years ago. This must be incredibly rare," Gideon said. "It would be wasted on me. Anyway, I need to keep my wits about me." In truth, he feared it contained a toxin. He felt terribly vulnerable and was wondering why he had followed Ostryd to such a remote location.

"Actually, that's the last thing you need—a clear head, that is," Ostryd countered. "You avoided telling me your name earlier, and you're avoiding drinking with me for the same reason: you don't know who to trust. But at least you didn't lie and give me a fake name. That's something to build on, isn't it?"

Gideon felt foolish for withholding his name, but he still wasn't going to volunteer too much.

"We should drink this rare treat for three reasons," Ostryd continued, holding up three fingers as he prepared to count them off. "One, I can explain how to unblock your magic. That's the easy part. But to succeed you will need to be completely relaxed and uninhibited. This is the strongest drink I know of, and you need to hurry if you want to help your friend. Two, unless you're as drunk as a wasp on a late-autumn plum, you won't believe what I'm about to tell you."

"Look, if you're going to tell me I must jump off the stable roof and fly to get my magic back, I'm not falling for it. Or I would fall. You know what I mean," Gideon replied. Ostryd thought for a moment, then cocked his head.

"Are you familiar with the phrase 'suspend your belief'?"

"Yes. It means no matter how compelling the argument, refuse to commit to it, at least for now," Gideon said, feeling slightly better at being able to demonstrate he wasn't the idiot Ostryd implied him to be around concealing his aura.

"Good, good. Now I want you to do the opposite. I want you to suspend your disbelief. I'm going to reveal some truths to you that oppose what you've taken for granted thus far. Relied on, in fact. You will want to believe I'm talking nonsense and suspect me of lying for some advantage. But listen when I tell you that this understandable scepticism will hamper your ability to reconnect with your magic. You need to accept everything I tell you as true, until you've heard it all. Then decide. There will be no jumping from stables or baking your head in an oven. The only risk I'll ask you to take, when you're ready, is to get drunk with me on the best wine in the world."

Gideon considered his options. If he kept his guard up and didn't overshare, his situation shouldn't worsen. And if there was a way to get his magic to work again, that was worth taking some risks. Helping Lu was just the start of it, not to mention showing her the value of charmers using healing magic. He could help more people if he could get Tuli's dying gift to work again.

"You said there were three reasons to drink with you," Gideon said. "What's the other?"

A warm smile illuminated Ostryd's face. "I'm celebrating! I told you earlier, I haven't met anyone like me, a slipper, for . . . well, I'm not sure for how long. Let me think . . ."

"A thousand years, you joked earlier, but what do you mean? You're what, about thirty-five years old? And what's a slipper?"

The man smiled and poured them both a healthy measure from his flask. He raised a toast, then took a long sip from his glass, swirling the golden liquid around his mouth. Gideon picked up his glass and sniffed the contents. His nose, trained to identify ailments and remedies, picked out cherries, walnuts, and a touch of cryroot.

"I'd take a slug if I were you. Now is where I'll begin to sound crazy. This wine was the best batch I made for King Lannis, and I'd dabbled in brewing for about two thousand years by that time." Ostryd paused to allow his claim to sink in. He wasn't surprised when Gideon put his glass on the table without trying it.

"I know. Insane, right?" Ostryd said. "I lose track every few centuries, so I'm never sure if I've calculated correctly, but I think I'm nearly four thousand years old. That's why I'm so careful with germs—one of the few things that can kill me. Come on, have a drink. You'll need it. That wasn't the craziest part."

"No one's immortal, Ostryd. I have medical training and can give you many reasons why you would not look like you were only thirty-five if you were truly four thousand years old. Whatever's in that glass has addled your mind, I suspect."

"If I'm just a crazy man, what have you got to fear? OK, silly question. This wine might be both poisoned and highly addictive, true. But when I tell you what a slipper is—and that, in fact, you're one—you'll be a smidgeon less sceptical."

"Perhaps if I knew why you were trying to help me and not trying to skrike me, it would help," Gideon said.

"I'll happily tell you. But ultimately, whatever I say, you will come up with a credible counterargument. It will eventually come down to you deciding to take the chance. But I have nothing but time—as do you, actually—so let's play your game. I want to help you because there are so few slippers. It's that simple. We should stick together. It's lonely living forever, having no one to discuss the ebb and flow of centuries with. I thought I was the last of our kind, to be honest, and that the others had been killed by the time weaver. It truly is a millennium since I last crossed paths with another slipper. And if I wanted to skrike you, I would have done it already. In fact, I can see you have considerably more power than I do, so what's to stop you from skriking me? Think about it. I should be hiding from you."

"Well, because I can't use my magic, of course," Gideon replied, wincing at the reminder of his situation.

"But I didn't know that at first, did I? I approached you even though your aura was lighting up the tavern." Ostryd's frustration was rising, but he took a breath followed by a sip of wine and continued in a more level tone as a sly look flickered across his face. "As I said, at some point you'll just have to take a chance. But let's try this thought experiment. If I wanted to kill you, why didn't I stab you through the heart earlier when I drew a star on your chest?"

Gideon rolled his eyes and stood up to leave. The man was clearly mad. The less he and Lu involved themselves with him, the better.

"What star? This is nonsense. I appreciate the warning about my aura, but I'm leaving."

"Stop . . . stop, I was afraid that would be too much for you," Ostryd said, his face creased with worry. He stood up and stepped away from Gideon, holding his hands out to indicate they were empty. He stepped as far away from Gideon as he could in the cramped space, stopping just short of the far wall, taking pains not to brush against it. "Just suspend your disbelief for a few more seconds and indulge me by looking at your chest. Please. What's the harm?"

It was only that Gideon was nervous of what the strange man would do if offended that made him decide to humour him. He unbuttoned his tunic, pulled his vest away from his chest, and looked down. In black crayon there was a six-pointed star on his chest and the words "Drink with the crazy man" written in bold letters.

Gideon's mouth dropped open, and he flopped back into his seat. He pulled his vest away a second time and checked the marks, rubbing them with his finger as his mind raced to figure out how it had happened.

"How in Ag's name did you do that?" Gideon asked.

"Interesting you should mention Ag, but I'll get to his involvement in good time." Ostryd sat opposite Gideon and pushed the untouched glass an inch nearer to the charmer. Both men sat for a long time appraising each other, then Gideon picked up the glass and drank it all in one swallow.

"OK, tell me," Gideon demanded, slamming his glass onto the table.

"Actually, I cheated," Ostryd said, then held up a reassuring hand. "I didn't write that there. You did."

"I did?"

"Yes. It was a gamble on my part. I worried you might recognise your own writing style, but with the angle, you twisting around and all, I hoped it would be different enough. All I did was promise you five gold coins if you wrote on yourself. The coins are in your purse, by the way." Ostryd paused while Gideon fumbled in his belt purse and found the coins. When Gideon looked up in confusion, Ostryd continued. "The tiny part I played in all this was to slip backwards through time. I paid you to write that, and then I went back to the moment before I asked you to write on yourself. Then I lied and told you that I'd written it."

"You . . . what?" Gideon croaked.

"That's why we're called slippers. We can slip up and down the timeline. And a by-product of this talent is we never seem to age. Now, don't go and leap off the stable roof. We're not immortal. We just don't age, and if in danger, we can slip back in time to dodge the threat. But an arrow or a germ in the wrong place will kill us as swiftly as the next man. But lead a cautious life, and don't attract the time weaver by tangling up his time threads, and you can live forever."

Gideon pushed his empty glass forward, and Ostryd refilled it with an approving nod.

"Who is . . . but what about . . ." Gideon wasn't sure what to ask first, but he was silenced by Ostryd's raised hand.

"You will have a thousand questions about time loops and such, I'm sure, and I'll answer what I can, I promise. But for tonight let's focus on getting you back in touch with your magic and helping your friend. Agreed?"

"But can't I just go back in time with some better gloves and boots for us?" Gideon asked.

"Definitely not. That wouldn't be good—or possible, even with our combined power. I can only slip back a few minutes, but we *can* do the next best thing. Trust me?"

Gideon thought for a moment, then drained his glass and placed it in front of Ostryd for a refill. He held out his hand. "My name is Gideon Strangelore. Apparently, I need to get quite drunk." Ostryd's face split in a wide grin, but he declined the offer of a handshake.

Chapter Twenty-Eight

The 470ᵗʰ Year of the Morde Dynasty

The day was dark, and Judd was dragging Brylee to the altar stones. She was desperate to escape but couldn't seem to find the will to reject him. Her parents stood silently to one side, nodding their approval. Her father had a raven clinging to his belt, gnawing its way through his stomach, which he stoically ignored. Nalik was there, a look of disgust on his face for the raven, his pa's acceptance of it, and his sister. He walked away, shaking his head.

Next, Brylee was at the Crow's Nest. Raegan wanted to hide her, but Brylee sensed that if she accepted her help, Gunnar would regain power over her friend once more. Judd was on the elevator coming for her. She rode the dragon to the ground and fled to the council chamber, where Mella led the council in turning their backs on her in a ritualised shunning.

Brylee forced herself awake, escaping the nightmare, but rose to a consciousness dominated by a thunderous, unrelenting headache. *This is the worst hangover ever*, was Brylee's first thought as the nightmare slipped from her mind as easily as water falls through fingers.

Wrongly assuming she was in the Wizard's Mark, Brylee lay still, her eyes closed while she forced an image of the room to mind, intent on making the fewest moves possible to get to the water jug. She recalled it sat on a small shelf near the window. As her senses returned, she realised she was not in her bed but on a cold floor. She was face down, her left arm numb beneath her torso. She tried to move and eventually leveraged her weight off it, then twisted her body to free it. She was barely aware as pins and needles rushed into her arm, the movement reigniting the pounding in her head, and she fell back into darkness. This time she didn't dream.

Brylee resurfaced. It was much later. The headache still assaulted her, but it was reduced to a maniac with a rubber mallet rather than a stone hammer. She lay still and opened her eyes. The room was dark except for a narrow shaft of light stretching almost horizontally from high up. It reached across to illuminate the wall opposite and a wooden bench, held level by a chain at each end fixed to iron rings sunk into the stonework. As her eyes adjusted, she could make out that the slot that let the light into the room was in a door, and on the floor below it were a jug and a bucket. She was in a cell, she realised. She crawled to the jug and discovered it was full of water. She sniffed it, but it had no particular smell, so she drank from it, finding it room temperature and refreshing. Then a wave of nausea rippled through her, which she fought to contain.

The water helped, slowly easing the pounding to a dull pressure, and this easing allowed her to focus. It took several minutes to piece together the last few things she could recall. Her stomach turned over from fear and she gasped at the vivid memory of Vekki invading her. Brylee had never been raped, but she had no doubt that the horror she had experienced could be called soul rape. Powerless, terrified, intimately penetrated, and completely at the mercy of evil.

Then her world lurched in a different direction gripped by the panic of being exposed as a charmer. She had the urge to run and hide, but there was only the meagre cover of the narrow bench.

Sweating and breathless, Brylee attempted to calm herself. She had often feared what such a discovery might mean to her family, but the reality was shockingly colder than her imaginings. Such worries were overshadowed by the realisation that she was unlikely to live long enough to witness her life unravel. Maybe it already had.

Then Brylee recalled Vekki being skewered and then skriked, followed by her own flight to the inn and her puzzlement at finding Buck, Vekki's man, dressed as a city watchman, directing another who was packing up her belongings. Then darkness.

Her nose reported a terrible stench. More than her own stale sweat. Unwashed men and buckets of waste, she surmised. That Brylee did not notice the stink for the past few moments was a measure of how groggy she remained. She shook her head in an attempt to clear it, regretting it instantly as the pounding increased. She drank more water as she examined her cell but found her earlier audit had captured everything with the exception of a thin blanket that lay folded on the bench. Brylee took stock of herself and, headache aside—which she connected to a large, sticky, egg-shaped bump on the back of her skull—she could find no other injuries. She was dressed exactly as she had been when she entered the Wizard's Mark, minus her knife and all her money and possessions, which were nowhere to be seen.

Why am I in a cell? Do they think I killed Vekki?

She levered herself to her feet, fighting through another wave of nausea. Steadying herself against the wall, she stepped into the beam of light. As best as she could in the dim conditions, she examined her clothing, looking for any trace of Vekki's blood. There was none to see. She was slightly relieved at that, realising that if Vekki's murder was the charge that held her there, hundreds of witnesses had seen the mysterious figure dousing the mage in red dye and pushing her from the balcony.

Then her chest tightened again. *Ag, no, do they know I'm a charmer?* Her mind galloped down that pathway, examining what she knew. Buck was part of the city watch, posing as Vekki's man. He had been clearing her room while Vekki lured her to the theatre. Who was her mysterious saviour? She numbly accepted that she didn't have answers.

Brylee walked to the door and stooped to look through the slit. Her hand rested on the door frame, which stung her, or at least it felt so much like a wasp sting that she searched for an insect as she touched the wood. She stepped backwards, upsetting the bucket, which was blessedly empty. Then she extended her finger back to the door frame and held it there. The frame and the door felt like they were fizzing with the buzz of angry bees, although she could hear nothing. She knew it was magic at work, but what type?

Remaining clear of the door, Brylee peered out through the slot. She saw a bright, wide corridor that was clean and neat. The jail cells she could see through the slot were square rooms with stone walls on three sides, but unlike her own cell, they were open to the front. The rear stone wall of each cell was punctured by a small, barred window. The open side of the cells bore floor-to-ceiling metal bars split by a narrow iron-framed door. She saw three cells, all occupied by one or two men, and sensed there were more cells outside of her constrained view.

Picking up her bucket, she struck the door with it and yelled for the guard. None appeared and so she kept banging and calling. At length, the man in the cell opposite stepped up to his cell's bars and yelled at her to be quiet. "For the love of Ag, charmer, they won't hear that. They're upstairs. Shut up and let us sleep."

Brylee sagged, almost touching the door, then caught herself. Her blood pounded in her ears, and her face was on fire. *If this man knows I'm a charmer, then who doesn't?*

"What makes you think I'm a charmer?" she asked.

"Well, y'in a charmer cell, aren't you? I've seen enough of them. Just be quiet. I have a good drunk to sleep off." That explained the need for a magically enhanced door. It had to be resistant to her magic.

The man across the corridor spoke with the broad, musical accent of Darrow. Darrow was in Mordeland's arid and barren Tikki region. Many of her seasonal employees were Tikki, so she knew the accent well. He looked like a manual labourer, his drinking paunch tempered by toil. He was ruddy around the nose, but otherwise his complexion was weathered. He wore his black hair short, had a scraggy beard, and stood about her height.

"Wait. Tell me where we are."

"This is the West City watch cells. Not a bad breakfast here, you know." He laughed.

"But the last thing I remember, I was in Follyton. That's miles from here, isn't it?"

"Aye, it is, charmer. But West City is nearest to Mage Wickham's manor. If I w'you, I'd make the most of the breakfast. Now shut up." He left the thought hanging in the air and returned to his bunk.

Brylee sat on her bench with her head in her hands. She tried to think of a way out of her predicament, then realised her brain was just spinning, and all she managed to do was scurry around her mind from calamity to disaster.

Perhaps an hour later she heard doors banging and a commotion in the corridor outside her cell. She walked over and peered through the slit.

Two men pushed a cart containing trays of food while a third who seemed to be their supervisor led the way.

"Feed the regulars first. Start w'Gavis here," the supervisor instructed, pointing at the man who had told Brylee to be quiet. The man approached the slot between the bars so food could be passed to him.

"I'm still not Gavis. He's in the cell at the end, like he was last night. But I'll 'ave his food too if you like," the man said, laughing.

"Right . . . right . . . we'll get it straight. You're Leach. No . . . Leach is in the middle. You're Jobb, right? You're the drunk, him's the rapist, and the other is a thief."

"That's right. Don't get me confused w'those two. You lettin' me out this mornin'?"

"Perhaps. You seem sober enough. As long as the warden signs off on your warrant, you'll be free to go. But he's away today, so maybe tonight or tomorrow."

Jobb scowled and returned to his bunk with his plate.

Brylee was about to call out to the supervisor, but he turned to her cell and addressed her door, keeping his eyes averted from hers, seemingly afraid to meet her gaze.

"Keep silent, charmer. We'll 'ave no witching words from you, or we'll slam the slot tight, and you can sit in the dark and starve. We'll feed you last. So as you know, Mage Wickham made this cell his'self, so don't think you can escape. The stone's thick and the door's proofed against magic. The key to the cell is locked away upstairs, so witching us won't help as we don't have access to the key. You behave, and we'll feed you and empty your bucket until the Mage takes you off our hands. You don't, well . . ."

"But I'm no charmer," Brylee said. "There's been a mistake."

"Then you have nuffin' to worry about, then. Wickham will let you go if there's no magic to skrike from you, won't he?"

"When's he coming?" Brylee asked in a quiet voice.

"Well, normally he comes straight away. But he's in the south, helping the war effort. You'll be our guest for at least a week, I imagine. Maybe two."

"Can I get a message to my family?"

"No, that ain't allowed. And that's enough talking. You're to keep silent until Wickham comes. When you hear us come down here, sit on your bed. We'll check you're seated then change your water and bucket and leave you your food. Don't leave your bed while the panel is up, and never talk to us. Any deviation from these rules, and we'll leave you to rot. Now, go sit on the bed."

Brylee wanted to argue but decided to comply and think things through before making her situation worse, if that were possible.

Once she was seated on her bench, the small panel in the door snapped open, and a hand reached through and pulled her half-empty jug away and then replaced it. A tray of food followed it in, and the panel snapped closed with a bang.

Chapter Twenty-Nine

"Jobb," Brylee called across the corridor. He didn't answer at first, but then he stood and walked to the front of his cell and rested his forearms against the bars.

"Are the guards always as daft as that one?" she asked. "He barely knows who you are."

"Normally worse. It's why I always make a point o' reminding 'em who's who. I don't want to get strung up being mistaken for Leach 'ere."

"Hey," Leach grumbled.

"You won't be able to talk your way out, though, if that's your plan. He wasn't kidding about not having access to the keys. The warden keeps them on his belt and will come down and supervise each release personally."

"I hope he'll listen. There's been a terrible mistake."

"There always is, lady. We all say that, right." Jobb wasn't the only man there who laughed.

"Look, Jobb," Brylee pressed, "if you're about to get out, can I beg a favour? I need a message rushed to my family. I'll be happy to pay, of course."

"You still got money on you then? That's normally confiscated."

"Well, no. But get the warden to confirm with me that he can release my money to you. If he won't, my parents will pay you when you give them the message. Please?"

"Where are they, and what's the message?" Jobb asked.

"Simply that I've been mistaken for a charmer and where I am. And I need help quickly. They're down in Haxley. We own Plainhand Estate. You know, Wispy Weed fingers."

"How am I supposed to get to Haxley? I've no 'orse, and I couldn't ride one if I did. I've never left Rostal. No, lady, I'm a day late for work as it is and will 'ave to make up the time."

Brylee's heart sank. She tried to persuade him, but Jobb had no interest in helping her. She was a charmer, and he wanted nothing to do with her release or otherwise.

She turned away from the slit, took a step to the left of the door, then put her back to the wall and slid down to the floor. She wouldn't be there to help her pa through his sickness. Who would help her mother when pa died? What would become of the businesses? Who would stand up for Raegan? Actually, Raegan was getting good at defending herself. And Raegan had Modwyn. An ache in her throat heralded the tears that soon slipped down Brylee's cheeks. She tried to hold them back, but then her shoulders began to shake and her nose began to run. She didn't have so much as a kerchief, so had to resort to her sleeve. She realised she wasn't as concerned about her impending death as she was already grieving the life she wouldn't live.

While Brylee slept, a man came from upstairs and stood outside her cell. He reached in with his magic to ensure she stayed asleep. Then he opened the door and entered her cell, standing over her for a time. He was curious and delighted about what he had found. He loved a good puzzle. Eventually, he left her as he had found her.

Brylee woke and ate. Jobb had been released while she slept, and another prisoner was in his place. A day passed, which she judged by the number of times her bucket was used and emptied. She cried again, fell asleep, and dreamt.

The dream was of herself as a child, riding Nugget, her first pony. Nugget was short, only eleven hands, and had a ridge of red bristles running from the foot of her mane and along her dappled back to the tip of her tail. Until then, being so young in her training, Brylee had never ridden bareback, but her teacher, Mr. Quippy, warned her that Nugget's ridge of bristles would chafe "more than a porcupine's quills." The sun beat down. It was springtime, judging by the lilac and cream-coloured nettle leaf that peppered the paddock's hedgerows. The scene felt somewhat familiar.

"OK, Brylee, remember what we practised without the pole across the jump. Canter towards the jump in a steady three-point post position, then some eight to ten strides away from the jump, transition into a two-point post position. Nugget's a good jumper and will know what to do. You just need to remain peaceful in the saddle and let her get on with it. Hold your body at the same angle over the jump and let her guide you. Once you're down, settle back into the three-point trot."

Brylee had spent the week first trotting and then cantering around the paddock and through the jump's gates with the crossbars missing. Today was her first attempt at a jump and the pole was set at four feet. It was Brylee's eighth birthday on Sunday, and she was determined to surprise Nalik by revealing that she could jump.

The initial circuit of the paddock had gone well, and Mr. Quippy had been encouraging as she made the final turn into the gate. Brylee felt relaxed and adjusted her position eight strides out, just as she had been taught. *Just let Nugget lead you over*, she told herself.

Just then a blue-collared hornet started fussing around Nugget's ears, which flicked back angrily in response. After the accident, Brylee recalled that Nugget had kept her mind on the jump. Had Brylee done likewise, things would have gone well. As it was, Brylee changed position, attempting to reach forward to swat the dangerous insect away. In so doing, she had upset her balance just as Nugget leapt. Instead of rising smoothly with her horse and staying about the same distance from the saddle as she would in a trot, Brylee tried to grab the saddle and when she realised she couldn't, she flung herself to the side. She recalled the crack her arm had made, and the memory of the pain threw her out of the dream and back into her cell.

Brylee lay there sweating and breathing hard, her right hand resting on her left arm where the bone had been broken. She had recalled the day many times but had never relived it through a dream. She lay back and slowed her breathing, thinking about the accident. It was three more moons before she could reattempt the jump. Mr. Quippy sat her on a stump before her next attempt.

"You'll do well today, Brylee," he said. "I feel partly to blame for your accident, you know. Something I should have told you then, I'll tell you now. There will be many occasions where you and the horse are at odds, but you must *always* ride the horse. You'll be tempted to bail or give up and let the horse take over. That's what got you in trouble. Even if you're running headlong into a wall, stay focussed and keep controlling the horse right through to the impact. You'll find that more often than not, that impact is averted or greatly lessened if you stay with it. Don't give up. Ride the horse right through the trouble. You understand?"

It was a lesson Brylee had taken to heart. Mr. Cleft, her weapons teacher, had once paired her with a gruff big lad called Brammer. It was a deliberate overmatch to teach Brylee a lesson for being too cocksure. Brammer swung his big practice sword at her at least a dozen times, but Quippy's principle of staying focussed through the impact allowed Brylee to deflect most of the blows, even if by just a hair's breadth. Brylee realised what the dream was telling her. *Stop giving up, lying there on the bunk waiting to be skriked. Use the time to ride the problem to the end.*

But what could she do? There was no way out of the cell. She had tried to tickle the lock, like she could at her parents' house where they were well oiled, but this one stubbornly ignored her. She had tried to heat it too, but it remained cold, although the fizzing sensation had increased somewhat.

She had been powerless against Vekki. She had fought with everything she had and even now panicked afresh recalling her life slipping away from her into the other woman. Wickham could hardly be less capable of skriking her than Vekki. If he came for her, he would kill her; she had no doubt.

Should she risk trying to reason with the guards and being shut in the dark and ignored? Could she bribe them in some way? There were three of them, so convincing them all seemed unlikely. And apparently they didn't have the key anyway. She felt the nausea rise again and fought to stay in control of her emotions.

Ride the horse, Brylee.

She racked her brain, only interrupting her useless thoughts to get lost in worry about her parents and what may already be going wrong. She had missed her meeting with Jyan. Had he contacted Mella? Brylee had lost track of time, but surely people back in Haxley would begin to miss her. They would have no idea where to locate her, though, even if they were looking.

It was hopeless. There was nothing she could do physically, due to the hardened cell and the jail protocols, which worked despite having idiots for guards. There was nothing in the cell that her small amount of magic could influence to affect her escape. The one positive, such as it was, was that her reserve of magic seemed to replenish much faster after being half skriked than it had before she was attacked. It allowed her to heal the various scrapes and knocks in a shorter time, and her reserves were already restored despite the poor-quality food. She would go to her death healthy, she thought, laughing to herself.

Then she realised there was something her magic could continue to work on in the cell: herself. Could that be useful? She remembered imagining a barrier between herself and Vekki, which had slowed Vekki down, if only for a moment. *No,* she thought, *that wouldn't slow a full mage down for long.* Aside from healing, she had only ever used her magic on herself to change her appearance slightly. The beginnings of a plan suggested itself. It was a long shot to be sure, and she would continue to seek a more realistic way out, but doing something was better than nothing.

She pictured Jobb, recalling as much detail as possible. He was about her size, with some obvious physical differences. Brylee made an inventory of which parts of herself she felt she could alter with her magic. She couldn't grow a cock, but she could shrink her breasts. She wasn't well endowed anyway, and for the first time in her life she was grateful for it. If they stripped her down, the game would be up in any case, but she would do what she could to look like a man.

She didn't rush, praying Wickham would stay in the south long enough for her to complete the task. She focussed on the skin on her throat, and over a few days a lump grew, similar to a man apple. She had nothing sharp, but by trickling magic into her hair two inches from the roots to harden it, she could snap the excess away to create a scruffy version of Jobb's shortcut. She threw the excess hair into the bottom of her slop bucket, trusting no one looked closely at what they threw out. Then she magicked what she had left on her scalp from its naturally sandy colour to his coal black.

She worked on the flesh of her stomach and hips and over the week became less curvy and obtained a small beer paunch. With great effort and experimentation, she convinced hair to emerge from her cheeks, although at first she had rashes and raised polyps. She lightened her skin colour all over and flushed her face around the nose to mimic a drunk. She made her eyebrows slightly bushy and all the while practised her Darrow accent. She had grown up with the accent around her and mimicked it often, but although her voice was deep for a woman, it was still too high for a man. When she tried to lower her voice, it sounded like a woman doing it and lacked the required gruffness.

Brylee removed the leather straps from her leggings and fashioned a binding that she wrapped around her chest. She had some success in convincing her breasts to shrink, but they still made her unmistakably female. She pulled the binding as flat as she could, almost so she couldn't breathe, then left her top baggy.

Brylee had no mirror, and the cell was dark, but going by feel, within what must have been more than ten days, she had caused a great deal of change to her body. It wasn't without its toll. She was thinner, she slept for longer periods, her skin had dried dramatically, and she felt wrinkles on her face. The latter detail was welcome as a disguise, but worrying nonetheless. She doubted she would ever be mistaken for Jobb, but she felt she must appear masculine enough to at least confuse the idiot guards.

Hour after hour Brylee worked on walking, moving, scratching, and all the other mannerisms she could think of that marked man from woman. As she did so, she thought through what she would say to Wickham and the guards that might convince them they had the wrong person. She thought of Vekki's comment about "smelling a charmer." Had she meant that literally, or had she said it just to torment Brylee? She shivered through her core, recalling the sensual evil in Vekki's tone. She had to try to get away before Wickham got close enough to smell her magic.

After many days her doubts built, and Brylee second guessed herself and switched tactics, deciding to conserve her magic and practise building a layer around herself as she had tried with Vekki. It might not work, but she acknowledged her disguise plan had little chance of success either. After just a day, however, she felt the hairs she had grown on her face begin to drop out and realised she had to expend magic to maintain the changes she had forced on herself; otherwise she would revert. Despite being trapped, she was glad Wickham's trip to the south had been extended far longer than she was told. Every extra day gave her a chance to improve her disguise, but she needed to be gone before the mage returned.

Her voice was still a weak point, and she obsessed about it. She experimented with magic on throat, then panicked when she lost her voice entirely. She was relieved when it returned several hours later. With some practice, she managed to lower it a little. It wasn't as baritone as Jobb's, but it did seem more authentically male.

Over what she estimated was more than three full weeks, Brylee spoke to no one. Through her slit she saw the occupants of the other cells change many times, with prisoners staying at most three days before being released or taken to a longer-term prison. She watched the guards and now had a feel for which were the brightest and the dumbest. She got to understand the flow of the guards' work and the procedures for moving prisoners in and out of the cells. She suspected they would treat a charmer differently, of course.

The warden was always the person with the key. It was clear he thought little of the guards, and the sentiment was returned. Any issues were made the fault of the guards, and they accepted it while the warden was present but often grumbled about it while delivering food or cleaning cells when not in his presence. It was all information Brylee tucked away in case it would be useful when her time came.

After perhaps four weeks, she was awoken by banging on her cell door. The familiar clench of panic gripped her, but she swallowed it down.

Ride the horse, Brylee, she told herself.

Chapter Thirty

"Sit on your bench!" yelled the guard whom Brylee had come to call Abe. She had given each guard a nickname starting with a different letter of the alphabet to help her separate them. Having guards grouped in threes with names starting with adjoining letters had been a way to help her memorise them, but the guards' shifts were unpredictable, and today was Abe, Kane, and Tall One, rather than the men whose names began with B or C.

Abe's shortness forced him to stand on his toes to look through the slit, and Brylee saw his head bobbing in the light. Once she complied, Abe opened the panel, pushed a box into the cell, then snapped the panel back into place.

"There's a jacket and leggings in the box. Put them on and do up the straps."

Brylee said nothing, just did as she was told. The clothing was some sort of treated blue canvas, and like the door it fizzed as it touched her skin. Brylee took care to keep some of her own clothing between it and her body to avoid contact with it wherever possible. Straps were sewn into the material, which buckled up to keep it close to her body. She was careful to leave it looser over her chest.

"Quick about it, charmer. Put the manacles around your wrists with your hands behind you." The manacles were of a similar but much thicker material and had locks that snapped shut.

"Stand in front of the door with your back to it, and lower yourself to the floor," Abe commanded. When she complied, she felt the panel open and then locks being applied to the manacles.

"Stand back!" the warden told the guards. Brylee heard the key in the lock. The door opened behind her, and she was helped to her feet and led out of the cell, through a door, and up some steps. The warden walked ahead of her, and neither he nor the three guards who flanked her met her eye. They were all terrified of her despite the fact she wore clothing she assumed was designed to suppress her magic. Brylee wondered if the material would undo the changes she had made to her body, but there was little she could do about that if so.

The corridor at the top of the stairs was similar to that of the cells, except the spaces were open and had no bars. It was clearly where the guards spent their time. There were chairs around tables, which had half-played hands of cards and gaming chips upon them.

Dreading every step, Brylee let herself be led through another door to an area better appointed than the guards' room. There were rugs on the wooden floorboards and pictures on the walls. They passed what Brylee assumed was the warden's office, judging by its desk and filing cabinets, then turned right into what appeared to be an interview room. It had a single table in the centre, a seat on one side, presumably for the prisoner, and across from it a bench that could accommodate four people.

The procession stopped, and for the first time the warden turned and looked at Brylee. She kept her eyes on his feet.

"Who's this then?" the warden said with surprise and impatience in his tone. The room was silent. Then Tall One spoke.

"It's the charmer, sir." It sounded like he was deliberately keeping the surliness from his voice. "Don't know his name, though. Unconscious when brought in by the city guard."

"Were you on duty that night, watchman?" the warden asked. His voice sounded pleasant on the surface, but malicious intent lurked beneath his words.

"Er, no, sir. I just recall the talk the next day. We don't get many charmers, so there's always gossip, sir. And as per your own instructions, no one is to talk to charmers for fear of being witched. So, no one's ever asked 'im his name, I guess, sir."

"Well, you're quite right, watchman," the warden replied. "The log does say that the prisoner was unconscious and unnamed, but it also mentioned the charmer was a woman. Is this someone you would consider marrying, watchman?" Brylee kept her gaze down but could feel four pairs of eyes studying her.

"Young female charmer, name unknown. Unconscious. Hold for Mage Wickham. That's the log entry, watchman. I see a scruffy, wrinkled male prisoner who appears to be well into his prime." The warden paused, waiting for a comment.

"Can't be, sir. He was in the charmer's cell."

The warden rolled his eyes and turned his attention to Brylee. "What's your name, man?"

"Jobb, sir," Brylee replied in her best Darrow accent, keeping her eyes low and her voice even lower. "I tried to tell the guard I wasn't no charmer, but he threatened to starve me if I spoke at all. I told them it was a mistake. Er . . . sir."

"Oh, I think you're a charmer, Jobb. I imagine some idiot wrote it in the log incorrectly, that's all. Wrote 'female' instead of 'male.' Wouldn't be the first time. We don't get many women in here, and the guards often get details wrong."

"If I may, sir, there was a woman in the cell opposite me on the first day," Brylee said. "The guard told her not t' drink so much, and he didn't want t' see her back anytime soon. I remember her because I was in for the night to dry out too. She weren't hard on the eyes, and I thought we could drink together, if you catch my drift, sir. Then later the guard started yelling at me about being a charmer." Brylee let her point drift into the silence. The warden looked stricken. She glanced up and saw him consulting the log. She knew he would find a man called Jobb there overnight, supporting the tale she was attempting to spin.

"Do you recall who brought you in, Jobb?"

"It was a big, beefy sergeant from the city watch, sir. Don't know his name, but bald head and a thick brown beard."

"No, you idiot," the warden growled. "Which guard put you in your cell?"

"I know he was much taller than this fella here but twice as wide. Scared me if I'm honest, sir." Brylee described the guard who had struck her over the last four weeks as the second densest. "He was also the guard who carried the woman in right after me. Had her slung over his shoulder like she weighed nothing, but she was at least as big as me. Another guard was helping. Average looking man, sir, except his eyes looked like they argued often about which way to look, if you know what I mean." The densest guard was cross-eyed.

"It wouldn't be the first time prisoners were placed in the wrong cells," Abe said, "especially by those two."

"Hang on," Kane argued. "Maybe this charmer can use magic to change his appearance. He's . . . she's trying to fool us, sir." They all looked at Kane and then back at Brylee.

"Honestly, man, have you ever heard of a charmer, or a mage for that matter, who can do magic on themselves? It's impossible. Their magic only works on others or on objects. Ag, what idiots.

Are they on shift?" the warden yelled. Spittle landed on Brylee, but she kept still.

"No, sir. Not until the weekend, sir." All three guards were at full attention. Apparently, the warden's wrath was to be avoided.

"I imagine the charmer wasn't secured properly and witched them into placing her into the wrong cell," the warden said. Brylee got the sense he was planting that idea into the guards' heads so that the prison gossip would support it if Wickham made inquiries. "Perhaps she wasn't really unconscious." He let that thought float too. He recalled his predecessor had been fired for mishandling a charmer. They had kept the wrong prisoner in custody, trying to make them perform magic, convinced they were being tricked. Wickham saw it as more bumbling. *Best to deal with things differently*, the warden thought. "Anyway, get this prisoner out of here immediately. I'll go to see Mage Wickham and tell him we made a mistake. I'll also make sure he's clear on where the blame lies."

Brylee wondered if she should make a pretence of asking for some compensation for being wrongly detained but decided to let things rest. The warden left the room, the guards released Brylee's bindings, and she slipped out of the magic proof clothing.

Ride the horse, Brylee reminded herself, trying to ensure her elation at fooling the warden didn't betray her. She remembered to do her best manlike walk, and even scratched herself in a few unladylike places too, but held off from spitting on the floor.

She let herself be led out of the room and through a large oak door at the end of the corridor that took them into the courtyard, which was open to the street. The warden was there, talking to a small man whose robes marked him as a mage.

Ag, it must be Wickham, she thought. Brylee kept her head down and forced her feet to keep walking, imploring her knees not to buckle. She realised she was holding her breath.

"Yes, that's him. The one we accidently locked up instead of the charmer," she heard the warden explain. Brylee maintained her steady pace and kept walking, feeling the mage's gaze on her.

"Stop, sir," Wickham called, his voice relaxed and courteous. Brylee considered pretending she hadn't heard, then accepted that wouldn't work. She turned and decided to risk focussing her magic on herself as a protective layer. She took a few steps towards the mage and stopped within earshot but still left as much distance as she dared in case a mage could actually smell a charmer. She was shaking with fear, but she knew everyone did around a mage, so that in itself didn't worry her too much.

"Jobb, is it?" Wickham asked, his voice still pleasant. "I appreciate you've had a terrible time of it, locked away unfairly for weeks, but I'd ask you for a few more moments of your time. I believe my apprentice was killed by a woman charmer, or the charmer witnessed her murder at least. I'd like to get a description of the woman you saw on your first night in custody."

Brylee really didn't want to be reconnected to that incident.

"Sorry sir," she croaked. "I'd surely help if I could, but I was drunk, and it was a moon ago. She was tall and had fair hair down to here." Brylee held her hand at shoulder level. "I recall she was a handsome gal, but more than that, I can't remember. And I best be off. My employer has likely already replaced me."

"That's so unfair, Jobb. I'll go see him myself and make sure he does the right thing. Look, come with me and I'll give you a silver bar, a bath, and a meal fit for a king in return for an hour more of your time. I insist we make this up to you, Jobb."

Brylee thought hard for ways to decline without raising further suspicion. The real Jobb would have jumped at the offer. No one turned down a mage, especially if they were offering half a year's salary and would prevent the person from being fired. Remaining in Wickham's vicinity was a huge risk, but there was no sign he perceived her as anything other than a wrongly detained drunk. Perhaps she would be able to provide a poor description that would throw the mage off track. She could certainly use a bath, not to mention some money to get Summer back from the stables and aid her escape from Rostal.

"Of course, sir. Did you say a tankard of ale came with that dinner?"

"There's a good man," Wickham said with a smile. He dismissed the warden with a wave and then led Brylee out of the courtyard and onto the street.

It was a short walk. They crossed a small square adjacent to the jail and continued along a broad avenue for one hundred yards. On the far side of a road that traversed the avenue was a brown stone wall that was twice Brylee's height. Set in the wall was a double gate, boasting a guard hut where three uniformed soldiers stood. As Wickham approached, the gate opened, and Brylee reluctantly followed the mage through it as the guards saluted.

Chapter Thirty-One

Most people imagined Lord Lessinger's leading mage would live in one of the magical raised palaces like the lord's House. But Wickham's manor was surprisingly modest. Although closed off from the city for security, there were no spacious grounds or gardens behind the walls. Everything outside the main building held an air of function over aesthetics.

Beside the main house was a small stable for Wickham's private coaches—he was one of the few allowed to ride on the surface streets—with a private circular road that led down to the main subterranean carriageways for deliveries and guests. Adjacent to the stable was a workshop where Wickham conducted some of his magical tasks and where he trained his apprentices.

The workshop mirrored the style of the main house, the ubiquitous blue-white hue with long, curved, sloping roofs reminiscent of mountain cabins designed to shed heavy snow. The window and door frames were oak, stained dark, with minimal ornate carvings or styling. Had they any less charm, the building would have been mistaken for a warehouse.

The manor itself had a total of four bedrooms for the mage and any guests, a bathing area complete with sauna, a main living room, a formal dining room, and Wickham's favourite room, his study. These spaces occupied the front of the house. At the rear were the main kitchen, the scullery, a storage area, and spacious rooms for his two live-in staff: his long-serving housekeeper, Rosemary, and her husband, Sage, who was a wonderful chef and an enthusiastic, if not talented, handyman. That someone named Rosemary had married a man named Sage provided constant amusement for the mage, and he took every opportunity to introduce painful herb puns whenever he talked to them. Other staff lived off site, arriving whenever needed.

The large oak front doors were nearer the gate that Brylee and Wickham had entered, but the mage walked Brylee down the side of the property and into the manor through the tradesman's entrance at the rear. If the chef was surprised to see his master enter that way, Brylee saw no sign of it.

"There you are, sir," Sage said. "Rose wondered where you'd disappeared off to. She's taken your meal up to your study."

"Wonderful, Sage. Can I assume there is too much food for one person, as usual? If so, we just require an extra plate, cutlery, and a tankard . . ." Sage had begun to move as soon as he saw Brylee follow the mage in and was already placing the required items on a tray.

"I know, sir. You were about to be droll and apologise for not warning us that your guest was 'cumin'. Will he be requiring a bath first?" Sage was deadpan in his delivery, and only a small wrinkle of his nose betrayed his reaction to the fact that Brylee had been incarcerated for nearly a moon without access to a bath.

"Actually, that's a good idea. I'd forgotten I'd deadened my sense of smell, and I don't want Miss Plainhand to stink up my study. Have Rosemary provide Miss Plainhand with some temporary clothing while her own is laundered or maybe replaced. And send any staff except the gate security home for the day, will you?"

Wickham had taken three steps before he realised Brylee's jaw had dropped to the floor. She looked ready to bolt at the revelation that the mage had not only seen through her disguise but also knew her name. She started to stammer in her Darrow accent, but Wickham cut her short.

"Oh, I think we can dispense with the charades now, Miss Plainhand. They sufficed for the warden, but I've known who you are for three weeks. I accept your need to disguise yourself, but please don't treat me like an idiot. I hate such things." From the corner of her eye Brylee noted Sage subtly shake his head at her, confirming it was not a good idea to treat Wickham's intelligence casually. "We have much to talk about, Miss Plainhand," the mage continued, "but a quick bath and some food will help us both focus. If I intended to skrike you, I would have done so at the jail. Take my word that as long as you don't make any stupid attempts to escape, you will be perfectly safe. At least for the time being. Come along, I'll show you the baths. They are quite good, actually." Wickham turned and walked to a door leading into the house.

Brylee was still thinking about running when she felt a gentle push of an invisible wall of hard air nudge her after the mage. One glance at Wickham's arched eyebrow confirmed it was him who was chivvying her along. If he knew her name, there would be no point in running home.

Would the Council for Magical Law protect Brylee if she could reach their offices? She had heard of such things. Skriking was against the law, even if a blind eye was turned more often than not. The hard air nudged her once more, this time a little more urgently. She accepted she was trapped and that for now, playing for time was her best option.

Brylee followed Wickham though the house, hesitating to peer around each corner, expecting further traps to be sprung. They entered a tiled bathing area with a large tub in the centre. Above it hung several pipes and levers. Wickham checked that the tub's drain was plugged, then pulled a red lever, which caused steaming hot water to flow from the pipe into the tub.

"Red for hot, blue for cold. The black one opens and closes the drain. There are several soaps and oils in the jars on the shelf. After a moon in that cell, you will need several cycles of washing and rinsing. Please use as much water and take as much time as you need. We have all day, and I want you in the best frame of mind." His voice was firm but not unkind. He seemed to feel for her predicament. "I appreciate you must be scared. Who wouldn't be when their worst nightmare has manifested? However, mark my words: how you handle yourself over the next few hours will have an influence over your future. Calm and thoughtful wins the day, eh? Remember that."

He strode away, then paused at the door. "Rosemary will show you to my study when you're ready. Oh, and don't shave off the beard. It's quite wonderful, and I need to study it."

Chapter Thirty-Two

Brylee locked and barred the heavy wooden door behind the departing mage, despite knowing he could easily breach it if he wished. She leant against the frame, tipped back her head, and closed her eyes. What did it say about Wickham's reassurances about not skriking her if she didn't trust him not to peek at her bathing?

On the far side of the washing area were glass double doors that led out onto a patio. Could it be that easy to walk out? She would try the lock at least, deferring the decision for every second she could.

Brylee strode across the room but froze when she noticed movement to her left. A yelp escaping her lips at being confronted by a scruffy, thick-set, bearded tramp who seemed equally alarmed at being confronted by Brylee. It took several breaths and what felt like a hundred pounding heartbeats to realise she was staring at herself in a floor-to-ceiling mirror.

That's what I get for doing magic on myself in the dark without a mirror, she thought. She certainly didn't look like herself. She had made herself appear masculine, but the thug who stood in front of her was very different from Jobb. In fact, he would have been insulted at her poor attempt at mimicking him. She would bathe and then examine herself in more detail.

Brylee continued to the patio door and peeked outside. No one was in sight. She turned the latch, and the door opened. She closed it again and weighed her options. Remain there, placing her life in the hands of someone with a ruthless reputation, or try to run. But Wickham knew her name, so where would she run, and what would the consequences be when he caught her? Even if she escaped, would he harm her family? Either way, a bath would help her chances.

It took some experimentation to get water flowing at the right temperature. Once she had the knack of it, she stripped off her clothes and unwrapped the bindings from her chest. She had the strangest set of bruises from where she had compressed herself too tightly. Who knew what damage she had done to herself with the magic? And not just to her chest.

Brylee lowered herself into the steaming bath. Once seated she pulled the lid off each of the soaps and inspected the contents. She settled on a transparent, viscous liquid that smelled strongly of citrus fruits and got to work.

Wickham had been correct; it wasn't until her third bath that Brylee felt clean. She heard a knock, followed by a woman's voice that said clean clothes awaited her outside the door and that she should come back to the kitchen once dressed. She stepped out of the tub and availed herself of the thick towels.

Brylee unbarred the door and snatched the pile of clothes. She stepped into the trousers and jerkin, which were both loose on her. Retreating to the mirror, she looked at her patchy beard and scruffy hair and was tempted to tidy herself with some scissors, which she found in a drawer. Although she resisted the temptation to groom, she slipped the scissors into her waistband and pulled the jerkin down to conceal them. Finally, she tugged on her boots, which would be essential if running became necessary. Having spent the time considering the virtues of fleeing versus staying, she had landed on the latter. With no more excuses for procrastinating, she folded her rank clothing and carried it at arm's length down to the kitchen.

Rosemary and Sage were busy with chores, which they paused as Brylee appeared. Sage took her old clothes and promised to salvage what he could. Rosemary offered Brylee some water.

"What did you make of Gil's—sorry, that's the mage's given name—his hot water system in the bath?" Rose asked as Brylee drained the glass. The water had a subtle citrus flavour. Wickham's kitchen staff seemed genuinely welcoming, and if they had any sense of Brylee's fate, they didn't show it. *How often does Wickham invite smelly strangers into his home through the kitchen to bathe them?* Brylee wondered.

"It's quite something," Brylee replied. "He seemed proud of it."

"Oh, that he is," Rosemary said with an infectious chuckle. "Come on, I expect you're hungry." Brylee suddenly realised she was ravenous.

Rosemary led Brylee along a corridor to a doorway just off the main hallway short of the front entrance. She knocked once, then strode inside. The smell of hot bacon, toasted cakes, and grou't assailed Brylee before she even stepped into the study. She felt her resolution not to eat anything offered by the mage crumble.

Wickham was at his desk, which was pushed against the wall, his back to the door and his head deep into some paperwork.

"Eat first, then talk," he instructed, gesturing towards a table piled with plates of food sitting under the window by the far wall. Brylee just stood, not knowing if it was wise to eat or not. Rosemary excused herself, and just before closing the door caught Brylee's eye with a smile and a nod towards the food, indicating Brylee should tuck in.

Two places had been set at the table. Wickham had not waited. There was evidence he had already eaten before dragging his chair to his desk. Brylee saw a cup of grou't and a small scone next to the mage, which he pecked at as he worked.

Feeling famished, she piled her plate high, rationalising that if this were her last meal before she died or escaped, it may as well be a good one, poison be damned.

As Brylee neared the end of her second helping—Wickham had promised a meal fit for a king, and Brylee chose to interpret that as in terms of quantity—the mage restacked the papers he was working on and slipped them into a desk drawer. Then he turned his chair around and regarded Brylee for a few moments. She took the hint, finished her last mouthful, washed it down with two big gulps of grou't, and then sat back to await her fate.

Wickham stood and walked over to a bookcase next to his desk. He ran a finger down a seam between shelves and, following a soft click, a three-foot-square panel swung outwards, books and all. From a hidden cupboard, Wickham brought out a flat blue crystal that was roughly the size of a small pony's hoof. He closed and magically resealed the cupboard, pulled his chair over to the food table, and sat across from Brylee.

"I'm going to call you Brylee unless you insist on something more formal," he said. "And I'd like you to call me Gil. It's important for us both to build a trusting relationship as swiftly as possible. You have some big decisions to make, and this Judge's Crystal will help us. Have you used one before?"

Brylee shook her head. "I've never heard of such a thing."

"I'm not surprised. They're almost as rare as a magic user who can change her own appearance." He smiled, raising an eyebrow.

"They have two qualities. First, if you cup it in your hand, like this, it will glow. That's how we know you're in full contact with it and not keeping a protective layer of hard air between yourself and its surface. Its second quality is that if you tell a lie while holding it, it will burn you. It's quite useful even on mages, as you can imagine."

"Listen, Mr. Wick . . . Mage . . . Gil . . ." Brylee stuttered. "I'm not here to lie to you. What do you want to know?"

"No, you misunderstand me. I want you to be confident that I'm being truthful with you, not the other way around. I have things to tell you, and it's important you believe me completely, for your sake as much as mine. But you need to know this works. Hold it and try lying." He held the crystal out until Brylee took it from him. It felt slippery and cooler than she thought it should. She cupped it like he had, and it lit up with a faint light.

"I don't want to get burnt," Brylee said.

"It's not a lasting burn, and you won't have blisters or redness. It will be evident to all that you find it hot but as soon as you drop the crystal, the pain ceases. Now, answer my questions please. What is your name?"

"Brylee Plainhand, but you already know that."

"How many winters have you lived through?"

"This will be my twenty-fourth year."

"Since you entered my home, have you acquired a weapon?"

Brylee's hesitation and rapid flush as she thought of the scissors tucked into her waistband would have betrayed her anyway, but when she shook her head, not daring to utter the word "no," a burning sensation shot up her arm and, as predicted, she dropped the Judge's Crystal onto the table with a heavy clang. It immediately dimmed.

"I always enjoy that," Wickham said with a boyish grin, his tone sounding more playful than mean.

Brylee shook her arm and rubbed her palm, then realised there was no lingering sensation. Her hand felt completely normal.

"Why doesn't it still hurt?" she asked.

"Because the lie is in your head, and the pain is in your mind, not your hand. There's no heat. The crystal makes you believe there is when you veer from the truth."

Brylee reached under her jerkin, pulled out the scissors, and placed them on the table, her eyes downcast. "Sorry."

"Not at all. Keep them if they make you more comfortable. I actually assumed you would steal a knife from the kitchen," he added with a smile.

Wickham picked up the crystal and held it so that it glowed. His face became serious, and he maintained eye contact with Brylee. "Listen carefully. I have some questions for you about Vekki's death. I'm not going to ask you to hold the crystal, but I hope you will answer me honestly. But whether you're truthful or dishonest, you have my word that you can leave here unharmed when we're finished, and I'll provide you with the silver I promised at the jail."

Brylee looked from Wickham's eyes to the crystal. His hand was steady. No pain, evidently. She felt a spark of hope and relief. She wanted to believe him, but she didn't trust that it could be so easy.

"Why would you do that? You can skrike me, and I bet the council wouldn't say a word about it. I appreciate the trick with the crystal, but I have to think a full mage can fake such things. You have a hard and ruthless reputation, Gil, and you sent your apprentice to skrike me."

He winced at her accusation and shook his head. "Actually, no. I didn't. I heard you were smart and resourceful, and you're proving to be both. That could be good, and I'll get to why later. And you've answered one of my questions already. I assumed Vekki had attempted to take your magic, but I wasn't sure. I had heard rumours she did such craven acts despite my forbidding all my apprentices from doing so."

"She didn't seem to be a rule follower, Gil, and she was savouring killing me." Brylee was surprised at how surly she sounded. A tremor shook her as she recalled her near-death experience. She resolved to try to keep that in check when she saw Wickham's lips purse. Pissing him off wouldn't improve her situation.

The mage didn't reply to her comment. Instead, he held up three fingers and lowered each, ticking off his next comments as he went.

"Three reasons I will not skrike you: because it's unethical, I would acquire only a miniscule amount of magic anyway, and more importantly, I believe you will be a better tool for me to exploit if you're alive rather than dead. Yes, I'm ruthless, but I'm not stupid. Skriking you would be worse than pointless."

"But there must be some trick," Brylee said. "Are you saying I can just go back to my life?" She was flabbergasted at her turn in fortune.

"Ah, perhaps you're not quite as bright as I'd hoped. What makes you think you have a life to go back to?" Wickham raised an eyebrow as he let the silence settle. "I promise you can leave here unharmed. I can't promise how long you will live once you've left. I'm just saying I am not your enemy, Brylee."

The rollercoaster of the last two hours was proving too much for Brylee, and she realised her mind was spinning in circles.

"You know nothing about me, Gil. What do you know about my life or any threats to it?"

"Wrong again, Miss Plainhand. I first stood in your cell three weeks ago marvelling at your transformation, and I've studied you many nights since. Your jail food was drugged." Wickham's tone was frustrated, but he took a breath and calmed himself. "Let me take back the comment about you not being bright. To be fair, I've had time to work everything out, but I've just sprung it on you. It might be simplest for me to lay things out from where I see them, then you can ask questions. OK?"

"OK."

"I came home from the south twenty-four days ago to hear my apprentice had been assassinated. She was killed at the theatre by one of the Namiduh Jou. The Jou are highly select and expensive assassins who mark their victims with dye as their signature. Each member of their group uses a different colour. They can only be hired through their leader, and the list of people who know that person's identity is small and jealously held. Vekki's death was witnessed by a few hundred people, as were you fleeing from her side."

"I didn't kill her," Brylee said.

"Obviously, but you're involved. Wait." He held his hand up to stop her interrupting. "You're involved but I suspect not of your own choosing. It took me less than a day to discover you were lured there by Vekki and three members of the city watch, namely Kepper, Fenn, and Sergeant Goss. It took me ten minutes with Goss for him to confess they were hired by a man who called himself Mr. Sod to work with Vekki to skrike you. When she was assassinated and you escaped, they panicked and put you under my nose, hoping I wouldn't make the connection and I would finish their job for them. If they'd just killed you, an investigation might have linked you to them, but no one ever follows up on a skriking, or so they believe."

"I don't think I know a Mr. Sod," Brylee said.

"I suspect you do. Vekki was not the first victim of the Red Assassin, as he's become known. She was the third. All were mages or apprentices. You can see why locating the assassin is a priority for not just me, but I'm feeling pressure from other mages who are worried they might be next. As should be clear by now, I have an excellent network for information, not just in Rostal but across all of Lanthe, including Haxley."

"You're telling me that all the effort you expended to find me was to see what I know about the Namiduh Jou? You aren't actually interested in me at all?"

"You're right—" Wickham didn't get to finish his reply because the Judge's Crystal jumped out of his hand and crashed onto the desk. "Ag, that hurts. Sorry, let me rephrase that." He picked up the crystal once more. "At that point in the story that was true. I wasn't really interested in you. But I am now, although not as a suspect."

"I guess the crystal does work on mages," Brylee couldn't keep a smile from her lips, which mirrored Gil's easy grin.

Wickham huffed. "Indeed," he said. "The critical question is why the assassin picked that particular time and place. Was he connected to you, with or without your knowledge, or was he stalking Vekki or one of the city watchmen? I'm happy to share that I've found nothing at all to link any of the Jou to you or the others. And I was thorough, even travelling to Haxley and your estate in disguise to work alongside my spies."

"What did you discover? I'm innocent, yes?"

"Yes," Wickham admitted. "I also had many descriptions of you, none of which resembled the person I found in your cell when I visited you while you slept. But I could sense your aura.

When I realised what you were attempting, I wondered if that played into whatever is behind the assassinations. But I don't think so. If Vekki had known how rare you are, she would have taken a different course, I think."

"If I'm not being stalked by the Jou, can I leave?"

"I'm confident you're not on their list, but that doesn't mean you're safe."

"I don't know of anyone else upset with me enough to want to kill me," Brylee said.

"Let me share some more of what I discovered in Haxley. I don't think I met one person who hadn't heard that you're a charmer, and soon to be a dead charmer at that." Brylee's world lurched again. She almost brought her meal back up.

"The hardest part of my research was discovering who was spreading that information. Common gossip spreads and bounces, and people embellish it. It's confused and hard to trace. I doubt, for instance, that you ever led eleven other ladies in a naked dance during the winter solstice."

"Er . . . no." Brylee replied, shocked that everyone knew about her and the rumours were expanding.

"On various pretences I spoke to your close friends, key employees, and your parents. I know much about your life and your history. I even know Fifi makes the best cassiaberry soup with those garell root croutons. She was kind enough to provide the recipe, which I have passed to Sage, but they unknowingly pointed me to one Gunnar Fenn."

"Ag," Brylee said, lowering her head into her hands. "He's mean enough to spread gossip. In fact, he would delight in it. But arranging a murder? That's quite a stretch. I think he might contemplate it, but he's not smart enough."

"Oh, I agree. As mean as a snake and dumber than an axe, that one. But if you follow him to a certain pub on a certain night, you find someone a little smarter who also has a good motive to want you out of the picture." He had leaned forward and lowered his voice without realising it to confide this information.

"I can't think—"

"A thug aspiring to be a lord. Judd Brown. I believe he is Mr. Sod, as the Olde Sod was the name of the pub where they confessed to me."

"Did you kill them?" Brylee realised how silly that sounded as soon as she said it. One could only hope, she supposed.

"No. And they don't know Mage Wickham was there with them that night. I was disguised and took some of my larger, rougher people who convinced them to admit their complicity. They believe they were visited by villains interested in taking over their territory. For now, at least."

"Then I need to get home and deny the gossip. It will already be impacting my business. And my parents. What can they be thinking?"

"Yes, your business is already suffering, and your parents are deeply upset. They don't believe the gossip, if that's any consolation. Your father even came to the jail but was told you were not being held there. That is my doing, I'm afraid. I need to finish my investigation before anything happens to you."

"Look, Gil, I appreciate I'll not be welcome in many places in Haxley, and I'll have to watch my back with Judd and Gunnar, but I can look after myself. I have to get back there." Brylee stood to leave.

"When we started this conversation today, I told you I wouldn't skrike you, and I listed my reasons, which still stand. For me. But like Vekki, there are many junior mages who are at great risk of being skriked. They have much less magic than me, and so to them, taking magic from charmers is a great benefit. They are desperate to get higher up the power ladder before they become a tasty snack for someone else. They won't be safe until they are almost a full mage. And while in Haxley, I saw two junior mages who had little business being in the town as far as I could tell. If anyone there knows your location, they'll hear. And you won't last a day after that."

Brylee flopped back into her seat. "What about the Council of Magical Law? Won't they protect me?"

"They'll try. For a short while. But in my experience, it just means even more mages will know about you, making you a bigger target. I'm sorry, Brylee. Gunnar and Judd essentially ended your life in Haxley when they exposed you."

"Then what am I to do?" Brylee wiped a tear from her cheek before she realised she was weeping. She wasn't sure if it was sadness or anger that had brought it on.

Wickham gave the crystal a nervous look. "I believe you have to die—at least to the outside world. If people believe you've been skriked by me, they'll stop looking for you. But you can never go back to your old life. I'm sorry, but that's gone already and you just have to accept it."

"No, there must be a way," Brylee said.

"You're welcome to stay here for a few weeks and think it through. Perhaps you will think of something I haven't. But I also have a proposal for you to consider. You won't love it, but you might not be able to do anything better."

"I'm listening," Brylee said.

"Despite the information network I direct, I don't have a clue as to the identity of the Red Namiduh. I've spoken to others who have investigated him before, and we have pooled our knowledge, to no avail. I highly suspect he's like you and can change his appearance. As far as I know only three mages could do that, and they all died centuries ago. It's an incredibly rare talent for a mage and unheard of for a charmer. No one else suspects it, but it would explain how this fellow has slipped out of various traps set for him."

"He's like me but not me. How does that help anything?" Brylee asked.

"If you can't go back to your old life, then work for me. I can't fix your reputation—it's too late for that I'm afraid—but in return for your help, here's what I *am* prepared to do. I can ensure Judd and Gunnar never involve themselves in your parents' business. I will help your parents run their business. I can arrange connections and investors, and if needed I can insert someone with experience as an advisor. I know how your father's sickness has diminished him, but perhaps he won't need any help because I'll ensure he's healed. I can't get your old life back, Brylee, but I can restore his. I can also give you a new one here, working for me."

Brylee didn't think for more than a second. "If you can heal Pa, then you've got me. I'm yours. Even if the other issue can be sorted out, I have to help him before all else, Gil. What do you want of me, exactly?"

"I want to train you to hunt down the Red Namiduh."

"You want me to kill a Namiduh Jou?"

"I want you to find him, yes, but you'll be my stalking horse. You will get me close to him so I can take him down. He's slippery and powerful, and I believe you'll need me to finish it. But a charmer who can change their skin? That would give us an edge he would not expect."

"Do you expect me to infiltrate the Jou?" Brylee's sceptical expression betrayed how impossible she thought that sounded.

"Oh, no. He's not one of them."

"But I thought . . . how do you know?"

"Didn't I say? They all work for me, and none of them use red dye."

As the conversation continued into the evening, Brylee agreed to spend the night and consider her options. As she closed the door behind her and settled into the sparsely furnished but quaint guest room, she noticed that Rosemary had left a plate of snacks, some lemon juice, and a vase of lilies by the neat bed.

She fluffed the two goose feather pillows and propped herself up on the bed, processing everything that Gil had dropped in her lap. On the one hand, she had to accept his offer to help her father. On the other, it rankled her that Gunnar and Judd would essentially win. And who would protect Rae? There had to be a way to entice Wickham or another mage to cure her father. Then she would take her chances with predatory mages.

Throughout the night she flip flopped between accepting Gil's offer and declining it. At some point she must have drifted to sleep because she suddenly awoke from a nightmare. As the sweat dripped down her forehead, she fought to recall it, but it evaporated even as she tried. All she could remember was that her presence in Haxley had brought a series of evil people to the town, which ultimately hurt everyone she loved. *That's about right,* she admitted.

A wave of rage gripped her, all of it aimed at magic. *Being a charmer, and magic in general, has brought nothing but misery and shame to my life. And now I'm beholden to a mage.*

By morning Brylee had chosen the path of leaving her Haxley life behind. She was stuck being a charmer, and that threat would always stalk her, but she vowed to learn what she could from Wickham that could help her defend herself. When she completed her contract with the mage, she would find a way to start a new life where magic played no part. She sighed. *At least my future endeavours will be all through brains and effort, not cheating with magic.*

Chapter Thirty-Three

The 467ᵗʰ Year of the Morde Dynasty—Three Years Earlier

Gideon wasn't a drinker, and he could count on one hand how often he had been as tipsy as he felt at the moment. *Why do people want to feel this out of control?* he wondered. He was already imagining where he might find some chalkleaf to settle the retching he knew would soon grip him.

"What I'm about to share with you took me more than twelve hundred years to deduce and then accomplish," Ostryd began once he had decided Gideon was appropriately intoxicated. "But those were different times and I had no one to guide me. And this information is certainly of the 'easy to explain, difficult to do' variety." On paper he had drawn a stick figure and written Gideon's name under it, and as he talked, he added details supporting his explanation.

"We've established that when you look magically into someone and see past their glow, you can make out their 'cord,' as you put it, but can't see where it vanishes off to. Correct?" He added a line to the drawing but didn't wait for Gideon's confirmation before pressing on. "A pipe rather than a cord or a tether is a more fitting description, as you will see. At least for this first part. Now, most magic wielders don't ascribe this pipe any value, and that's if they see it at all. And most can't. A few people have better than normal eyesight, and a fraction of mages and charmers have a sharper magical sight. With practice I'm confident you'll be able to see the end of the pipe, but mastering that trick quickly is one of three problems you face in regard to reconnecting with your magic swiftly enough to help your friend."

"Should I start trying now then?" Gideon slurred.

"Not yet. Just listen. This pipe links us back to a much thicker conduit." He drew a thicker line; the stick figure was connected to it by the thin line he had already drawn. "These pipes carry our magic from the source—and don't worry where that is for now—to our bodies. Every living thing needs magic to live. A flea has a tiny spark and an elephant a great deal more. The size of the living thing is part of it, but how much thinking we do, how emotional we are, and some other factors determine how much we need. A huge tree doesn't need as much as a cat, for instance. We store a little magic in our bodies, but it is replenished through the little pipe from the big pipe." Ostryd put arrows on his sketch and raised an eyebrow.

"Yes, following you so far. I think," Gideon replied, fascinated despite his impatience.

"Every living thing has some magic, and most things have just enough to be alive. But some of us have a little more and learn, mostly through trial and error, how to use it to change the world around us. We call these people charmers. Typically, charmers are born with a slightly thicker pipe connecting to the main conduit. You don't know how many people I've studied to work this out, by the way," Ostryd said with a proud gleam in his eye.

"Is the glow our soul?" Gideon asked.

"Interesting question," Ostryd replied, sitting back. "My belief is that the magic powers three different types of our thinking—emotional, logical, and spiritual—and is what powers our souls, if we have such things. I think the glow is a product of the magic working in the same way that a fire gives off light and heat when the fuel burns. But let's stay focussed, eh? So, how do you think a charmer becomes a mage?"

"Well, skriking, obviously," Gideon replied, trying to apply what he had just learned to deduce how skriking worked. "I assume you take someone's stored power and add it to your own." As he spoke, however, he recalled his experience with Tuli. "Actually, I think you take their glow, but you also take their pipe. Is that it?"

"Yes, exactly, and that's why people die soon after being skriked. Once they burn up the residual magic left inside, there's no way to replenish it. Essentially, the person who does the skriking takes the other person's pipe, vastly increasing the speed at which they can draw magic out of the larger conduit." Ostryd added another stick figure and several lines to his drawing. "For charmers, most of their magic is consumed just by living, and a small portion is left over for charming. When you add a second pipe, that new supply can all be used for magic. That first step is most noticeable."

Gideon recalled the process of pulling Tuli's pipe into himself, then those of his colleagues soon afterward, and was once again overwhelmed by the horror of his actions. He raised a hand to his mouth. He couldn't share this with Ostryd. He would think him a monster.

"Immediately after skriking, a person has two pipes, theirs and the new one they acquire," Ostryd explained, "but they wrap around each other and soon dissolve into a single bigger pipe. Now, when I look inside you, I see a tangled mess of small and large pipes. This tells me you recently skriked many people—too many at once, and that the consolidation process is going badly. In several millennia I've never seen anyone acquire more than one or two at once, so you, Mr. Strangelore, are quite unique. No wonder you became a slipper." Ostryd didn't seem to hold any judgement against how Gideon came by so many pipes, but seeing as his nasty secret was so easy to discern, he felt a pressing need to explain himself.

"My sister was mortally injured, and I was trying to heal her. She was a more powerful magical healer than I, and she knew it was a lost cause. She pressed her pipe into me. I didn't take it." Gideon felt his guilt deeply as he confessed, unable to hold back. "Well, not at first anyway. Once it touched me, I sort of pulled it in greedily, but I'm horrified by my actions."

"That's quite common. The 'gift' is how most charmers take their first step towards becoming a mage, and they feel terribly guilty about it afterwards too. I'm curious about how you acquired the others, of course." Ostryd paused expectantly. Gideon felt sick, but he was committed now.

"In the moment I took my sister's pipe, I saw many other pipes floating nearby. In the confusion, that greedy feeling I had for Tuli's glow sort of took over, and without thinking I captured those pipes too. I think I killed all the charmers at the HAC even though they were in another building. You have to believe I didn't intend to hurt anyone." Gideon finished in a desperate rush, ashamed because he felt that at some level, he had been intentional in grasping at the pipes.

"Oh, I do. I do. Don't worry," Ostryd reassured him, raising his hand to quell further declarations of Gideon's innocence. "Even a powerful and experienced mage must work hard to take a single pipe from even a weak charmer. They usually succeed, but it's an effort. Taking so many at once by force is impossible, trust me."

He sat back and looked afar. "When a person is killed, their pipe disconnects and hangs around for a minute or so. Maybe someone or something killed the other charmers, and by fortunate timing, you were there to harvest them."

Gideon slumped down, closed his eyes, and with a long breath released all the guilt he felt from potentially having skriked his HAC colleagues. *I still accepted my sister's power, but I'm less of a monster, I suppose,* he thought. There was a long silence as Gideon processed his relief. Ostryd seemed preoccupied with what he had just learned too. Eventually, Gideon brought his mind back to understanding his predicament.

"If mages skrike to build their power, why don't they just steal the pipes of regular people? There are many more of them, and they can't defend themselves either."

"I'm not sure," Ostryd said. "For some reason if one doesn't have a surplus of magic flowing into them, they aren't vulnerable to skriking. I've thought a lot about that but have never come up with a rational explanation. But I'm glad that they can't."

"Is the mess of piping why I feel powerful yet can't access my magic? Do I need to straighten it out first?" Gideon asked.

"It's certainly not helping, but your issue lies where the mess of pipes joins the main conduit," Ostryd explained, going back to his diagram. "For everyone except slippers, these small pipes plumb straight into the side of the main conduit and are firmly attached. But for some reason, in our case our pipes wrap around the conduit but don't pierce it. Somehow the magic still makes its way across into our pipes, but our loops are free to slip up and down the main conduit because they're not joined on. It takes a lot of power to slip, but that's why we're called slippers—because we slip up and down it. You see, in addition to carrying magic, the main conduit is actually the timeline. Somehow magic and time are linked. Your issue is that your pipe is only partially wrapped around the conduit. It can't close into a loop because your guilt is preventing the end of your pipe from reattaching onto your own pipe to form the loop. It's trying but failing."

"My guilt?" Gideon asked.

"I have hardly any experience with the looping phenomenon. There were so few of us to study. But I fully understand why the smaller pipes refuse to consolidate at times, so I don't see why a loop should act any differently. Pipes seem to have a consistent nature and behaviour.

"To recap," Ostryd continued, building to a conclusion by counting on his fingers and pointing to his drawing, "Your first challenge will be to see all the way to the conduit, which you can't at the moment. Your second challenge may be to mentally steer the end of your pipe so it wraps properly around the conduit, ready to close. It's the pipe's nature to want to do this anyway, so it might turn out to be easier than the final challenge, which is to dissolve your emotional block, thus allowing the loop to complete. That will be the hardest of all."

"Why is that? Why does guilt prevent these pipes from connecting correctly?" Gideon asked, afraid of the answer.

"As I mentioned earlier," Ostryd said, "these magical links are fuel for the body's thinking, emotional, and spiritual activity, and I think the fabric of the pipe itself contains aspects of these things. The pipe's behaviour is influenced by intense, negative emotions, such as shame or guilt. For most of us, skriking feels deeply shameful and as you can imagine, such affairs of the heart aren't quickly resolved by the mind."

The more Gideon recalled Tuli's death and his own role in it, the more his emotions welled up and choked him, even if discovering he hadn't killed all those charmers was a big relief. If he knew then what he had just learnt, could he have reattached the pipes to his fellow charmers? Of course, he hadn't known about any of this then, but neither had he even tried to find out what had happened to them. For a moment he thought he imagined hearing Tuli's voice in his head asking if he would have kept their pipes, even if he could have restored them. He blinked and shook that thought away.

"Being drunk could conceivably hinder your first two challenges, Gideon," Ostryd continued, "but if you're going to let go of whatever emotions you're bottling up, you need to first let go of your inhibitions. The wine will help with that."

As Gideon sat quietly, Ostryd could see a battle playing out on the younger man's tortured features.

"My sister, Tuli," Gideon said in a voice so quiet Ostryd had to lean forward to hear it, "for her entire life she selflessly put aside everything to support my dream. After warning me, begging me not to be impulsive, I acted rashly, and as a result, a man stabbed her. Right there in front of me. I could argue it was correct of me to be bold and act as I did. And it was, I think. But had I thought for one moment that . . ." He trailed off. Ostryd waited, letting Gideon's admission take up the space for a time.

"One day, Gideon, if you get over your shame and guilt, it will be because you've agonised over it for years and rationalised it three ways to Sunday. But no logic will be involved in your change of heart, whatever you think. It will be a purely emotional response. One day, without rhyme or reason, and not because of your self-torture, you'll forgive yourself or perhaps just permit yourself to let it go. There is no way to process all that in one night, of course. And you don't have to. Just allow yourself to leap straight to that choice. Put the self-doubt and self-torture aside. Help your friend now rather than wallow in guilt. If your friend loses her hand because you're self-indulgent and wallowing in the past, that decision will be one more thing you will hate yourself for in the future."

"But that's crazy. I'm responsible—"

"Nothing will have changed. You'll just accept it," Ostryd said, cutting off Gideon's protest. "But here's another perspective. You should now live for thousands of years and see many changes in the cultural norms as the generations play out. Shame and guilt result from feeling you have broken a moral rule and are at risk of being shunned by those you value. Intense shame leads to feeling we are unworthy of being part of society and our deep-seated drive to be valued by others stems from being connected through the magical time conduit. Do you follow?"

Gideon nodded, so Ostryd continued. "Shame relates to you being an unworthy person, but guilt relates to a specific bad thing you did. There's a big difference. You're not bad; you just did a bad thing. Embarrassment is similar, but it relates more to a breach of social rules. It can even be funny in hindsight. Passing wind in church. Slipping clumsily. You can look back and laugh. Ask yourself, did you truly break a moral rule that killed your sister, or was your rashness a poor choice in the moment for which you should feel guilty but not ashamed? Or were you right, but your timing was poor, which is embarrassing? Your sister died because of the way someone reacted to your embarrassing timing. Therefore, the blame is with them, not you."

"Sorry, I see what you're trying to do, but it's such a stretch," Gideon replied. But part of him wanted to respond differently. It was the cold, dark part that wanted to grab Tuli's gift, even as another part of his mind rebelled.

"And which moral rule did you break? Is it a valid rule, Gideon?" Ostryd asked. "When I was born, women were literally treated as the property of men. If a man chose to kill or sell a woman, no one cared. Is that how I should measure my morals today? Of course not. Then why must you remain bound by the rules of today if you will live for a thousand generations? I'm not saying you're a god or anything, but your moral compass must transcend that of a single generation's culture. You need to accept you're outside, exempt from today's standards. Here, another sip." A drop of wine had somehow escaped the lip of his glass, and Ostryd brushed it off with his cloth.

What was it Lu had said? Gideon tried to recall. Tuli's death was wasted if he gave up now. He could go and be a non-magical healer, as she had suggested, but now he believed he could be so much more, even more than a magical healer. Now that he grasped the concept of building his powers, he could be an incredible healer, perhaps for eternity. That unsought outcome seemed attainable if what Ostryd said was true. It would happen in time. But if he waited, Lu and the village healer with the growth in his chest, two people who had been kind to him, would suffer unnecessarily. If he took the shortcut to where he would go in time anyway, he could save Lu's hand, restore her warrior's dignity, and cure the healer too. All he had to do was accept his . . . well, his actions, as Ostryd argued, were not completely to blame. And was it his fault society hated charmers or that Arkly was a killer?

Something snapped within Gideon, and he felt an immediate sense of relief. He thought he heard Tuli whisper to him. *Accepting this enhanced gift of healing is more precious than anyone else's individual needs, even yours. Don't be so selfish, Gideon . . .* He recognised his subconscious was responsible for the advice, and it was his tiredness and disturbed emotional state suggesting these messages were coming from his dead sister.

Disturbing as it was, he knew it was his brain's version of "If Tuli were here she would say . . ." He had always listened to her advice.

But did you? her voice asked.

He was just one man, but he could do such good for humanity. He promised himself—no, he promised Tuli—that he would never be bound by the world's moral rules, which were designed for people who lacked the wisdom that he would acquire over time. Instead, he would create his own rules to support the good he would do. He wondered how much power Ostryd had accumulated.

As Gideon buried his conscience in a shallow grave of questionable rationalisations, he relaxed, and at that moment his magical pipe slipped around the conduit, forming a perfect loop. As his negative sense of self was replaced with a growing feeling of overconfidence, the barrier that had prevented the loop from closing vanished. He felt whole. Gideon reached out and channelled heat into the wine glass. The wine bubbled, then the glass shattered. He smiled.

Chapter Thirty-Four

The dawn was beginning to leak in through Ostryd's small window when the sound of unsettled horses in the stable below intruded on Gideon's efforts to trace his pipe to the conduit.

"Has the morning shift arrived to prepare the horse teams for the day?" Gideon asked, even though Ostryd's expression told him otherwise. Ostryd put a finger to his lips, then waved a hand to douse the neverdark. They listened closely but heard nothing but snickering and stamping from the stalls. Ostryd cracked open the door, then stepped onto the small landing at the top of the stairs. As he scanned the area below, Gideon eased out behind him.

For several long breaths, there was nothing out of place. Then a small movement drew Gideon's eye to the bushes at the corner of the street. Sitting low on her forepaws was Shanna, her tongue lolling and waving in time with her panting. She glared at him in annoyance. Then, unseen by Ostryd, the cat got up and slinked away.

"I think it's time I went back to Lu," Gideon said. "She must be wondering what happened to me by now."

"Whatever spooked the horses seems to have stopped," Ostryd whispered, eyeing him suspiciously. "Take Lu to the tavern. I'll walk over now and get you a room. They'll be up by now, preparing dough and warming the water. You and I have much more to discuss after we've both slept. It was a long night. Listen, Lu knows you're a charmer, but no one can know about slippers, OK? We'll speak about that again when we get back here, alone."

Gideon did up his tunic and pulled his cloak around himself before skipping down the stairs feeling better than he had since Tuli died. It took a moment to orient himself, then he turned and followed the waterfront to the east. He hadn't gone far when Lu separated herself from the shadows beside a boatshed.

"I was worried about you," she said, her tone sharp. "What happened? I waited and then searched but eventually had to risk Shanna coming into the village to track your scent. What were you doing up there?"

"I met someone who can help us, but that's not the best news."

"How do you know we can trust him?" Lu asked. Gideon wondered for a moment how she knew it was a "him" but then realised Shanna would have let her know. "It's not just your hide at risk, you know."

"I don't know how far to trust him, actually," Gideon admitted, "but he's a charmer, like me, so he has just as much to lose. But listen, great news." Gideon reached out and touched her injured hand. "I've got my magic back. Much stronger than before. Now I can save your fingers." As his words registered, he watched Lu's face. She bit her top lip, and the injured hand unconsciously rose to meet it. Her eyes closed, and tears splashed onto her cheeks. A sob of relief escaped her.

"Truly?" she croaked. "I'd reconciled with my fate. But . . ."

"I know. It's amazing, isn't it? Listen, I feel so much better. I know I've been awful these last few days, but I met Ostryd, the charmer, and we had a drink together. Perhaps it was the alcohol or some drunken debate, but I feel like a weight's come off. I see everything quite differently now."

"How did you get your powers back?" Lu asked. Gideon realised he and Ostryd would need to get their story straight on a number of things, so he deflected her question.

"It's a long story, and I need to do something before Deni wakes up," Gideon said, taking Lu's elbow and leading her towards the healer. "I noticed he's sick, and I'm going to heal him in return for his generosity, but I don't want him to know I'm a charmer."

When they reached Deni's house, Lu slipped into the room Deni had lent them and gathered their belongings. She left a note on the kitchen table explaining she had changed her mind and wanted to try to find another solution. He might think it odd, but he would probably put it down to fear.

Meanwhile, Gideon found a small glass vial, which he filled from the batch of sleep syrup that Deni had just cooked. *That was only last night,* Gideon realised with surprise. It seemed like another lifetime. He crept along the corridor towards the soft sound of snoring emanating from Deni's room, which grew louder as Gideon opened his bedroom door. Without entering, Gideon used his HAC training to reach out with his magic and located the small nerve cluster at the top of Deni's neck. He applied a technique that caused Deni to slip from sleep into unconsciousness. He had often practised sedating injured people, though not normally from ten feet away. He grinned, realising how much more power he now had.

Entering the room, Gideon rolled Deni from his side to his back, then poured a dose of sleep syrup into the man's mouth, careful not to pour so much as to choke him. Deni's breathing slowed and deepened, then Gideon realised he was holding his own breath, which he let out with a whoosh. The drug relieved him of the mental burden of holding Deni asleep with his mind, allowing Gideon to concentrate on healing the man.

Lu appeared and asked how it was going. Gideon was torn. He felt self-conscious healing someone in front of Lu, but he also had an urge to impress her.

Perhaps it's best if the warrior doesn't know too much, Tuli whispered in his mind. Gideon started in surprise, then decided to analyse these odd appearances of Tuli's voice at a more opportune time.

"I'll be here for a while," he told Lu. "Can you go to the porch and keep a lookout?" Lu gave him an odd look, then nodded and left.

The HAC often imported sick people from Quartt for their charmers to practise on. Based on this experience, Deni's lungs should have taken several sessions for Gideon to clear of blight, and Gideon should have needed long rests in between to recharge his reserves. He had planned to start work on Deni that morning and then sneak back and administer additional treatments over the following few days. But with his larger connection to magic, he completed the procedure in one twenty-minute attempt and didn't feel depleted. Gideon was delighted with himself and considered waiting to see Deni's face when he discovered he had a new lease on life, but eventually he decided he shouldn't take the risk. There would be other occasions when he could enjoy people's gratitude for his efforts.

Were you always so vain? Tuli asked. He shook the voice out of his head.

Gideon turned Deni onto his side and left him to sleep off the syrup. As he was leaving the bedroom, he saw the healer's purse on a small table. *It would be right for you to take a fair fee,* Tuli's voice whispered. He thought of the gold coin that Ostryd had given him. Then he shook his head again. He didn't need Deni's money. He collected Lu from the porch and headed up the road to the tavern with the warm morning sun on his face and a spring in his step.

Chapter Thirty-Five

Ostryd met Gideon and Lu outside the tavern's closed front door.

"You have a warrior's grace," he said to Lu, who stiffened with suspicion at being so easily identified as a Mobi'dern, then flinched as she remembered she wasn't. "Don't worry," he continued, reinforcing his words with a quick hand gesture. "I have an eye for such things. It's your muscle tone, stance, and the way you flowed across the street. Come, we have to enter through the kitchen door. Are you hungry?"

Lu shared a glance with Gideon as they followed the strange man up an alley. She had felt suspicious, not hungry, a few moments ago, but as they approached the kitchen door and the rich, salty tang of fresh baked bread assaulted her, she realised it had been over a day since she had eaten. Her stomach grumbled without a care for her dignity.

A wash of heat from two flame-fired ovens greeted them as they stepped out of the cool morning air. Lu took in what at first seemed a chaotic scene, with every cupboard wide open as a small, energetic woman danced from counter to counter, pulling out item after item as she prepared to embark on the remainder of the day's baking. It took only a few moments to see that each ingredient fell neatly into a bowl or cup, and the chaos was an efficient ballet of motion that simultaneously produced a dozen dishes. She paused and popped a finger into a jar of white liquid, drew it out, and sucked it clean, then wrinkled her nose and tipped the jar's contents into the sink.

"Mosh, the cream isn't fresh!" she yelled towards the pantry. A bald, wizened man emerged with a quizzical expression on his sleepy face. "Run down to the dairy and get some fresh cream," she said. "Hurry now. Can't you see we already have mouths to feed?" Without pausing to watch the old man wander out the door, she turned to Lu, Gideon, and Ostryd with a tray filled with rings of bread, butter, honey, and a thick beef spread that had magically appeared in her hands.

"Here, Ostryd," she said, pressing the tray toward him. She saw Lu's bandaged fingers. "Oh dear. What have you done? Hang on." She disappeared into the pantry and came out with a small jar of red powder. "Mosh will get some warm water for you. Mix in this much," she held her fingers close together to indicate a pinch, "and it will clean any wound without stinging. Well, not too much. So, who are you? I'm Jax . . . with an X." She crossed her arms into an X shape for effect as she tilted her body and gave a hearty chuckle.

Lu took the powder, warming to the woman's easy way and confidence. She was about to introduce herself when Ostryd cut in.

"This is Lyn, and that is Dak," he said, pointing at Lu and Gideon in turn. "I appreciate you letting us in at this hour, Jax. Lyn and Dak were trapped in bad weather in the mountains, and they're exhausted. Is it OK if we sit in the bar and eat this delicious fare, then they can get some sleep?"

"Of course, and the water is boiling, so I'll bring some tea along shortly. Go on, I have to bake," she said, shooing them away and turning to shuffle the contents of a frying pan that was sizzling on the stove.

"Are these all of your belongings?" Ostryd asked once they were seated in the next room. He pointed at the pile of oddments they had commandeered from the pursuing soldiers.

"Yes. We had to leave the last place in a hurry," Gideon explained. Lu felt uncomfortable as Ostryd ran his eyes over her, as if taking inventory. He pointed at the short sword and dagger in her belt.

"They don't suit you, and you both need proper travel packs. Most people pay little attention to strangers hereabouts, but to anyone trained to watch, you stand out like foxes among hens. Eat your fill; it's all paid for. I'll be back shortly." He stood up and left through the kitchen.

They ate slowly, savouring the firm bread, which they smothered with butter, honey, or beef. After a while Mosh brought in two cups and a steaming pot of tea, which he placed on the table in front of them. He also left some clean cloth strips and a bowl of warm water, explaining it was to use with the red powder. Then he left, running to carry out the next barrage of instructions Jax threw his way from the kitchen. Lu tried to pour the tea, but it was awkward with her bandaged hand, so Gideon took over.

Gideon unwrapped her hand and reassessed the damage. His magical sight saw below the surface, and his training allowed him to quickly build a plan of how to repair the frost damage. He added the powder to the dish, as much to satisfy Jax as from medical need. Then he located the nerves in Lu's wrist and elbow that would inform her brain of pain in her hand and mentally clamped them off. Then, using his magic like a scalpel, he began removing all the flesh that was unsalvageable.

The hardest part of reconstructing Lu's hand was replacing some missing tendon. He could stimulate growth and replacement, but her body had been honed and shaped by decades of training. Using Lu's good side as a template but allowing for the differences between right and left handedness, it took Gideon about thirty minutes to recreate the basic structure.

"It's amazing how much more power I have now," Gideon said as he worked. "It replenishes almost as fast as I can use it. But I'm tired, and I don't want to make mistakes. This tendon needs to settle for twenty-four hours before I refine it and then repair the muscles and the flesh." He began to wrap her hands in the makeshift bandages.

"I can't watch, but I can't feel a thing either," Lu said. "I've never experienced magical healing. I can see why you are passionate about every village having access to such talents."

Gideon sat back and frowned.

"What is it?" Lu asked.

"Nothing. It's just at the HAC, we would administer a drug-based pain reliever and sedative to our patients. I don't have one handy. I can't maintain the magical pain block indefinitely. The traditional drug would take over once I remove the magical force. When I go to sleep, you will lose pain protection."

"That's alright, Gideon. Don't forget, I'm a warrior. And it's been agony for several days. It'll hurt, but . . ."

"Oh, I think this will hurt a lot more. I've completed some significant restructuring. Hmm, hold on, let me try something." Gideon reached into the small but strong glow of magic deep within Lu's chest and drew out a thin stream of it. He attached it to the two pain blocks he was maintaining in her arm. It took him several attempts, but by the time Ostryd returned, Lu's innate spark of power was maintaining the block without his help.

"See, Tuli? I think I've just invented a new procedure." Then Gideon shook his head and laughed at his own stupidity, talking to ghosts. But Tuli *would* have loved this.

"Ag, what are you doing?" Ostryd asked. "You're determined to get caught, aren't you? What do you think people will make of the smell you've created? You've got to think, man." Gideon felt foolish. Ostryd was right, of course. He should have done it at the stable, or out in the countryside. The flesh he had magically cauterised stank. Ostryd ran around cracking open the windows, then went to a decorative vase on the mantle and removed some fennel leaves, which he threw into the fireplace. A musky odour rose into the room, softening the acrid smell.

"Here, these are for you," Ostryd said, handing them each an empty travel pack. Gideon's was a typical backpack, made of thick canvas and lined with pockets and loops to hang items. Lu's had more structure than Gideon's and stood firm, where his collapsed on the floor. The canvas on her bag was strapped across a square frame, and it was longer and thinner than Gideon's.

"Open the cap on the top, Lyn," Ostryd prompted, using the false name he had assigned to her in case they were overheard. Lu pulled the cap, and it flipped up easily, falling away to hang on a thin, leather chord. With the cap removed, Lu saw a sword handle. She pulled it, and the sword came out easily. Her jaw dropped.

"It's a Mobi'dern blade. Where did you get it?" She held it in her left hand and checked it for straightness, nicks, and other issues but realised it was in excellent condition. In fact, it was of exceptional craftsmanship, the sort that would only be carried by a clan leader.

"The pack has a hidden scabbard, and if you set up the shoulder straps correctly, you should be able to fast-draw the sword in an overhead scorpion strike," Ostryd said, drawing a perplexed glance from Lu as to how he knew Mobi'dern terminology, which was not supposed to be shared with outsiders. "Take care of it. It belonged to an old friend." She wondered again where he had gotten his hands on a blade that her clan would jealously protect but decided not to pursue it, at least not for the moment. She slid the sword back into the pack and concentrated on setting up the straps to allow comfortable carrying and fast access to the blade once her hand was repaired. Recalling how just a few hours ago she had resigned to never holding a blade in that hand again, she felt her throat constrict and her eyes burn.

"I suggest we all get some sleep," Ostryd said. "Dak, I'll come to your room at around sixteenth bell and teach you how to mask your aura. Don't leave your room until we've got that light under control. And no more magic, OK?" With that he turned and left.

"I slept through most of the night," Lu said. "I'm going to go out and visit with Shanna for an hour or two."

"I'm exhausted," Gideon replied. He opened his purse and took out two of the five gold coins Ostryd had given him. "If I give you a list, could you procure some herbs, salves, and other medications and a small pack to carry them in? Also, some better clothing for the weather?"

"Yes," she replied, taking the coin. "And before you meet Ostryd this evening, you're going to tell me what you know about this man and why he is helping us and giving us gold."

A foreign thought flitted across Gideon's mind that perhaps he might regret telling Lu that Ostryd had been so generous.

Chapter Thirty-Six

Shall I come to you? Lu offered to her big cat. She was rewarded by Shanna's warm, welcoming response.

I have a sun patch where the ground is heated if you'd like to share it. And a porcupine. You can help me avoid its sharp spines.

Lu accompanied Gideon up to their room. She left her supplies there but not the new pack with its sword. Lu had no intention of leaving such a rare weapon in such an insecure setting. She retraced her steps through the tavern and slipped out the back door while Jax had her head buried in her pantry.

The streets were fully awake with people bustling about their business. The skies were clear and the sun warm, but the breeze that was building from the lake was cold. It wouldn't look odd for her to pull her cloak's hood up to her face, so she did.

Lu's first stop was the Sandrick bank, where she had them break the gold coins from Ostryd into something less conspicuous. Next, she visited the market, which was made up of two dozen carts converted to stalls, and a maze of small pens and cages for livestock. She bought some fresh fruit and cheese. Jax would no doubt supply them with wonderful food, but Lu felt better having a separate supply in case they had to leave quickly. As she passed a farmer's stall, she spotted an ox's thigh bone. Shanna could bring down small deer, but the marrow-rich treat would please her. She offered an image of it to her cat and thought she detected an undignified purr.

Two stalls were peddling warm winter clothing, and Lu spent time identifying low-cost but good-quality items she would collect on her return from her visit with Shanna. There was no point in carrying it around all morning. A small deposit and a promise of later payment were sufficient to secure agreement from the stall owners to hold her items for a few hours. As she completed her negotiations, the door to the apothecary squeaked open, so she stopped there next.

Something about the maze of jars, boxes, bowls, and small plants had always drawn Lu to such places. The astonishing range of colours and perfumes easily outweighed the tightness of the space, where every available surface was crowded, and a small number of smells were truly awful if she got too close. Behind the counter a young girl in her early teens, appropriately named Nettle, was a delight and a fountain of knowledge. She was quick to explain that she always opened the store, so her only parent, her mother, could sleep late. Her mother ran the store late into the evening and stayed up to the early hours preparing the many herbs, oils, soaps, and a thousand other items for the shelves. Nettle flushed with pride when Lu had her admit she collected many of the goods in the afternoon once her school lessons were finished. Lu liked that Nettle had a cheeky but subtle upselling technique and deliberately let herself be persuaded to buy more than she had intended.

Lu acquired everything on Gideon's list and added some quality leather oil and boot wax, a modest whetstone, and a small amount of tiki paste, which she would dilute and use to keep her new blade's razor-edge true. Her chores done, she made her way out of the village via the backstreets and alleys and set off up the hill to meet Shanna.

As Lu entered the clearing, the big cat was in the process of rolling from one side to the other, as much to warm another part of her body in the sun as to make it easier for Lu to scratch her tummy. For two hours the pair groomed and played while Lu caught the cat up on events. As was typical, the cat cared little for much beyond hunting, sleeping, and ensuring Lu was whole and happy, but she did sniff Lu's partially repaired hand suspiciously when the warrior explained how Gideon had worked on it. Otherwise, she listened patiently, though she was intent on working her way through the ox bone so not a lick of marrow was missed.

When sated, the cat rested her large head on Lu's lap and looked sullen. *Your loyalty to him grows, but increasingly he smells like meat that once was good but is now rotting. He has changed since Tuli died,* the cat complained. *Can we not leave him now that he has a new friend? There is good hunting to the south. Perhaps now you're without a clan, I can find a mate. I would share my brood with you.*

Lu laughed, surprised that her killer cat was feeling maternal, but her humour faded quickly as she considered the first part of the request. She scratched Shanna between the ears while she considered if she should abandon Gideon. She did find some merit in the idea.

Lu's deliberations were disturbed as the cat raised its head to sniff the air. She shared the thought of several horses and riders, perhaps half a mile distant. *The horses smell of the breed soldiers prefer, and I smell tar, like that of a fire arrow. They come slowly from the south, heading for the village.*

Lu sprang to her feet, gathered her belongings, and stored them in her pack. She checked that the cap on the scabbard was loose and the sword accessible. Then she loped off towards Sandrick and flashed a request to Shanna to inspect and follow the approaching riders. The cat rolled to her feet and slunk away into the bushes, licking the remaining marrow from her lips.

Well ahead of the approaching group, Lu joined the main road to accelerate her journey back to the village. She hadn't gone far when a lone rider appeared around a bend ahead. He was coming towards her at a fast canter, heading away from Sandrick. He slowed as he drew level with Lu and reached down to rub the side of his mare's neck.

"If you're heading to Sandrick with that injured hand, lady, you might think twice. Our healer died in the night."

"Deni?" she asked, immediately cursing herself for revealing she knew him.

"Yes, he died in his sleep. He had lung rot, you know." The man sat up straighter in the saddle. "I've been given the authority to ride south with the funds to attract a replacement. But it may take a week or two. There's a healer in Tarc if you need one. Follow this road back the way you came and take the right-side path at the mountain's summit. Follow that road for three days, and you can't miss it. Good luck." Without another word he kicked his mare's flanks and rode up the hill.

Chapter Thirty-Seven

Lu burst into Gideon's room, and his eyes flew open as he jerked up from his dreams. Despite bolting up, he was far from awake, and Lu had to repeat herself twice before his mind caught up. Shanna was stalking the soldiers and flashing images to Lu. She identified them as members of the Nuulan guard by their garb and pennants, although she recognised none of them. They were accompanied by a young Bredden acolyte, identified by the yellow scarf wrapped around her head, which revealed only her golden eyes.

"I don't imagine this is a coincidence, Gideon. We need to move. Come on, get up. We have to leave the village."

"We need to get to Ostryd. He has information I need. We'll have to convince him to come with us."

"Let's get out into the hills. We'll be safe there. We can return at night to talk to your friend."

"Do you think the locals could describe us well enough?" Gideon asked. "We both entered town wearing cloaks we took from our pursuers which are common enough and bear no sigil. Only Jax, Mosh, and Deni have had a good look at us. Bredden and Nuulan's Guards have no jurisdiction here anyway. We left Raile behind on the other side of the mountains."

"Well, we don't need to worry about Deni," Lu said as she explained what the rider had said. "He was such a nice man. I thought you said he was healed." Gideon slumped down on to the bed and shook his head.

"He was. He was healthier than he had been for ten years. I'd swear it."

"Well, something happened. Come on, let's go!" Lu ordered, passing Gideon his new pack as she added her supplies to her own. "Shanna says they will enter town shortly."

Gideon didn't budge. "What are you implying? That I didn't heal Deni?" he asked, his voice a notch louder than normal.

"Quiet! I know you did your best for Deni. I'm just trying to hurry you up. Look, I walked through the market this morning. There'll be some who might remember me." Before Lu could elaborate, the door that she had latched and locked behind her flew open. Having heard no one approach, she was caught off guard. Her sword was drawn and scything towards the threat just as Ostryd stepped into the room. She cursed herself for her lack of control. She was rattled, and her instructors would be ashamed. Had her right hand been available, the little man might have even been injured, such was her lack of discipline.

"That door was locked," she said.

"Charmer," Ostryd said by way of explanation, pointing to himself, the lock, and then her sword. "Put that away and calm down. I could hear you from the top of the stairs. Relax. There's no real danger. If you keep calm, that is."

"But—"

"Yes, three Nuulan guards and a Bredden acolyte, I know," Ostryd said, cutting Lu off. He took out a clean hanky and laid it across a chair, then sat on it. He held up his hand and started counting off the reasons he felt they were safe. "I pay people, so I know these things quickly. Deni . . . he'll be missed. Jax is a close friend. She won't betray me. Lu, my associates tell me you kept your hood up in the market. You were just part of a busy crowd. I've sent someone to convince Nettle's mother that a grove of sidle root has been discovered at the edge of the mine, across the lake. It's rare enough she will send Nettle on the next boat to harvest it. It leaves in an hour. She will be gone overnight. If your pursuers stick around until then, we'll come up with another plan." He lowered his hand and beamed.

"You arranged all this so quickly?" Lu asked, shocked. She exchanged thoughts with Shanna, who confirmed the group had just split up. Their leader and the acolyte had ridden into the village while the other two had separated and circled around Sandrick. They would watch for anyone fleeing, she supposed. Whoever was leading them was cunning.

"I received a pigeon from Tarc in the night. The group arrived there two days ago. They have an aggressive way of seeking information. It was expected they would arrive here after twelfth bell today. I assumed you're their quarry and have had my associates working to cover your tracks since the message arrived. It pays to be well informed. Had they surprised us, I might have had to kill them. Acting so openly would have meant having to disappear from this part of the world for a few years, which would have been inconvenient and upset my business at the mine."

"So we just sit here and hope they don't find us?" Lu asked.

"Yes, for now," Ostryd said. "If you're discovered, I'll know. Then we act. I advise you to focus on getting your sword hand functioning. Three armed men wouldn't worry you if you were whole, would they?"

Lu was embarrassed to be reminded of her weakness but accepted he was right. Her inability to defend herself had made her defensive, ironically. Still, she didn't like being protected by or beholden to this stranger. First the gift of the sword, now his protection. *Why didn't I sense I was being watched in the market?* she wondered, further decreasing her faith in her current abilities and discipline.

Gideon had observed the exchange, but his mind was distracted. What had happened to Deni? While others discussed their safety, his mind replayed how he had cleared the man's lungs of blight. He was confident he had left the man able to breathe better than he had in years, and he had even taken the time to regenerate the cells in Deni's airways, to ensure there was no infection or stress. A warning from his teacher at the HAC crept into his thoughts, causing his stomach to fall away. The heart adapted to poorly oxygenated blood over time, and if the blight was reversed too quickly, the vessels in the heart could split. Deni had probably died of a heart attack. *I never thought the instructors stressed these things enough,* the part of his mind that sounded like Tuli said, giving him the excuse he needed.

"Gideon," Ostryd said, cutting into his thoughts. "Let's work on your ability to conceal your aura. I told you that our magic is a mixture of spirit and emotion. If that acolyte is sensitive, and most are, she might detect your brightness. If you come close enough to her, that is."

"I've never heard of such a thing," Gideon replied, his brow furrowing.

"It's not so surprising when you think about it. It's something the Bredden clerics have exploited for centuries. Some charmers never truly discover their abilities or, out of fear, suppress them. Clerics recruit such people and instil a hatred for us like no other. Acolytes are unknowingly using the very talent they are taught to despise to see or sense the magic in those they hunt. A sensitive acolyte can be fanatical and should not be taken lightly if you want a long life, Gideon." This was meant as a subtle reminder not to share with Lu that both men were slippers.

For the rest of the day, Ostryd instructed Gideon in the art of shine shadowing, the slang name for masking the glow of magic. Gideon discovered it was fairly simple to hide one's magical glow. He imagined a layer around the glow and concentrated on making it opaque by spreading a small amount of magic around that space. This made it less obvious he was a charmer, but it also created a different problem. All living entities should exhibit some light. If he masked completely, he would look flat and dull and stand out to the observant. Ostryd explained that the trick was to shine but just enough and in the right way.

"I've never worried about shining before," Gideon complained. "Why now?"

"There is not a great deal of visible difference between a non-magical person and a charmer with modest powers—no offence to your previous abilities intended, of course," Ostryd said. Gideon did find it irritating to have been thought of as so weak, but he said nothing. "As I believe I mentioned, the first increase in capacity, which you inherited from your sister, manifested outwardly as magic, as opposed to burning inwardly to maintain the body and mind, as it does with Lu here," Ostryd continued. "Charmers blend in well with the population if they haven't *inherited* additional strength." Gideon warmed to the substitution of "inherited" in place of "skriked," which stirred his self-loathing each time the memory surfaced.

With a few hours of practice, Gideon was able to create a shadow around his glow, which let just enough shine through to look authentic. With Ostryd's help, he even managed to regulate it so that he shadowed his shine evenly in all directions and not just his front, as it had initially.

"That's enough for today," Ostryd said. "Tomorrow we will begin to learn the subtle art of flexing the shadow to reflect your emotional state. Once your pursuers leave town, we can go sit in the tavern. Now that you know what to look for, you will see all the different shades and variations at play in the crowd. You'll also be shocked that you didn't see it before. Everyone is when they see it for the first time."

Throughout the day there had been discreet knocks on their door, and Ostryd had stepped out to receive updates on the activities of the Nuulan guards and the acolyte. As in Tarc, they had upset many people with their brash attitudes and probing questions but seemed to make no progress in their hunt. They were staying in the same tavern but had paid for just one night. It was anticipated that they would move on in the morning.

"You must also learn to maintain your shine shadow when you sleep," Ostryd warned. "I plan to leave town in a few days, and I would like you both to travel with me. I have business in Lidanah, on the Quartt-Lanthe border. I've arranged to travel with merchants who leave the day after tomorrow. We will be inconspicuous travelling as a group. If you will permit me, I'll introduce you, Gideon, as my aide. We can share a vardo." Seeing their bemusement at the term, he expanded on it. "That's what they call a tall, enclosed wagon equipped to live in hereabouts. I will teach you how to maintain your shadow while you sleep, starting tonight. Lu, you can also travel as part of the group, but make it appear as if you are on your own journey. That way the two of you will look less like travelling companions."

Gideon and Lu exchanged questioning glances and then reached a silent agreement, accepting his offer.

"Good, good," Ostryd said, standing to go. "Now, it's a long shot that the acolyte will detect you tonight, but you shouldn't risk sleeping unshadowed so close by, Gideon. I have a spare bed at the stable. You should come to me tonight. Lu, you're welcome to stay here or come and sleep in a stall if you like." Lu felt indignant at the offer of a stall, which she declined. She planned to slip out and spend the night with Shanna anyway. And this time she was determined to avoid being watched by whoever had tailed her through the market.

"Lu, when the tavern shuts down, come across to the stables and I'll work on your hand some more. If that's alright with Ostryd," Gideon said. He was looking forward to learning more about time slipping, which he suspected was the real reason Ostryd had invited him to sleep at the stables. There was no spare bed in the room he saw there. He expected he would have to sleep in a stall, but that was better than he had fared for the past week. He agreed that the sooner Lu was fighting fit, the better.

Chapter Thirty-Eight

Della-ki unwrapped her yellow shasha from her head, rolled it rather than folded it to avoid unsightly wrinkles in the silky fabric, and placed it on top of her pack. She lifted the Bredden Triangle and its chain from around her neck and clutched it between her hands. Cleric Oliver had awarded it to her at the completion of her training and uttered the -ki suffix, denoting her acolyte status for the first time. It was a moment fixed in her mind. She protected the symbol of Ag jealously. She removed all her clothing, and as he had taught her, she knelt naked at the foot of her bed to pray. There would be no scourge for her sins without a father present, but the ritual still had to be honoured.

Each night of the week since she had been tasked by the cleric to track Gideon, she had prayed for the same things: that Ag would guide her spiritual growth through the order, that her first assigned quest would be successful, that Ag would keep her family safe, and that Ag would care for Cleric Oliver. He was tough and ruthless, but his age was taking its toll. She had also prayed that either she or Mudda-ki would sense the charmer or receive word of his detection elsewhere. She hated being so cold and away from her sisterhood.

Mudda-ki, her sister acolyte, was trailing two days behind them, disguised as a tinker's wife. The man she accompanied was actually a tinker, in the employ of the Bredden Order, and together they would covertly trawl the waters that Della and her team stirred up.

Those were the prayers of the past week, but her prayer tonight was delightfully different. Several times during the day she had felt the magic. It faded and grew repeatedly, like a lighthouse at a great distance. She had decided not to react to it overtly. She had not even told the captain who accompanied her. Therefore, tonight, in addition to asking Ag for his guidance and protection, she asked him for the wisdom and guile she would require to tease out the man with the perverted spirit of a charmer and end him. Cleric Oliver had been clear: the man could not be allowed the chance to defend the charge of murder of his fellow students, which had been levelled against him after he escaped.

Once her prayers were complete, she saw to her nightly ablutions, then slipped under the covers and closed her eyes.

As usual she slept soundly until dawn and awoke refreshed. While she dressed and ate the dates that she had purchased at the market, Della considered her options. Her interviews the day before had yielded next to nothing. A healer had died after a period of deepening illness. That did not seem relevant. The owner of the tavern, Jax, was hiding something, but most tavern owners had secrets from the Order. Brothels, gambling, and alcohol were all denigrated by her faith. Was there more to it than that?

Gideon was a healer, so Della had paid close attention to every apothecary they had passed on their trek. They had found his medical kit at the HAC, left behind in haste. Would he replenish it at some point? Was the errand the apothecary's daughter had been dispatched on suspicious or coincidental?

Della would probably have categorised all these potential leads as false had it not been for the tingle of magic she had sensed throughout the day.

Of the Mobi'dern and her prida, there was no sign, although judging from the cat prints at the scene of the murdered trackers nearer to the HAC, the warrior had been with Gideon at some point. It was hard to imagine the soft-bodied man getting this far without help, so she was probably still close by.

As she wrapped her shasha around her head, she made up her mind. They would continue that day at a fast pace. They would not want a direct confrontation with a Mobi'dern and prida of Lu's reputation, and if she were nearby, her cat would certainly stalk Della's group until they were well out of town. Yes, that was the way. Let them relax and then let Mudda-ki sniff them out. Mudda-ki had messaging pigeons to send word out to Cleric Oliver. Her own group would go to the next village, two days hence, then circle back.

Della wrote a coded note for Mudda-ki, then concealed it in a thin, flat wooden box. She added a blob of tu-gum and palmed it in one hand.

As she paused at the bar to thank Jax for her hospitality, Della pressed the note to the underside of the bar, where Mudda-ki would know to look when she arrived a day or two later.

As she mounted her pony and turned it west, Della could feel the charmer growing and shrinking his aura once again and wondered what would cause him to do so.

Chapter Thirty-Nine

Lu left the stable while flexing her mostly repaired hand. Gideon believed one final session would be required before she could begin practicing her sword work. Keeping to the shadows, she made her way to the market square. She couldn't see anyone following her, but her instinct told her otherwise. The market was empty, with most stalls wheeled back to their owners' homes to be refilled with wares for the following day.

A light drizzle had begun to fall, coating the stone slab walkway in front of the apothecary with a thin film of water. The alley along the side of Nettle's store was covered and remained dry. Lu entered the alley and noted two sets of damp footprints, two men judging by their size and pattern, and added her own wet trail alongside them. At the end of the alley, she turned right.

After two more right turns, Lu was back at the entrance to the alley and expected to see a fourth set laid by her stalker, but she was disappointed. She carried on past the apothecary, stopping and peering in windows as though she were taking in the night air before turning in for the evening. The feeling of being watched persisted. At the end of the street, she doubled back and picked up speed.

Four stores past the apothecary, Lu ducked into a different alley and broke into a sprint. At the end of the alley, she leapt onto a brick ledge, then continuing the vertical momentum, she pushed off and back across the alley to plant her foot on a windowsill. Without breaking her stride, she tacked back across to the bracket securing the downpipe before stretching for the roof's gutter and swinging her body up onto the tiles, relying on her good hand to take most of her weight. She rolled into a crouch under the lower end of the wooden eves, sank back into the shadows, stilled her breathing, and became invisible.

Nothing moved in the alley or the back lane, but Lu could hear the occupants of the house she had just scaled moving around. After twenty minutes their movements stilled, and the night sounds were reduced to the patter of drizzle and a gentle hiss as it ran off the rooftop and down through the gutter.

Lu was about to relax her vigil when lightning lit the sky, backlighting the silhouette of a head peering over the rooftop on the far side of the service road running along the rear of the stores. Her night vision ruined by the flash, she extended her other senses to the fullest, focussing on the spot where she had seen the watcher. It was too far to feel actual movement, but her brain translated the faint sound of someone creeping across the tiles and the vibrations of the wood shingles flexing under the weight of a person moving away to her left.

Lu stepped off the roof and landed without a sound under the assumption that the watcher had dipped behind the ridgeline to mask their movement. A dozen or so silent strides brought her to the wall of the house her pursuer was perched upon, and she circled to the left through another alley to emerge in the street behind her quarry. She was about to mount the drainpipe when a shape detached itself from a shadow under a water trough to her rear and stood.

"We could play the shadow dance all night, but it's cold and wet, and the storm will make things unpleasant," said the strong and feminine voice of a hooded figure dressed in black. *You move with the warrior's grace,* her hands flashed in Mobi'dern sign.

Lu nodded. *As do you,* she signalled back. "You have the skill but do not carry the sword. Are you also severed?"

The woman peeled the hood back from her face and shook out her blond hair. "My sword is in your pack," the woman explained, stepping forward in a non-threatening manner. "Ironically, its name is Lightning. I assume that's what gave me away? But I am not of the Clan. My grandmother was, and she taught me much before she died. What is your prida?" The woman's tone reminded Lu of an excited child's, and now that she was closer, Lu reappraised the woman's age. She was perhaps eighteen summers, no more.

"I have a mountain cat, called Shanna. She hunts to the south," Lu replied, swinging her pack off her shoulders and opening the scabbard's cap. "I cannot take another's sword. Here."

"No, keep it. Giving it to you was my idea. I have others, and in truth I am not a swordswoman. Give me a bow and then you will see my skill." She laughed.

"I can't. This is a rare weapon. It should stay in your family," Lu persisted, holding the sword out flat with both hands.

"My father has many rare things, Lu," the woman said, signalling refusal with her hand and that Lightning should be put away, out of the rain. "My grandmother was Da-Stone. My mother named me Brightstone in honour of her. My father, Ostryd, says your companion is a rare man, but he has not told me why. The way he speaks of him, almost like found family, I thought it best that such a rare man be protected by a rare woman with a rare sword. I like the symmetry. I have many swords that I feel more comfortable using anyway. Can I meet your cat? Shanna?"

"My cat would like to meet the granddaughter of a legend," Lu said as Shanna mentally accepted the offer. "Your grandmother led the defence of Merker's Keep? Where I think she died?"

Brightstone didn't answer; she just turned towards the hills with an enigmatic smile.

Chapter Forty

Why is this voice of Tuli so toxic and mean? Those were never her qualities, Gideon thought, wondering about the part of his mind where his sister's voice persisted. He was lying in an uncomfortable stall, feeling cold and vulnerable. Ostryd waking him every time he dozed off to tell him his shine shadow was waning had made for a long night. It was only in the small hours when Ostryd was too tired to continue that he left Gideon to rest. *I don't understand why you now sound so sour and angry. If anything, I was always the sharped-tongued, bitter, and impatient voice in our family.*

That was before I was killed and you decided to leave me for dead. After your impetuousness instigated the actions that killed me, he replied to himself, though in Tuli's voice.

"We've been over this. Ostryd said when I master time slipping, I will only be able to go backwards in time perhaps a few minutes at the outside. A week is already out of the question. I can't come back and save you."

Would I be so quick to believe him if it was your life, Gideon? If I arrive at the afterlife, and our mother is there, I won't be able to stand the shame of being associated with your failures. Imagine what she will think of me.

"Tuli, it's not failing if it's impossible, is it? If I could, you know I would." On top of everything, Gideon felt embarrassed he was arguing with himself and resolved not to, but his guilt, which he thought Ostryd had helped him put aside, kept pecking away in the form of his sister's voice.

You caused my death with your arrogance, Gideon. Your soft, weak body slowed Lu down in the mountains and she almost lost her fingers. Yes, you should feel guilty and ashamed, but where was that when I was alive? Did you ever feel guilty at all for my sacrifices? And you killed poor Deni with your incompetence, didn't you? Gideon had no answer to his own questions, but the voice was relentless, making him feel nauseous.

Now, instead of leaving no stone unturned to come back and change events so I can live, you just accept the word of this stranger. What if he's wrong? What if he's as ignorant as you, and this time weaver could help if you approached him correctly? A force that polices time should be able to fix your mistakes.

"Ostryd isn't ready to share everything about the time weaver, I've—"

Exactly. Why is he keeping this secret? What are his motives? You let him deflect your questions too easily. Where is the fire you showed Arkly? You're prepared to battle if it's for your ego, but you don't put in the effort to help those whose death you caused.

Gideon's mind fell silent, but his stomach flipped and he retched into the straw. He had shocked himself. Once again he wondered if he was, in fact, talking to himself, or if Tuli was somehow reaching out to him through his tangled pipes. Perhaps there was some of her left, lurking in the conduit. He would ask Ostryd if such a thing was possible.

"I'm sorry, Tuli," he whispered. All he received in response from his accuser was a sullen, empty silence.

"Gideon, didn't you hear me?" Ostryd called from the stable doorway. He had clearly been calling out while Gideon was distracted. "And tighten up your shine shadow. It's too bright again. Come upstairs. Jax sent over some breakfast, and we have things to discuss." Ostryd turned on his heel and marched out. A moment later Gideon heard his boots on the stairs leading up to his room.

Gideon stood and stretched out his aches as best he could, then brushed away the dust and straw from his clothes. He would be more determined to get answers this time, he resolved.

There were two plates on Ostryd's small table, each with bread, cheese, and meat. Gideon realised Ostryd preferred not to share a plate given his obsession with cleanliness. There was also a steaming pot of tea to share. Ostryd poured for them both, using a cloth to hold the pot's handle.

"I want to talk to you about your plan to set up a healing centre in Quartt," Ostryd began. Gideon regretted mentioning it the night before. He had sensed resistance. "I credit my lengthy survival to a few crisp rules, Gideon. One, don't draw attention to yourself. Ever. Two, remember you literally have all the time in the world, so be patient, not reactive."

"Can you give me some examples?" Gideon asked. He was determined to steer the lesson around to the time weaver but was curious.

Procrastinating, not curious, Tuli insisted.

"Of course. I've had hundreds of urges to set up altruistic or selfish enterprises that would involve me taking an overt lead," Ostryd said, "but then I imagine the questions: 'Why doesn't he age?' 'Should we try to take over his business interests?'" When you leave the shadows, there are always questions."

He plucked some cheese off the plate with his left hand, grabbed a heel of warm bread with his right, and paired the two. A bite and a sip of tea later, he continued. "I've been slighted and attacked many times. At first I was filled with the urge to retaliate. Sometimes I did with no issue, but sometimes . . . well, let's call them near misses, shall we? Then I wised up. Now every person I've despised becomes dust, yet I go on. Patience will seem hard to you now, but soon, waiting thirty years for someone to die or for an opportunity to have someone else ruin them for you or buy them, while you remain in the shadows, will seem like a blink."

"But the concept we were promoting and testing at the HAC could provide tangible benefits to humanity," Gideon argued. "It would be a sin not to pursue it."

"And so it will come to pass," Ostryd said in a placating tone, "in fifty or a hundred years, without you sticking your neck out where someone can chop it off. Do you want to make a moment in history or experience all of it, forever influencing it subtly from a position of safety?" He chewed another mouthful and then reached over and took a strip of dried meat and worked through a bite of that too.

"Which brings me to point number three. An arrow, a knife in the dark, or too many damned germs are threats to take seriously," he mumbled through his mouthful of food. "If you don't have time to think, you can't slip back and avoid the threat. Germs can be in you for a day or two before you even know you have them. They nearly did me in twice. Obsessive cleanliness and surrounding yourself with loyal protectors are critical. How many people do you think I have in my employ here in Sandrick?" He took another piece of meat from the tray and inspected it.

"You mentioned some associates. Four?"

"Eighteen. Most make up the group of merchants I mentioned yesterday. They all work for me, but we pretend we're strangers. I play the part of a traveller, a mummer, or a banker, joining the group to move from place to place, and some of them change roles too. Others travel seemingly separately and arrive at our destination ahead of us and reconnoitre."

"That's amazing," Gideon said, realising that living forever wasn't as straightforward as he had imagined.

"In a few moons we will arrive at one of the thirty or so properties I own in Mordeland, in addition to others in other countries. We will stay for a few moons, then assume a different disguise and move on. Every five years or so I disband the group and set up another."

"This must be costly," Gideon said.

"Yes, it has a high price, but when you've acquired sixty lifetimes of wealth?" He shrugged. "I have letters of credit at all the banks under many different personal and business names. None of them are excessively large, but add them all together and I'm as wealthy as the Elect himself."

"How do you remember it all?" Gideon asked. "Most people's memory begins to weaken after sixty or seventy summers. Do you write it all down?" He noticed that Ostryd's eyes flicked to his trunk.

"You'll develop your own methods, Gideon. As for making money, I've made a significant portion of my wealth from cards and dice, believe it or not. I see how the cards come out, then slip back and alter my bet. No big wins, and I'm sure to throw in some deliberate losses. Just slow, steady, relentless accumulation. If I genuinely get lucky and win a large pot that would draw too much attention, I slip back and lose it."

Gideon saw an opening to move the conversation where he wanted it to go. "With all this slipping, aren't you worried you will bring this time weaver fellow down on you?"

"At my property at Troll Lake—that's in east Lanthe—I keep my personal library. I'll let you read it in time. It covers the time weaver and everything else I've learnt and documented. You're not wrong about memory, but I started my life organising records and documents, and it's still a passion." Ostryd laughed. "I'll begin teaching you to slip tonight—if the acolyte leaves town, that is. I'll give you the basics of it now."

That library is valuable, Tuli whispered.

"It is obvious that everything we change when we slip could circle back on itself and cause chaos," Ostryd said. "If I could go back far enough to kill my grandfather before he begat my father, I wouldn't be born. Therefore I couldn't go back and commit grand patricide. Do you follow me?"

"Yes, of course. That's the sort of thing I've been curious about," Gideon replied. He leaned forward and put his elbows on the table, drawing a glare from Ostryd. He removed them, embarrassed to have put germs near the food.

"For a few things, such as the grandfather example, it would be a problem, but not for the obvious reason. The gods care nothing for loops or whose grandfather survives. I have it on good authority that magic is sent to the world by the gods, and it is supposed to flow down the conduit and disperse in a similar fashion to lightning leaving the clouds to be absorbed by the ground.

"However, sometimes slipping activities, such as the grandfather example, draw their ire. They don't care about us praying or fiddling with our crops, moving the sun across the sky, or any of that nonsense today's church claims for them. Just don't create any big issues for them. If you're lucky, only the time weaver will come and sort it out. If he can't, the gods have been known to destroy the whole world and start over. What do you make of that?"

Gideon lifted his cup to his lips to mask any sign of what he thought. Instead, he asked the obvious question. "But there's still the small stuff. If you see how the dice fall and then slip back and change your bet, you will win money fated for another. That money might have made a significant difference to their life and, therefore, the entire world."

"Possibly," Ostryd said. "That's another reason to keep your bets small. But the reality is neither the gods nor time itself seem to care about it, and things just sort themselves out. Throw a large rock in a stream, and the current just flows around it. The same amount of water ends up in the sea. The momentary splash is reabsorbed, and the flow continues as if nothing happened. If the water splashes on the land, it soon evaporates to become rain, and the sea still beckons. Time is the same. As long as you don't block the river, it sorts itself out."

"I mean no disrespect, Ostryd," Gideon said, "but just because nothing bad that you know of has come of it in your case, it doesn't mean your theory is accurate. You can't possibly know all the ramifications of each slip, can you? And the gods sending magic being like clouds and lightning?"

"I don't claim to have proof, boy," the older man said. "And it's not my theory."

"Well, whose is it then? I'd like to meet them," Gideon said.

"I really don't think you do. It was the time weaver himself who told me when I caused him a massive headache nearly four thousand years ago."

Chapter Forty-One

Nearly 4,000 Years Ago

"Ostryd van Hyke, we are lighting your candles, and if you don't come down right away, Jord and I will blow them out for you," Trina called from the bottom of the ladder.

"A few minutes more, my love. I don't want to lose my place," the archivist replied a little too sharply. Two boxes from the shelf he had just cleared were balanced on the top of the ladder, and he was intent on squeezing them onto the shelf above, although it was already bursting. Ostryd had spent two long days rearranging the entire section to make space for the Zyph priest's recent discovery. He was almost finished translating, categorising, and labelling the fascinating history, some of the oldest ever found, and he wanted to store them in an orderly fashion.

"Those dusty old documents are much older than you, Ostryd. Another hour while we celebrate your thirty-third year won't do them any harm. Come down, please."

Ostryd recognised the growing disappointment in his wife's voice. He was neglecting her. Again. He had promised to be more mindful, but once again he had become wrapped up in his work. His heart melted. He loved Trina dearly, but he could be overly task focussed. He was when she married him, of course. He placed the boxes back onto the shelf he was trying to clear and scurried down the steps.

"I'm so sorry, my love. I just lose track of time, which is ironic, as this new find discusses the time magic of the aggar. Perhaps something in that last batch will inspire me to do better." He chuckled as he folded Trina into his arms and kissed the top of her head. Her arms went around him, and she snuggled closer.

"Come on, you two!" Jord yelled from the other room. "I didn't spend an hour wicking this birthday candle only to watch it burn on my own."

"Why is he here?" Ostryd whispered. "He pays you too much attention, and I don't like it."

"Sshhh . . . he'll hear you. He's the only chandler we can afford, and the hours you work means we burn a lot of oil and tallow. It's a wonder you haven't gone blind. Yes, I agree he has a crush on me, and yes, he makes me laugh, but you know I only go for men who aren't hairy, and he's practically an ape." It was a joke that always eased Ostryd's jealousy.

If only he knew the truth, she thought, pulling away as she squeezed his arms.

They walked out of the library and stepped across the narrow alley to Ostryd's workshop. No flames were allowed in the library due to the vast number of rare works it contained, so filing was a daytime chore, relying on sunlight through the windows. Anything that needed to be worked on or studied took place in the workshop. The alley provided a firebreak in case of accidents.

In the centre of the table next to his life candle was a plate of peeled fruit and sugared cake. Beside those stood four freshly poured mugs of fizzing apple juice. At his birth, Ostryd's mother had chosen a deep purple life candle for him, as during her third trimester she ate little but blueberries, a fruit she hadn't enjoyed before or since.

At the end of his first year, a single wick was sunk into the centre of the circular nine-inch pillar candle. Ostryd imagined he could vaguely recall seeing that solitary flame, but he admitted, when challenged, he was probably recalling a different occasion. Perhaps his younger brother's first birthday. Each year an additional wick was added by the family until his eighteenth birthday. From then on, a chandler would need to be employed to remove all the used wicks and replace them, adding an extra one each year. It already looked crowded with thirty-three, but he hoped to at least double that number in time.

"Am I too late?" Nessa, their cook, asked as she bustled through the door with a small plate of cured fish.

"No, we're just about to start," Trina said. "Quick, take a glass."

"Let's see if the old man has enough wind left in him to see off all the flames in one blow," Jord joked. Ostryd railed at the snide comment and noted how Jord edged towards Trina as he said it. The man was four years his junior and had repeated the same snarky comment ever since Ostryd left two candles burning on his twenty-eighth celebration.

Ostryd set down his mug, squared up to the table, and leaned in as he filled his lungs to capacity. He gave a mighty puff and shook his head furiously. As his lungs emptied, he was aghast to see three flames had survived his blustery onslaught. His final gasp snuffed one, but two escaped. Jord laughed with glee, and the women joined him, but their humour rang a little of pity to Ostryd's red ears.

Angered, Ostryd fixed the image in his mind from seconds earlier of leaning in to blow the candles and wished he could go back to that moment. Unconsciously, he relaxed his grip on the time conduit and let himself slide back to that moment. He repeated his attempt, this time moving his head more deliberately and extinguishing all the candles, gripped by a dizzying sense of déjà vu. He shook it off and still had breath left to quip that Jord's wicks did not stand as straight and tall as they once had. He was still unhappy that Trina's laugh, although more joyous this time, had a whiff of relief about it, and the look she gave Nessa was unfathomable.

Ostryd shrugged off his concerns about his blowing prowess and Jord. He found himself a little surprised that the toast he made next to "family and friends" felt quite genuine. He was touched by many of the fond memories and words of love that circled the table over the next hour and was almost sorry when the group broke to do their chores.

Jord said his goodbyes and, following a brief discussion about future candling needs, departed. To Ostryd's relief, he didn't linger as he gave Trina his familiar hug goodnight. If anything, it was shorter than the hug he gave Nessa.

"Can I help clear this away?" Ostryd offered, hoping not to so he could hurry back to his filing while the light held.

"No, no, I'll help Nessa in the kitchen. But before you go, we have a final gift for you." Trina held out a small box. Ostryd unwound the pretty wire-lined ribbon that encased it and removed the lid. His eyebrows lowered, and his face crinkled when he saw a thick masculine ring of copper with a blueberry mounted as a gemstone. He pulled it out and touched it, which made both women hoot with glee.

"I told you he would think it was real," Nessa said, the hands that had held Trina's wrist in shared anticipation at his reaction flew up in a delighted clap.

"Nessa found the purple stone in the market," Trina said. "I repurposed an old copper ring for it, and we both spent several nights polishing the stone to resemble a blueberry so it would match your candle. Do you like it?"

"I do. It's lovely. It truly is. Thank you both," Ostryd said, putting the ring onto each of his fingers in turn to see which one it suited best.

He hugged each of them and then took his leave, marvelling at the way the ring caught the daylight as he crossed the alley back to the library.

He was halfway back up the ladder when it struck him how cold it was growing now that the sun was dropping low in the west. *Another glass of that apple juice will keep the warm blood flowing*, he thought and then set off back to the kitchen.

As he reached the door, he heard the two women talking in low voices.

"I'm glad he cleared the candles," Nessa whispered. "He seemed quite anxious about it."

"And did you see the way he stood up to Jord? I don't like seeing him jealous," Trina said, "but it keeps his attention away from us, my love." Ostryd's jaw dropped as he stepped into the kitchen and saw Trina, unaware of his arrival, reach up and place her hand on the back of Nessa's neck and draw her down into a delicate kiss.

He backed out of the room, caught between the silliness of feeling bad about intruding when he should feel anger and the foolishness of being blind to the affair his wife was having with their cook.

By the time he crossed the workshop, the swirl of initial emotions had resolved into a growing sense of betrayal and anger. He turned and faced across the room. He should go back in there and confront them, but what if Trina loved Nessa more? Could he lose her? He had a history of being neglectful, after all.

Ostryd didn't know what he wanted to do, but he could feel his rage building. He felt so trapped, battling a dozen fears about the future. What would the future be like if he left her? What would the future be like if he said nothing? Would the future be better if he put her ahead of his other priorities?

It was too much. He took off the ring and with an explosion of anger flung it across the workshop towards the kitchen door. As soon as it was airborne, he regretted his rashness and wanted to take it back, but it was too late. Ostryd thought of the moment just before he launched the ring, but his mind, bursting with rage and injustice, could not draw him back in time. He braced himself for the unwanted confrontation that was inevitable now, but there was no sound of the ring hitting the wall or the floor and no reaction from the kitchen. Instead, with a quiet pop, the ring vanished from its trajectory in a flash of green light.

Flummoxed by seeing it disappear, Ostryd's immediate anger left him. He crossed the room and searched, but there was no sign of Trina's guilt gift. Confused, he wandered across the alley into the library and closed the door.

If he was shocked before, he was stunned to find a tall man standing in the middle of his library holding the blueberry ring out to him. The man's blue eyes were wide, and his narrow brows raised. He cocked his head slightly and leaned forward.

"How in this world did you accomplish that?" the man asked. Then his eyes rolled into the back of his head, and he collapsed like a pile of books falling from the shelf.

A moment later, Ostryd shook himself free of the shock and ran to kneel at the man's side. He turned the man's head, expecting to see blood or bruising from the fall, but there was none. The stranger looked like he had simply fallen asleep, except for his pallor and clammy brow.

As Ostryd rolled the man onto his side, he swallowed his feelings and decided to hide his discovery of his wife's affair until he could process it. He picked up the ring from where it had fallen and hid it in his waistcoat pocket. He couldn't bring himself to wear it now. He resolved to mention it was too snug and would need adjusting at a future trip to the coppersmith.

Aside from a steady heartbeat and relaxed breathing, the stranger didn't flicker so much as an eyelid or twitch the corner of his mouth for two straight days. The healer attended, was greatly puzzled, and prescribed rest. He helped Ostryd undress the man and roll him into the guest bed. He returned every eight hours to check on and clean the patient, noting with surprise that the man's bladder and bowels were as dormant as the rest of him.

A Zyph patriarch—senior to all but the apostle in the local Aggar church—knelt by the man's bedside for an hour after morning and evening prayers and mumbled religious words, to no effect. It was as if the man's soul had departed but forgotten to inform his body to die and fade to dust.

On the third day, Ostryd was translating a text from Old Aggar in his workshop when the man walked through from the bedroom dressed in his recently cleaned clothing as calmly as if returning from a summer stroll. Ostryd leapt to his feet, tipping over the inkwell—thankfully not on the sacred text. The man repeated his earlier question in an impatient tone, as if there had been no break or dramatics since he had last asked it.

"How in this world did you accomplish that?"

Ostryd had spent over forty-eight hours going in circles about his feelings for his wife and waiting to ask the stranger a similar question.

"How did you, sir, pluck my ring from thin air so it would appear in your hand in my library?" he said, feeling affronted by the man's lack of observance of the niceties of society. All accusation and no introduction. "Entering someone's house uninvited to do magic on one's jewellery and entering the library, a restricted—"

"If my bluntness offends you, I don't care. You provided me with little choice, sir." The way he said "sir" sounded wrong to Ostryd, as if the man were mimicking his own use of it rather than understanding the word's nuance. "You created a rupture on a scale rarely seen. It was all I could do to get there in time to save your world."

What is this man ranting about? Ostryd wondered.

A noise from the kitchen drew the stranger's attention. He looked about, orienting himself, and then pointed towards the alleyway. "Your book storage room lies that way, correct?"

"They are sacred texts, and that library is the private property of the Zyph Church. Do you have permission to be there?" Ostryd was not a violent soul, but he picked up the letter opener from his desk and stepped forward. *Would I be as brave if someone threatened Trina rather than my books?* he wondered, his face flushing with shame at the thought.

Misinterpreting the reddening as mounting anger, the stranger raised his hands and stepped back. After several breaths passed, Ostryd relaxed his stance somewhat.

"It would be best," the man began in a friendly, even tone, "if we could start over. We need to talk in private. I don't care where, but the timeline is dangerously unstable here, so can we agree not to slip? That would be a really bad thing to do as things stand."

Ostryd thought the man seemed genuinely worried about something serious, but he couldn't fathom what it might be. Appearing out of nowhere and making things disappear and reappear elsewhere—a type of magic unheard of—then accusing Ostryd of causing some issue were all signs that he should show the man the door and forget about him. But one didn't become a preeminent archivist without having boundless curiosity. He felt his sense of survival taking second place to his inquisitiveness.

"We can talk in the garden, I suppose. But I'm keeping this . . . dagger handy," he said, using the letter opener to indicate that the man should turn left along the alley.

"My name is Levinial, but call me Levi," the man said once they were seated on the two seats that Ostryd and his wife used to spend time on together, looking across the valley and talking as the sun set, though they did less so in recent times.

"Ostryd van Hyke, Chief Archivist to the aggar Church, attached to the Zyph Priesthood," Ostryd said, asserting some authority. "You didn't say what your profession is, Levi."

Levi considered the question before replying. "In your study of the aggar, have you come across the term 'time weaver'?" Levi asked with an ironic chuckle. Ostryd missed his humour, struck by the phrase, which seemed familiar.

"I'm translating some ancient texts, and I've come across a similar phrase. I wasn't sure if it would be 'knitter of eternity' or 'artisan of endless moments.' 'Seamstress of time' was another possibility. Aggar is so vague in written form that the intonation is critical, you know. It could be 'time weaver,' I suppose. No idea what it is though. Why?"

"That's my profession. When people like you slip back down the timeline—that's what we call it when you go backwards in time for a few minutes—sometimes you create a mess. Too big a mess and the gods cancel the world and start over. My job is to watch many worlds for such things and prune anything dangerous before things come to the gods' attention. 'Time weeder' might be more accurate, but the first aggar created the term 'time weaver,' and it stuck."

Ostryd blew out his cheeks and shook his head. "It's only because I've begun to read these texts that I give your words any credence, Levi. I don't know how you know things about the priesthood I'm only just now discovering, but take my advice: don't talk about it openly. People here will think you mad at best, heretical at worst. But where you're mistaken is I am not a magic wielder. Not a jot, I'm afraid." He held his hands up as if to show it.

"I suspect you have some latent magic, Ostryd, even if it never shows itself. Do you often have the feeling something you have done or seen is happening for the second time, yet have no specific memory of the previous experience?"

"Often, yes, but I have an active imagination and a flair for predicting events and behaviours."

"I'm here to investigate, but all I know so far is you had a massive emotional seizure during which you pushed four ounces of mineral from your time to almost one hundred years into the future. Nothing can ever be moved forward. Ever. I thought it was impossible, but here we are. The scale and urgency of the mess you created meant I had to take risks to retrieve the item, which almost drew the wrong sort of attention from the gods."

"Nonsense. I wouldn't know how to . . . whatever you said," Ostryd said, oddly feeling a little proud of himself. Then a new worry formed in his mind, and he gripped the letter opener more tightly. "Are you here to . . . *prune* me?"

"Actually, I couldn't even if I wanted to. You appear to be tied to my future now. If I prune you, this world will certainly rupture."

Chapter Forty–Two

The 467th Year of the Morde Dynasty

"What I don't understand," Gideon said, "is if you were uncovering magic relating to time slipping and this aggar church, why have I never heard of either? Is this another mage conspiracy?"

"In this case, no. In the millennia after the aggar created our world, mankind had knowledge of him—it—and its role in the order of things. However, there is no record of any direct communication with this being, or how we know of him. But the aggar's lack of interaction with people allowed doubts to grow in people's minds. Religion evolved to be faith based rather than fact based. Two millennia later, even what had been written down in the early days was lost. Few but the Zyphs maintained the oral histories, and what was passed down focussed on behavioural expectations and moral standards. Knowledge of the source and true nature of magic and its relationship with time was lost. We worship and curse Ag today, of course. Ag's roots stem from the aggar, but it has evolved to be thought of incorrectly as a deity in its own right in a faith serving the clerics' agenda."

"But you know about time magic?" Gideon asked, obsessed with that topic and caring little about various faiths.

Ostryd nodded. "Its absence was part of my deal with Levi. His experience was that worlds who know about but ban such things nearly always have people who ignore the prohibitions and create chaos. Worlds where it isn't discovered, and the aggar fades from memory—if it were ever known about—are far more stable."

Ostryd stood and stretched, then retook his seat. "At Levi's encouragement, I ensured my translations of the earliest records omitted such information, and I even created fake originals for when subsequent scholars took an interest. But the original translations are still in my library."

"If the time weaver and the aggars are so powerful, why don't they just magically remove all evidence and reform people's memories or prevent slipping in the first place?"

"I asked the same question, but in truth their ability is incredibly limited," Ostryd said. "An aggar can create a world and the life on it. He can design and create new species with new behaviours. But once they are formed, he has no influence on them. His magic forms the timeline, but using our analogy, he is just funnelling magic down a pipe with no control of what happens to it thereafter."

"Incredible. I understand why we thought him a god in one sense, but why pray to him?" Gideon found himself reassessing his faith. He was never devout, but he said prayers often and donated to the church after each harvest. *What a waste,* he thought. "What about this time weaver, Levinial?"

"Limited too," Ostryd said, enjoying sharing his knowledge. "Levi's analogy was that raw magic, produced by the gods, has a specific tone or flavour. But as a natural consequence of the aggar on each world processing that magic, they alter its flavour subtly, each in a unique way. Levi's innate magic is drawn directly from the gods, therefore it does not match that of any world. As a result, using his magic can cause bigger issues than he set out to repair."

"It seems like an imperfect system," Gideon said. "One would think gods could do better."

"Apparently this whole thing is a big distraction to them. Levi never implied they were lazy. Nothing like that. They're just not interested, that's all."

"What can Levi do? What powers does he possess?" Gideon asked, trying not to appear too interested.

"As much as possible he avoids moving through time when he's part of the world. That's what caused the issue in my case. I have many details in my original translation of the aggar texts in my Troll Lake library, but essentially, he works as follows . . ."

Ostryd looked around for a clean sheet of paper to draw out his explanation but plunged ahead without one. "The aggar of a world contacts him because there is an issue on the timeline preventing the smooth distribution of magic. Levi borrows an amulet the aggar gives him, which is tuned to that specific world. With that Levi can travel instantly anywhere on the timeline and anywhere in the world. He told me time and space are two sides of the same gold piece. But while 'riding the amulet,' as he called it, he can't interact with our world, just observe, and he cannot travel close to the disturbance itself. While riding the amulet, he narrows down where and when the issue is occurring, then goes further back, steps away from the amulet, and manifests, as he calls it. He becomes part of that world in that time and place."

Does he leave the amulet unguarded? Tuli asked. Gideon was curious but thought it better not to pursue that angle at this moment and let Ostryd tell his story.

"Once manifested, using his magic would cause problems. My sending the ring forward caused a huge issue, but that wasn't apparent at first. Levi manifested and spent a moon among us learning our culture and languages so he could interact without drawing attention to himself. Then he came to investigate. All he knew until he reached the moment I created the issue was that something odd was afoot. He had left the amulet in a distant hidden place for safety, so ironically there wasn't time to fetch it to use native magic to deal with the issue. He had to use his own flavour of magic. To minimise the risk to the world, he wrapped his magic within my magic. Then he leapt forward in time and returned with the ring."

"And his magic didn't end the world," Gideon said. "Obviously."

"No, but it almost killed Levi," Ostryd replied. "He returned to his physical body but had no link back to what he calls the Gods' Space—his specific source of magic. His surge of incompatible magic used in our world had severed his link. He was cut off for two days, eking out the residual power of his body until he eventually reconnected. It took him several more days before he was fit enough to leave us."

"Where did he go?"

"He returned to where the amulet was hidden, I assume, and then left our world."

"And you never saw him again?"

"He visited me once more, about five hundred years after our first meeting," Ostryd said, a look of satisfaction flickering across his features. "During his initial stay, as he couldn't prune me, he taught me just enough time magic to survive but not to be dangerous with it. I've shared the basics of that with you already. He had never seen the sort of tension in the conduit between us that led him to think our futures were intertwined, so he thought it best I stay healthy. When he returned it was a brief visit. He explained the tension was still there when he manifested, but he had developed a better understanding of it. There is a future wrinkle in time, some event that involves me. When it occurs, the wrinkle will smooth out and the risk will disappear."

"Can he not ride his amulet to see what it is?"

"No, there is history, lined up behind the ever-moving 'now,' a line that continually extends. The future hasn't been created yet, but the substance that the timeline relies on to form is ahead of us, waiting for us to solidify it into our collective experiences. I don't understand that, but Levi can start at the beginning of the world and ride forward, but he cannot normally visit past the 'now' point because there is nothing for him to visit."

"So where did you send your ring?" Gideon asked, fascinated by Ostryd's story.

"That was the problem. He likened it to me creating an island in the future with no path to it along which he could ride the amulet. He used his incompatible magic to leap the void and then return. With the ring gone, the island dissolved, but its residue has a touch of us both. Although he estimated I caused the issue about one hundred years in the future, the remnants of the island is the wrinkle drifting ahead of us, part of me and part of him. When we overtake it, it will sort itself out. I hope I've proven myself trustworthy enough to avoid pruning when that day comes, but I've had sixty lifetimes, so I probably can't complain."

There was a knock on the door, and Lu entered, followed by a woman a few years younger whom Gideon didn't recognise.

The woman has terrible timing, Tuli complained. Gideon felt disoriented, and for a moment his vision clouded. When things cleared, he found he had stepped across the room to the door. Presumably, he had stood up too quickly and lost his balance because he realised Lu and Ostryd were staring at him.

"What?" he asked, trying to account for the last few moments.

"No need to be rude," Lu said. "I just came to let you know you can relax. Shanna reports that the acolyte is many miles distant. If you don't like my timing, put a sign on the entrance." She stormed out and slammed the door. Gideon didn't recall uttering a word. Baffled, he spluttered that he was caught up in his mind, trying to comprehend everything Ostryd had shared.

"Did I speak out of turn?" Gideon asked. In his mind he wondered if Tuli had somehow acted.

"Oh yes, boy," Ostryd said. "Your precise words were 'Wait to be invited before barging in, woman.' A little rough, I felt." Gideon agreed, but he still had no recollection of speaking.

"Let's teach you to slip," Ostryd said. "A useful skill for taking back harsh words."

Gideon put the odd experience behind him, excited to learn the new skill.

Chapter Forty-Three

Slipping required little more than picturing the moment he wished to slip back to, relaxing his grip on the conduit of time, and allowing himself to be drawn back to the moment desired, in much the same way as juggling six balls merely required that a person toss and catch them in sequence. In Gideon's case, this analogy would include never having seen a ball until twenty-four hours before and almost three decades of listening to scholars who insisted that juggling was impossible.

Gideon spent the day placing a card face down, announcing a guess as to its value, turning it to see what it was, then attempting to slip back to the moment just before his guess to state it with certainty. It was well past sixteenth bell—and partially courtesy of two glasses of Jax's wine—when it happened. His vision flickered for the briefest moment, and the card he had just turned over remained face down. He was so bored by the repetition and surprised by the slip that he nearly forgot the card's value. He glanced at Ostryd, who appeared unaware of anything amiss and was studying some papers from his trunk.

"King's Beggar," Gideon announced, replacing his original and incorrect guess of Knave's Mistress, and turned the card. The image of a threadbare panhandler raising his bowl towards the retreating back of a king who had passed him without acknowledgement—both figures bearing the same features—stared back at him. He let out an undignified squeak of delight.

"What?" Ostryd said.

"I did it. I slipped!" Gideon said. "Rather than trying to relax my grip, I imagined myself pushing the loop backwards, and, well, you know." He grinned like a simpleton, expecting praise.

"Hmph," Ostryd grunted. "Most people find it best to learn it like breathing or catching, an action not thought about. But well done, I suppose. Keep at it. It's a bit like riding a horse. Once you get the rhythm . . ."

Miffed that Ostryd wasn't more encouraging of his swift mastery but pleased with himself regardless, Gideon bent to the challenge with renewed enthusiasm. He went through all thirty cards twice with mounting frustration before he slipped for a second time. Fifteen cards later he succeeded a third time. By eighteenth bell he was slipping four out of every five attempts and feeling quite smug that Ostryd was completely unaware of his success. This raised a worrying thought, though.

"Ostryd, if a threat burst through the door right now, and we both slipped backwards at the same moment, would our pipes tangle? It is one conduit after all, isn't it?"

"Well, they don't tangle, no," Ostryd said. "Think about when you slip your pipe. It doesn't slice through or catch on the millions of others fixed to it."

"Why is that?"

"I doubt what we perceive as pipes are truly pipes at all. It's a convenient but limited metaphor. For example, the conduit extends moment by moment to infinity, but a pipe cannot. Anyway, are you having much success? Unless you tell me, I won't know."

"Oh, yes, actually. About four out of five times I can do it," Gideon said. He did it one more time to prove his prowess.

"Your shadow shine was nicely stable until you finished that second glass. Your unconscious mind has assumed the duty of regulating the shadow for you." Gideon flushed with pride until Ostryd continued. "I've never witnessed anyone pick up these skills as quickly as you. I imagine all that training at the HAC has made you more adept than most of us at assimilating new magic and skills."

The sound of boots thumping up the stairs announced the arrival of a visitor.

"I expect this is Addy, my wagon master," Ostryd said. "I'll introduce you. See if you can slip while he's here."

Addy had a firm knock. Ostryd released the lock and ushered in a tall, gangly Abbonite who was perhaps in his late fifties. The air of competence he projected seemed to define the man more than his narrow features or bald, tattooed pate. Addy swept his gaze around the small space, missing nothing.

"Welcome," Addy began, prefacing his message with his emotion in the traditional Abbonite way. "Pleased to make your acquaintance, Mr. Strangelore. Jax is enquiring if you will be taking dinner at the tavern tonight or if she should send a meal here." At first surprised that the man knew his name, Gideon recalled Ostryd had sent people to follow him on that first night, and Addy would be privy to some basic facts about him.

"Good to meet you too. May I call you Addy?" Gideon replied, then he pushed himself back in time to the moment Addy stepped into the room and watched the scene repeat. This time he responded with "Addy, it's good to meet you too." Neither man noticed anything amiss.

"Let's go join the others, shall we?" Ostryd said. "Have Brightstone and Lu returned?"

"Consideration," Addy said, wrinkling his nose. "Yes, and they have gone to the baths." Gideon was suddenly conscious of his own lack of cleanliness.

"I would also welcome a bath. I've only washed in the bedroom ewer since arriving," he said.

"Good, then that's agreed," Ostryd said. "You do that, and I'll tidy up here. Tell Jax we'll be along in about an hour for some food and to try our luck at cards."

Gideon's eyes turned to Ostryd, but he didn't see any knowing glint. He decided he wouldn't want to play a game of bluff with the fellow.

After Addy departed, Gideon held back for a moment to tell Ostryd about his latest success at slipping. They agreed Gideon would join a game or two of dice or cards later that day and test his skills at the table.

Ostryd opened his trunk, took out a square token, and passed it to Gideon. It had a complex pattern with a ten-digit number engraved upon it.

"Take this to any bank in Mordeland and use it to withdraw funds as you wish. The account is in the name of Fennymoor, and they will ask you for a code number. Add two to each odd number and subtract one from each even number on the token to get the correct code."

"That's exceedingly generous, Ostryd," Gideon said. "Of course, I'll return anything I borrow with interest."

"As you wish," Ostryd said. In a rare personal gesture, the older man reached out and rested his hands on each of Gideon's arms. "It matters not; there is so much money. I'm just so relieved to have met someone to share it with who won't die on me. Go to the bank before you bathe, and obtain some small coin for the table. Ensure you lose it all. This is a test of your slipping. There is no need to demonstrate your prowess at gambling."

"I must say, I'm excited to try this," Gideon said.

"And no more alcohol. Even I can't maintain a convincing shine shadow after a few glasses."

Gideon left Ostryd to his papers and walked outside. It was the last few moments of dusk, and the light was spectacular. He sauntered back to the tavern feeling happy about how things had turned out. Two weeks earlier, he was a frustrated charmer. A few days ago, he was running for his life, almost dead from the cold. Today he felt he could do anything he wanted. He thought about thanking Ag for his good fortune but realised he would have to reassess his view of religion after what he had learned about the aggar.

You're happy. Have you already put aside your grief for your sister? Tuli sniped. Gideon didn't attempt to answer. He had already resolved to talk with Ostryd about the time weaver and make some plea on Tuli's behalf.

It should be on your behalf if you missed me like I would you. And that old man won't share such information. Troll Lake holds the key. We must get there without delay.

Gideon ignored the barb as he stepped around a tinker's wagon that had stopped outside the tavern and went inside. He waved at Jax, who was talking to a young woman traveller at the bar, and then went up to his room to collect the spare set of clothing Lu had provided. As he passed through the tavern on his way to the bank and the public bath house, the fiddler struck up a jig, and Gideon whistled an echo of it as he strolled down the street.

An hour later, Brightstone sat to Gideon's left at a table for five and passed him a plate full of dinner pudding, cooked in the traditional Northern Region manner, dark and crispy topped above a fluffy base. The batter had been placed in a hot pan directly under the roasting beef, the meat's juices allowed to drip over it to ensure it browned well. Extra drippings had been added to the gravy, with a generous pinch of salt. Gideon accepted the plate, cut a healthy slice, which he added to the beef and roasted vegetables already on his plate, and passed it to Addy, who was sitting to his right. Lu and Ostryd already had their meals and had started to eat.

The bar was lively. Gideon took a moment to study the shine of those present. He was amazed, as Ostryd had predicted, that he had never observed the subtle variations before. The colours and tones were similar in all, but they were a shade brighter in people who were more exuberant and a shade dimmer in those who were less so. If he had noticed in the past, he would have assumed it was just a variation in the room's lighting rather than an aura emanating from within. He wondered if he could tune this information enough to win at cards without slipping.

Aside from the woman traveller he had passed earlier, who was now sitting with the tinker, he saw a few new faces. He supposed most people who could afford Jax's reasonable rates ate there each day rather than spend time away from their work to prepare food.

"Addy," Ostryd said, quietly enough that only those at the table could hear him, "please plan to leave town four days from tomorrow. Lu will pose as Brightstone's aunt. There is a similarity in their looks and movement from their training, which will make that connection seem natural. Gideon here will be my cousin and share my vardo. Please brief everyone on two things." He held up two fingers to count off his points. "First, if anyone asks, they have both been with us since we left Nuulan last fall. Second, Gideon will be with us indefinitely. Lu too, if she wishes. We have yet to discuss this with her. Everyone will treat Gideon's instructions as orders, second only to Brightstone and me."

Gideon was taken by this warm show of trust. Ostryd had clearly decided to adopt him, which suited him, but his own view of their relationship was less certain. What Lu, Addy, and Brightstone thought was more evident.

"Most surprised," Addy said. "It will be as you order, Mr. van Hyke, but the others will wonder why you have embraced this pair so quickly when you are typically slow to trust." Lu was about to add her own voice to this when Ostryd held up both hands to halt the discussion.

"We are kindred spirits is all anyone needs to know."

The conversation was slow to recover, but it did. Over the meal, Lu and Gideon got to learn some of Brightstone and Addy's backgrounds and felt much of the former's wit and love for sarcasm, at their own expense. When the meal ended, Lu slipped the remainder of the beef into her napkin and begged off to visit Shanna. Brightstone gave her a look, and Lu happily extended an invitation to join them. Addy excused himself to pass on Ostryd's instructions and begin the process of advertising their departure. With such a sizable caravan heading out, many others would seek to join them, and there was safety in numbers. Addy would vet the applicants but include as many as possible, and he needed to ensure adequate provisions were stocked for the journey.

Ostryd joined a card table, where he appeared well known and well liked. He introduced Gideon as Dak. Gideon sat and watched the first twenty or so hands until he felt he had the rhythm of things. If Ostryd slipped during any of the games, Gideon couldn't tell. The older man won slightly fewer hands than he lost, but overall the hands he won were a little bigger, so he came out ahead.

As arranged, Ostryd excused himself to go relieve himself, and Gideon took his place. He played a few hands before attempting to slip. He struggled at first, but then the knack of it returned. After an hour he found he could slip almost at will, and as instructed, slowly and deliberately, he lost all his coin, which made him enormously popular at the table.

As Gideon lost the last of the coin, the woman who he had seen with the tinker interrupted the group. She had visited all the tables in turn, and theirs was the last.

"I just wish to inform you good folk that the tinker will be open for business at the market for the next two days. I have a talent for reading palms and communing with spirits, should anyone require that service. And goodnight to you all and good fortune on your cards."

"It's a little late for that," Gideon said, as he excused himself and trudged over to the stable for another night of interrupted sleep. If only he had the power of foresight instead of slipping, he would have known the truth of that statement.

Chapter Forty-Four

By the third night, Gideon's shine shadow persisted while he slept. Using a similar technique to the one he had invented to pinch off Lu's nerve centre and prevent pain, he fixed his shadow in place. Ostryd reported the shine didn't vary as Gideon dreamt, as most people's did, and declared it good enough to allow Gideon to return to the tavern and a comfy bed. As a result, both men were in better humour the next morning.

Lu had spent most of each day out with Shanna, sweating through sword drills to recover the dexterity and strength in her hand. It still had some way to go, but she deemed it ready to begin sparring. Addy introduced her to the three men and a woman who were mercenaries hired as their caravan's guards. Lu took two of them to a quiet clearing well out of town and sparred with them until they were worn out. She returned to Sandrick to eat and sleep before repeating the process with the other pair. For the last two days she had made solid progress, and she began to feel lighter due to her growing competence. That all four of her sparring partners thanked her for teaching them new skills made her feel useful, something she realised she had missed lately.

While Lu was training, Gideon spent time with Addy, who introduced him to all the members of the caravan. Gideon joined Addy and his buyers to help them acquire their supplies for the upcoming journey and to begin to build credibility that he was a long-standing member of the party. Gideon saw why Ostryd retained Addy; he was efficient at planning, frugal when provisioning for their journey, and deeply respected and well-liked by the group.

Brightstone had been cautious around Gideon at first, uncomfortable with the ease and speed with which Ostryd had accepted him into their tight family. Ostryd had suggested she show Gideon the items she had inherited from her grandmother. She took the charmer to her room, located at the far end of the stable building, which was the mirror of Ostryd's own. She recounted the stories associated with each of the weapons she withdrew from her trunk, a history that Gideon found fascinating. But what seized Gideon's attention was three thin, old leather-bound manuals on Mobi'dern lore, each much older than himself.

The first was on human anatomy—ostensibly used to teach the most vulnerable parts of the body to damage in a fight—boasting magnificently detailed images of human anatomy. The second was a book on poisons, part of the black art of assassination that the Mobi'dern shunned but needed a thorough knowledge of to counter effectively. The last was a book of Mobi'dern healing techniques. Seeing Gideon's enchantment with her heirlooms softened something in the young woman, and the two of them spent several hours over the next few days going through the books together and sharing their thoughts.

Lu and Gideon were enjoying a late lunch reviewing the departure plans for the following day with Ostryd, Addy, Brightstone, and the two senior leaders of the caravan. Gideon had only been a passenger in such undertakings and was astonished at the planning required for such a journey to operate smoothly. Shanna was hunting well to the west when she picked up the scent of riders heading towards the village. She investigated and shared an image to Lu of the Bredden acolyte and her men travelling at a slow but determined pace back towards Sandrick.

Lu estimated the group would arrive in three to four hours if they didn't stop to rest. Other than Addy and Brightstone, Ostryd hadn't told anyone on his team that Lu was a Mobi'dern—he had explained her fighting skill as a passionate hobby—so Lu covertly hand signalled to Ostryd that they needed to speak urgently and in private. When Ostryd dismissed Addy and his men, Lu shared the news of the approaching danger.

"Should Lu and I depart now and overnight with Shanna?" Gideon asked. "We could meet you on the road tomorrow."

"I don't think that's necessary," Ostryd said. "Your shine shadow is sound enough, especially if you keep to your room. If we're seen departing as a group, and you're treated as if you have been part of the caravan for a long time, it will dispel suspicion. If you're noted to have joined it after we leave, should we encounter the acolyte again, that will only draw attention."

Everyone saw the logic in Ostryd's words, and by the time Della-ki entered Sandrick, Gideon and Lu had retired for the night. Each had their own room now that Ostryd's largesse afforded them the luxury of privacy, and it made it less obvious they were associated with one another.

Ostryd remained playing dice in the tavern to observe the acolyte's arrival and behaviour, covertly protected by his mercenaries and Brightstone. Aside from virtually interrogating Jax about recent comings and goings, Della-ki and her men seemed content to rest after their day's ride. Following their meal, they retired for the night. Ostryd settled all the accounts with Jax, including the cost of the breakfast they would have before departing in the morning.

At fourth bell, about an hour before the dawn, Shanna woke Lu with an urgent thought: *There is smoke in the air.* The stables were on fire, the cat observed from the treeline. As Lu shook her head free of sleep and processed the message, she heard frightened whickering and the frantic kicking of horses.

Lu pulled on her clothing and slipped into the hallway. Pausing outside of Gideon's room, she could hear nothing but his gentle snoring. She decided to let him sleep while she investigated. With the acolyte so close, she hoped he would have the good sense to stay in his room if the ruckus woke him. Tiptoeing along the corridor, she listened outside of the rooms occupied by the acolyte and her men. She could hear movement, the sounds of people settling in for the night. She crept down the stairs and out into the alley and then sprinted towards the stables.

As she sprang onto main street, Lu narrowly avoided being trampled by stampeding horses having just escaped the flaming stables. As she was recovering her composure from the near miss, Addy ran up to her from out of the darkness, breathless and as white as a sheet.

"What is it?" she demanded.

"Heart sick! Miss Brightstone is murdered, and Mr. van Hyke's room is ablaze. It is much too hot to approach, but I fear he must be inside. I can't see him elsewhere!"

"What? How?" Lu asked. She ran to the burning building. Addy caught up with her when she was forced to stop due to the fierce flames.

"Broken hearted . . . I found Brightstone here at the foot of Mr. van Hyke's stairs. She was alone with her sword in hand but was felled by several arrows," he explained. He led Lu off to one side, where he had dragged the dead woman. Lu bent and did her own quick inspection, but it was obvious Brightstone was well beyond help. Lu turned away, brushing her eyes dry before addressing Addy.

"What were you doing there?" Lu asked, not accusing but trying to grasp his story.

"Self-critical! I was asleep in my vardo and was awoken by the horses' screaming. By the time I ran to the stable, she was dead and there were flames coming out the door."

"And you saw no one else?"

"Regretful! Many were arriving just as I was. Together we found Brightstone where she had fallen. She was killed protecting Mr. van Hyke, it seems."

Lu inspected the scene, from the marking on the ground to the angle Addy described the body had been found. She couldn't come up with an alternative explanation or see any evidence from the ground that Ostryd had tried to come to her aid. She did determine that Brightstone didn't have her bow, her preferred weapon, and had been hit by arrows from several directions at once. There was nothing more to do until they could access Ostryd's room, but that side of the stables was swathed in flames.

Over the following fifteen minutes, Lu and Addy helped run a bucket line from the wells to the stables. Eventually, the blaze was subdued enough for Addy to pick his way up and into Ostryd's room. While he was inside, Lu walked to where Brightstone's body had been dragged, and her heart tore again as she looked down at the broken woman. Her hand traced the signs for *Go with the warrior's grace* as she bowed her head in respect.

As Addy trudged back to report what he found, his posture informed Lu that it was not good news.

"Deep sadness!" he said. "Mr. van Hyke is dead."

"Did he suffocate?" Lu asked, feeling sorry for Addy, who was obviously fond of his employer.

"Disbelief and anger! No. Initially I thought it was suffocation, as there was no sign of a struggle or anything to the contrary. The damage from the fire makes it difficult to know anything with certainty. But as the fire didn't shoot Brightstone with arrows, I thought to look more closely. There is a gash across his throat that the fire didn't cause any more than it killed his daughter."

Addy sent two men to collect what was salvageable from the rooms of the deceased and then accompanied Lu back up to the tavern. They found the main bar busy, Mosh and Jax serving an early breakfast to those who had fought the blaze and helped to round up the horses. Most of the tavern's occupants were up, including the acolyte, but Lu was pleased to note that Gideon had kept to his room.

She went up and knocked, then bade him to get dressed and follow her out of the back door. He was keen to understand what the commotion was, but she insisted they walk in silence until they were well clear of the crowd. They made their way to Deni's house, where Lu had arranged to meet Addy. When they arrived, she informed him of the tragedy.

Gideon was bereft. He had so much to learn from the ancient slipper, whose generosity had affected him deeply. He felt himself plunging back toward the depressed and desperate state of the first days of their escape. First Tuli, then Deni, and now Brightstone and Ostryd. What a nightmare. He expected some jibe from Tuli about his shortcomings, but it struck him that as disconcerting as it was for part of his mind to appear to think independently, he had been drawing much comfort from hearing his sister's voice. He was so lost in thought that he was surprised when Addy spoke to Lu.

"Suspicious! When you went to fetch Gideon, I observed the acolyte and her men for several minutes. Outwardly, they mirrored the shocked emotions of the room, but judging by the crafty looks they shared when thinking themselves unobserved, I believe they were secretly celebrating. The tinker and his woman were with them too, and the woman is now wearing a shasha. Do you believe they killed Ostryd and Brightstone? I don't know what to think."

Gideon burned with rage at the thought. How could they deprive him of the future that Ostryd had made possible? His first reaction was to implore Lu and the men to take revenge. They had more than enough strength for an ambush.

Is that truly the best course? his sister asked. *The acolytes were searching for a charmer and a Mobi'dern. Let them return to Nuulan and report that the search is over. It's a tragedy, yes, but why waste it?* Gideon railed at her calm and lack of anger, but she continued anyway. *Ostryd implored you to play the long game. Will you now sully his memory with such thoughtlessness while his corpse still cools?* Gideon blanched at the contempt Tuli showed for him. However, her logic seemed sound. As Lu and Addy shared their anger and desire for retribution, he struggled to work through the problem in his mind.

"What do you think?" Lu asked of Gideon, pulling him from his thoughts.

"I completely agree with you both," he began, letting anger he no longer felt flare on his face. He struggled to keep the self-loathing from his voice. "But I can't help thinking if Ostryd were here, he would point out two things. First, he confided in me that he placed me in the chain of command of this group for a reason. I'm sure he wasn't expecting a disaster this soon, but he had begun to groom me as his replacement mentor for Brightstone. He has even given me access to his finances and shared knowledge about his many resources, and hoped I could pick things up if anything . . . Well, you know.

"Second, it feels terrible to benefit from their deaths and worse to leave their killers untouched, but the acolytes will now return and report they have killed a charmer and a Mobi'dern. The hunt for us will end. Therefore, any repercussions to the remainder of Ostryd's party are also neutralised. They think they have silenced the filthy charmer and are happy. If we kill them, the hunt will continue. Alternatively, I can access Ostryd's funds to keep this group together. There might be people other than Brightstone whom Ostryd would expect us to care for."

"I liked Brightstone, and she is descended from Mobi'dern royalty," Lu said. "She deserves vengeance."

"If you will stay with me, Lu, I would like to bide our time for six moons. Then once we are well forgotten, I can help you get all the vengeance you like. I'll hold the acolyte down, and you can look her in the eyes as you slit her throat so she knows why she's dying. Then I'll bring her back from the edge so you can kill her a second time. But let's not let this tragedy be a waste. Neither Ostryd nor Brightstone would want that, eh?" Bile rose in Gideon's throat as he manipulated Lu. But then he recalled that he had made a silent vow to himself to rise above such things and work toward a position where he could openly do good in the world. If short-term sacrifices were needed, however repulsive he found them, so be it.

There was a long silence, eventually broken by Addy.

"Reluctant but supportive! I think, as you say, Mr. van Hyke would have thought about such things the same way. And I would feel good about us paying out the remaining moons on the contracts of those in the group and not have them concerned that the Bredden Church pay them any heed. They are good people with families at home whom they care for and send coin to support."

"Lu?" Gideon asked. "I will continue to need your support. I wouldn't have made it this far without you."

"Where will we go then? To Quartt, where it's safe?"

"Ostryd's death has left us free and clear with no need to hide anymore. But I'm known in Raile, including to some of the Council of Magical Law, so we must go farther west, where we should be safe. I want to go to Ostryd's estate at Troll Lake. He mentioned it was a central base for his activities. We might discover heirs or people he would want us to pass his legacy on to. Perhaps not someone as close as Brightstone, but someone else Ostryd would want protected. It is the least we can do," Gideon could see his words had swayed Lu.

And to visit the library of time magic, brother, Tuli whispered.

Chapter Forty-Five

Gideon and Lu spent several hours in their respective vardo wagons sorting through supplies and possessions acquired over the previous few days. They delayed returning to the tavern for their remaining items until the acolyte and the group left and Shanna had confirmed they were well away from the area. Even so they were cautious in their approach, watching for further treachery.

Gideon closed the door to his room and pulled the pack gifted to him by Ostryd onto the bed. From the side table drawers, he withdrew his new medical kit, and from the small armoire he retrieved the clothing he wished to keep. He folded those and made a separate pile of items he would ask Jax to pass on to people who needed them once they left.

Bundling the items he would keep, he attempted to fit them into the pack, but it was already too full, so he flipped the pack over and dumped its contents onto the bed to repack. On top of the pile were the three leather-bound manuals from Brightstone's collection and two small pouches of the type in which he stored freshly mixed medicines. There was also a small notebook and a dozen tokens such as the one Gideon had used to access Ostryd's bank accounts.

He knew Lu had already asked Addy to have someone collect all Brightstone's effects and anything that survived the fire in Ostryd's room. He had already thought to claim the rare books and hoped Lu would similarly honour Brightstone by taking control of the other heirlooms from Da-Stone. He wondered how the other items belonging to Ostryd and Brightstone got into his pack. He replayed events of the last few days. He had hoped to bring the books back to his room to study, but the young woman had been understandably wary and refused. It reminded him he didn't know Brightstone well and that the short but warm connection with her in her room going through the books would be all he ever experienced of her. *What a waste*, he thought.

Then a disturbing thought struck him. The acolytes must have taken the items and planted them in his room to shift suspicion. Beset by panic, he shoved them to the bottom of the pack. Would Lu ever believe he wasn't involved if she saw them? Should he dispose of them? But what would Brightstone or Ostryd be doing with the medicines? He opened each pouch and sniffed the contents. Both had the vague aroma of bee breeze. He thought of

Deni—another tragedy he had caused—and the healer's more rustic approach to using arrowroot in his sleep syrup. In one pouch he could smell cadium. Wetting his finger to taste each one, he noted the bitter twang of boresbain in the other. They were probably two different sleeping drafts, but why would they be there?

You're hopeless, brother. Gideon heard pity and frustration in Tuli's nattering. *It was I who did what you were too weak willed or frightened to do.*

"What do you mean?" Gideon asked.

There is no attempt to incriminate you. Go take charge of things before you let this opportunity slip through your fingers.

Gideon was confused. What was she talking about? She did something without his knowledge?

While you slumber, brother, I can do what I wish. We cut Brightstone's bowstrings and added two ounces of lampsdraught to some milk we took her.

"Brightstone?" Gideon whispered. "That much wouldn't put her to sleep."

No, but it slowed her reactions greatly. Hobbled so, she was no match for the acolyte's men. Even so, she caught me the first two times I pocketed her books, but I slipped and tried again until I stole them without her noticing. Ironically, using cadium to make the poison tasteless was an idea I read in her own book of poisons yesterday.

Gideon grasped how lampsdraught made with cadium would act as stated, but he couldn't comprehend why or how his sister had acted at all. He felt nausea rising and a sense of being mentally cast adrift at sea.

I concluded you were not strong enough to do what is required to find the time weaver and compel him to come back and save me, so I took control of your body and took decisive action because you would not.

As understanding came to him, Gideon was so horrified he began to gag, diving for the ewer just in time. When he recovered enough to think, he went through his memory but could recall none of the actions Tuli claimed to have carried out. *I've lost my mind,* he thought.

"What have you done?" When Tuli didn't immediately reply, he continued. "And Ostryd?" Gideon didn't want to hear her, but he felt so adrift he needed answers.

He was easier, trusting fool. We took him a bottle of Jax's best bower brandy and a bottle for ourselves. He was so delighted that we were so germ conscious, he agreed to regale us at length with tales from his life. The poison I put in his bottle was in his system for almost an hour before he felt it. I suspect he tried to slip away from it, but our betrayal was too far into his past by then. He could do nothing to save himself.

"What was it?" Gideon asked, a moth to a flame.

A little devil's breath, to loosen his tongue and make him compliant, and lillynurse. I chose lillynurse because it's slow to give us time to get his secrets before it fully took effect but also because it's a psychedelic.

"Why was that important?"

Tuli's voice was full of smug pride. *With this combination of medicines, we went through his trunk's secrets with him. He fought us, but he told us everything. Even about things that were not in the trunk. In the back of the poison manual, I wrote down all his financial entities and how to access them.*

"No, I meant why the psychedelic?" Gideon said, fearing he had already guessed the answer. "Why was that necessary?"

This time Tuli's voice sounded superior and condescending. *Oh, this is the best part. Why I acted. After our visit with him, we slipped a note under the acolyte's door, knocked, and then hid in our room. The note was an anonymous tip from a discontented Wig. After they killed Brightstone and entered Ostryd's room, the drug made his shine shadow completely erratic, and I expect he was lit up like a Harvest Fire festival. They won't doubt they found and killed their prey.*

Chapter Forty-Six

The 470th Year of the Morde Dynasty

In the massive cavern, the air hung motionless, undisturbed by movement, sounds, draughts, and people for centuries. It was so still that an observer could have been forgiven for thinking they were looking at a painting.

In the centre of the space, a small column abruptly turned green and the air seemed to still even more, but then the column flexed, and Levinial appeared. In his left hand he grasped the time-riding amulet that held him separate from this world. After a brief look around, he set down the amulet and manifested into flesh-and-blood form. A ripple of air pushed outwards by his solidification moved fronds of rock grass at his feet for the first time in a long while.

He inhaled heartily. It was always the tastes and smells that excited Levinial most in these first few moments. He craved them. When not attending time-repairing duties, he hovered in the space of the gods as intelligence without form. There, sights and sounds remained rich memories, but sensations of touch, taste, and smell were pale and distant to him. Although he retained a faint sense of the zesty bite of citrus, a sharp briny seaweed, or dank woodsmoke, such memories didn't flare his emotions or inspire a distinct recollection as they did when he was whole. He missed them until he manifested in the cavern of the aggar and its jamboree of smells embraced him. His heartbeat increased as his mind recognised that the loneliness of the gods' space would be temporarily relieved by interactions with people.

No weaver had met the gods whose void they share but Levinial had sensed their vast presence. Master Weaver Garalon relayed their reason for creating time weavers. When they performed their great feats, the gods' magic left an irritant called naether that they wished gone from their space. Their solution had been to create a mechanism enabling naether to efficiently drain away. For this purpose, they created aggars as both a gateway from their space and to control the process.

The creation of an aggar marks the beginning of a new world. Initially, the aggar uses the naether drawn from the gods' space to create a physical but sterile world where time does not exist. A mountain forms first around the aggar, who resides perpetually within an enormous cavern under that peak. Naether is pressed outwards to form barren lands and seas beyond. Once the empty continents are formed, the aggar begins to create life.

Each living thing, be it a worm, leaf, or tree, is attached to the aggar by a life-link. Through this link it draws naether from the gods' space via the aggar to fuel its existence. The more complex and intelligent the life, the more naether it consumes. People are the best consumers of naether as their intelligence, emotions, and spirituality burn brightest. Making life which reproduces leaves the aggar with only the task of attaching each new life, strand by strand.

As the aggar pushes the gods' waste outwards to fuel all life in the world, it creates a by-product: time. The world moves forward in time, leaving the aggar in the past. Millions of strands of time weave together to form the timeline, reminiscent of an umbilical cord connecting a mother to her child. Most people have a link barely adequate to sustain their life, but those able to draw a little more can use the gods' energy to change their world–they call it magic.

Neither the gods nor the aggar care how events in the world evolve, provided that naether is consumed voraciously. Inevitably, a magic wielder will, knowingly or not, use magic in a manner which disrupts the smooth flow. A little turbulence is acceptable, but a blockage, or an Unravelling, results in the gods' spawning a fresh world and terminating the broken one. This distraction for the gods can be averted if a time weaver can locate the cause, influence events, and reestablish a smooth flow.

As the centre of magic, the cavern is imbued with a blue glow that illuminates everything evenly with no obvious source. There is a background aroma like the pungent sweetness of a lightning bolt on a rainy night, but it is a fragrance overlaid with so much more. The magic's ozone tang is scented by the prototypes that the aggar had chosen to retain as if his cavern were his personal museum.

Four acres of dusty desert with lush cactus formed one square of the cavern floor. Two acres of cedar forest, rich with moss merged into another two acres of rainforest, and so on, creating a patchwork of ninety acres that echoed the diverse woodlands in the world outside. Nutty, musty corn. The iron watermelon of fresh snow. A million variations of plants and habitats, created, modified, and loved before being released into the world many millennia ago. Cherished examples of his favourites preserved and sustained in a place where time and magic flowed. While plants and land could stand frozen and timeless, animal life could not, and so the space was devoid of such things.

Levinial scanned the dazzling patchwork of biospheres containing the sources of the smells. The aggar of this world had a keen eye for arranging his archive in an orderly and aesthetically pleasing manner, with tidy pathways of stone separating them. Since they were created, the paths had only ever been touched by the feet of the time weavers arriving and departing to attend to their duties.

The practice for attending a duty on a world was begun by answering the summoning of its aggar, arriving from the gods' space at the moment the world was conceived. From there the time weaver collected the amulet attuned to that world's magic. They rode that device down the timeline to a place as close to the blockage they were tasked to investigate allowed. Unable to manifest at that point due to time turbulence, the time weaver backed up to where manifestation was achievable, and from there they began to work.

Levinial's experience suggested this was the best time to begin. It was roughly two and a half years after the event he determined had started the chain reaction leading to the temporal disturbance. As far as he could estimate, it was about four to six of this world's moon cycles until "current time," when the conduit's turbulence reached catastrophic proportions and the Unravelling began.

Although rare, a time weaver could perish in solid form. Therefore, after manifesting, the amulet was always left in the aggar's cavern. This allowed the aggar to recall it for a replacement time weaver, if needed. More importantly, it prevented the amulet from falling into the hands of a local magic user, who might use it to cause chaos.

The aggar's first prototype had been water and algae, which formed a stalagmite-stalactite ice formation resembling a pair of hound's teeth. Levinial set the amulet on the lower tooth for safekeeping. He would return there when his task was complete and retrieve the device to ride back to the beginning of time and then onwards to the gods' space.

As he walked naked through the many paths to the cavern's entrance, he paused occasionally to savour the experience. He sank his toes into the sand, caressed plants, and laid in the grass. He picked fruits and fungi, savouring them. Time weavers always manifested with an empty stomach, making the first meal particularly special.

Just inside the cavern's entrance, he found clothing and supplies left by the last time weaver. *Was it me or has another time weaver been here since my last visit?* he wondered. The magic in the cavern had preserved everything perfectly, even though it had probably sat for hundreds of years. Rather than coins, which would date him, the cache included gold, silver, and copper bars of varying sizes, plus a small sack of gemstones. Flints, weapons, an eyeglass, and a series of maps sat ready.

Next to the clothing was the codex. Levinial picked it up and walked to a spot near the entrance where sunlight streamed into the cavern and sat down to read it. The codex was written in the highly efficient symbology used by time weavers to document the main languages, cultures, and history of each world. Each time weaver updated it at the end of their mission when they replenished the supply cache. Even though the gods created time weavers to learn at an accelerated rate, it still took many days to assimilate the contents. The information would be dated, but it still served as an invaluable base as he took his first tentative steps out into the world.

From his pre-manifestation observations, Levinial estimated the blockage would form several hundred miles northwest of the cavern. Once he finished studying the codex, he would head in that direction and find a small town where he could perfect his grasp of the language. There he would create a story about himself he could share as needed and acquire such things as the coin of the day as well as identity papers that the locals might employ.

At the top of his list of priorities was researching the events on the day the time turbulence began and their consequences. To do this, he needed to find libraries and scholars.

Levinial sat and consumed the contents of the codex and ate his fill from the landscape around him. What he took would not grow back, so he was careful not to over-pick any one parcel of produce.

On the fifth day, his research complete, Levinial picked up a pendant from the cache and strung it around his neck. The jewel allowed him to step out through the magical barrier that barred all animal life, including and especially people, from entering the cave. Unlike the inhabitants of the world, weavers retain their link directly to the gods' space, drawing on pure naether to live. The naether on any world is changed subtly by the aggar's processing, and the two are incompatible. Using pure naether to perform magic on a world, risks causing an Unravelling and must be avoided at all costs, hence the use of the aggar's amulets to access the cavern and travel time and space.

Stepping out, he emerged onto a rocky slope, where a series of angular boulders hid the cave from view. For miles around the zone emanated an intensely uncomfortable feeling due to the flow of magic in the cavern. This deterred settlement and exploration, so it was highly unlikely anyone would see him amongst the rocks. He gazed at the landscape, relishing the sights. Noting the sun's position, he set out to the north to begin his investigation.

Chapter Forty-Seven

As Winter dismounted from his grey stallion, the combination of his chiselled features, rangy, muscular frame, and easy confidence turned the heads of women and men alike, if for different reasons. As he loosened his riding jacket and handed Bastion's reins to his apprentice, Sirius, Brylee made sure she mimicked the effect he had on the women nearby and stole glances while studiously not looking his way.

Brylee considered this morning an important test of her abilities to evade detection. Winter was arguably the best hunter in Wickham's network. The mage had tasked Winter to train her in the very skills she now employed, and the tracker knew her well, no matter the disguise they had dreamed up together. Knowing her father had been cured and that her business and friends were protected by Wickham's contacts, Brylee had vowed to help in the hunt for the assassin. She was driving herself to live and breathe the tasks required and become the best spy she could be in a short time.

Winter came to this market just outside the city at the same time most weeks to buy fresh produce—he loved to cook and share recipes with Sage—and was familiar with the bazaar's faces and rhythms. Always alert, he would notice anything unusual or out of place. He would scrutinise and catalogue each face as his gaze trawled the crowd, and all this without any conscious effort on his part. He could also read the magical auras in the crowd. Had he been raised in Raile, he might have been inducted into the Bredden Order as an acolyte—he had a small amount of charmer in him—but instead it was Mage Wickham who benefitted from his acute senses. Winter had worked for Wickham since boyhood and was his most trusted soldier.

For the last few moons, Wickham had trained Brylee to use her magic as a mage would. It was necessary for her to survive and save her father, but it made her sick to her stomach with shame, and she felt that the gods might fling it back in her face down the road.

They determined her natural magical capacity was still quite modest even though it had expanded due to her near skriking by Vekki. Wickham provided Brylee with a necklace with three oblong yellow Galei stones suspended on a silver chain, which he believed was the only such device in existence. Galei was a mythical god of memory, and the stones appeared to have a memory for magic. Wickham infused the stones with his own power, and in the same way a water skin held water until needed, the Galei stones retained magic for Brylee to draw upon. She could draw great power from the stones quickly or a smaller amount more slowly, but once they were drained, she would need to rely on her own innate capacity until Wickham recharged the necklace.

He also taught her simpler traditional magic, such as how to harden air, how to heat and cool with magic, and levitation, while Brylee attempted to teach him how she changed her own body. Try as he might, however, Wickham couldn't affect his body in any way. That skill seemed to be outside of the realm of general magic and more akin to the rare magic of the stones and the Judge's Crystal. He also couldn't use techniques to change hair colour or body structure on other people. He was frustrated but unsurprised.

With the added capacity of the stones, Brylee soon learnt to rapidly change her own body, which was a useful skill for a spy or hunter of assassins. But there were limits. She could change her hair and skin colour in moments. She could also grow her hair or curl or straighten it in minutes. Body mass, such as muscle and fat, took hours instead of the days it had taken her when she was in the prison cell. There wasn't much she could do about her unusual height, but Winter taught her ways to alter her posture, such as stooping without appearing to, which was almost as good. She could never pass as a short, skinny person, but soon she could drastically change her appearance and her voice and, to some extent, even her smell.

While learning how general magic could affect the colour of certain vegetation, Brylee hit on the idea of dying cloth with an algae that she found was particularly easy to alter in colour. Without Winter's knowledge, Rosemary and Brylee made several outfits that Brylee could vary in colour in seconds using minute amounts of magic. She could even do it without the stones, although that was a little slower. She was wearing such an outfit at the moment, and it was a large part of the test she had planned.

For the test, Brylee had grown her hair into a ponytail. lightened her skin and phased the colour of her tunic and jacket to two complementary blues. She had also altered her features to be more pinched and narrow and made sure she stood in a way that emphasised her height. Under Wickham's guidance, shadow shining had become an unconscious act, but she checked her aura anyway as she paid for two apples. She did not allow herself to look directly at Winter, but she remained peripherally aware of him as he shopped three stalls away.

Winter's mind was occupied with reviewing Brylee's afternoon weapons practice. In her teens, her parents had provided her with a good fighting instructor, and her own determination and desire for toughness ensured she had made good use of that time. He found that Brylee was already competent with a knife, sword, and bow. Over the two moons since Wickham had asked him to teach her to fight, track, and be stealthy, he had improved those skills threefold. Brylee would stand well against many soldiers, and a Mobi'dern would respect her. Although they would still beat her, it would not be easy. Against the Red Assassin, however, she would need to be even better than she was. Ideally, she would never have to face the assassin directly; that task would fall to Winter or the mage, but should things go awry, and if she needed to fight such a person, other tools might be better. The day's lesson was on preparing poison darts and the use of blow pipes, which were small enough to hide in her clothing.

As he lifted a bushel of skyleaves to his nose and confirmed their freshness, a woman he had noted as new to the market smudged in his peripheral vision.

Smudging was an unconscious technique natural to most people, but many spies cultivated it as a conscious skill. When used unnaturally, and awkwardly, it could seem false to a trained observer, which was why his subconscious drew the woman to his attention. Smudging was the use of one's aura, body language, and other faculties to influence the perception of others. It could complement charm to make a person more attractive. It could also deter approach if one was feeling frosty, encouraging people to sit elsewhere rather than close by, or the opposite. Everyone did it to some degree, although most were unaware they were doing it.

Winter didn't react outwardly to the mental alert. Instead, he replayed what his memory had recorded about the woman. Blonde, tall, almost alabaster skin, shopping unaccompanied. Nothing about her seemed threatening. Winter's instincts suggested she was aware of him, encouraging him to pass her by. Now that she had piqued his curiosity, however, that wasn't going to happen.

Winter put the bushel down and picked up a second, smelled it, then held it out to the stall's owner to add to the bag of items he had already selected. He sensed the woman move away from the stall she had been inspecting to another one behind him. He asked the vendor to hold his goods for his return while he browsed, then went to the stall behind him and across the aisle to cut the woman off without it seeming too deliberate. He would close in and find out what she was about.

Brylee smiled inwardly. She sensed Winter had become aware when she deliberately smudged him in a slightly clumsy manner. Now she needed to deepen the hook she had just set in him. For the next two minutes, wherever Winter shopped, appearing to take no notice of her, Brylee moved to shop somewhere just out of view. She let him herd her towards a tavern set between the two narrow rows of stalls to which their subtle dance had taken them. She worked hard not to make it look easy or obvious. She glanced back to where Winter had left Sirius and noted the apprentice had disappeared. She expected Winter would surreptitiously signal his apprentice to go take up station at the rear of the inn she was heading towards.

Brylee jerked her head up, then looked back and forth as if spooked. Then she strode into the inn as if realising she had no option but to escape that way but made herself act nonchalant—slightly too nonchalant, she hoped. Without looking around, her senses told her Winter had sped up in pursuit. She had just moments to act.

She had chosen the inn because like many, to enter it one passed through the first door and then a second one six feet farther inside, so that in the colder moons, heat would not escape the building as easily. She was prepared to use a quiet booth in the inn to affect her change if she was forced to but was relieved the short space was empty as she stepped through the first set of doors.

As the outer door closed, with a flash of her knife she lopped her ponytail off close to her head and shoved the hair into a pocket. She drew on the Galei stones and changed her remaining hair to black and added tight curls. She also altered her skin from pale white to a dark tan. She pulled a string inside her jacket to release extra cloth, which fell to make the short jacket a mid-length coat, adjusted perfectly for the stoop she now affected.

Even with these rapid changes, Winter might still make the connection, so as Brylee magically softened and rounded her facial features, she changed the colour of her outfit from complementary blues to white with a tan coat. Finally, she pulled a small cap from another pocket and set it on her head to hide her rough haircut. In the time Winter made four or five strides towards the door, a completely different Brylee was walking out the door, which Winter held for her. This time Brylee smudged him ever so subtly as she let her eyes land on him, then looked down demurely in the way most women who unexpectedly encountered him responded due to his good looks.

Winter entered the bar area and then stepped sideways so he would not be silhouetted against the door as he paused and let his eyesight adjust to the dimmer conditions. He scanned all the booths and tables, confident his quarry had carried on through the bar and kitchen and would be intercepted by Sirius at the rear entrance. Ignoring the half-hearted complaints from the proprietor who, like most, was intimidated by Winter's size and sense of purpose, he stalked through the kitchen and out the rear door, only to find Sirius waiting expectantly.

"You saw no one?" Winter asked. "She wasn't in the bar or the kitchen. Perhaps she went upstairs."

"Ahem," Brylee said as she bit into an apple and leaned casually against the fence to the side of the yard, having looped around the building's perimeter. "Looking for someone, Winter?" She tossed him the other apple she had purchased, which he caught in his big hand without even glancing at it. He shook his head, turned, and walked back through the market to retrieve his purchases from the stall where he had left them.

As he walked, he replayed the events. When he was certain that Brylee couldn't see him anymore, he allowed himself to smile, remembering he had even held the door for her. She was a quick study, and he was keen to find out how she had done the costume change so quickly.

Chapter Forty-Eight

Gideon watched Brylee Plainhand smile as she left the market, a slight swagger in her step. At the market's gate she paused and seemed about to glance his way. *Watch it,* his Tuli side warned. In the years since assuming Ostryd's empire, he had worked with several mages to perfect many of their techniques. With his significant power, it was a small matter to use hard air to overturn a basket near Brylee to distract her.

The woman had proven extraordinarily difficult to track—and not solely because she could rapidly alter her appearance. This convinced him more than anything that she was what the time weavers called a salient. Ostryd's Troll Lake library was fascinating in many respects, but Gideon had found it devoid of anything concerning the time weaver. Distraught, he wandered the estate in a dejected funk, believing he would never find Ostryd's secret trove concerning the aggar and their time weavers. Several times he had visited a renovated folly that stood on a shallow bluff overlooking the lake, feeling a comfort there, away from Lu and the staff.

The inside of the folly was laid out like a reading room with large windows, but it had no torches or fireplace, and it reminded Gideon of Ostryd's description of his fire-safe archive where he had first encountered Levinial. That revelation initiated an obsessive search of every nook. It took him a day to discern where the hidden niche was located and two more days to locate the magic-activated latch that released the hidden door. Three weeks of devouring the contents of the ancient documents had presented him, he hoped, with the key to locating a time weaver. He would locate and follow a salient.

Levinial had revealed to Ostryd that the blockages he removed sent turbulence back down the timeline, with the disturbance growing weaker and weaker until the nexus point. The nexus was the triggering event whose ramifications built up to eventually form the blockage. Those individuals whose lives were critically bound to the events were termed salients. Their magical link to the time conduit reverberated with the turbulence, whereas all others remained unaffected. These time tremors were how time weavers located the players contributing to the impending temporal breach. Gideon accepted he might wait centuries before a time weaver came to the world, but when one did, they would be tracking salients.

Gideon had spent the entire journey from Sandrick to Troll Lake perfecting techniques such as shine shadowing, reading auras, slipping, and studying the links he and others had back to the conduit. During that process, he made two key discoveries. First, after hours of concentrated effort, he believed he could discern the turbulence on the conduit which, in his ignorance, he had assumed was the conduit's normal state. If it was indeed turbulence, then a time weaver could already be on his trail.

In two moons of intensive study, Gideon had gone from discovering, then being able to see his own link, to being able to identify the conduit with clarity. Now it felt like he could command his vision to blur from the physical to the temporal plane, and millions of links bristling from the end of the conduit appeared, presumably touching all life on the planet. In fact, he felt the conduit was not one large pipe but rather all the links intertwined like the threads in a rope. Among that massive tangle, some links stood out more than others, and they proved to be Lu and other people sharing his journey through life. Geographic proximity didn't appear relevant to those links being more distinct. It was as if time grouped people together according to their past and future interactions as opposed to physical distance. In the more distinct group, two links resonated with the turbulence: his and Brylee Plainhand's.

Of course, at first he had no idea of her name or where Brylee was, and it took moons of experimentation to confirm that the turbulence felt slightly more or less pronounced if he travelled in various directions. It took another two years of travelling the world to home in on Haxley. Just a few moons ago, sitting on the deck of the Crow's Nest on a cold, snowy night, he had found her. He had been playing dice, slipping occasionally to top up his funds but focussed on the comings and goings of the patrons when she walked in and sat at the bar to talk with the proprietor. Gideon saw immediately that the link he had followed those many moons connected to this woman, and to the surprise of all at the table, he let out a sound of glee, despite having just rolled five low dice.

Gideon hired two men and two women skilled in covertly following people and set them to observe Brylee and report back everything they learned about the woman. He set another on a clandestine search of the southern lands that bordered Backalar. Ostryd's library contained his journals in which he claimed to have lent Levinial a horse to facilitate the time weaver's departure. The time weaver returned by horse courier, and Ostryd took the opportunity to track the horse's movements back to a smaller border town, where the trail went cold. Gideon was keen to complete that search, feeling the information could be crucial at some point.

In parallel with tracking down Brylee, he had to deal with the other salient: himself. His own link to the conduit stood out: it was turbulent and looped around, rather than attached to the timeline. It marked him as a slipper. He couldn't do much about the latter other than tighten the circumference of the loop so its nature was less obvious, but he had developed a technique that dampened the vibrations on his link. If the time weaver came looking, it was Gideon's hope he would go unnoticed compared to Brylee's far more tempestuous activity.

Brylee's swift departure to the Brown Estate and then to the region's capital gave his tracking team a headache, but they soon caught up with her at the Creative in Rostal. Her abrupt disappearance the following day threw his team completely. At their request, Gideon travelled to the region's capital and used his magical link tracking ability again. Eventually, he found Brylee in the employ of Mage Wickham, but much about her had changed. A new face, a slightly thicker link to the conduit, and a far larger magical ability than such a link should provide. She also had a new name: Senna, a fictitious distant niece of Wickham's housekeeper.

As Gideon paid for a pastry, he watched Brylee depart the market after whatever game she had played with a large man and noticed another man also covertly observing the woman. The man was hooded and standing in the shadow of the Smith's Shop, fixated on his quarry. Gideon blurred his perception into the magical realm to study his link to the conduit. He was shocked to see it was not attached, instead drifting off in a different direction and fading to nothing, with a significantly different colour to all others.

I see you, time weaver, Gideon thought.

He spoke to the leader of his tracking team, instructing him to leave one person loosely observing Brylee but switch the rest of their resources to observing the newcomer.

Chapter Forty-Nine

Levi's journey back to the nexus location he visited earlier while riding the amulet found the buildings shuttered and derelict. He went to Raile's capital and searched the odious Bredden cleric's libraries. He found nothing of the nexus location other than a suspiciously brief report of a mass poisoning some years earlier and a claim that the culprit had been killed in mysterious circumstances in a mining town in the north. It soon became clear that anything concerning magic was shunned and largely written out of their history with a staunchly conservative prejudice.

By contrast, the Library of the Council of Magical Law contained a great deal concerning magic, including the politics of mage versus charmer and of the failed experiment that was the HAC and its tragic ending. This extensive library also gave some insight into quandaries he had wrestled with since leaving the aggar's cavern. When he initially inspected the time conduit, he sensed two salients. One was unusually faint but generally akin to this world's population. After a few weeks it faded from his senses as its resonance from the blockage evaporated. This had been known to happen if its owner died, or if events changed the course of the future and the individual was no longer salient to the temporal crisis. When a time weaver acted, changing the course of history to prevent the crisis, all salients' links returned to normal.

It was the other salient's vibration that was more intriguing, as it had the signature of a primi, one of the first people. Was this why he was so drawn to the woman? In the early millennia of any world, almost all people are imbued with unfiltered naether as their bodies accepted the flow of magic from the timeline without mutation. After hundreds of generations, however, the population evolved to be far less effective at absorbing pure magic. By the time a world reached the age of this one, perhaps only 5 percent of people retained the amount of naether required to be deemed a primi. The alternative scenario was for primis to be intentionally bred out of existence, essentially becoming extinct.

Levi hadn't scoured the codex for details of their extinction, but ancient relics such as Galei stones were mentioned in the libraries, proving primis' prior existence. The origins of such magic appeared to be at least 12,000 years ago.

As he watched the woman he had initially seen at the rooftop tavern, two thoughts wrestled for his attention. The first was to wonder if a recessive gene was responsible for the primi power reemergence. The second was that he was even more attracted to her than he'd suspected. A new feeling for him. *Duty,* he reminded himself, shaking off the sensation.

Although discouraged by the gods, it was common for time weavers to have physical relations with the inhabitants of the worlds they visited, but they strenuously avoided emotional entanglement with the people they investigated. Most time weavers took pains to avoid any emotional complications because their time was limited on any one world. But enjoying any and all experiences while manifested, including sex, helped counter the long periods of isolation in the gods' space between assignments. Levi had taken many such opportunities but had never felt the likes of the emotional response to a person as he did at the moment. He had always scoffed at the notion of love at first sight, and although he wasn't ready to accept that was his affliction, it seemed like such a thing was possible. He was so taken with the woman that he failed to notice several people detach themselves from their activities and follow him out of the market.

On leaving the cavern, Levi had walked twenty miles to the nearest township, Fallow's Green, and was pleased to note that not much had changed since the codex's last update. He walked around just listening to conversations and observing social conventions for two full days before entering a bank and exchanging some silver and four small gems for the coin of the realm. He spent a week in the Freely Given Inn, becoming comfortable speaking the common language while shopping in the markets for updated clothing and supplies more fitting to the time period.

As had been his practice during other manifestations, Levi searched for a companion who would travel with him for the first few weeks so he could learn about contemporary politics, geography, and customs. On his fifth day in Fallow's Green, he found such a man and introduced himself as a refugee from Backalar, the country to the south that appeared to be gearing up for war.

Robb Piscator had been a Mordeland ranger for over forty years prior to his retirement two summers ago. Ranger Robb, as the locals still called him, was a restless soul and soon found retirement not to his liking. He had already fulfilled several private contracts escorting travellers or ferrying valuables and was quick to agree to be Levi's guide for a moon.

Piscator's easy-going nature and depth of human empathy impressed Levi and was evident in the unusual adventure they had on their journey together. As they travelled through Quartt, they came across a woman and two men who were camping by a stream. They failed to respond to Piscator's call as they approached seeking space at the fire for the night. It was soon clear that all three had consumed sufficient narcotics to render themselves unconscious for many hours. Levi and Piscator left the camp the next day, and the group still hadn't regained their wits.

"Aren't rangers supposed to arrest or report such people?" Levi asked as they sat around the fire. Piscator argued that his duty was to ensure everyone was safe and, if so, to let them live how they wished as long as they weren't harming anyone. Piscator had tended to each person in turn, repositioning them so that if they vomited, they would not choke. He also restocked their water and other supplies and built up their fire before leaving camp.

On other occasions when Levi was probing for information on the world's conventions and behaviours, Piscator revealed he had experienced love and overpowering physical attraction, but Levi had disregarded his tales, sure he would not suffer from such a weakness. Now Levi regretted parting company with the ex-ranger several weeks earlier seeing as he couldn't ask the many questions that were forming since he first set his eyes on the primi woman. He was sure there were ways to prevent such emotions and move on.

Levi enjoyed Piscator's companionship and found their conversations eased the loneliness he sometimes felt due to his role protecting worlds. Over the past three millennia, he had made several visits to this world and enjoyed many of the companions he met. During his unusual encounter with the scholar, Ostryd, he sensed the man's attachment to Levi's life force. In discussions with Master Weaver Garalon, Levi had determined that Ostryd's connection was tied to some act that the time weaver and Ostryd were destined to do that would affect them both in some way that was important to the world's future. He noticed he could not sense Ostryd on the timeline, and it troubled him to the point he considered returning to the cavern and using the amulet to investigate what had happened to the ancient scholar. Then the woman turned and smiled at him, and thoughts of Ostryd were put aside for later consideration.

Brylee had spotted the tall man in the heavy cloak watching her as soon as she walked away from Winter. She maintained her grin and swagger at besting her trainer despite her concern over the stranger's presence. He certainly wasn't overly skilled at concealing himself, so she determined he was neither a spy nor an assassin. Perhaps he was a mage intent on skriking her. Had her aura slipped? She didn't think so. As she led him along the street, she felt no overt hostility. In fact, she felt quite the opposite. Despite his intensity, he had a warmth about him. She decided a direct approach was best. Rehearsing the tricks that Wickham had taught her to fight a skriker—which would not fend off a full mage for long but would frustrate a lesser being—and checking that she could draw on the Galei stones, she picked a tactically advantageous spot and turned to face him.

"Can I help you, sir?" she asked, offering her most disarming smile.

The man was a conundrum. He was taller than Brylee by a hand, and his physique had the long, ropy muscle of an athlete or cavalryman, but his movements lacked the fluid grace one would expect from someone who has worked hard enough to produce such a build. He had no signs of calluses and no visible scars, and there was an awkwardness about him, as if he had been transformed from a wolf to a man and was just becoming accustomed to his new body. But where his gait was imperfect, his face was not. As he pushed his hood back, the face that was revealed made her freeze until she admonished her schoolgirl self to restart her bodily functions and settled her heartbeat.

His bushy blond hair stood in tall, unkempt spikes, bristling out from a widow's peak offset slightly from the centre of his square forehead. His stubble angled down, narrowing from strong cheekbones to a firm jaw, framing what Brylee imagined were full lips had they not been pinched as he studied her with discomforting intensity. She noted his atypically large nose was eclipsed by the purest, most piercing aqua-blue eyes she had ever seen. Those eyes seemed intent on laying her soul bare. Brylee wasn't sure how long she stared at the man, but his lips twitched mischievously before his demeanour became serious, and he spoke in a deep, smoky voice. He had a faint accent that she found difficult to place.

"My name is Levinial, and I need to talk to you in private."

Chapter Fifty

In the countless interventions he had completed, Levi found that one of two strategies worked best, depending on the circumstances. If the situation involved several salients, it was usually best to remain in the background and observe matters as they developed. Often those salients never knew of his existence. When there was just one salient, it was better to use a more direct approach. Often the issue was one of ignorance rather than intent. On worlds where primi existed, salients were typically aware of their abilities but perhaps not of the implications of using them in certain ways. But in this instance, with the salient being the only primi for 500 generations or so, he suspected she had no idea what she was or what damage she could cause.

For her part, Brylee sensed something dangerous about this stranger, something alien. She could not identify what unsettled her to the point she was afraid to refuse to talk to him. She supposed he was a powerful mage, so she felt it best to retreat to be close to Mage Wickham for protection.

"I'm staying with Gil Wickham," said Brylee, gauging the man's reaction when she mentioned the most powerful mage in the region. "We can talk discreetly at his house, and it's only a fifteen-minute walk from here. There is no privacy in the market." She sensed no reaction to Wickham's name, but after a moment's consideration, the man gestured for her to lead the way. As much as her body appreciated Levi's appearance, she found his simple shrug of agreement faintly annoying, and she wondered why. He was imposing on her without explanation, seemingly confident she would comply. Men had done that most of her life, and it always annoyed her. *It's because you fancy a roll with him, but he's making you uncomfortable,* a small part of her mind whispered.

As they fell into step with each other, the light breeze carried Levinial's musky scent Brylee's way. As it registered, she became excruciatingly aware of how it added to the thrumming in her blood, which was already stimulating her womanly places in delightful ways. *OK, he's attractive. Get a grip, Plainhand,* she chastised herself.

"Do I know you?" she asked, hoping to change the course of her thoughts.

"We've never met," he replied. "And I don't even know your name, I'm afraid." Brylee choked back the urge to blurt it out. She wanted to learn more about him first.

"What brings you to Rostal?" she asked.

Levi thought about her question, wondering how much to reveal while enjoying the simple act of walking with her, how confident she was in her strength, and how her deep brown eyes sparkled with curiosity. Levi was attracted to curiosity, a trait he believed was one of the most powerful forces in nature. Not only did it invite learning, it also undermined prejudice and bias, fostered perspectives other than our own, and typically led to growth in whoever practised it. He looked around the market and saw that no one was paying them any heed, but he didn't want to say too much until they could not be overheard.

"I'll reveal more in private; I assure you. But for now, let's say I'm interested in current and future events, and I have reason to believe you're on track to become entangled in a problem you would not wish to be."

Brylee's throat tightened, but she said nothing as she wondered if those events involved the Namiduh Jou and her search for the Red Assassin.

"I also have a deep interest in archaic magic. Call it a by-product of my work, if you like. I hadn't noticed them until coming this close to you, but those stones in your necklace fall into that category. This increases my confidence that you're the person I've been looking for these last few moons."

As he spoke, Brylee's hand flew to her Galei stones, and she drew on them to harden the skrike barrier she had prepared in case of attack. But Levinial seemed to have no such intent, and he held his hands up to reassure her when he saw her flinch. Again, she felt piqued at the ease at which he put her on the defensive, but it wasn't an act of flirtation or aggression.

"Don't worry; I don't collect such things, and I have no ill intentions towards you."

"Are you a mage, Levinial?" Brylee asked, not ready to drop her guard.

"My friends call me Levi," he said with a disarming smile. "And the answer to that question is somewhat complicated. I'm not a mage in the sense you mean. My magic would be dangerous if I used it here. But I could, like you, draw on those stones." Again, he held his hands up in reassurance. "That would make my magic safer, but I have no intention of doing so."

Brylee bit back a retort to the effect that if he drew on her stones, it wouldn't be safer for him because she would gut him. She warned herself he could be lying, but she sensed he was being sincere. She let herself relax somewhat. When she realised she was gazing into his eyes, she shook her head.

"Levi," she said, choosing her words carefully, not wishing to lie more than necessary, "You can call me Senna, and if you're inferring I'm a mage, I don't claim to be one."

"That doesn't surprise me, as I will explain. I have some sense of the tensions between the common folk, charmers, and mages. Is that the correct terminology for magic wielders?"

"Where are you from?"

"Not from anywhere you will have heard of." He chuckled and shook his head. The warmth in his laugh and the way his eyes sparkled and lips twitched stoked her fires once more. "But I've travelled extensively and pick up languages quickly, although I often find myself confused by small idioms and nuances."

As they passed a bakery, the smells took their small talk to the subject of the various artisans and storefronts they passed. They were so wrapped up in that subject that they failed to notice that several people, including Gideon, took turns following them as they walked. None were close enough to overhear their discussion, but the ease at which they followed would have disgusted Winter had he seen Brylee's complete abandonment of the skills he had taught her just because she had met a pretty boy.

"Here we are," Brylee said as they reached the gate. A nod to the guards allowed them to enter. Brylee led Levi down the side of the house towards the kitchen.

Get in there after her, Tuli urged Gideon.

Following a brief conversation with two of his mercenaries, Gideon went to stand near the guards, where he knelt to adjust his boot. On the far side of the street, his two men began to argue. The argument quickly escalated into pushing and shoving, drawing the guards' attention and causing them to step away from the gate to watch. It wasn't as far as Gideon would have liked, and he had to slip back through time eight times before he managed to sneak past them and into the shadows of the tall walls.

Gideon let himself into the house through the unlocked double doors of a bathing room, his attention drawn to the clever arrangement of taps as he thought about how he could put them to use in the several small hospitals he had anonymously sponsored.

He encountered no one as he crept down corridors, but each time a floorboard creaked, he slipped back a few seconds to change where his feet fell. He approached a room where he could hear Brylee and the time weaver's voices as she introduced him to another man. He stepped into the adjacent room and closed the door behind him. A small amount of hard air in the lock would stop anyone from surprising him.

He walked up to the adjoining wall and examined its construction, determining it was made of wooden studs that supported thin oak panels. He pulled a small couch away from the wall and at a spot that would be hidden when the couch pushed back, used his magic to cut around a panel and remove it, placing it against the wall. He didn't dare repeat the trick and remove the panel in the room next door, but he did make a series of tiny holes just above the floor level, which enabled him to hear every word that was spoken in the next room.

Chapter Fifty-One

Brylee took Levi to Mage Wickham's study. There was something unsettling about the stranger other than his good looks, and she wanted Wickham to be present to handle any trouble. She knocked and then entered, waving Levi in behind her. Wickham was seated at his desk.

"Gil, this is Levinial, and he apparently has an urgent need to talk to me confidentially despite having no idea who I am." Brylee paused to let the oddness of the request register with the ever-suspicious mage. "I was hoping we could use your study and that you would sit in."

The mage started to protest the interruption until he looked around, at which point he stopped mid-sentence, cocked his head to one side, and clamped his mouth shut to prevent what was going through his mind from spilling out thoughtlessly.

"Of course," he said. "Take a seat."

"I'd be pleased if you called me Levi," the time weaver said as he took the offered seat, "and no offence intended, but what I have to share with Senna is for her ears alone."

"Senna is my housekeeper's niece, and I consider her under my protection, Levi." Wickham drew himself up and made his tone more formal. "I'm not sure *what* you are, but you're not what you seem, are you? And until I understand exactly what you are and deem you no threat to her, I'll be staying."

Levi considered his options, wondering if withdrawing and observing developments might be the wiser course after all. He let his energy roam around the office while he thought, feeling a pull from the bookcase. He sensed that hidden behind it were more objects of power, which he associated with primi magic. He realised his eyes had wandered towards the discovery and that Wickham noted his attention being drawn to that spot. He watched the mage gather his magic and erect a barrier that would prevent Levi getting far from the chair in which he was sitting.

"What do you mean when you say you want to find out what he is, Gil?" Brylee asked. "I can feel he's different. He claims to be a type of mage who can't access his power without creating danger."

"I'm not sure," Wickham admitted. "All life has energy, and mages have large quantities of it, but other than scale, a mage's energy has the same quality as everything else's. But Levi's feels different from anything I've ever sensed. Not large in quantity but foreign. I'm hoping he will explain."

"Well, you're right and wrong," Levi said, deciding to take a direct approach. "I'm from somewhere else, which explains why my magic feels different. And if I call upon it here, I can cause the same issue I'm here to prevent. But should I choose to access it, I would become perhaps the greatest mage you have ever met. Not being able to draw on my magic usually makes it hard to get people to take me seriously, but in this case I could make an exception by drawing on the magic of Senna's necklace."

Brylee shared a look with Wickham, then she turned to Levi. "Why do we need to take you seriously, and how does it involve me?"

"Normally I would describe myself as a policeman of sorts, but a ranger I met recently described his role as being present to ensure everyone's safety. That seems more appropriate as a description for me than someone who enforces laws."

"Do you think I've done something wrong?" Brylee asked, worried Levi had somehow linked her back to Haxley.

"No, but you or someone close to you will do something perilous soon, in perhaps a few weeks."

Wickham and Brylee shared another look. They planned to begin the hunt of the Red Assassin in the next few days, and both of them wondered if that was relevant.

"Trust me when I tell you that whatever you do, intentionally or otherwise, could mean the end of this world," Levi continued. "I know that sounds dramatic, but I mean it quite literally. My purpose here is to ensure you don't cause the crisis that is already brewing. I'd like to call myself a time ranger, as that sounds more fun, but the term used by the gods is 'time weaver.' I guess they see us as unknotting their timelines without causing them to unravel."

"I don't believe in prophets or oracles," Wickham said, "and if I'm being honest, most days I doubt there are gods, Levi. What is it that you think Senna will do?"

"I have no idea yet. I wish I had the skill of an oracle. Some who have the old magic, such as Senna here, can see echoes of the future and are the origin of what you think of as oracles, but I don't have that skill. All I know is that a crisis is forming, and it is echoing through Senna here. My work involves becoming familiar enough with current events to predict what will happen and to determine how to prevent the calamity while doing the least amount of damage."

Rosemary chose that moment to appear in the doorway, knocking on the wood frame. She opened her mouth to ask if refreshments were needed, but Levi drew a thread of magic from Brylee's Galei stones and lifted everyone in the room except the housekeeper out of the time flow. To Brylee and Wickham, Rosemary simply froze with one foot in the air, her mouth open mid-sentence.

Levi was impressed at how quickly Wickham tried to access his own magic to defend what he thought was an attack on his housekeeper. The astonished look on the mage's face increased when he realised he could no longer access his magic. Brylee, on the other hand, did produce an effective threat. A knife appeared in her hand, which was now at his throat.

"The woman is in no danger, I assure you," Levi reassured the others. "You were likely about to tell me that time-related magic was impossible, so I took the opportunity to conduct the demonstration I mentioned earlier. I've temporarily lifted the three of us out of your timeline. For your housekeeper, time is continuing, and she will notice no difference. If you put away your knife and take a seat, I will restore matters."

After a pause, Wickham nodded, and the knife vanished as Brylee sat back down. Levi placed them back into the time flow, and Rosemary's step continued.

"Would you like some refreshments?" Rosemary asked, as if nothing had happened.

"I would love a cup of tea and maybe a bite to eat," Levi said, covering the awkward silence as Brylee and Wickham tried to make sense of what they had just experienced. After a long pause, Wickham nodded and said she should set up a full spread in the dining room and to shut the door to the study as she withdrew.

When they were alone once more, Wickham adopted a tone of rebuke, partly to cover his embarrassment, pointing out how it was hard to trust a stranger who claimed not to be able to use his magic there, then plainly did so a moment later.

"Well, I did say I normally had no opportunity to demonstrate who I am," Levi replied with a sheepish look. "In my defence, I didn't use my magic; I used yours. I assume the stones around Senna's neck contain your power. I apologise for taking a small amount without asking, which I said I wouldn't. That is quite rude. The idea just came to me, and I acted."

"Let me recap," Brylee said. "You're a time policeman of sorts, here to stop me ending the world—"

"Or someone connected to you," Levi said.

"Or someone close to me, right. But you have no idea how this is supposed to come about. Earlier you said I have old magic. Could old magic create this crisis you're worried about? I use these stones because I have a paltry amount of magic. So little, in fact, that I don't think I'm the problem you're looking to solve." Brylee realised the amount of indignation that had built up within her was partly because Levi believed she would do something so dumb it would end the world and partly from the embarrassment of not having much magic in the face of these two men who valued it so much. After a lifetime of wishing she had no magic, she was confused as to why she would care, but the situation irked her.

"In nearly all cases I find the cause is someone who has the rare ability to slip up and down the timeline or manipulate time in some manner, which is not typically part of the skills that someone like yourself possesses. But there have been occurrences where primis—that's the term for users of the original magic— have caused rifts in other ways."

Brylee felt somewhat relieved at that but was annoyed that Levi ignored her claim about her meagre powers. *Why does what he thinks matter to me at all?* she wondered.

"Again, Levi, I have almost no magic compared to a mage," Brylee said. "I can do small things on my own, but without the Galei stones, I'm next to useless."

Levi sighed in frustration at Brylee's naivety and lack of respect for his wisdom. "Senna, not only can you draw power without the stones, you're also probably the only person in this world who could create Galei stones. You wouldn't be the first person I've had to prevent from destroying their world due to ignorance."

Brylee sucked in her breath and stood up, crossing her arms. "You accost me in the street, ask me to speak with you privately, then call me ignorant?" Brylee's outburst elicited several emotions in Levi. It shocked him how her fierceness caused a physical response within him that he did not recognise. It combined with his exasperation that she was twisting his words and beating him with them. He found himself on his feet too.

"Now, look," Wickham said, his sharp tone drawing their attention to him. "Senna, sit. What Levi undoubtedly meant is there are powers that he has knowledge of and we do not. So we're ignorant of them not because we're stupid but due to lack of opportunity to learn, which I hope Levi will rectify if we give him the chance." He was right, of course, but her emotions were screaming about him siding with . . . with . . . this hunk of sexiness.

Get a grip, she told both parts of herself in much the same tone that Wickham had used on her.

"Levi, please sit too," the mage said in a slightly less chiding tone. "Perhaps our meeting will be more productive if you explain how you think we should proceed from here."

Levi shook his head at his own reaction, wondering how this woman could have such an effect on him. "Look, I'm sorry if my choice of words was poor. If I had never learned that striking a flint against dry wood could start a blaze, and I accidently created such a delightful spark, why would I not keep making sparks?" He was relieved when Brylee offered a somewhat reluctant nod of acceptance, which lowered the room's temperature. "What I need is information," he continued. "We don't know for sure if Senna is the trigger of events, just that she's involved. But if she is the trigger, then disaster might be averted simply by my educating . . . sorry, explaining the benefits and pitfalls of her powers so there are no accidents. Then again, maybe my doing that will cause the issue. You can see how tricky these things are. If you haven't thought about it already, you will, so I'll just say it: if I killed you to terminate your involvement, your death might be the trigger, as you may be destined to prevent the catastrophe.

"When I first arrived here some moons ago, I felt the signature of another salient person. It was faint, and I've lost track of their thread, but they might re-emerge as the person who triggers the crisis.

"It seems that whichever path you take could lead to trouble," Brylee said, feeling silly at her earlier childishness.

"Yes, but that is my role. I've been in this situation more times than you've drawn breath, and I would say most times I've sorted things out before—"

"Most?" Brylee asked, her tone laced with concern and, to her regret, some misplaced, fear-based blame. "What sort of percentage of success do you claim?"

"I can boast far more success than any of the other time weavers. In only a few hundred cases could I not prevent the gods from ending a world." Noticing their shock, he quickly carried on, "But remember, those worlds would have ended without my intervention. Perhaps one in a hundred could not be saved, and of those which continue, perhaps only in one in ten is there a significant upheaval. In all the cases where there has been a negative outcome, lack of information about the circumstances has been a factor. If I can see all the factors, in most cases no one even notices a problem. And in many cases my intervention improves the outcome." Levi tried to suppress the pride he felt recalling some of those occasions but acknowledged part of him wanted Senna's approval.

"That makes sense," Wickham said. "So once again, how should we proceed?"

"One thread is visible to me, and that is Senna's," Levi replied. "We should stay joined at the hip from now on, or at least until other information emerges. And she should do nothing without my permission." He saw Brylee bridle at that. "Permission that will not be unreasonably withheld, of course. Second, I need to seek any others who might be salient. I felt one other, as I said, but it has faded. I must wait for that person to reappear and be ready to react accordingly, especially the closer we get to the crisis point.

"Third, I need to find a man who likes to remain in the shadows. His future is tied to mine due to events in the past, but I can no longer feel his presence. If he still lives, it would be good to know why I can't sense him, and if not, the circumstances of his death may point to events to come. His name is Ostryd van Hyke."

"I can help with the last thread," Wickham said. "I have the means to conduct an exhaustive search across Mordeland if you can provide me with a starting point."

"I'm not comfortable being joined at the hip for weeks," Brylee said before any decisions were made on her behalf. She quieted her inner voice, which wanted nothing more than to grind hips with Levi. "We have a . . . confidential search to begin, Gil."

"That's true, Senna, and I have fresh news about that," Wickham replied. "I've already asked Winter to assemble a small party to accompany us to Yarrow. He will need to hire some mercenaries who are up to the challenge of facing the assassin, and that will take several days. But I want you on the road before the opportunity evaporates. We have reason to believe the person you're searching for will be in Matalon in three weeks. Let's go eat Sage's food. I think more clearly with a full belly, and Levi has dropped a lot on us to process. I'll catch you up about your assignment this evening."

In the next room, Gideon replaced the panel and pushed the drawers back into place before retracing his steps to the street. His mind was racing in response to what he had overheard. The time weaver and a mage of Wickham's standing looking into Ostryd would soon lead them to him. He felt the noose begin to tighten.

Go in there and kill them all, Tuli said. *You're not without power yourself, you know. You have the advantage of surprise.* He ignored her, sensing a time weaver, a mage, and Brylee—as well as whatever these primi skills were—would be too much for him to overcome. He needed a plan. Gideon considered taking a sleeping draft, one strong enough to prevent Tuli from taking matters into her own hands while he slept, but first he needed to talk to Lu. If this Winter person was hiring skilled fighters, who better than an ex-Mobi'dern?

Chapter Fifty-Two

The meal was awkward. Levi realised his knowledge of time and primi magic was good leverage to persuade Senna and the mage to collaborate with him. Refusing to answer their many questions until they capitulated frustrated and yet intrigued them. Instead, Levi kept taking the conversation back to the delicious food and what they knew about the cooking methods. This was easy in one sense, as he missed such things in the gods' space, and he was genuinely enthralled. But in another sense, he found maintaining this tactic difficult, as what he wanted was to get closer to this woman, not aggravate her further. But perhaps annoying her would be better for both of them in the long run.

As the meal ended, Levi suggested he return in the morning to allow them time to discuss matters. He also realised he needed time to think. Something about the woman got under his skin. He served a greater purpose and prided himself on keeping on task. Somehow this woman had him confused and emotional. *No one does that to me,* he chided himself. *I have a duty to the gods which . . .* He was about to think his duty was more important than a roll in the sheets but once again, he felt his emotions flare, defending her. *She is more than that.* The mage offered him a room in the house, which Levi declined, but then he sensed the mage was considering using magic to stop him from leaving, so he decided to head that off by offering an olive branch and a welcome distraction.

"We both have our secrets," he began, "and I believe working together will help us both with our respective missions. But we need to build trust, so before I leave, I want to offer two tokens of good faith. I will give you some general insights into primi but not the specifics until we know we can work together. Now you know the term, no doubt you can find out much about it in your libraries."

Wickham looked like he was considering accepting but then he asked what the other token would be.

"I gleaned that there are artefacts of older magic concealed in your study. I'll share what I know of them but not how to create them. Both of these tokens I offer without conditions as the first bricks in a trust bridge that I hope you will build with me."

Brylee was frustrated by Levi's reluctance to trust her, yet part of her knew she was being unreasonable. His unusual phrasing and accent were a constant reminder of the time weaver's alien nature, but she still perceived him as a man first and assumed that, like her father and most men of her acquaintance, his reluctance was shaded with misogyny. Was he being condescending because she was a woman, or was he merely being cautious? For the sake of learning more, she decided to swallow her pride and accept Levi's offer. Wickham acquiesced too. They retired to the study, where the mage opened his secret cupboard and brought the Judge's Crystal and three other items over to the table.

Levi correctly identified the functions of each object and provided enough small nuances about each that Wickham was fascinated and eager to learn more. While examining the artefacts, Levi outlined the reason Brylee was a primi.

"Let me make sure I understand," Brylee said as he finished his explanation and handed the last artefact back to Wickham. "The gods' waste is what we call magic, and as it flows into our world, we disperse it as our life energy or to perform magic. This flow of magic from the source is also the flow of time. Compared to a primi, mages are relatively inefficient consumers and processors of magic—no offence intended, Gil."

"None taken. This is fascinating."

"If I accept that," she continued, "I see I could make something hotter or stronger than a mage, but how does efficiency allow me to make a Judge's Crystal when they can't?"

"That is an excellent question," Levi said. It was a genuine compliment, and he enjoyed how the woman blushed and sat a little taller as a result. "It's about force of will and how the mind works. Belief, you would call it. Because non-primis have evolved to lose the ability to work with raw naether—what you call magic— they have imposed on themselves somewhat artificial limits. With much training they could learn some of the old skills, but because it's hard, they fall back on what they know. They know science. They know things can be hot or cold, hard or soft, light or heavy, and it's simple to visualise the mechanics of these transformations and direct their magic to perform them. It's much harder to visualise how one might change the base nature of something. Over the aeons, this gap in knowledge becomes a certainty in their minds, that magic cannot work that way. This false belief hardens into an obstacle they can't overcome with their minds."

"What does changing the base nature mean?" Brylee asked, her eyebrows crinkled in a way that Levi found delightful.

"Remember, the aggar created this whole world from nothing but naether. He didn't just change wood into iron or water into wine. He took raw magic and created iron and wood from it, along with every other substance. Enough naether can do almost anything in the right hands. Your world doesn't have to be limited by your sense of reality. With proper training, you can imbue crystals like the Judge's Crystal with the ability to bind to their users' minds."

"How?" she asked, both doubtful and excited. Levi was flattered that she was so intrigued.

"The first technique is meditation. A discipline in thinking, specifically to clear extraneous thoughts from your mind. Next you learn how to apply naether through that empty mind. This discipline is important. If you're trying to make a brick and impulsively think of a cake, you might create the cake by mistake. Throw in emotions, distractions, and so on, and you precipitate a crisis and have a visit from your friendly time weaver." He smiled as he made his joke and was relieved that a warm understanding followed the initial look of annoyance at his gentle teasing.

"But these are lessons for people I collaborate with. I'll return tomorrow and we can talk more." Without waiting for their reply, he drew from her Galei stone, lifted himself from their time long enough to walk out to the street, then severed his connection. To Brylee and Wickham, Levi simply vanished into thin air.

When he was outside, he rested against a stone wall, as if its coolness could quiet his racing emotions. His stomach squirmed at the thought that his perspective and grip on the situation wasn't solid. He needed to reassert himself and his confidence. As he walked away, he tried to recall Senna's faults and blemishes, but he found he excused, rationalised, and admired each characteristic he had seen so far.

"Well, this day didn't go as I expected when I woke this morning," Wickham said as he poured a brandy for Brylee and himself. They sat in silence, sipping the fragrant liquor and processing Levi's revelations. Eventually Wickham continued.

"How did your test with Winter go, by the way?"

Brylee walked him through the events at the market. "Do you suppose my ability to change my appearance is an example of old primi magic?" she asked.

Wickham nodded. "What do you think of Levi's proposal to work together?" He had already made up his mind to accept the idea, but he wanted Brylee to get there on her own, seeing as she was the one who would be "joined at the hip" with Levi.

"What about finding the Red Assassin?" Brylee asked. She was confused about it all, and she felt loyal to Wickham, as he had effectively saved her father's life, not to mention her own.

"If we take Levi at his word, and that's a big if, it's a simple decision," Wickham said. "I'm under pressure to find the assassin, yes, but compared to allowing the world to end, the pressure I'm under stems from one individual who is frightened she's next on the assassin's list. She'll die if the world ends, of course. The problem for me is I don't trust that individual at all, and I certainly wouldn't share any information about or from Levi with her. We have to be seen to start our search at least."

"Who is this individual, and why do they think they're a target?" Brylee asked.

"The assassin's first victim was Mage Garrick the Lesser of Yarrow in the first weeks of the year 468. The second was Mage Alleg Ordel in the summer of 469. Vekki was the third. Each was marked with the assassin's signature red dye. It's Alleg's sister, Alleph, who believes she is at risk, and she happens to be the daughter of the head of the Council of Magical Law, hence the pressure on me to use my spy network to locate the assassin."

"But why does she fear she's a target?" Brylee pressed.

"She and the captain of her guard provided a description of the killer. The captain vanished soon after the attack, and Alleph claims she was threatened with promises of retribution for speaking out and for pursuing the matter."

"Claims?" Brylee asked, picking up on the doubt.

"Alleg was, and Alleph is, a lying, cheating opportunist, so any claim she makes would be suspect but this one especially so, as Alleg's skriking occurred in a building that was sealed by guards before anyone could escape. No one matching Alleph's description of her brother's attacker was found."

"That's odd," Brylee said, her curiosity engaged.

"And despite the assassin's warning, Alleph convinced her father to expend significant resources hunting for the assassin. She recently received another letter from the assassin, in red ink, reminding her of the consequences of her actions. She's since tried to call off the search, but she stirred things up so much that every mage in the nation is worried, so the search has a will of its own."

"When we first met," Brylee said, "You stated that your interest in me was partly because you thought the assassin and I might share the rare talent of magically altering our appearance. If Alleph's claim and description of the assassin are true, do you think the assassin was interviewed by the guards but altered their looks?"

"Yes. I admit it's a stretch and that she lied or was mistaken is more likely. Either way, the 'set a poacher to catch a poacher' ploy is not a huge advantage, but it wouldn't be expected. And if the assassin suspected you, a complete change of your appearance might save your life."

"What makes you think the assassin will be in Matalon? Why send me there?"

"Every five years the Council of Magical Law holds a symposium led by the top level of the organisation. It will be in Matalon in two weeks. Alleph must attend with her father. It will be the most secure location outside of the Elect's residence, yet the supposed warning letter threatened her death if the search is not called off before the first day of the event. I'll be there too. The party that Winter is putting together will represent my security detail. You will pose as my administrative aide, looking after my chambers, meals, and so on. Rosemary will accompany us and will carry out that role for you, allowing you to use your talents to sneak around the compound and see if you can pick up the assassin's trail."

"And if we agree that Levi can accompany us? What role will he assume?"

"A new apprentice or maybe an advisor on magical antiquities. There are several options. That won't be an issue."

"Is there any chance Levi is the assassin? His vanishing act just now could be how he escaped the scene of Alleg's murder." Brylee didn't believe her own suggestion seeing as it was at odds with the impression she had of the stranger, but they had to explore every possibility.

Wickham winced. "That hadn't occurred to me. But keeping him close is the best way to handle that potential scenario. In the meantime, I suggest we both learn as much as we can from him. Agreed?"

Brylee's emotions roiled. She found Levi incredibly attractive but annoying too. All this was a distraction from the mission she had vowed to undertake to repay Wickham for saving her father. She was curious about her primi ancestry, but magic hadn't served her well in the last few moons. Did she want more of it? She was torn.

"Listen," Wickham said, sensing her inner turmoil. "You're contracted to me to hunt for the assassin. When that's resolved, you don't have the option to return to your life in Haxley as a charmer. But as a powerful primi-mage, you could probably do whatever you wished." He saw her resistance crumble at the words and a look of hope he hadn't seen before seeped into her eyes.

"Then I think we should plan what we say to Levi over breakfast," Brylee said.

Chapter Fifty-Three

Lu felt Shanna open their mind link. *Tak was less curious today, and Smak less lazy,* the cat sent. *We were able to keep pace and are now hunting mice and rabbits in the scrub atop the ridge, just ahead of you.* Lu smiled, knowing Shanna would feel her smile's warmth.

Lu hadn't met the male Shanna had chosen to father her cubs, but she knew that Shanna thought him lazy and that her boy-cub had inherited that trait. She found him hard to move after a meal, a little too fond of sleep, especially when the sun was warm. Tak, by contrast, was always busy. More inclined to play games with the quarry than kill it or while away the best hunting hours investigating her prey's warren, intent on understanding the world. Motivating her small pride to travel for fifteen hours each day to match Winter's demanding schedule proved difficult for Shanna.

Lu had offered Shanna the choice of accompanying her on her latest mission for Gideon or to take her pride back to Troll Lake. The cat surprised her by opting for the former. Shanna had explained that with Smak close to reaching sexual maturity, he would soon need to leave the pride. If he didn't find a mate or show the desire to take up the nomadic life of a male, the time was fast approaching where Shanna would have to drive him away. Tak would want cubs, and Smak might see them as a threat. Yarrow was good territory for their kind, which increased the chance that Smak would wander across a female who would capture his interest and make the natural transition less painful. Lu felt for Shanna, as not only would she lose her son to the wild ways, but their disgrace at the HAC also prevented her from offering her cubs to the Mobi'dern as prida candidates.

They had struck out from Rostal four days earlier and spent three of those days on the well-maintained roads that stretched east towards Nuulan, stopping each night at inns that were used to catering to intercity travellers. That morning their route split off the main road and into Leppary Forest. They had spent the whole day beneath its thick canopy, which blocked much of the sun's light but little of the rain that had come down in waves throughout the day.

Winter's group of travellers consisted of Mage Wickham and his advisor, Levi; his staff Rosemary and Senna; Winter's apprentice, Sirius; and six mercenaries, including Lu. Winter put

Sirius in charge of the mercenaries, but Lu's experience and prowess in the fighting arts led to her being designated as his second.

Since the HAC tragedy, Lu hid her exile from the Mobi'dern from strangers so as not to reignite suspicions among the Bredden clerics. During her interview with Winter, Lu had bested him and Sirius in hand-to-hand combat and weapons trials, only exposing her Mobi'dern fighting style on one occasion, which she explained away as a trick picked up from working alongside the fabled warriors on an assignment. Shanna kept well out of sight, and Lu kept the sword that Brightstone had given her hidden in the travel pack that Ostryd had provided, keeping a lesser blade at her side for appearances.

With other leaders, being a deputy might have meant Lu would do all the hard work, but Sirius proved to be a fair boss, and she admired him for taking on at least as much as he gave her. He admitted he wanted to learn the fighting arts from her and scheduled sparring sessions as time allowed. She felt Shanna's amusement across the link and realised the cat was reacting to her own recalling of the previous night's sweaty wrestling session with Sirius, which she hadn't minded in the least, letting it go on longer—and become physically closer—than was necessary.

The day's rain, dripping relentlessly through the trees, had made the track slippery and slowed their progress. After a moon of dry spring weather, the rain brought out a deep, earthy scent and kept away the insects, which on balance was a blessing. The delay meant that when dusk fell, they were still two hours from the inn where they had planned to stay overnight. Rather than risk a horse turning an ankle on the slick path, Winter directed the group to make camp. They pulled fifty yards off the track and found a well-used clearing. In no time they had collected wood and started a fire. Soon the meaty smell of one of Rosemary's stews was working on their saliva glands as they strung lightweight canvas across tree limbs to keep away the worst of the deluge.

Gideon has camped here, Shanna sent, accompanying her words with a mental image of the location. The man wanted a report each night, even though there was little to tell other than they were headed to Matalon, and he didn't appreciate how hard it was to slip away from the group. He was particularly interested in Levi and Senna and requested that she befriend both of them but did not explain why. Although the pair had apparently just met before the mission, Lu observed an obvious chemistry between them.

For the four days since leaving Rostal, most of the trail allowed them to ride two abreast. Levi spent his time either with the mage or with Senna in conversations too quiet for the others to overhear. It provided little time for Lu to get to know the man one on one. They had fallen into a routine each night where, after a brief meal and use of the baths if a village boasted them, Wickham and Levi would stay up in one of their rooms talking late into the night, and Senna would attend to them, providing what refreshments or other things they required. All three would be exhausted the following morning.

After Senna and Rosemary passed around stew, cheese, and a heel of bread each, Levi and Senna settled their bedrolls near each other and talked quietly. The mage quickly fell asleep. Although Lu had learned almost nothing about Levi, she had taken the opportunity to ride with Senna when Levi rode with the mage. An easy, natural camaraderie had sprung up between the only two young women in the group, yet Lu still found Senna to be a puzzle. It was rare to see a household worker so comfortable on horseback and so uneasy about making and serving food. Her hands had neither the rough calluses to match the farming stock she moved like nor those of someone used to washing dishes and clothing or polishing and cleaning. Lu found herself warming to the woman, nonetheless, and she put it down to Senna's openness, curious nature, and confidence. So far, she had allowed herself to be gently rebuffed when enquiring about what Senna heard Levi and Wickham discuss in those late-night meetings.

Sirius took the first watch, so Lu pulled out her cleaning bag and declared she was going to wash at the narrow river just visible through the trees. She walked until she was out of sight of the camp before shouldering her bag and breaking into a loping run. Six minutes later, Tak and Smak leapt out in a mock ambush, smothering her playfully before their mother crept out from the bushes and joined the fun. The greetings complete, Shanna led Lu to Gideon's camp.

Lu interrupted a meeting between Gideon and a man she hadn't seen before. She eavesdropped as she approached, learning that the man had been dispatched to the southern border to locate a cavern. Apparently he had some success, because Gideon was delighted but tamped down his joy when he sensed her arrival.

Lu gave Gideon a brief report. As had happened on a small number of previous occasions, Lu noticed that Gideon moved and spoke with some of the mannerisms of her old friend, Tuli, his sister. Sometimes it was like he was recalling her, but other times it was so pronounced it made shivers run up Lu's spine. He asked a few basic questions, then sent her back to Wickham's camp. She walked back into the treeline and communed with her cats for a few minutes. Then with a last rub of Shanna's ears, Lu trotted back to the river, washed up, and strolled back into her own camp and went to sleep.

Since their initial discussion, Brylee felt Levi had been aloof and cool towards her. She found it something of a relief, although part of her resented it. She had been worried when Levi first mentioned that the key to unlocking the supposed magic within her was meditation. He had a way of unsettling her, which didn't help her focus. She had imagined long moons of silent soul searching that required a patience she did not possess. She would prefer to throw herself headlong into trying, no matter the risks. She was relieved when the time weaver explained that as most magic was the work of mere moments, it was the ability to become hyper-focussed for just a few seconds that was critical for most tasks. That, she knew, she could master quickly enough.

In exchange for being joined at the hip until the temporal crisis, Levi had agreed to train Brylee to use her talents safely. "Good magic hygiene," he called it. After the crisis was resolved, he would stay as long as required to ensure she would not be a menace, but she would have to develop the full breadth of her skills on her own from that point onwards.

Each evening and when riding on easier trails during the day, Levi drilled Brylee in various tasks of mental discipline. He had her think through various mundane tasks in extreme detail, such as how to clean and sharpen a blade, picturing the layers of folded steel as they narrowed to the edge, where the edge was sharpest or nicked, and how to angle the stone to the blade's edge. He also had her focus on how to scrub a pot, including how to shape the rag just so to get into each crevice and turn it in the light and scour it for any last blemish. She pictured each item's curve, stain, and scratch, its smell, the glint of light, and the sound of each action.

At the same time, with her consent, he drew magic from the Galei stones and entered her mind, where he initially monitored and chastised her when her thoughts wandered or if she tried to shorten the task to avoid boredom. As she developed more discipline, he introduced more and more distracting thoughts, which she gradually learned to ignore.

As they lay on their bedrolls, Brylee sweating as she concentrated on the mental task that Levi had demanded, which included cleaning her horse's hoof of every imaginary molecule of mud, the time weaver was lost in her beauty. He had initially suppressed the irrational attraction he felt that first day in the market, but the more time he spent with her, the more she infected him. Part of him was annoyed by it. He didn't know how she had got under his skin, but she was burrowing deeper. Another part of him sulked when she rode with Lu or Rosemary, worried about what she thought of him, or sought her if she was out of sight. That part of him had blossomed with each interaction until his duty was a distant whisper.

Back at Wickham's manor, he had thought Senna physically attractive and was surprised how much he was drawn to her. When he witnessed the transformation from her disguise to her natural self—a different face, body shape, and expressions—his desire didn't change one iota. That was his first clue. It was her spirit that was calling him, not just her body. As he discovered her mind, her values, and drives, how her soul embracing naether made a music so similar to his own, he knew it was not a simple crush. They were spirit mates. *Crap,* he thought. *This is a problem.*

The realisation that he was lying next to his spirit mate panicked him, so he escaped back into the task of testing her concentration. He plucked a memory from her mind from two days earlier of an accidental sighting of Winter, bare to the waist, washing in the communal bathing trough, the sun glistening on his skin and the dawn light highlighting his muscles. He changed the memory so the man's leggings were lower than they had been, revealing more of his flat, muscular belly as he turned to scoop more water. The top half of his buttocks was now visible. He pressed the memory into Brylee's consciousness. *Why am I showing her another man's attractions?* he wondered.

"You asshole," she whispered through gritted teeth. He had to admit, she kept enough of her focus on her task, and her concentration didn't waver. He also noted that she didn't have the expected excited and embarrassed response to the image, which pleased yet puzzled him. Was she not attracted to Winter? Did she like Levi? Or she was not attracted to men at all? If they truly were spirit mates, she would be attracted to Levi. Did he want that? He lay there attempting to make sense of things while she finished her practice.

When Brylee had mentally removed the last fleck of dirt from the image of the hoof she held tightly in her mind's eye, she put down the dirty cloth amongst the pile of mud scrapings below the imaginary horse. She inspected her work from every angle. She gave the hoof one last brush with an imaginary finger, then let the vision fade from her mind and relaxed onto her bedroll. She became aware of the cooling sweat on her body, the sound of raindrops dripping from the leaves around her onto the forest's mulch, and Levi's scent and steady breathing. *Why did he show me that particular image?* she wondered with annoyance.

When setting up the rules for her training, Brylee had baulked at giving Levi full access into her thoughts, partly because of some embarrassing ones about the time weaver himself. She had never reacted to a man as she had to him. She was physically attracted to him, as she had been to other men, but she was also drawn to him, craving his company. With the whirlwind of recent events, she hadn't had time to decide what to do about it. There was no point in pursuing anything meaningful with a man who would leave the world in a matter of weeks and who might have to kill her to save everyone else. Yet a quick roll in the hay didn't feel right either.

In one of their first lessons together, Levi explained that she could close off parts of her mind and certain memories, then showed her how to do it. She hid her feelings for him there, along with the pain of her brother's passing, her panicked fear of her near skriking, and the secret parts of her that she didn't want him to see.

Brylee glanced across the small space between their bedrolls and noticed how the firelight reflected in his eyes. Masculinity, mystery, intelligence, kindness, and a tough purposefulness. She hid how her mind and body reacted to him in her memory vault.

Levi could sense the chemistry building between them even though he looked away from the woman beside him, who was holding his full attention just by breathing. *We need a distraction,* he thought.

"Sorry about that picture," he whispered. "It was a poor test. I think you're ready to try some simple primi magic."

Brylee was gripped by excitement and dread. What if she caused a crisis? What if she couldn't perform magic? What if she could?

"You already do primi magic, Senna," Levi said, sensing her concerns. "What do you think changing your own appearance is? Admittedly, your technique is terrible, but—"

"Terrible?" Brylee said with a disgruntled tone, almost loud enough to be heard by those nearby. Levi reached out a hand to reassure her, surprised yet again at his poor choice of words but also tickled at how sensitive she was.

"I meant untrained, of course, but brilliant given you had no one to learn from. Sorry, poor choice of words. I've just relearnt your language. Could you cut me some slack?"

Brylee was barely listening to him, instead picking over her own emotions. Why was what he thought so important?

"No, sorry. My fault," she said, letting out a long breath. "You were about to teach me some magic."

"I was, but I think we just proved we're both a little tired and emotional. Let's pick this up at the inn tomorrow, where we can have more privacy."

He pulled his cloak over his shoulders and turned his back to Brylee, ending the conversation. Incensed yet relieved, Brylee lay staring up at the canopy of trees, her mind in turmoil until fatigue claimed her and she drifted into a disturbed and uncomfortable sleep.

Chapter Fifty-Four

Brylee whirled towards the sound of a twig snapping, nearly losing her footing on the slimy rocks in the riverbed. She covered her nakedness with her hands and sank low into the water.

"I'm sorry," Lu said, emerging from the trees and gesturing towards the grey, sluggish water. "Do you mind? The men are all at the other spot, and Winter wants to leave soon to make up the time lost yesterday." Brylee's mind was so occupied with Levi that she hadn't heard the mercenary approach. She relaxed and began working some soap into her hair.

"No, of course," she said with an awkward laugh. "I was startled, is all."

"I should have made more noise," Lu said while thinking the opposite. She had all but stamped on that twig to get Senna's attention after the rustling of bushes and stomping of feet had failed to herald her approach.

Brylee looked away as Lu casually undressed without a care about her nakedness in front of another woman. Lu was still wading into the water when Brylee glanced back. She was astonished at the depth and solidity of the mercenary's wiry muscles and thought Lu looked like a goddess with her black hair let down. The mercenary had a womanly grace that she hid when among the men while dressed in her fighting leathers.

Realising she was staring, Brylee dunked her head under the chilly water. She came up for air and combed her fingers through her hair to ensure the soap was rinsed out.

They finished their cleansing in quiet companionship and emerged together onto the rock where their clothes were warming in the morning sun.

"I would ask for some fighting tips," Brylee said, "but you seem to have your schedule full sparring with Sirius."

Lu laughed. "It's fun to keep throwing him down on his back. At least he's past the stage of trying to go easy on me because I'm a woman. Maybe I'll let him win a few to keep him interested. But you and Levi are a strange couple." She stopped at the look of consternation on Brylee's face.

"We're not a couple," Brylee said.

"Sorry, I know you said you only met him a week ago, but the air sizzles when you two are deep in whatever it is you two talk about all day," Lu replied.

Brylee's heart dropped for a moment thinking Lu meant the air sizzled with magic. Then blood rushed to her cheeks when she realised what the mercenary was inferring.

"He's a little intense for me," Lu continued. "I like my men to be more . . . unrestrained."

"If I'm honest, so do I," Brylee replied. "Normally I go for the competent woodsman or farmhand type. They need brains to catch my interest, don't get me wrong, but focussed on horses, growing crops . . . you know, nature. Not on my mind, if you know what I mean." Brylee didn't quite understand why she was being so open with Lu, but she welcomed some feminine interaction, realising how much she had been missing Raegan.

"Don't we spend our lives trying to get men to look at us for our minds and not our tits?" Lu said with a laugh, feeling guilty at deliberately being vulgar in an effort to manipulate Senna into opening up, as Gideon had requested. She didn't quite convince herself that her genuine liking for the woman would have resulted in her asking similar questions. "Is that your background? Farming?"

Brylee's heart skipped again, wondering if she had said something to undermine her cover story of being Rosemary's niece and assistant.   "What do you mean?"

"I don't really mean anything, Senna. Just girl talk," Lu said, unsure if she was pushing too hard. She wasn't used to this sort of work and was unsettled by it. *Give me a foe with a sword any day,* she thought. She decided to press a little more anyway. "You just don't seem like the serving woman type. You ride so well, are comfortable sleeping under the stars, you seem pretty handy with that sword, and you're so strong, you look like you should carry furniture for a living, not clean it."

Brylee was shocked at how easily her disguise was undone. The Red Assassin would see her coming from a mile away.

"I grew up on a farm in southern Lanthe," Brylee said a little too quickly, eager to bring her tale back to the story that she and Wickham had concocted, which was mostly true, with key elements that would identify her as Brylee Plainhand replaced. "Mostly crops and stable work. My aunt took me in when the farm was sold and I had nowhere to go. The mage lets me help with his horses, and I've taken over growing some of the plants he uses in his magic."

"I wondered," Lu said, nodding. "But you don't have the calluses a farm girl would have either."

Brylee silently kicked herself. She had used her magic to remove her calluses when she took on the disguise of a maid, but clearly she hadn't thought it through. She drew on the Galei stones and formed slight calluses but kept the skin colour unchanged instead of the lighter shade of a natural callus. Then she held out her hand.

"Oh, I do, look. They're hard to see due to my skin tone. I have oily skin, so mine are softer and less obvious than most of the farm girls. I've always thought it's a blessing."

Lu inspected Brylee's hand, unsure what to make of the calluses that she would have sworn hadn't been there when Senna offered her bread at dinner the previous evening. Her reflection was disrupted by an urgent thought from Shanna.

Four men who smell like soldiers are approaching your camp. Should I hunt them? The cat sent images of the four riders in leathers, with swords and longbows. They were either mercenaries or bandits.

No, she replied. *Stay hidden but close in case I need you. Protect the cubs.*

For Senna's benefit, Lu made a show of pretending to listen to the rustling of the trees, looking around as if noticing a disturbance.

"The hairs on my neck just stood up," Lu said. "I have a bad feeling. Let's get back to camp."

Brylee listened as she peered into the bushes, but she couldn't detect anything. She followed Lu nonetheless.

At the campsite Lu approached Sirius while buckling on her sword belt and explained she had heard movement through the trees to the south. Sirius issued orders to rearrange the mercenary team into a protective ring around Wickham, Rosemary, and Levi. He was surprised to see Senna had drawn her sword and looked like she was going to join the defence.

"Rosemary, have your niece come stand with us," Wickham ordered, subtly reminding Brylee of the role she was supposed to be playing. She sheathed her sword and joined the inner group but stood between Rosemary and the threat.

With a hiss, an arrow flew out of the trees and buried itself in the thigh of the mercenary to Lu's left. Two more thunked into a tree to her right as she ducked. Two more slapped through the leaves of a bush near Wickham. The mage took two steps forward and threw up a wall of hard air. Several more arrows clattered into it, falling harmlessly to the ground. There was silence for a few moments, followed by the sound of horses racing away into the forest. The attack was over in a dozen heartbeats.

Rosemary ran to the injured mercenary, who had collapsed to the ground, grasping his leg and crying out in pain. She removed her scarf and used it to staunch the bleeding. Wickham strode over and inspected the wound.

"It's in his muscle," he said. "I don't think any bones are broken, and it missed the artery." He used his magic to cauterise the blood vessels. "Give him some poppyroot to numb the pain. He'll be OK if we can get him to a healer." Rosemary went to her horse to fetch the prescribed herb.

"Bandits?" Winter asked. "Odd they would attack a well-armed group such as ours."

"I assume they fled once I put up the barrier and they realised I'm a mage," Wickham replied. "I'm just sorry I didn't shield us immediately. I've never been attacked so blatantly before, and I was taken aback."

"There was a healer in Theeze, the last village we stopped at," Sirius said. "I don't think we'll see another for two more days on our route to Matalon. Should we go back?"

After a brief discussion, Winter dispatched one of the other mercenaries to escort the injured man back to Theeze while they pressed on to the mages' meeting.

As they broke camp, Rosemary whispered to Wickham and Brylee that Levi was as white as a ghost and hadn't spoken since the attack. They went over to find he was recovering from the shock of the attack and the ensuing bloodshed. Levi let them believe that he had been frightened by the raid. He couldn't tell them he was terrified because he had been moments away from reaching out to his own natural magic source to kill the attackers and protect the group, particularly Senna. His incompatible magic would have caused untold chaos.

Winter took Lu to inspect the section of trees that the attack had hailed from, and they soon discovered the tracks of horses and other signs of the raiding party. Winter postulated that perhaps there were three to five riders. Lu knew from Shanna's reports that there were four, who had galloped towards the sun after the attack, but she kept that information to herself.

Back at camp there was a brief discussion about pursuing their attackers, but Wickham quashed the idea.

"An attack and withdrawal against a larger, well-armed group might be designed to draw off some of our number and whittle down our defences while others attack from our flank," he argued. None of the group believed it was simply a group of bandits who fled when they realised they had inadvertently attacked a mage. The party mounted their horses, returned to the trail, and took up a brisk trot, determined to make up for time lost the previous day. Winter rode with Wickham and Levi with Brylee. Lu rode point, and Sirius was rear-guard behind Rosemary and the remaining mercenaries.

"During the attack did you notice anything odd about the attackers with your magical senses?" Levi asked Brylee once they had settled into the rhythm of the ride.

"I didn't even see them," she replied.

"But you could see their aura, no?" he pressed, recalling that Brylee had shared how she had become aware of her own aura and how she had learned how to control her shine shadow.

"I see auras as the glow that people emit from their skin," she said. "I couldn't see any skin."

It struck Levi that she was unaware of the links people had back to the source. He explained it to her, but despite fifteen minutes of concentration, she couldn't catch a glimpse of her own link. Levi realised that although the population of most worlds remained adept at seeing energy links, some worlds lost the skill, and this was one of them. How could he have forgotten? He recalled reading such a note in the codex.

"May I use your Galei stones to open your mind and help you see it? It's harmless and painless," he assured her in response to her concerned reaction. "But the effort will drain most of the power from the stones. Gil will need to replenish them before I can teach you more." After a long, thoughtful pause, she nodded. "This will also make you more able to access other primi skills as your needs develop," he added.

Brylee sensed the necklace heat up as Levi drew on the stones' power. She also felt unnatural sensations at the base of her skull, but they were not painful. After a moment the world about her lit up so brightly she yanked her mount's reins and pulled up short, causing the riders behind her to scatter to the side of the trail to avoid a collision. Everyone at the rear of the party drew their swords in anticipation of another attack. Twigs and leaves rained down as the hard air barrier that Wickham threw up around the group sliced through several small tree limbs.

"I'm OK," she said when she realised what her abrupt halt had done. "I . . . I just felt a little lightheaded," she added to cover her embarrassment. "It's passed. Let's carry on."

"Drink some water," Levi said, offering his own water skin. She took it despite having her own, aware of how intimate his gesture felt. After taking a sip, she handed it back, thanked him, then kicked her mount into a trot, marvelling at the world around her once more. Every living thing was brighter and sharper than she had ever known, and each living thing had an internal glow and a thread leading off to what she initially thought was the sky but quickly realised was to somewhere else. Somewhere "other," where they joined together in a massive river.

"What did you do? Did you create this?" she whispered in awe.

"It's been there forever," Levi said. "I just helped you to see it. This is the energy of life. Look at the ground."

Brylee did and realised it remained dark, except for where shoots of new growth emerged. "Now look at Lu. See how her link is full and strong and feeds the bloom of energy within her? Where that bloom manifests at the outer edge of her being, her skin, is the aura you could see. Look at Gil's, how his has a dark film around it, his 'shine shadow,' as you call it."

Brylee looked at each person in the group, noting their similarities and differences. Wickham's link was as thick as her wrist, whereas everyone else's was thin, the girth of her little finger. Levi's was even thicker than Wickham's, but it was a different shade, and it didn't connect to the source, vanishing into the distance instead.

"You see how both of our links thrum? A small vibration?" Levi asked.

"Yes, what is that?"

"It's the turbulence I am here to investigate. That's how I identified you as being linked to the crisis ahead. You and I are both affected by it, but that is normal for me, as I'm here to rectify things."

"Amazing," Brylee said, her head swivelling around as she attempted to take everything in.

"I could see the aura and the links of the four attackers," Levi said. "One of their number's link tremored too. It stopped at the moment that arrow struck our mercenary. Then his aura returned to normal."

"What does that mean?" Brylee asked.

"I think it means the mercenary's injury was a stepping stone to the future crisis. Somehow it relates, part of the chain of events. My investigations contain many such clues, but they are tricky to piece together. I'll share this discovery with Wickham later today."

It was a long, arduous day. With the Galei stones drained, Levi couldn't supervise Brylee's training and said she needed time to let her mind acclimatise to the new information. She was distracted by every tree, squirrel, and bird as he answered many questions during the journey.

By mid-morning they reached the village they had fallen short of the previous day. It was nestled at the base of a mountain pass. After a brief stop to replenish their supplies, they began a steep climb. Although the air was cool, the sun beating on their backs was fierce. Soon the steep, rough terrain forced them to dismount, and no one but Lu had breath to discuss matters. They reached the mountain village of Shepherd's Nook at twilight, feeling sweaty, tired, and hungry. After visiting the warm sulphur pools around which the village was built and taking a cold dip in the nearby tarn to wash off the smell of the hot springs, the group tucked into the inn's delicious fare.

Later, as Lu slipped away to rendezvous with Gideon for her daily report, Wickham, Levi, and Brylee met in the mage's room. While Wickham recharged the Galei stones, Levi caught him up on his suspicions about the attack and the changes he had made to Brylee's magical sight. Wickham had heard of such links and their being the basis of auras, but as he had never been able to see them himself, he hadn't given them much credence. After a brief examination, Levi declared that Wickham's lineage meant his mind had evolved so far from its primi beginnings that it would never be possible for him to see the links, even with Levi's help. Wickham hung his head and grunted in disappointment.

"I don't understand," Brylee said. "Gil is so much more powerful than me. Why can't he see them?"

"Being able to channel a greater quantity of magic doesn't mean he can handle magic the same way as you," Levi replied. "Lu can run all day without stopping, whereas Winter is breathless in ten minutes, but he can lift twice as much as her and for a much longer period. They are both strong in their own way."

He studied Wickham's link for a few moments. "I think you call the process of inheriting another's magic 'skriking,' yes?" They both nodded, so Levi continued. "There are three ways to obtain a larger capacity to draw magic from the source than the norm. The first is to assume another's link, either by force or as a gift; that's skriking. The second is to inherit a larger capacity than the norm from your parents. This family disposition may stem from your ancestors skriking to acquire that capacity, which they pass on to their offspring. The third method is to use your magic to increase your link's capacity to feed you with naether."

"We've heard of the first two methods," Wickham said, "although we didn't understand there are actual links. I've never skriked anyone, but those who have shared their experience describe pulling the other's magic away from the person and holding it close until it remains with themselves."

"I'm not surprised," Levi replied. "In this world it seems rare to see the links, and besides, most of what you think you understand is technically wrong or at least incomplete. Our minds represent complex things in ways we can comprehend even if the truth about them is different. As on most worlds, your scholars have made a hard science around what they think they perceive. These models are sufficient for a society to operate, but they only get you so far. And the limitations and omissions built into your models hold you back, as I've said before."

"Can you give us an example?" Wickham asked.

"At camp last night, Rosemary heated water for that delicious tea by making a fire and suspending a pot full of water above it," Levi said. "Similarly, a blacksmith will start a fire in a furnace to heat coals and use that heat to shape metal. But do either of these people really understand fire? They know aspects of it. They know that whatever fuel they use for the fire is consumed. They also know that the volume of air available can affect the fire's heat and colour. But what is fire?"

"I see your point, but how does this hold us back?" Wickham asked.

"You're a mage of some ability, Gil. How would you create fire here and now?"

"Basically, I would choose a fuel, like wood or paper or even certain types of gas, and pour magic into it, picturing fire in my mind until they ignited. How else?"

Levi laughed. "Like this." He drew on the Galei stones and formed a ball of flame in midair. The blaze didn't reach for the ceiling, nor did it smoke. The flames licked around each other in an intricate pattern that formed a sphere. Then he reshaped them into a more traditional fire where the flames reached upward. Then he spun the blaze around so it flickered upside down.

Mesmerised, Brylee plucked a piece of kindling from the stack by the hearth and pushed it into the flames. Nothing happened. "That's a trick," she said. "It can't be real fire because it's not hot."

"You equate fire with heat and expect it to rise," Levi replied. "That's its natural tendency, I agree. It's what it knows to do. But its nature can be overridden. Look." Levi took the kindling from Brylee. As he did, he accidently touched her finger and almost got distracted by the resulting surge of warm emotions. He pushed the stick into the flames as she had, and this time it caught. Enjoying their puzzled faces, he snuffed out the flames as if they had never existed.

"Everything is made from naether, and everything that is created from naether knows how it should behave, its nature imprinted into it as part of the creation process. I call it a thing's attributes. My observation of your world is that most of your magic revolves around pouring energy into the task of making a thing do what it already knows how to do, forcing it to do it faster, slower, or more or less. You heat water to make steam or freeze it to make ice. Water knows how to react when temperature changes its internal energy levels, but you don't try to make water into rock."

"Is that even possible?" Wickham asked. Levi nodded, explaining that it took a great deal of energy to do such things and that a lot of water was required to create a small amount of rock.

"But there are exceptions to how this world behaves with its magic," Levi continued. "Air doesn't know how to harden, for example, and this is a great insight as to how primi magic works. I believe this is because air is invisible and mostly intangible, wind aside that is, so your minds are willing to treat it with more flexible rules. You've been teaching Senna to create hard air. How do you explain it?"

"He has me visualise anchoring it to the ground," Brylee said. "I form that concept in my mind, and pour—or trickle, in my case—magic into how I visualise it."

"How would you do it if you were out at sea, on a boat, where there was no ground?" Levi asked.

Brylee shook her head, perplexed.

"I would use the boat's mast as the anchor," Wickham said.

"And in a bottomless ocean, swimming with no boat or land in sight?" Levi pressed. "Could you create a platform of hard air or water and step up onto it for safety?"

Wickham shook his head. "I couldn't do it. I would drown."

Levi laughed. "But Senna could. With some training, that is. Although when the Galei stones ran dry, she would plop back into the sea, of course."

In Brylee's mind she saw herself as a half-drowned rat. That Levi found this funny annoyed her. She drew herself up, anchored the air near his cup to the table in front of him, and pushed. His tea spilt into his lap. As he yelped, she felt terrible, having forgotten it was so hot.

"Oh, Ag, I'm so sorry. That was stupid," she said as she leant forward to help wipe the worst from his leg, then pulled her hand back when she realised where she was touching him. To her relief he laughed even harder.

"That was very . . . instinctual," Levi mused.

"How can she harden air in such a sea where I could not?" Wickham asked, cross with their childishness when there was such knowledge to be gained.

"The ground knows how to be hard and stationary. So does a ship's mast, at least with respect to a ship's deck. What you think of as an anchoring thought is just your mind's representation of what you're truly doing. You're creating a bridge between ground and air and transferring the knowledge of how to be hard or rigid, which the ground already knows, to the air. When you pour magic into that process, you're forcing the ground's attributes into the air, essentially teaching it how to be hard for the duration you hold the concept in your mind."

"Is that what real magic is?" Brylee asked. "The ability to borrow attributes from one thing and impose them on another."

"Yes, but it's a shortcut. The aggar created everything from naether. He made the original set of blueprints, then mixed and matched them as needed. With magic, you are essentially mixing and matching what he created. But why not create the attributes rather than borrow them? Floating in the bottomless, boatless sea, if you could hold the attributes clear and crisp in your mind, you could impose them on the air or the water without a source or anchor point. Magic is about imposing a set of attributes on naether, the gods' waste product. It doesn't matter where they come from as long as they are crisp and clear. You don't need an anchor; you just need a sharp mind."

Brylee and Wickham met his explanation with a blank stare.

"Think of it like this: naether is like clay and can be formed into anything. Doing magic means releasing energy from the clay that forms the clay into something. What it becomes depends on the attributes imposed on it. These attributes are embedded in the clay when it was formed originally. For example, a leaf is created from naether. The tree draws more naether from the source and feeds it to the leaf, and embedded in the leaf are the attributes of growth. So, as energy is released, the leaf consumes it, puts it to work, and grows. It also knows how to burn if you apply heat, which is also naether. Or you can impose new attributes that override the behaviours inherent to the leaf and turn it into something else entirely. What you call ironwood, by contrast, is wood from which you've removed the knowledge of how to burn, scratch and bend, replacing those attributes with the attributes of metal. It still looks like wood because you didn't think to change the attributes controlling its look and feel because you didn't know you could."

"I partly understand what you mean, Levi," Brylee said, "but again, why can I do things that Gil can't? Are you saying my mind is more flexible or that I'm smarter or sharper than Gil? You keep talking about my mind being more efficient at processing naether. Are you saying I'm better at moulding clay? What are you talking about?"

"On another world I met one of the most powerful primis I've ever encountered," Levi said. "He was a farmer by trade, so maybe your farming background will help your mind assimilate it this way."

"How do you know I have a farming background?" she asked, shocked by his knowledge of her past.

He shrugged. "Your head contains many memories of you farming. Anyway, this farmer realised that to form something from nothing, he had to visualise its attributes in their entirety. He had to imagine its shape, weight, colour, every last aspect of its composition and behaviour. This is why I've had you sharpening your focus through the exercises you've been doing. The farmer likened it to growing turnips."

"Are you saying my brain is a turnip now?" Brylee asked, a mix of humour and anger in her voice, which Levi found unsettling. He placed a steadying hand on his cup.

"Uh, no," he said, wondering if this analogy was wise. However, he plunged forward, unsure where else to go. "The farmer likened each collection of attributes to a turnip. Up close, each turnip is different. If he could visualise all the differences, he could create a turnip from nothing but naether. In fact, he could create one hundred identical turnips. But if he could hold what made each individual turnip different in his mind, he could create one hundred unique turnips, including their ability to pass their differences on through their reproductive cycle. Of course, what he meant is at each spot in the field, if he had the right grasp of a thing's attributes, he could create a potato, a cabbage, a rabbit, a tree, or even a person. A person's attributes are much more complex than a turnip's, of course, but they don't take up any more space."

Brylee's head was spinning. "Are you saying I can imagine more vegetables than Gil? I'm so confused."

Wickham laughed. "No. He's saying you have a bigger field and are a better farmer than me. A better feel for growing things from nothing or mixing cuttings from one thing to make another. Your mind is more fertile soil for this sort of thing. Right, Levi?"

"Correct," Levi said, relieved that Wickham had provided the words to get himself out of the corner into which he had painted himself. "A farmer with a more suitable field. You're not a turnip. Gil can cook turnips. He can borrow the attributes of salt to make it taste better. But he doesn't have the capacity—the field—to store these collections of attributes or the sort of mind to unpack them into different combinations or come up with completely new attributes. By the way, the aggar didn't create Galei stones. Your people created that blueprint by adding new attributes to an existing crystal."

"I'm not sure I understand," Brylee said in exasperation, "but who can teach me to farm turnips if not Gil?"

The joy in Levi's face drained away, replaced with sadness. He felt a stab of hollowness that almost consumed him, and his hand drifted unconsciously to rest over his heart. The others noticed his swift deflation and leaned forward in concern but said nothing.

"Not me, I'm sorry to say," Levi replied. "I would dearly like to, but I have to leave once the crisis is averted. But I hope to teach you how to visualise, unpack, and store the attributes of things and how to impose your will on them before I go. I fear I will never see the beautiful gardens I expect you will make, Senna."

Brylee's throat clenched, astonished and touched as she watched a tear form in Levi's eye and trickle down his cheek. Feeling flushed, she realised her own eyes were brimming in response. She took a gulp of ale to quench the surge of strong emotions that his tenderness had ignited within her.

Levi drew a small, circular, flat stone he had found that morning from his pocket. He gave it a quick polish before handing it over to Brylee. "Your first lesson," he said. "This stone has few impurities, so it has a relatively simple set of attributes. I'll teach you how to interrogate it and then extract and hold its attribute of hardness in your mind. Then we'll throw the stone away, and you'll learn to apply the attribute of hardness from your mind to harden water, air, or anything else you choose."

Chapter Fifty-Five

The village of Shepherd's Nook began life as a deep cleft in the soft chalk cliffs on Mount Gillian where herders sheltered from the worst of the elements. It was tucked away near the centre of the deep plateau that, from afar, looked like a seat cut into the mountainside. Over the centuries a network of tunnels had been carved for the storage of food and for people and livestock to take shelter during the snowiest moons.

One winter, bandits took over the tunnels and began charging the shepherds to shelter there. An odd symbiosis took hold over the following decade. Shepherds bartered for increased comfort, including use of a tavern, a brothel, and a small general store. Centuries later the town had grown from this modest start. The tavern, the Shepherd's Nook Arms, remained almost unchanged, and the tunnel's storage capacity supported the needs of the entire town.

At each overnight location, Lu knew to seek Gideon near the largest warehouse, a commonly known landmark in all villages, and it was there that she found him standing in the shadows. She confirmed that Wickham's itinerary remained unchanged and listed the places they expected to stay overnight. She described the attack on the party, the injuries suffered, and their speculation about the bandits. Gideon listened, but to Lu's practised eye, he didn't seem as shocked or bothered as she expected. His only question was to confirm that neither Senna nor Levi had been injured.

"Any other news?" Gideon asked. Lu had the sense the man was keen to give her some news of his own, but he wanted her to finish first.

"Yes, actually," she replied. "But I'm not sure it's relevant. I overheard Winter and Sirius discussing security arrangements for the mages' event, specifically a threat from someone they referred to as the Red Assassin." She noted Gideon didn't seem too interested in the information, but she completed her report anyway. "I asked Sirius about it later in the day. He seemed put out that I overheard them but explained there was a rumour that one of the Namiduh Jou was targeting someone at the event. That's why we'll be taking extra precautions when the time comes."

"Interesting," Gideon replied, but Lu sensed he didn't find it relevant to the mysterious mission he had asked her to undertake.

"The day after tomorrow, your itinerary has you overnighting at the Farmer's Quest Inn at the Harding Ranch," Gideon continued. "The road that leads to the inn follows the long, narrow Euse Lake for about five miles. Where the road first meets the lake is a fork. The group will turn right for the inn, but I want you to leave the party and take the left fork. This mission hasn't yielded the information I expected, so I'm cutting my losses. Make your excuses before you reach the fork, and we'll break off and head home. If you take the left fork, I'll meet you at the next town. We can circle back to Troll Lake from there."

Lu felt disappointment well up. She was enjoying the journey and getting to know Senna. She hadn't met many women she respected, and she had begun to hope they might become friends. She also really liked Sirius. As they shared their evening meal, she had shocked herself when she realised she had been daydreaming about herself, Shanna, Tak, Smak, Sirius, and . . . the daughter they had. She dreamed that the daughter might share a bond with Tak, as she enjoyed with Shanna. Never before had she had a maternal thought, but something about the man had her dreaming of creating her own family.

"I'm actually enjoying the assignment," she replied. "Why don't I meet you back at Troll Lake later? Shanna wants Tak to explore Yarrow anyway, perhaps find a mate for himself. You go. I'll catch up to you at some point."

Gideon was surprised by Lu's refusal to go along with his plans, but it wasn't the first time. The woman had a mind of her own, which could be annoying at times. *I told you we should have sent her packing years ago,* Tuli whispered, but Gideon ignored his sister. Instead, he slipped back through time to the point where he had just explained the fork in the road and replaced the words he had first used to explain why she should separate from the group at that point.

"It's essential you leave the party at the fork," Gideon said, his tone insistent. "My plans have changed, and we must head north, I need you with me."

Lu had no awareness of Gideon's manipulation of time, but her feelings and reply were much the same. Gideon thought hard, then had an idea. He slipped back to the same spot and made another attempt.

"The next town down that fork is Le Faette. My network heard that an old friend of yours will be there. Da-Jeef, your Mobi'dern leader from the HAC, is using it as a meeting point to gather one hundred warriors who have been tasked with protecting the mages' meeting. You've helped me so much, so why not slip away for a night and see if you can convince Da-Jeef to look at Tak and Smak as potential pridas? I know it's a long shot. She doesn't have to tell anyone they're associated with Shanna, does she?"

"I'm not sure," Lu replied. Motivated by helping Shanna and her cubs, her mind was already creating excuses to give Sirius as to why she wanted a night off. "I'll tell Sirius I know some potential replacements for the mercenaries we lost who live in Le Faette. I'm sure if I vouch for them, he'll agree to consider them. I can rendezvous with Wickham the next morning and explain that my contacts were not available." After confirming some more logistics, Lu melted back into the night to meet with Shanna just outside of town.

Gideon remained hidden in the darkness by the cleft and ran through his plans to ambush the time weaver's party. His action that morning had removed two of their defenders. Now that Lu would be out of the way, success would depend on surprise and his ability to separate the time weaver from Wickham. He needed the mage dead first, and if he could kill the time weaver, he could take the time weaver's amulet. It would admit him to the aggar's cavern. Once inside, Gideon believed he could find the time-travel amulet the time weaver used. If he could learn to activate that, he could go back and save Tuli. He waited for her to weigh in on his plan, but she was unusually silent.

Chapter Fifty-Six

Winter and Rosemary had risen early and picked through Shepherd's Nook's marketplace for fresh provisions. They ate their fill as they shopped while the rest of their party breakfasted on the buffet provided by the inn. Afterwards, the group roused the horses from the warm stables and saddled them for the next leg of their journey. They all met outside the baker's shop, where their haul was distributed across the group's saddlebags. As they trotted out of the village, clattering over the stone bridge that spanned the stream they would follow down the eastern slope of the mountains, Rosemary fell into step beside Brylee. Brylee had hoped to ride alongside Levi, partly to discuss her overnight magical progress, but more because she felt increasingly drawn to the man and craved his companionship.

As Rosemary shared what she had seen in the market, Brylee tuned her out so she could practise what she had learnt from Levi. He had explained that her mind would probably adapt quickly to seeing links and auras and had predicted that by morning she would be able to switch her vision from seeing such things to ignoring them. It was dazzling and distracting to see the complex webs of links. She had two types of vision now: her normal vision and her magical sight. Her mind could superimpose the latter on the former and, with practice, she would be able to switch her magical sight on and off at will. Once she gained that ability, she would be able to see magical elements when her eyes were closed. Levi's prediction proved correct, and Brylee spent the first few miles of the journey practising this new ability.

By midmorning Brylee felt she had enough of a grip on her magical sight to experiment with the next phase that Levi had explained. She was to pick an object and focus on it until she could see every intricate detail and then press in further until the vision blurred into perceiving the components that made up the object.

At the top of her mount's halter was a metal stud that she used as the object of her attention. It took no more than a few moments to realise she wasn't ready to try while bouncing along on the back of a horse. She felt dizzy to the point she almost fell. Levi spurred his horse, and in a few strides he was at her elbow, steadying her. She was touched but embarrassed, her emotions in turmoil.

They paused for an hour at noon, during which Brylee sat on a rock and tried again. The nausea returned as she zoomed in on the rock but was nowhere near as severe as when riding. She felt like she was just beginning to make progress when Winter called for them to mount up for the next leg. Time had sped by, and she had forgotten to eat. She pulled some dried meat and bread for herself and an apple for her horse from her bag. Then she swung up into her saddle and nudged her horse sideways until they fell in step with Levi as the party moved out.

Brylee shared an account of her successes and failures with Levi, who advised patience, though he was clearly impressed by her progress. She felt like a schoolgirl being praised by a teacher she had a crush on. This realisation brought her back to an idea she had been wrestling with overnight instead of sleeping or practising her magic. She knew she was dangerously drawn to Levi. In her limited experience with such emotions, she had preferred the direct approach. "A romp in the hay," as Raegan always referred to it. Her impetuous side wanted that with Levi but was held back by a new part of her psyche, which thought Levi might be "the one." That part of Brylee insisted she slow down and let the relationship develop. As her two selves argued, she realised the clock was ticking. Levi intended to leave in the next few weeks, although it appeared he would do so with some regret.

Brylee's emotions were in knots over Levi until she was struck by an idea. She planned to share it with him after that night's lesson, but she remembered how Levi had rolled over and escaped to sleep in the rainy forest when emotions ran high. She decided to put it to him there on the trail instead where she would be difficult to avoid. She took perhaps the deepest breath of her life and dove in.

"Levi, I'm going to be blunt. I wouldn't normally be so direct, but, well, that is . . . I would, I guess. Raegan is always telling me I hate to chicken out of . . . well, what I mean to ask is . . ." Her feeble attempt petered out. She felt completely out of her depth. She reminded herself how much she hated emotions. Despite her turmoil, Levi gave her an encouraging smile.

"Go on," he prompted.

"It's just that . . ." She stopped again. Was this really the time? What if he thought she was needy and weak? Or that she was reading too much into how he was responding to her?

"Senna, you don't strike me as someone too scared to talk about something," he said.

"I'm not scared," she shot back, bristling in her saddle. "I'm trying to be sensitive, alright?" Another long silence. *Ag, what the hell?*

"Look, I like you," Brylee said, feeling her face burn. "A lot. And I think you like me. But you aren't planning to be around long, right? And I had a thought about what we could do about that. If you want to, that is."

Levi's face flushed and his features softened, like a weight had been lifted from his soul. He grinned, urging her to continue.

"Well, it just struck me as odd that a time weaver doesn't have much time. You know, to . . . well, to explore if we're right for each other, if you take my meaning. And I'm not saying we are. It's just that we can't find out, can we? Anyway, I recall you saying that when your mission is over, to get home you hop on this timeline thing and follow it back to the beginning of time." She paused, hoping he would fill in the gaps so she wouldn't have to ask and risk looking even more vulnerable than she felt.

"Go on," was all he said, in a way that seemed like he was prepared to be vulnerable too.

"What if you hung around for another fifty or so years after your mission concluded and then rode back to the beginning of time? It seems to me you would get home at precisely the same time either way, yes? If we decided things worked between us, well, I'd be dead before you were even missed."

Levi had been fretting over his own quandary and had decided not to tell Senna about it, but now it seemed pointless not to.

"I do like you, Senna. A lot. And I must say I'm impressed with your grasp of things. Unlike the turnip fiasco, you've nailed how the timeline works in this context."

Brylee shrank at the mere mention of turnips but realised Levi was deflecting with humour. But deflecting from what?

"But there's a . . . a wrinkle. Perhaps that's an understatement. I wasn't going to mention it because doing so might unduly influence you, though in a good way or bad, I'm not sure," Levi paused, then decided to commit to what felt like an act of folly. *Damned if you do and damned if you don't.* "We've discussed magic and naether ad nauseum, but an aspect we haven't touched on is how it relates to what you might call the soul or spirituality, if you like. Part of what makes us, well, us because individualism stems from how our bodies consume naether to live. Naether fuels us, but how our minds burn this fuel is reflected in our character. Are we good or evil? Confident or insecure? Analytical or free thinking? I have enough understanding of how your mind works to see that we burn naether almost exactly the same way."

"That's a good thing, surely," Brylee said, worried about where Levi was going with this.

"Yes and no." Levi said, looking sheepish. "In our case it's so close a match, and we're so linked through whatever crisis is closing in on us, that with the thrumming on our links, we've . . . I think the best word in your language is 'synchronised.' It's complicated, but we've connected on a spiritual level that has nothing to do with how we have interacted as people here in the world. It's called having a spirit mate."

"Again," Brylee said, "it sounds like a good thing."

"Yes, but here's the problem." This time Levi rushed on, afraid he might back out if he didn't explain things now, but it felt like his heart was breaking. "Spirit mates will *always* fall helplessly in love with each other. It's a by-product of the synchronisation. You think you like me a lot, but what if you can't help it? I don't want you to be with me because your will has been overtaken by something other than your heart."

Part of Brylee agreed. What if Levi was being forced to like her by this quirk of nature? But part of her didn't care. She wanted him.

"Does it matter? Love's love, isn't it? No matter the cause." Brylee wasn't sure she believed what she was saying, but she was otherwise stuck for words. It was too hard to wrap her head around. But she continued. "If you stick around, you know, afterwards, we have the rest of our lives—my life—to untangle our feelings and decide if this is genuine. And if not, you can just slide off down the timeline."

"Sorry to make this so complicated," Levi said. "I wish it were simple, believe me. The moment we started synchronising, this body that was formed when I manifested began to draw on the magic of this world. It's a sluggish process, but I'm slowly weaning off the magic from the gods' space to this world's magic stream through you."

"Is that a problem?"

"It means soon, if it is not already the case, I will be incompatible with my home magic. As soon as I return there, that magic could kill me. I might not be able to revert." They rode in silence for a dozen strides while the implications of Levi's admission sank in.

"You should leave now then, before it's too late," Brylee said, her hand at her throat. She didn't want him to leave, but she didn't want him to die either.

"I can't. It will take longer to get back to the cavern to step back into the timeline than we have. The crisis is already upon us. I thought we had weeks, but I can feel it looming quickly now. Things are accelerating towards the Unravelling. It could be hours or a week at most."

Brylee was terrified by the spectre of the looming crisis, but her heartache at Levi's predicament was more profound. She felt deeply ashamed of the relief that washed through her that he wasn't about to take off into the night. She didn't want to dwell on the crisis. She didn't understand it, and she couldn't engage with it. She focussed on where her heart led her instead.

"If you're stuck here, is it so bad? You'll live forever as the most powerful mage ever. If you're beginning to consume our naether, combined with your knowledge."

"And then there's us," Levi said, meeting her eyes with warmth and excitement. Then he shook his head, and his lips pinched in concern. "I won't live forever. This body I manifested in is aging just like yours. But we can age together, and for that I would give much, if we survive the next week, of course."

Humour again, Brylee thought. *Why is he deflecting? Is it resentment?*

"Is that why you're hesitating to explore what we mean to each other?" Brylee asked, the idea making her feel indignant. "I'm the cause of you losing your immortality. You're dying because you met me, if not today then over the next few decades."

"Not at all, actually," Levi said, his voice louder than he intended. "The chance to live for maybe fifty years creating something meaningful, rather than popping in and out of worlds, never attached to anything or anyone is . . . I'd make that exchange in a heartbeat if I could share those years with you."

Brylee had been shocked by the anger in his voice, but as his words sank in, her heart swelled, and she teared up.

"But I want you to choose me for who I am," Levi said, his tone frightened and vulnerable. "Not because we're spirit mates or because you feel sorry for me being stuck here. My life would be shortened but enriched. I want your love, not your pity. I also want you to be certain this is the best for you regardless of what that means to me."

Brylee's throat was so tight, it was hard to breathe let alone answer Levi. She wanted to tell him she was sure she wanted to try out a relationship, but that seemed so selfish despite his admission.

"You know," he continued, his voice hollow and dry, "there's a possibility that if I go back, I might *not* die. But frankly, forever without you? It seems so dull." Then Levi shook himself, as if chasing away a daydream. "My duty is to deal with this crisis and return. These swirling emotions are distracting me from focussing on saving this world. Forgive me if I don't act due to my duties. My fear of losing you because of the Unravelling is . . . I need to be a time weaver right now. For all of us."

Part of Brylee's mind knew he had to focus to save the world from the Unravelling, but was he committing to wanting her regardless? That's what she wanted, but was that because circumstances were daring her to leap into the unknown with him down an emotional slooper? *I'm not afraid to,* she told herself. However, it was that internal voice that often got her into trouble, she realised. Doubt wrestled with excitement, and frustration chafed at hope.

They both sensed enough had been said, and they needed time to process their thoughts. By unspoken agreement they rode in silence for an hour. There were moments when she couldn't see the trail ahead because she was blinded by tears, which she hid by staring at the opposite side of the path from where Levi rode. She hated crying. It made her feel foolish and weak. Yet she was wise enough to recognise the tears were of many flavours. Some were about the words he'd uttered with selfless consideration for her, making it clear that he wanted her. Others were for a future with something meaningful enough to counter what she had lost with her family, business, and friends like Raegan. Still others were from her fear of becoming a mage, for she had to accept that was one outcome ahead of her, and it had enormous implications. Some tears were laced with the fear of challenging a deadly assassin who might end the new opportunities and hopes that had been gifted to her and helped fill the void in her heart.

Brylee also knew she was burying a hard, squirming worm of a truth deep in her soul. A life with Levi, and even what he was teaching her now, meant letting magic into her life to a degree that terrified her. Magic had been at the root of everything she felt shame about and had always resulted in problems. Accepting it felt like deciding murder and theft were acceptable. *Yet I'm deliberately keeping those thoughts chained up in the dark,* she thought. *Why? Because I'm lusting after Levi?*

When they spoke later, it was about simpler things: food likes and dislikes, music, the majesty of the mountains, the pretty details of the wildflowers, anything but magic and a future together. But the more they rode on avoiding the topic, the more Brylee worried their choice not to discuss the future would cause a chasm to form between them. So she took the conversation back to a more practical rather than emotional aspect of their dilemma.

"If you stay," she began, glancing at Levi to gauge his mood, "won't your mere presence here mess up the future timeline? Change what is meant to be? Might another time weaver arrive to chastise you?"

"I doubt it. We have an expression: 'Time will flow its own way.' The phrase captures the way time adjusts and adapts. Time is surprisingly robust."

"I don't understand. If it's robust, why do we need time weavers?"

"You wish I hadn't come?"

Her eyes flew to his, concerned he was upset, but she realised he was grinning. "Idiot," she said, grinning back.

"The trouble with this world is that it confuses logic with magic," Levi explained. "You all get stuck on concepts such as what if someone went back in time and killed their grandfather before he had sired the killer's father. It makes sense logically, but remember, time isn't a flow of logic; it's a flow of naether or magic."

"And that differs how?" Brylee asked, almost rolling her eyes in response to his thought that she might leap to the conclusion he was hoping for rather than confusing her further.

"Magic isn't burdened by reality. It can be anything if properly crafted. You think of time like a river, always flowing in one direction. It's not an awful metaphor, but people forget rivers have other features. Within the flow are eddies and whirlpools that swirl around and around. The weather can suck water up to form clouds downstream, which blow upstream and drop rain onto soil that rejoins the river. Get it?"

"Er, no. Sort of . . . no, not really."

"Do fish understand waterwheels?" Levi asked, his eyes twinkling with a smile.

"What? You're killing me with this. Now I'm a fish? I thought I was a turnip."

Levi was about to apologise, but then he saw her grinning back at him. "Touché. To be honest, in this metaphor you're more like a tiny organism that isn't aware of the river. At least a fish knows how to navigate currents." Levi sighed for dramatic effect. "Killing your grandfather is like a magical whirlpool. Yes, things get confusing as water rushes back upstream, pushing aside the water that would have flowed through for a moment, a day, or a hundred years. Maybe the whirlpool is caused by a rock beneath the surface. But eventually, either the rock erodes or the water level changes, and the whirlpool slows and dissipates. Eventually, all the water flows down the river and everything is fine. Time will flow its own way. It will right itself. Its current endures."

"So, what happened to the grandfather?"

"As the whirlpool rotates, sometimes he's alive, sometimes he's dead, and sometimes he's both."

"You're giving me a headache." Brylee looked up at the sky and took a deep breath.

"Only because you're being logical. You want to think about it from the perspective of one of the participants in the conundrum. But magically, at least for a while, several different perspectives can exist simultaneously. Magic isn't one dimensional. It's multidimensional. It prefers order, but it's robust enough to tolerate competing alternate realities for a time. Whirlpools."

"So, why time weavers?"

"The flow can tolerate, adapt, flow around, or overcome almost any eddies or minor blockages. But people who practise time magic, who go back in time and deliberately alter things, such as killing their grandparents, sometimes don't stop there. They continue messing with things until they cause a problem so big the river breaches its banks, or they build a dam. Remember, time is just a convenient waste disposal for the gods' naether. If one world gets clogged up, they destroy it and replace it with another. Problem solved. They don't spend time sorting through the details of why it's clogged. They despise stooping to such maintenance, so they created us to do it for them. But they didn't grant us the power to replace worlds, so we have to manifest here and work out how best to keep things flowing."

"And how do you do that?" Brylee asked. "Kill the meddler?"

"Rarely. We try to change as little as possible. The river is normally struggling already, so we make the most subtle changes we can to restore order to the flow. The more time can sort out what it needs to flow smoothly, the better it will work out in the long run for everyone."

"If you stay here, you know, with me, how do you avoid being a problem for the river of time?" Her voice was tentative but hopeful.

"Swim smoothly with the current with gentle strokes that make the fewest ripples. If I stay, I will change the future, but that doesn't matter as long as the flow continues."

Upon reaching the Lame Goat for their night-time stop, the horses were stabled, brushed, and fed. Rosemary spoke to the innkeeper and got the keys to their rooms. Wickham told the party they were free to have an early night and catch up on their sleep. He announced he would wash up and buy dinner in the tavern before turning in. They all mounted the stairs and filed into their respective rooms. Levi had the last room farthest along the corridor, and Brylee's was adjacent to it. They found themselves outside of her room, alone.

"How are you feeling?" Levi asked.

Brylee laughed. "Look, I only admitted I liked you."

"A lot. You said you liked me a lot," Levi shot back, taking a step towards her.

"Then you laid this spirit nonsense on me and essentially told me you're dying," Brylee said in a mock-serious tone. "Not the romantic gesture I expected from Sir Levinial, time weaver of the gods."

"You may have to teach me about things like romance," Levi said, taking her hand and holding it close. Brylee slid her other hand up and across Levi's shoulders, grasping the back of his neck. Finding his hair, she pulled him into a soft kiss. It was a long moment. As it broke, she reached behind herself, pushed open the door to her room, and pulled him inside.

Chapter Fifty-Seven

Levi had slept with many partners in many worlds, but as he sat awkwardly at breakfast with Wickham's party surrounding them, he reflected on how it had felt last night. It was like the first time—more heart than body, although he had to admit his body was more than cooperative. He felt content with his choices, even if in the end he and Brylee—she had whispered her real name to him and the reason for the subterfuge—couldn't work things out for the long term. *Long term,* he thought. *What is that now?* How quickly his perspective was changing.

By contrast, Brylee's head was a whirlwind of doubts. She had lost everything because of Gunnar and Judd. Now she was living under a tentative contract with Wickham, yet she felt the beginning of a friendship between herself and the strange collection of people he thought of as family. Into this mix landed Levi. She was infatuated and was willing to risk everything with him. But what if this was truly the impact of being spirit mates? She had said they could explore where things went and try to discount that effect, but what if she found she didn't like him in the long run? Could she push him away now that he had nowhere else to go? It didn't help that despite the loving, warm words shared between them as Levi left for his own room in the early hours, he could barely meet her eye now at breakfast. *He's just being cautious with our secret, as you insisted*, she told herself. Yet the doubts continued to cruise around in her head like sharks in the sea.

"Lu knows some quality mercenaries who used to live in Le Faette," Sirius said to the group. "It's a small town just off the trail today. I've agreed she can divert and see if they're available to replace Kurt and Ulla. She'll rejoin us tomorrow morning."

"You should go with her," Wickham suggested, a twinkle in his eye. Lu wondered if he had noticed their attraction too.

"Your guard is already depleted," she said through a mouthful of oats, not knowing how she would explain meeting Da-Jeef and the Mobi'dern.

"Yes, but we're back on a main road today, out of the wilds, and it's a much shorter journey to our next stop," Wickham said, a note of finality in his tone. "I've decided to rest here for the morning anyway. If we leave after lunch, we'll still make the Harding Ranch by nineteenth bell. I never travel with more than two guards, and I still have Winter and Ben. What I need is a full complement of guards when we get to the Meeting of Mages. That's where I expect trouble may occur. If there are quality fighters in Le Faette, Sirius can have his pick of them."

Lu wanted to argue, but the idea of her and Sirius being alone on the road and overnighting in another town tempted her, especially as he seemed keen to join her. She let herself be persuaded, her mind already suggesting ways she could navigate the web of lies she had spun around herself at Gideon's behest.

The two of them set out while Wickham took Levi and Brylee up to his room. Wickham said it was a good time for Brylee to practise what she had learnt while not tottering precariously on horseback, but in reality he was fascinated with Levi's revelations and wanted some quiet time with the time weaver to get answers to the many questions that were spinning in his head. He was so engrossed in formulating questions that when Brylee revealed she had confessed her real name to Levi, he simply accepted her reasoning: that Levi had already discerned the falsehood in her mind, without suspecting that their relationship had progressed.

So distracted was Brylee by the night's events, especially now that Levi seemed to be all business in the cold light of day, it took several hours for her mind to settle enough to regain the level of focus she had achieved just the day before. Only after Wickham declared a break so he could empty his bladder, during which Levi inquired how she was doing and said he wished they could be alone together, did she manage to centre herself enough to make any progress.

When Wickham returned, he had news. "A messenger from Sage caught up with us. As you had asked, Levi, I set my network to search for Ostryd van Hyke. He was hard to trace, seeing as he used many aliases. But we found out his fate. I'm afraid he was killed in a suspicious fire up in the Northern Lands, a place called Sandwick. Does that help?"

"Is there more information on the circumstances?" Levi asked.

"Not about his death. All I know is Mr. van Hyke had a sizable estate and based himself out of Troll Lake, back in Lanthe. The odd thing that caught people's notice was that Mr. van Hyke had named a man he recently met as his heir. He was a bit of a recluse by all accounts. Does it mean anything?"

"I'm sure it does," Levi said, "but I have no idea what it could be. We should investigate further."

Lunchtime arrived, but it seemed the wrong time to stop training, so food was brought to Wickham's room. They let Winter know they would stay for one more hour.

Brylee was bearing down on the stone, her magical sight boring into it for all she was worth as she gripped the arms of her chair, a sheen of sweat glistening on her brow.

"I get a sense of what makes the stone a stone," she gasped, her throat tight with effort. "But it's akin to smelling a roast from afar when you've never eaten meat and trying to visualise the taste and texture of the joint. Hot, salty, corky, aromatic, but I couldn't describe the joint of meat."

"Let alone the cow," Levi said. "Oh!" he exclaimed, smacking his hand on his forehead, "I'm a fool. I've never taught anyone before; forgive me. You're so clever, Brylee. Keep using your magical sight, just as you are. I know I said it's not sight but that thinking of it as such helps your mind with the process, so let's expand the same metaphor. Use your mind to try to taste what you can see. Touch it. Smell it. Listen to it. What sound is it making? Bring in all your senses."

Brylee considered the suggestion. She didn't like the idea of tasting the stone, but smelling and touching it didn't seem too weird. She imagined herself extending those other senses into the stone, and it instantly came into a different level of focus for her. Not that she could describe in words what she was sensing, even though she felt at some level she understood it. It was something beyond language.

Levi had told her to interrogate the stone to learn its attributes, so she tried that. *I command you to reveal what makes you a stone!* Nothing. Everything in her world was about the stone now, and she was oblivious of the room and the people in it. *Tell me!* Still nothing.

"Don't demand to be its mistress," Levi's voice whispered in her mind. *"It wants to tell you. When you harden air, you just form the bridge, and the ground shares its secrets with the air without much encouragement. Be its friend or even its lover. Seduce it; don't bully it."* The way he said "lover" almost caused enough distraction to break her concentration.

With effort, Brylee shifted her emotions in the same way she did with her father when he annoyed her. With him she had to take a breath and remind herself he was old, he loved her, and he had given her so much. She softened, striving for a different mindset and feeling for the stone. *What are you, you lovely stone?* Abruptly, she knew everything that was the stone. It came to her so swiftly she lost concentration, and everything faded, including her knowledge of the stone's attributes. But for a moment, she had known.

Her hand flew to her neck where the Galei stones had become so hot they were burning her skin. She had not noticed the pain, being so absorbed in her task. She yanked them off, breaking the thin silver chain that held them, then dropped them to the floor as they burnt her hand.

"Well done, Brylee," Levi said. "Your first major breakthrough. That was incredible, wasn't it?"

Wickham picked up the Galei stones by the chain and felt their heat. "I don't know what you did, but these are drained. Put them in your pocket for now. I'll recharge them tonight. I want to get going as soon as you gather yourself." He was obviously grumpy and feeling left out.

"But I think I understand it now," Brylee said.

"The mage is right, Brylee," Levi cut in. "Rest your mind for a few hours. It will be easier next time. I promise. Here, drink some water. It will help reduce the headache you'll have for the afternoon."

It didn't take more than a few steps for Brylee to realise how much she had taken out of herself though the morning. It took over half a bell for her to feel well enough to mount her horse without feeling dizzy. She wanted to ride next to Levi, to pick up the threads of the previous night, but she was disappointed when Wickham claimed the spot next to her, full of fatherly concern.

The last of the mountain's downward trail petered out two hours into their ride. They passed a fork in the road, and Wickham explained it was where Lu and Sirius would have turned off the trail that morning. The lake was beautiful, with light ripples being nudged around by the breeze. Spring shoots lifted their heads above the soil, spilling whites, yellows, and purples across the grassy hillside. Brylee engaged her magical sight and looked at the lake. Without the Galei stones to supplement her meagre power, things were not as clear, but she could make out the glow of schools of fish glimmering in the long reeds lining the shore.

Two hours later they stopped at an area that had been widened into a resting place. A small stream trickled into the lake, from which they refilled their water skins. As Brylee knelt to fill hers, a dark red bloom near her elbow caught her attention. She knew it from somewhere. It felt significant. Then she placed the memory. Bellyberry. She snatched some off a bush and rushed over to where Winter and the mage were conferring.

"Is Harding Ranch where Jyan Harding lives?" Brylee asked. "The grou't seller? Bellyberry is crushed and used as a catalyst in his roasting process."

"Yes, he and I go way back," Wickham said. "It will be lovely to see him."

"Maybe," Brylee replied. "But he knows me as Brylee Plainhand. I didn't connect Harding Ranch with Jyan. I met him the day Vekki attacked me. I even chose the name Senna because the sweet old man initially mistook me for someone I resemble. I think he would know me again now."

"That would be awkward," Wickham said. With his mind he reached out to the Galei stones in her pocket. "We don't have time to fully recharge the Galei stones, but I've put enough in them for you to change your appearance."

"But what about the last mercenary?" Brylee asked.

"When we get close to the ranch, Winter will send him off on an errand. Once he's away, make yourself unrecognisable to Jyan. That should do it. Now let's get going. We should pick up the pace if we want to make the ranch by dusk."

When they remounted, Levi pushed his way in so that he fell into step with Brylee. Wickham pulled ahead, somewhat put out, taking a position with Winter at the front. Rosemary rode with the remaining mercenary, bringing up the rear.

Two hundred yards along the path, a ridge ran down from the hills to their right and formed a small hillock that blocked their path before falling away to meet the lakeshore. A century ago, someone had carved an archway through the hill to allow travellers to continue uninterrupted. The Hardings had made a point of ensuring the most amazing blooms festooned the site, creating a novel feature marking the entrance to their lands. Brylee and Levi smiled at each other, both of them noting the romantic symbolism that might mark the start of their journey.

As Wickham and Winter led the group into the archway at a fast canter, their mounts shied suddenly, sensing a transparent wall of hardened air. Although the horses' keen senses saved them from the worst of the collision, the abrupt stop catapulted the riders into the wall with a savage force that was punctuated by a sickening crunch. As Rosemary and the mercenary pulled hard on their reins, managing to halt them and stay atop their mounts,

Brylee and Levi only avoided impacting whatever had taken Wickham and Winter down by flinging themselves to the ground.

As the disorientation subsided, Levi found himself flat on his back. He sat up. Three men had emerged from the bushes and were holding crossbows on Rosemary and the mercenary. He looked around. Winter's neck was clearly broken. The mage had a terrible gash on his head and was unmoving. Brylee was slowly pulling herself up onto all fours, shaking her head to clear it. Levi felt the clench of hardened air envelop him as a fourth man, a noble judging by his clothing, stepped out through the archway. Levi could barely move, but from the corner of his eye he noted that Brylee was frozen in the grip of hard air too.

Levi reached out to the Galei stones, which were nestled in Brylee's pocket, but there was not enough stored magic to lift Brylee and himself out of the timeline. He had never felt so helpless. Other time weavers had perished on missions, but he didn't think it could happen to him.

The noble pulled his sword and rushed the few steps to where Levi lay. Levi blurred his sight into the magical realm and saw the man was a powerful mage, and, on closer inspection, a slipper. He didn't have time to think much more before the man plunged his sword into Levi's chest, piercing his heart.

Brylee's head was just clearing as she saw a stranger stab Levi. She tried to fling herself at them to prevent it but found herself locked into stillness by hard air. Memories of Vekki's cruel face loomed over her, turning the choking fear for Levi that had assailed her into frenzied panic as she flashed back to her near-death moment. But somehow she held onto her need to save Levi. She pulled herself back, her breathing rapid and her eyes bulging with the effort to break free, but she was utterly immobilised.

The man stood over her, a sad look on his face, as if at some level he hated what he was doing. Then she felt the pull of skriking tugging at her soul.

No, no, no, no, no! she shouted in her head. The attack was far stronger than Vekki's, and there was no fighting it. *Get a grip. If you don't act, you will die. Use your magic!* she yelled at herself. *Ride the horse.*

She glanced through her magical sight just in time to witness her link to the source ripping away from her and being drawn into the man standing over her. It felt like most of the world's light had been blown out like a candle. Her sense of reality was diminished and distant. Without the ability to replenish her life force, let alone perform magic, she knew she was dead. Then the world skewed and twisted around her. Overwhelmed by a massive wave of vertigo, she blacked out.

Wickham was in a dark place. He felt one side of his face pressed into the dirt, a heavy trickle of warm liquid on his other cheek. Blood, he realised. He opened one eye. The light hurt so much he nearly fainted. His vision was focussed afar and hard to shift. A few hundred yards up the path he saw Sirius and Lu galloping to their defence. *They came early,* he realised, although he sensed it was not early enough. *A shame.*

With effort he wrestled his focus nearer. Levi was on the ground, the tip of a wicked blade protruding from his chest, dripping blood into the mud. Yet somehow the time weaver had a few breaths left in him. A stranger was standing over Levi, rooting through his clothing.

Wickham couldn't move his head; he was too weak. He couldn't see Brylee anywhere; he hoped she had survived. As darkness overtook him, he said a small prayer for Rosemary, hoping she would be spared to return to Sage. They would be well provided for in his documented wishes.

Levi lay there, laughter bubbling up through the blood in his throat. He coughed. The slipper was above him, yelling, not understanding where Brylee had vanished to. The man's anger only made the situation seem funnier. *The irony,* Levi thought. He looked at his link to confirm it was no longer thrumming with turbulence, but it was, which meant that world's source of magic was entering its crisis. He had caused the Unravelling to commence. In his panic to save Brylee he had done the only thing he could. He had reached for his own magic from the gods' space and flung Brylee back through time. The massive invasion of foreign magic to this world had breached the riverbank. Yet he had created a chance, though a small one. If Brylee could keep her wits about her, she could survive. He had given her the means. At least for about four years until she reached the same point on the timeline again where his actions had likely begun a rupture that would end everything.

With one more cough, he spat at the man towering over him. The man reached down and took the aggar's amulet from Levi's neck. *This stranger wants access to the cavern,* was the last thought Levi had as the world faded around him.

Chapter Fifty-Eight

The 466th Year of the Morde Dynasty–Four Years Earlier

The darkness lasted but a moment and with the return of light, albeit blurred and fuzzy, the nausea twisted Brylee inside out. The clenching grip of hard air had evaporated, leaving her to collapse forward onto her face in the wet mud. She flopped sideways, her hip crunching onto the gravel and her lungs gasping for air.

I'm wet through. Has it been raining? was her first thought, followed by a terrified recollection that her magical link to the source had been skriked away from her and she was dying. Despite her natural vision remaining blurred, her magical sight was crisp. She had a link. *Thank Ag! But how?* Brylee noticed the links in her vicinity were all the wispy tendrils of plants and small animals. There were no people close by according to her magical vision. She tried to switch back to see through her eyes, but the darkness encroached again, heavier, thicker, and swirling until even her magical sight slipped from her determined grasp and she fell back into unconsciousness.

It was nearly two bells later when Brylee awoke to the nervous whickering and snorting of a horse. She became aware that she was lying on her right side, her right ear, cheek, and hand hot in the sun. Her body ached, and her clothing was dry where it faced the sky but damp where it contacted the ground. *How long have I been lying here?* She heard footsteps approach across the gravel track. She tried to sit up and open her eyes, but her world lurched sideways and she felt sick again. She flopped back down and held tight to consciousness, screwing her eyes up to block out the light.

"Easy there, lass. Keep still," an old man said. She could tell by his shuffling gait that he favoured one leg over the other. "You've fallen from your horse, I suppose, although he doesn't seem to be about anywhere now." Brylee noted his raspy accent had the singsong tones of a Yarrowman. She felt his cool hand on her hot cheek, lifting and tilting her head. "Here, sip this. It's just water. Slowly now."

The cool liquid helped immediately. Her head stopped spinning, reducing her nausea. The stranger helped Brylee into a sitting position. With some effort, she opened her eyes, and with a few more sips from the man's waterskin, her vision cleared completely. She took in her surroundings. The lake, the arch through the hill, the grass, the bushes, and the dark red bellyberry. But there was no sign of Levi, Wickham, or the rest of her party. Nor were there any scuff marks where the horses fell, arrows, or any other signs of ambush. Just a large red hops cart protruding partway out of the arch harnessed to a large farm horse and an old man peering down at her, his face full of concern. He looked a little younger and had no cane, but there was no doubt in her mind who he was.

"I'm Jyan Harding," he said as if to confirm her thoughts.

"The Grinders man, I know," Brylee replied, unable to clear the fog from her mind. "We met in Rostal three moons ago. What must you think of me, not following up on our meeting?"

"You have me crossed with another, lass. I haven't been to Rostal for at least three years and don't know what a Grinders man is." Jyan wrinkled his face and scratched his ear. "Let's get you up off the ground and into the cart. You've bumped your noggin. We should get a healer to look at it."

"I'm so confused. Perhaps you're right," she said to buy time to understand whatever game Jyan was playing.

"I'm afraid you're a bit heavy for me to lift at my age, young lady. Can you stand? Here, steady yourself on my shoulder." It took a few attempts and the rest of his waterskin, but Brylee eventually stood and made her way to the cart. She crawled up onto the flat bed and then propped herself up against its wooden siding.

"What are you doing out here all alone?" Jyan asked once he had the cart turned around, swaying and creaking its way back through the arch towards his ranch.

"There were six of us. I think we were ambushed by bandits. But there's no sign of anyone. I don't understand."

Jyan suggested she sleep. It was clear there had been no ambush. The rain had been light and could not have erased the signs. He assured her that the answers would come soon enough. The swinging of the cart and the clip-clop of the horse soothed Brylee back into the darkness.

Brylee dreamed of Vekki's skriking attempt, but this time she felt no sense of panic. She was a third person watching events unfold in the theatre box. Vekki had her, and was lustily sucking away her life force, an exquisite, primal expression tainting the apprentice's pretty face. Slowly, the curtain behind Vekki parted. In one flowing movement, the Red Assassin stepped out and skewered Vekki from behind. The assassin held Vekki and Brylee with hard air for a while. Brylee forced her vision to the magical realm and watched the assassin claim Vekki's link to the source for his own. She couldn't see the assassin's face due to his outfit, but she felt that unlike Vekki, he took no pleasure in the skriking. The assassin turned his head and stared at her. Wanting her to see his features, he reached up to remove his hood. Then Brylee awoke with a start.

"The assassin is a mage!" she gasped. Despite witnessing the assassin apparently skriking Vekki, she hadn't processed or perhaps had blocked out the implication. She looked around and found herself alone. She was lying flat on the back of the cart. Its rocking had shifted her as she slept. Jyan was on the steps of his house, evidently having just told his servant she was injured. Men and women jumped into action. Some came to her, fussing and helping her down. Another rushed away to fetch the healer. In no time she was sitting on a couch in Jyan's home, hot mulled wine being pressed into her hands by a kind old woman who was introduced as Inka, Jyan's sister. At Jyan's instruction the room was cleared, and Brylee was left alone with the healer, a young blonde man named Barrow. He poked and prodded as he asked her some questions.

"Do you know where you are?"

"I think this is Harding Ranch, and that's Jyan Harding," she replied.

"How many fingers am I holding up?" She told him three, which seemed to please him.

"What year is it?"

"It's four seventy of the Morde Dynasty," she replied, tiring of his questions. Barrow pursed his lips and tutted.

"Have a think about that for a second. Four seventy?" he said, tilting her head back and examining the large goose egg that had formed since she hit her head after leaping from her horse.

"It's not four seventy?" she said, thinking she had misunderstood his question.

"It's four sixty-six, not four seventy. Can you tell me your name?"

Four sixty-six? she wondered. *How could that be?* She thought that perhaps she didn't want to know.

"Who is the head of Trinity's councils?" Brylee asked, not answering Barrow's question. The man listed them off without thinking, intent on peering into her eyes while having her follow his finger from side to side. He had named the Trinity leadership from a previous cycle.

For the remainder of the examination, Brylee thought through the events as she could recall them. Wickham would never have left her on the ground, and there was no sign of her horse or a struggle. How did she lose four years? *What did Levi do? Whatever he did saved my link.*

Jyan slipped back into the room. "Is she alright, Barrow?"

"Her head has been banged about, and her memory is scrambled, but no bones are broken. If her memory doesn't sort itself out after a night's sleep, she should see a mage," Barrow said. "If one will see her, of course."

"I think we could convince one," Jyan said. He turned to Brylee. "Tell me, deary, what do we call you?"

She pondered his question for a moment. "I think you call me Senna."

They fussed over her some more, then took her to a guest room. As she entered, a maid was removing a pan of hot coals from between the sheets of a large bed ornately framed in black wood. They left her to undress, and soon she was enjoying the warmth of the bed and the simple cotton sheets. The maid also brought her some soup and explained that Inka and the healer had conspired on its ingredients and that she should eat as much as she could without inducing nausea.

When the maid returned later, Brylee was fast asleep. She slept until noon the following day.

"Welcome back," an old man's voice said before she had even opened her eyes. The accent was of Quartt, not Yarrow. Therefore it wasn't Jyan. She sat up and looked around, her hand absently rising to examine her head, but there was no longer a bump or even a bruise. A bald man with a grey beard—a mage, as identified by his robes—was sitting in a padded chair. His shrunken, hunched body rested on the seat's tall back. She checked her aura, which was as it should be. Then she flipped her sight and looked at her link. It was small and tight. Was she even a charmer anymore? She didn't dare test herself in the presence of someone who might decide she was a tasty snack. Her skin crawled as she recalled her two experiences with magical predators. The mage's link was thick, but it had an ancient look to it, and it didn't pulse with vitality.

"I've mended everything I could find wrong with you, Miss Senna," the mage said. "Young Jyan was worried for you and sent a message and his best carriage for me overnight. Imagine such a thing. As if I don't own a carriage. I arrived just after sunrise, and I'm glad I made the effort. It's been too long since I saw Jyan and Inka. But you didn't need my healing abilities, aside from that bump and a few scratches. But they say your memory is stirred up."

"I'm glad to be the cause of your reunion, sir," Brylee said. "And I'm also grateful for your attention. If there's a fee, I'd like to settle with you, but I still feel somewhat disoriented."

"Not at all." The old man smiled and leaned back deeper into the lush chair. "No fee. A favour for my godson, Jyan."

"Thank you," she said. She spotted her clothing, which had been cleaned. Then she felt vulnerable lying in the bed.

"Is it OK if I dress?" He nodded but made no move to give her privacy. *He is a healer, I suppose.* She felt self-conscious stepping out in her underclothes, pouring water from the ewer into the delicately patterned bowl, and washing up in his presence, although he wasn't paying her too much attention. He had taken to examining his nails.

Once she was dressed, Brylee walked to the window and pulled back the drapes. The location of the ranch house had no doubt been chosen for the view. Rolling field after field of ale hops were strung on wood and wire as far as her eye could see.

"Where does Mr. Harding grow his t'Yuk beans?" she asked.

"t'Yuk beans?" the mage replied. "I don't believe that's one of his crops. I doubt they are grown anywhere in Yarrow, as I have never heard of them." *Not yet,* Brylee thought, surer than ever that Levi had somehow transported her back in time. *To save me?* Her heart leapt at the idea.

"There's no fee, as I said," the old man said, leaning forward again. His expression was cryptic, though there was a glint of curiosity in his bright eyes. "But I would like the answer to a question or two. If I like your answer, perhaps I'll pay you instead."

"Of course, sir," Brylee replied. She would be guarded with her answers, but she knew to be cautious and polite with any mage, however friendly he seemed.

"I'm curious about the stones in your pocket," he said, his gaze intent on her reaction. "They were on the table when I arrived. The maid put them back into your jacket when she returned your clothing. How did you come by such . . . clever jewellery?"

Brylee's mind raced as she strove to keep panic from her face. If it was the year 466, Wickham would have no idea who she was. If she claimed they were his and this mage followed up, he would think it was a lie. How could she explain what she was doing with Galei stones? Her instincts told her not to pretend she didn't know what they were.

"I know they're of a certain type of value, sir," she began. "To the right person. I was on the way to Rostal, in Lanthe. I had a mind to ask Mage Wickham if he was interested in buying them from me. I understand he collects such things."

The mage eyed her with curiosity, his head tilted to one side. "Thank you for your honesty. I thought you would pretend not to know their power. You don't have the look of a mage or a charmer." Brylee knew that by "look" he meant "aura." "Would you tell me how you acquired such a rare antiquity?"

Brylee thought long and hard about her answer. The mage sat patiently. "It's a strange tale to be sure, sir," she began. "One many would attribute to the blow to my head or call me a liar. Could we leave it that a man I met gave it to me in return for some work I am doing for him?"

"For it to be of value, the Galei stones need to be filled. These are almost empty," the mage said. Brylee was sure he would press further, but instead he laughed, clucked his tongue, and waved the tension away. "Don't worry, Miss Senna—if that is, in fact, your name. I'll leave you with your secrets. If you answer my next question just as honestly, I'll even do you the favour of charging the stones for you. I'm sure whatever their purpose, it would be better done with them full, yes?"

Brylee nodded, her pulse increasing at the thought.

"What do you intend to do now?" the mage asked. "My question stems from wanting to ensure that my godson faces no peril from you. He is a lovely man but quite naïve in some ways."

"To be honest, sir," Brylee said, feeling relieved she could answer the question so easily, "I'm not quite sure. Events have changed dramatically for me, and I need to think about my circumstances. But I can assure you I have nothing but goodwill towards Mr. Harding."

As if the mention of his name summoned him, the door opened and Jyan's face appeared. "Ah, good, you're awake. I hoped you were. Have you had a chance to be introduced?" Jyan asked as he stepped into the room, his face beaming just as it had when Brylee had first encountered him in Rostal. She shook her head.

"This, I'm proud to say, is my godfather, Mage Garrick the Lesser of Yarrow," the old man said.

"That's a bit formal, so call me Elijah, please," the mage said with a wink.

Brylee's eyebrows shot up. In a little over one and a half years, Garrick the Lesser would be the Red Assassin's first victim.

Chapter Fifty-Nine

It didn't take much more than the smell of lunch to coax Brylee out of the bedroom and to the table. Inka was already seated with a large glass of wine in her hand. Jyan and Garrick shuffled over to their seats, neither of them too sound on their feet.

"Please sit," Jyan said. "No ceremony here. Some wine?" He was pouring a much smaller amount into his and Garrick's glass than Inka had for herself, and Brylee intuited the farmer wasn't too pleased his sister had taken so much. But he said nothing to her, and it felt like a typical scenario.

"Just some water, please," Brylee replied. "I think my head has enough to contend with without confusing it with wine." She was glad of the excuse to keep a clear head, surrounded with so many potential traps she could easily talk herself into. "At some point I would like to taste your ales while I'm here," she added so as not to seem ungracious.

During lunch, Brylee only had to field one or two harmless questions. By unspoken agreement the group seemed to think it wise to leave her to take things at her own pace, at least for now. The strong appetite she had brought to the table dulled, and her mind filled with worries as it caught up on the implications of the last twenty-four hours. Or was it four years less a day? No, it was late spring when she saw Levi last, almost summer. This was early spring, the sun still digging winter's icy claws out of the land. She could barely grasp the situation. What terrified her was seeing Levi stabbed, his life seeping away, and Wickham and Winter lying seemingly lifeless on the ground. If Levi had called upon his magic to save her, would the world even exist four years from now? Something of those terrors must have shown on her face as she realised Jyan was asking if she needed to lie down.

"Ah, no, sorry. I was just trying to remember things. It's frightening not quite knowing what to trust about your own thoughts." As Brylee spoke, she felt Garrick's gaze pass over her and determined he was scanning her with his magical senses. The old mage offered no opinion. Inka reached over and put her hand on top of Brylee's. Then she let go, refilled her glass—almost to the brim this time—and gave her brother a pointed look. *She is sassy,* Brylee thought.

"Really, sister," Jyan said, a mixture of frustration and concern in his tone. "Elijah, tell her please. Drinking wine all afternoon can't be good for her."

The old mage laughed. "Do you think she'll listen to an old man like me?" He gave Inka a covert wink.

The conversation changed to farming matters. Jyan was especially pleased when they found Brylee could contribute insights into growing, distribution, and crop marketing. After an hour, Brylee's appetite was sated and Inka was wavering in her seat, her eyes repeatedly checking that the wine bottle was still empty, as was her glass.

"I think I'll go sit in the living room by the window," Inka said. "The light on the fields is beautiful at this time of the afternoon." When Garrick stood to escort her, offering his arm, she didn't object, and the two left the room.

"Is she OK?" Brylee asked.

Jyan laughed. "Don't worry about her." Then he leaned in close. "The large chair by the window is perfect for sleeping off the effects of lunch." His face filled with concern. "Inka lost her husband recently. It's been hard for her. She's often lost in her cups like that, sometimes for days. I find I'm running the business on my own most of the time. It used to be the three of us. I find it quite hard, to tell you the truth. I'm not a young man anymore."

"That's so sad. And hard for you, doing the work of three."

"Now there's an idea," Jyan replied. "Look, I know you need a few days to recover from your accident, and perhaps you have plans that will take you somewhere else, but you know how hectic a farm gets at this time of year. Planting, fertilising, hiring, meeting suppliers, customers, and whatnot. If you have nowhere better to be, I'd like to talk to you about a job here at Hardings. I don't know what yet, but you clearly have experience, and I have more than I can manage."

"I'm flattered, but I'm not sure where I need to be. I'm feeling quite lost. Can I think about it?" He nodded, but she could tell he was already making plans for her, and she felt that she would like the idea. The Jyan of the future seemed to know his Senna well. Perhaps this was meant to be.

Back in her room, Brylee took stock of her situation. Many ideas filled her head. Perhaps she could warn her future self about Judd Brown, Gunther, and Vekki. Or warn Wickham or even Levi. She could change her appearance and visit Nalik. Oh, to see her brother again. But could she stand to lose him once more? Could she prevent his accident? Should she? Brylee tried to recall what Levi had warned her about time, about loops and disruptions.

Could she—should she—save Mage Garrick from the Red Assassin? What a tangle.

After several hours she wandered out onto the wrap-around porch and stood alone, looking over the fields. It was well before dusk dimmed the world, but the moon had already risen and was big, bold, and mysterious, looking down at her. From her experience losing Nalik and later everything she loved in Haxley, she recognised the stirrings of grief tugging at her heart when she thought of Wickham, Rosemary, Winter's grumpy perfectionism, and especially Levi.

Brylee remembered using her magic to save the woodsman she found dying by the Haxley road. It was one time she hadn't regretted having magic in her life despite the shame she had felt after acting. She remembered Raegan's insight about how the world might be better if more people could use magic to heal and how that notion flared again when she learned of her pa's poor health from Fifi. Brylee had lived her life resenting magic, fearful of it, and in some ways the last few moons had reinforced those feelings. Or had they?

Magic had saved her and Judd from the bandits, and she couldn't completely resent saving Judd despite the harm he had done to her subsequently. And despite public assumption to the contrary, Wickham only seemed to use magic to help, as did Garrick. Even Levi claimed to bend over backwards to preserve worlds from themselves with minimal negative impact. He was magical, but that didn't define the man. The more she thought about it, the more Brylee felt that perhaps not embracing what she was had been the problem. If she had developed the ability to see magical links, she wouldn't have been surprised by Vekki. She would have had a shine shadow. Gunnar wouldn't have messed with her either if she were a mage and not a charmer.

Something clicked deep inside. Rather than hide from herself, if she was going to put things right she realised she would have to become what she had always shunned. She was surprised to discover that she found that thought inspiring.

Having decided on an initial set of priorities as she stared back at the moon, she became fierce and determined and promised that heavenly body that she would prevail and not grieve.

As a worst case, she needed to be back at the arch by the lake in four years' time. She would need magic, allies, and the ability to heal wounds like Levi's, if that were even possible. *My world isn't limited by reality,* she reminded herself. *Anything is possible with primi magic.* Letting events play out exactly as they had—with minimal, if any, meddling—would present perhaps the least additional trauma to the timeline. She did not want to compound whatever Levi had done at the point he sent her back in time. *I must swim smoothly and make the fewest ripples if I want to find Levi where I left him.* Perhaps a better option would present itself, but for the moment she would focus on regaining or expanding her magic, learning to heal major trauma, and learning as much about the Red Assassin as possible. It was time for action, not self-pity.

Perhaps she should offer to apprentice to Mage Garrick. Apparently, he was one of the best healer-mages of the age. That would give her the opportunity to protect him from assassination, and until she could recover her own magical strength, he might be willing to top up the Galei stones on occasion. She would also learn more about Ostryd van Hyke. Levi had thought he played a part in things.

Her initial decisions made, Brylee slipped out of her room and found Garrick sitting in a chair opposite Inka, who was snoring. When Brylee asked him if she could be of service and expressed a desire to learn healing and magical theory—she wasn't ready to divulge she had the potential to perform great magic and suggested her apprenticeship would be of the non-magical sort—he thought about it and then proposed a deal. He already had an apprentice, whom he had contracted for the next two and a half summers. If Brylee helped his godson with this farming cycle and assisted in choosing foremen and managers who could support Jyan, then Garrick would consider her for the apprenticeship when the time came.

The next morning at breakfast after a sound sleep free of doubts, Brylee committed to helping Jyan, at least for the current growing cycle. He was delighted. By sunset she had her own room in the loft of the house, not unlike her room in Haxley. She also had her own horse, a stallion called Whipcrack, and was touring the fields nearest to the property with Jyan, ensconced in the nuances of hop farming.

Chapter Sixty

That spring and summer, Brylee worked as hard as she ever had back home. By summer's end Jyan and Brylee had hired first-rate growers, sellers, and shippers who eased the burden of day-to-day work. Their team expanded their market share across Yarrow by introducing some fruity radlers, an ultra-hoppy ale of a pale, hazy hue, as well as the darkest stout in the region, which Brylee had secretly modelled on Plainhand Estate Sludge.

Garrick had been as good as his word and had topped up the Galei stone before leaving for his own manor. Over those first few days at Harding's Farm, Brylee tapped into that magic to subtly change her features and colouring so that no one working there would link Senna to her future self too easily. Since then she had only lightly tapped that source when practising her technique at interrogating the properties of various things and applying them to other objects in small quantities.

Just after the last field had been fallowed for winter, when the air smelled of a snow that was yet to fall and puddles froze overnight but melted by noon the next day, Dara, the maid, split the dawn's silence with a loud, baleful keening. The whole household rushed to the source of the sad cry to find Dara kneeling beside Inka's bed, the old woman's hand clutched in her own. Tears tumbled down Dara's cheeks as she mourned for the woman she had worked for since childhood. Inka would have looked as though she were resting in a peaceful sleep if not for her white-grey pallor and blue-purple lips. Brylee backed out of the room, leaving Jyan, Dara, and other close domestic staff to say goodbye to Inka and comfort each other.

When Jyan emerged into the kitchen some time later, Brylee had the ovens lit, hot food and drinks set up, and a ready hug for the man of whom she had become quite fond. Garrick arrived by lunchtime, and the three of them ate lightly, drank heavily, and then retired to the living room viewpoint that Inka had almost lived in of late and perhaps haunted still. They told stories of better times, many of which were outrageously funny and often so rude they caused Brylee to blush, shocked at the old men's revelations. At her best, Inka had been a force of nature. Garrick believed Inka's broken heart drove her to drinking, seeking to numb herself with wine until her liver gave out. He thought she was now back with her husband, causing him trouble and leading him astray once more.

Inka's death ceremony, known locally as a sky funeral, was delayed past the three days that Yarrow tradition demanded, as many from afar wished to attend. Garrick used his magic to maintain a cold space to preserve Inka's remains for three weeks until the last of many coaches struggled up the long drive from the main road. It was pulled by a pair of tired white geldings.

Brylee was wrapped up on the porch, snug in a swinging chair and deep in her thoughts, when she heard shod hooves rattling up the cold, hard path. She looked up, finding the carriage's ornate heraldry and sigils familiar, though she could not place them. She stood as the carriage swung around to stop next to the entrance. A footman jumped down from the bench atop the vehicle, swinging his arms and mashing his gloves together to warm his fingers before opening the coach's door.

The door behind Brylee wheezed open, spilling light across the porch as Jyan shuffled out, tugging a warm cloak around himself. The footman opened the carriage door and unfolded the wooden steps. A moment later, Mella Stonebrook descended, looking tired and dishevelled. Jyan's face lit up and he hopped down to meet her. The pair fell into the hug of good friends too long apart, brought together in sad circumstances.

"Sunny crops, Jyan. I was so sorry to hear such sad news," Mella said, looking up at him and clutching his cheek. Brylee's heart had raced for several seconds before her brain reminded her that Mella would know Brylee as a young, wiry girl of nineteen summers not yet grown into her body. She was unlikely to recognise her today, even without the subtle magical modification she maintained. So it was something of a shock that after introductions and a goblet of warm wine in front of a roaring fire, Mella flagrantly grilled "Senna" about her heritage, convinced there must be some familial link to Luka and Celeste Plainhand back in Haxley.

Two days later, following a poignant ceremony and a lively, drunken wake around a seven-foot-tall pyre that burnt long into the night, Brylee was sitting in the chair opposite the one in which Inka used to nap when Mella bustled into the living room. Out of respect, no one had sat in Inka's chair since her death, but Mella plopped into it without hesitation.

"I'm not being disrespectful," she began in a mildly chiding tone, seeing Brylee's reaction to her taking Inka's seat. "It's such silliness that's making poor Jyan so depressed. We need to turn him around before he follows his sister down the same macabre path."

"I think he knew it was coming," Brylee replied. "Inka's passing, I mean. Looking back, I think he began grieving her parting moons ago. Now that she's gone, he's at a bit of a loss about how to react."

"Maybe," Mella replied, although she was shaking her head in disagreement. "The Hardings are sweet, hardworking folk, and I love the man dearly, but they've always had a bit of a disposition towards glumness. Jyan's always needed a project to perk him up. What should we make him do, do you think?"

"Doesn't he choose his own projects?" Brylee asked with a laugh, realising how much she missed the rascally older woman.

"Nonsense. Where would be the fun in that?" Mella smiled back. "I think he needs a holiday. Do you think you can handle things here for a moon or two . . . or three? I'm going to tell him to go exploring, and I won't brook any argument about it. He will thank me in time. You see if he doesn't."

"I can certainly keep things ticking over here until spring planting. To be honest I expect it to be pretty quiet. Have you thought about where you're sending him?" Brylee asked, raising an eyebrow.

"No. That's the thing. Do you have a suggestion?"

"Actually, yes," Brylee replied, sitting straighter. Ideas that she had been kicking around for the summer but didn't know how to get traction with rushed forth at the opportunity that Mella might represent. "He should travel the Rainbow Archipelago, especially the Green Isle. I hear they grow a strain of t'Yuk bean that can be crushed and heated to make an interesting drink. Jyan and I have been discussing ways he could make use of the acres at the north of his estate, and I think if tempered with bellyberry, which we have in abundance, he could grow t'Yuk here."

"What would be the point of that?" Mella asked, leaning in, not committed but curious.

"Well, wine, ale, and tea are fine drinks later in the day, but none are a rewarding way to start your morning. I hear ground t'Yuk has quite a kick to get you going. A nice complement to ale and a similar supply chain and customer base. I've even had a few ideas about new ways he might sell it."

Mella approached the idea with Jyan at their next breakfast. She pointed out how depressed and woolly he was that morning and said he was going to find a fine example of what was missing in the world: a breakfast drink to get the brain going and shake off the morning fog. Jyan was intrigued, and when Brylee confirmed she would be honoured to take care of the ranch in his absence, he took up the idea as if it were his own.

Mella and Brylee let him embellish the notion, adding his own touches and ideas, sharing the occasional conspiratorial glance. Jyan was well hooked and Mella smugly reeled him in when Brylee had a thought to make her own mischief.

"You know, Jyan," she began, the seeming paragon of innocence, "my duties will keep me here, but would it not be more rewarding if you had someone to share the trip with you? Someone with business acumen, who knows farming in the organisational sense? Why don't you take Mella with you?"

Mella protested, a little too hard in Brylee's opinion, yet it all fell together so swiftly she began to wonder if accompanying Jyan on a trip had been Mella's intention all along, as much the point of her visit as Inka's ceremony.

A week later, Jyan and Mella set off in Mella's carriage with a convoy of carts stacked with trunks. Brylee thought she could hear the old man explaining the joys ahead to Mella for the twentieth time as they turned the corner onto the main road.

Brylee enjoyed the silence of the house for the first two weeks. With the help of the Galei stones, she practised talking to the polished pebble that Levi had given her to train with, which she now treated as a cherished keepsake. She interrogated its attributes, taking its hardness, colour, temperature, and other characteristics and applying them to the air or water she kept in a small glass in her room. It was something she had worked hard on since arriving at Jyan's, but now the slower workdays and increased privacy helped her concentrate far more.

On the fourteenth night after Jyan's departure, Brylee realised that at some point she had stopped extracting the attribute from the stones and instead was applying them to the water from her memory alone, something that apparently Mage Wickham had never achieved. She flushed with pride at her achievement but also felt a wave of unexpected unease. Such powers would change her life in many ways.

Brylee went to the kitchen for a plate of food and a glass of milk. When she returned, she saw a messenger trotting through the light snow up the driveway. She pulled a cloak from the hook by the door, slipped into her fleece-lined boots, and stepped outside to greet him.

"Mage Garrick the Lesser sends his compliments," the prim man began. "He asks if you're free tomorrow night to dine with him at his manor." Brylee guessed that the old man, realising she was alone but for the staff, was just being neighbourly, so she accepted. She told him to give his mount to one of the stable hands, then to warm himself and take a bite to fortify himself for his trip home on that cold, murky night.

The next evening Brylee dressed in warm clothing and then set off on Whipcrack, opting to travel across the country, eschewing the road. The moon was full, and the air was clear and crisp. She enjoyed the journey as much for the view of the stars reflecting in the river as she did that the direct route shaved half a bell off her travel time.

Garrick set a generous table, including roast beef, gravy, carrots, and roasted potatoes. It was just the two of them, as his apprentice, Jia, was away for the week, travelling from village to village seeing what she could do for folk and practising the techniques she had learned. She would often return with all manner of gifts that the grateful patients insisted she accept despite her insistence no debt was owed and it was her honour to help. The gifts included herbs, baked goods, even livestock on occasion.

They talked while they drank their way through a carafe of white wine. Whenever Garrick turned the conversation towards seeking stories from Brylee's past, she steered him away, asking about magical healing techniques instead. She was as eager to protect her history as she was interested in learning anything that might save Levi in just over three years' time.

Garrick called out to his maid to refill the carafe, but his call went unanswered. Brylee offered to fetch the bottle, but the old man's pride hauled him to his feet. As he stepped away from the table, he turned to finish a thought, and his foot caught the edge of the carpet. He twisted, falling backwards onto the table and sending several items crashing to the ground, which was where gravity dragged him next, and he thudded down on top of them.

Brylee leapt up and raced around the table in a few quick strides. He was laughing at his own clumsiness, clutching his waist.

"Forgive an old man's drunken feet," he said with a chuckle as she helped him sit up. Brylee was beginning to relax, assuming Garrick would have but bruises to his hip and his ego when he coughed once, then again, and then a third time. It was the last cough that brought blood to his lips. For a moment they both stared at each other, then Garrick looked down at his body, engaging his ability to scan inside for damage.

"Damn it to Ag," he cried, his eyes wide.

"What is it?"

"I've broken a rib, and it has poked its way into my lungs." He turned carefully to ease the pressure. "This is bad. If I move, I'll make the wound bigger." He coughed again, more violently this time.

"What can I do?" she asked. "Can't you fix it?" He shook his head, and she remembered it was a rare ability for anyone to perform magic on their own body.

Just then the maid came in and rushed to Garrick's side when she saw him on the floor leaning on his dinner guest.

"Send a rider to Camberton. Jia should be at the Tipsy Butcher Tavern. It's the only inn there," he said, gasping. "Hurry now. I don't have long." The maid and Brylee shared a look. Both knew the round trip to fetch Jia could take longer than the old man had.

When the maid left, Brylee decided to act, risking exposure of her hard-kept secrets. Mostly because it was the right thing to do, but a small part of her, which she felt ashamed about, whispered that the mage had to live for another year at least so he could be killed by the Red Assassin if she were to save Levi.

"Lie still," she said to Garrick with a sense of authority she didn't feel. "And don't ask questions. I think I can help, but I need to concentrate." She looked into his body with her magical sight, drawing on the Galei stones. Her experiments over the last two weeks had left the stones depleted. She reached back and undid the clasp, then removed the necklace, pressing it into the mage's shaky hand. "I need magic. Pour as much as you can into these stones and I'll draw it out again. It's a way to transfer your power to me." He looked at her in bewilderment for a few moments before he realised what she needed him to do. Closing his eyes to help him focus, he set to it.

Brylee realised that if she pushed his rib backwards, clear of the puncture site, more blood and fluid would flow into his lung, which was already struggling to remain inflated. But even if that wasn't a problem, she wasn't sure how to manipulate the bone. There was no air to harden. Could she harden his blood and move that as she had with air? She wasn't sure she wanted to experiment. If she ripped his lung further, he would die before she could work out what she was doing. *Your world is not limited by reality*, she recalled Levi saying.

Brylee's mind whispered to the blood and tissue that surrounded the rib. *What makes you, you? Tell me your secrets.* Then she did the same with the tissue that comprised the wall of Garrick's lung. It took a little longer to get a feel for that, but with some flattery, the lung's lining shared what it knew of itself. She held all this information in her head as if it were a cherished picture. Then she imposed the blood's attributes onto the tip of the rib. She imposed energy into that concept, wishing it into existence as she drew on the Galei stones. The tip of the bone obediently melted and became blood. Her confidence growing, Brylee repeated the process, teasing the rib to turn to blood a fraction at a time until the bone still blocked the hole but had been reduced back to where it pierced the lung.

Brylee turned her attention to the lung's wall. *It should know how to heal itself,* she thought. *I just need to speed it up. Then I can melt the bone back a little farther so it won't cause more damage.* She pictured what she wanted, leaning on the lung's knowledge of itself to regrow. But no matter how much energy she poured into it, the lung failed to respond. She checked the Galei stones' reserves. Despite Garrick pouring his power into them, her efforts were depleting them; they were nearly empty.

What's wrong with you, little lung? Won't you talk to me? Help me?

"I'm too old," she felt it was telling her. She realised that the ancient mage's body had aged to the point it was forgetting how to repair itself and regenerate. Realising she needed younger tissue, she talked to her own lung. It took a while, but she eventually teased out what was different between the old and young tissue and applied those elements to Garrick's wound. Gradually, the hole slowed its bleeding and began to close around the blunted rib. As the hole narrowed, Brylee focussed on closing the hole further while also melting the rib back farther.

When the hole had repaired itself, Brylee examined the lung, which was saturated with blood. She imposed the attributes for air on the blood, and some of it began to change, but then the Galei stones ran dry. Glancing up, she saw that Garrick had fainted and had stopped adding his power to the process. Had she done enough?

With nothing more she could do magically, Brylee pulled the tablecloth down and wrapped it over them both, feeling deathly cold. Exhausted, she closed her eyes for a moment. That was how the maid found them when she rushed back into the room. She peeked under the cover and noted Garrick's bleeding had stopped and his colour was returning. She elected not to disturb them other than to ease the pillows around them as she was able. Then she sat in a chair and watched them sleep, which they did peacefully for four hours until Jia rushed in to help.

Chapter Sixty-One

Brylee woke first and immediately received a barrage of questions from Jia. The apprentice had enough skill to detect that Garrick's lung lining had not repaired itself using the normal magical method. Brylee deflected the questions by feigning ignorance, suggesting Garrick must have healed himself. Jia was quick to point out that she thought that impossible, to which Brylee shrugged innocently. It was soon clear that Garrick didn't take on idiots to be his apprentices. Jia was immediately suspicious. Brylee felt the younger woman scan her magically from time to time, trying to solve the riddle.

Garrick slept for the next five days. Brylee shuttled back and forth, tending to her duties at Hardings and sitting by the mage's bedside. Jia had to work hard to reduce a fever that settled in from an infection on the third day. It finally broke on the evening of the fourth day, and his fifth day was peaceful. When Brylee arrived to check on him on the sixth day, Garrick was awake and eating heartily. Jia was in his room and reluctant to leave, so Brylee waited until she could finally talk privately with Garrick.

"How much do you remember?" she began.

"I remember feeding you magic through the Galei stones," he replied. "And I recall you using it to do some extraordinary magical feats, for which, of course, I'm grateful."

"Is there any chance your memory is . . . blurry?" Brylee asked coyly.

"I certainly told Jia it is. She's been quite persistent. And who can blame her? It's not often one sees evidence of a miracle, is it?" He paused to take a sip of tea from a chunky blue cup. And I don't think you've been entirely honest with me, young lady."

"I haven't lied to you," Brylee said, her eyes meeting his. "There are just things I'm obligated not to share, even if I could explain them."

"Well, I suppose that's one reason I'll keep your secret, Senna." He sighed. "People would think me a daft old man claiming a woman without even the power of a charmer had more talent than a mage."

"There's another reason?" Brylee asked.

"You saved my life? I like you? You intrigue me? You seem to have a purpose that feels . . . vital. I can't explain it. Call it an old man's intuition."

"It is vital, my purpose," Brylee said, wondering if she should say more. "I've been told by someone, who I have reason to trust, that my actions in the future might save us all. But I have to be ready when the time comes. I don't know much except that I will need to heal a man from a dire wound if I'm to be successful. I have considerable ability with the Galei stones but almost no medical knowledge to direct it, hence my interest in apprenticing with you."

"Yes, I see that now. Well, I'm grateful to you, and although your purpose sounds a little far-fetched to me, I'm happy to begin teaching you as soon as Jyan's back and we can work something out."

Brylee considered telling Garrick that he was to be assassinated at the turn of the year but held her tongue. *I have time to think about it, and I must swim with the fewest ripples.* Try as she might, she couldn't picture a scenario where she would let this man she had become fond of fall to the Red Assassin.

Three moons later, Brylee was setting seedlings into pots in the nursery, pouring a little magic into each one as she had with the daighberries that fed her Wispy Weed stock, when she was distracted by a commotion outside. She slid off her gloves and wiped her brow with her sleeve as she slipped through the nursery's glass door and went to investigate. A procession of wagons laden with sacks was being led up the driveway by a plain white carriage, and Jyan's bright face beamed through its window. Soon the yard was filled with people welcoming him home, keen to hear of his adventures.

"No Mella?" Brylee asked, noticing Jyan was the carriage's only occupant. A sad look crossed his face, but he shook it off and beamed anew.

"Uh, no. She is a fun companion, but quite . . . active. I fear I didn't generate enough intrigue to keep her attention. We said our fond goodbyes at Grovesport. She has returned to meddle with politics in Haxley. But let me show you these t'Yuk beans," he said as he marched back to the nearest cart, not waiting for her to follow. When Brylee caught up with him, he had already sliced open a sack using his pocketknife and had a handful of beans. He passed them to her and then led her inside, all the while explaining their merits and how he thought it was best to sow them in the northern pastures.

As spring gave way to summer and both crops were planted, Brylee felt the team they had hired had things well in hand, so she broached the topic of her moving to live with Mage Garrick as his apprentice. Jyan was distraught at first. Was it because he had neglected her, so taken up with planting his new crop and experimenting with the mature beans he had brought home with him? He had valued her in his life since his sister died. It became an emotional evening, but he understood she had her own life to lead and would be just down the road. By the end of the week, Brylee had transplanted herself from one house to the other and was up to her neck in textbooks and lessons from Garrick and Jia.

As summer passed into fall, the shadow of the Red Assassin grew taller in Brylee's mind. She began to pay close attention to any new faces at the house and spent more time visiting the inns in the area, attempting to find ways to detect his presence. Using money she had saved from her wages, she hired three men: one to join Garrick's staff under the cover of gardener and the other two in the local villages. The three became her spy network to vet strangers as the year progressed. She took a week to help Jyan bring in the harvests and then over a dinner at Garrick's, she explained she needed to go away but would return at the year's end. She felt guilty telling a white lie, that she had word that a relative of hers in the town of Sandrick in the Northern Regions had fallen sick beyond the healer's abilities and she needed to attend to them immediately.

She knew nothing of Ostryd van Hyke other than that Levi deemed him salient and that he would die in Sandrick sometime in the next weeks. Over the summer, Brylee had worked with local dressmakers to create a wardrobe of clothing, which she dyed with the algae she had discovered in Rostal. This enabled her to change its colour using magic from the Galei stones. She knew she could achieve the same end by tweaking the material's attributes with her primi powers, but that would take time and power from the Galei stones that she couldn't spare.

The following day, she set off on Whipcrack. That night she arrived at the first inn she had chosen for her journey north in the guise of a man. It took ten days to reach Sandrick, where she took a room at the Iron Rock Tavern. She observed the comings and goings for a week and was beginning to despair that she would never locate Ostryd when someone she recognised walked into the tavern and turned her heart to ice. She stood, a wave of hot rage gripping her, and for a moment she was intent on killing the man. It was the man who had driven a sword through Levi's heart. With great effort, and constant reminders that she must swim softly and make few ripples, she was able to sit and observe another man who came over to talk to Levi's assailant.

As Brylee watched the meeting, she switched to her magical vision and examined their links. Levi's assailant had a link of some girth, but it was twisted and confused. It had the tremor of turbulence that had marked her own connection to the crisis that Levi was investigating. Her own link had lost its tremor now that she was living in the past, and she often wondered what that meant. The other man's link was smaller, not much bigger than a charmer's, but she spotted something that she hadn't seen before: neither link was attached to the source. The smaller one was looped around it, and the larger one was flailing around it, touching it but improperly connected.

For the next few days, changing her guise often, Brylee pieced together the network of people surrounding the two men, including, to her great surprise and disappointment, Lu. She had grown fond of the woman, only to find she had been playing them and presumably spying for the assailant. She watched the arrival and departure of the Bredden acolytes. She also helped pass buckets of water to quell the night-time fire, which she later discovered had taken Ostryd's life.

Brylee thought about following Gideon, perhaps asking to join the caravan he seemed to be overseeing, but instead she had to withdraw. It was time to get back to intercept the Red Assassin. She vowed that if Gideon turned out to be the assassin, she would kill him, damn the timeline. It would just have to sort itself out somehow.

Due to the worsening weather, it took ten days more to travel home. When she got there, things were not as she'd left them.

Chapter Sixty-Two

Brylee had pushed late into the night to make it home rather than spend another night at an inn. She arrived at Garrick's house after second bell in the morning, surprised to see lights on behind the shutters. She walked Whipcrack into the barn, removed his tack, and settled him into a stall with some fresh hay and feed before entering the house. She had reverted to her "Senna guise" on the road but did a quick check in the looking glass by the front door. Sometimes, when her cheeks were frozen from the deep chill of winter, her skin was reluctant to change as instructed. When she was satisfied with her features, she stripped off her warm riding clothes, hung them on the coat rack by the door, and then stepped into the kitchen.

Jia was rearranging logs in the stove to encourage a large pot of water to boil, but when she saw Brylee, she put down the poker and stepped over to give her a hug. She made no attempt to hide her red, puffy eyes, surrounded by black circles.

"What happened?" Brylee asked, assuming the assassin had struck while she was travelling. Yet, according to Mage Wickham's investigation, the attack wouldn't happen for another week.

"It's Elijah," Jia cried, fresh tears springing onto her cheeks. "His heart."

"Is he . . ." Brylee's own eyes filled, about to brim over. She drew in a deep breath, as if that would keep the tears in.

"Oh, no . . . not yet. But soon, I think," Jia said, pushing her brown fringe away from her eyes to better wipe them on her sleeve. "He keeps asking for you. It's like he won't let go without saying goodbye to you. Jyan's been by every afternoon and sits by his bedside. They share a late meal and talk when Elijah has the energy."

"His heart . . . how?" Brylee asked. "Was there an incident?"

"No. He's an elderly man, and his heart's always been a liability. I've done all I can, but it's just his time. Anyway, go on through. He was awake asking for you again when I came away to get water for his tea. I'll bring it when the water boils."

Brylee pushed the door to Garrick's bedroom open and poked her head inside. Her hand flew to her mouth. The deflated, grey figure propped up against the pillar didn't resemble the vibrant, rascally old man she had last seen. She hardly recognised him. His eyes were closed, and she was about to withdraw when he whispered her name.

"I'm here," she said, hurrying to his bedside and grasping his withered hand. "I'm sorry I went away. You didn't tell me your heart—"

"Well, it got me this far, didn't it? I didn't want to worry you." The corners of his mouth rose as he spoke, and his hand twisted to grip hers.

"The Galei stones are low, but otherwise I think I could help." They had spent the summer with him teaching her everything he knew that might repair a heart, and with her primi magic, she believed she would be able to generate younger heart tissue, as she had done for his lung. She started to magically examine his heart, seeing immediately he had suffered a massive heart attack and the damage was extensive. Garrick's eyes opened, and he stared up at her, noting her tears and concern.

"You know, I think you could," he said. "You're a miracle; that's what you are. I'd never imagined such a person existed. But I don't think I have the capacity to draw much magic now to refill the Galei stones. Anyway, that's not what I want. I'm tired, and I want to choose a different path. I have a gift for you... before I... go. Just, give me a moment."

Brylee waited impatiently, wanting to shake him so he would at least try to replenish the Galei stones. After a few moments, she realised he was sleeping. She reached out with her left leg and hooked it around the chair, pulling it closer. She sat holding his hand and watching him breathe until Jia entered and made tea for all three of them.

"He's stable at the moment," Jia said. "It's how he's been since the attack. He'll sleep for a few hours now, I think. But he will go soon. Tomorrow, maybe. A week at the outside."

For the next five days, Brylee only left Garrick's bedside to sleep when Jyan visited, and even then only when he promised to fetch Brylee from her bed if Garrick stirred. She wanted to convince the old fool to fill up the Galei stones so she could work on him. For the brief moments Garrick stirred, however, he wasn't coherent.

For those five days she worried. Any day now the Red Assassin should show up. She had learned from her gardener-spy that no one in her mini network had seen anything that sounded unusual at the house or elsewhere. Brylee kept her short knives close by and reserved the remaining power of the Galei stones to supply her in the use of various types of magic that she had devised as weapons. But another part of her worried the Red Assassin would not appear. What if Garrick just died of natural causes? Would the hunt for the assassin happen? Would Wickham take her into his employ? Would she ever meet Levi? She missed Levi terribly, and she was surprised that such intense feelings could evolve so quickly.

The year turned, but there were no celebrations. The only change to the bedside routine was that, on New Year's Day, Jyan was late to Garrick's bedside. His duty to host his household's feast for the staff kept him at Hardings for longer than he wished.

On the seventh day after her return from Sandrick, Brylee became frantic. This was the day Wickham believed the attack would happen. She attempted to dissuade Jyan from his afternoon visit, suggesting he looked worn down and a day's rest would do him good. He had agreed to see how he felt, but in the end couldn't sleep. In fact, he rose early and stopped to pick bellyberries on his way over. It was an unusual fruit that matured on the bush into the fall, with the berry buds forming just as winter set in. The first warm days in the new year saw the buds burst, revealing fresh scarlet fruit. They were too small, unripe, and bitter to eat and wouldn't be harvested for four moons, but they let off a beautiful aroma, similar to a cherry but with a tang of mint.

"I know Elijah loves this smell. I was awake anyway, so I rode out and picked some for him," Jyan said, placing a bowl of the crushed berries on the bedside table. "I've left more in the kitchen. The smell will fade quickly now that I've broken the skins, but there's enough for a few days . . ." His voice broke as he shared a look with Brylee that said he didn't expect they would need much of the additional supply.

Brylee left the two men alone and snuck around the house, checking that every window and door was secured and visited every place she felt an assassin could hide in wait were he already inside. She had recalled her spy network to the property and checked in with each of them to verify that they hadn't seen anyone and that they were alert at their posts.

Jyan stayed until a bell before nightfall. When he left, Brylee took up the vigil. She was so keyed up that she jumped when Garrick called her name.

"Ah, there you are. I think it's time for your gift, Senna." He spoke as if continuing their conversation of a week ago, sharp and with his wits about him. "Now, I don't have much left in me, so please just do as I instruct. No arguments, you hear?"

She nodded, not sure at all what he meant.

"Good. Now, with the vision you use to see inside a patient, look carefully at my chest. You see here? Something like a cord that glows?" He pointed to where his link to the source left his body. Brylee could see it plainly but had never shared the fact that she could with the mage. She doubted he could see much more than the stub of the link. Few people could. But she told him she could see it now that it was pointed out to her.

"Good. Now, you have to take it. You have one too, and you have to take mine and merge it with your own." He stopped, seeing how wide her eyes had grown and how she was shaking her head. "Ah, I suspected you knew about our links. Now, don't be silly. This isn't skriking. It's my gift. If you don't take it, it will be wasted."

"No, Elijah," she cried. "I can't. I won't!"

"You will, Senna. Is that even your name?" he asked, cocking his head to the side. "Never mind. You're a miracle starved of magic. You're a noble woman, Senna. You could be the most talented mage of our age if you had your own power. Some mages inherit their power from their parents, but many start off like this, with a gift from one of us who has no use for their own anymore to another they deem worthy. That is how I ascended from a charmer over ninety summers ago. I had planned to give mine to Jia, but I sense your need is greater, and I think your heart is purer, although there is nothing wrong with hers. Take it."

Brylee's head and heart were spinning. She didn't know what to do. She didn't want to take Garrick's link. It would end him, and it would mean there was no murder by the Red Assassin. What would happen to Levi?

With an effort, Garrick tugged at his link until it broke. It hung in the air between them, the glow that remained in his body dimming quickly.

"Say goodbye to Jyan for me," were his last words before his eyes lost focus and the glow faded entirely. Brylee felt as if her own heart had stopped. She didn't dare breathe for fear she would either take the offered link or it would fade if she moved even a hair. She realised it was too late for the assassin to play his part, so with mixed feelings, she reached out with her senses and touched the wavering link. As she felt it, a wave of greediness took her and she drew his link into her own. A feeling of euphoria swept through her, which disgusted her.

The power of Garrick's link, massive compared to what she had as a charmer, flowed into her. She was so disoriented by the power she felt that her head spun. She fell to one knee, disturbing the bedside table. The bellyberry bowl flipped, tossing the crushed contents onto Garrick's face and chest, creating a bright red splatter.

"Sorry," Brylee said without thinking. As her senses settled and she regained her composure, she looked down. It was as if the Red Assassin had visited and left his mark. Brylee's brain refused to process anything for several seconds, but then the pieces fell into place. *Time will have its way. Do I impersonate the Red Assassin? Could I actually be the Red Assassin? Is this time eddying, trying to right itself? After all, the Red Assassin can change his features.*

As if to ground her spinning thoughts, Brylee reached down and closed Garrick's eyes. Then she sat down to think. Jia and the staff had turned in for the night, so she had time to take stock of this twist of fate. She forced herself to gather her many and disparate thoughts. If she were the Red Assassin, that meant she would have to kill Vekki in cold blood in the theatre. Well, the woman had attempted to kill her, so . . . But even if she could do that, which she doubted, there was still the assassin's next kill, Mage Alleg. He wasn't a nice man, by all accounts, but she couldn't kill him in cold blood. There was no way. *Swim carefully, make few ripples.* What did that even mean now?

Half a bell later, Brylee was still sitting there, trying to unravel the mess. What stayed with her most throughout was the red mess on her mentor's face. If time had conspired to create the mark of the assassin, could she ignore it? If she became the assassin now, it didn't commit her to murder later, did it? If she wiped away the mess, then there would be no assassin in the future, and her hopes and perhaps the future would unravel. *Ag, what the hell?*

She thought about how she could pull this off. Only one part of it seemed difficult. Could she? She took her dagger from her belt and held it over Garrick's weak, treacherous heart. He wouldn't have wanted to die for a mission he didn't understand, but she had to believe he would forgive her for what she had to do next. *Perhaps I'm saving the world by doing this,* she thought, knowing she was trying to build a case she didn't truly believe. Before she could second guess her idea, she pushed down. The knife went in easily. Garrick didn't move, although Brylee half expected him to leap up in pain, accusing her. With his heart stopped, not much blood emerged until she tugged at it with her new power.

The hard part done, Brylee kissed Garrick's forehead, apologised for her intrusion, then said a quiet prayer for his onward journey and another for her own soul, which she suspected she had just damned. She thought of all those times she had put on her one dress and attended the cathedral, full of doubt and cynicism. Why was she so scared for her soul now? She set those thoughts aside with a deep breath.

"OK, now for some real magic," she said, squaring her shoulders and drawing Garrick's gift into herself. First, she focussed on the berries. It took fifteen minutes to get them to reveal how they needed to change to be less like fruit and more like dye. When she understood, with the massive power of a full mage flowing into her, the transformation took but a moment.

So familiar was she with magically altering her clothing, it took less time than it had with the berries to turn her garb into something that resembled the pictures Wickham had shown her of the Namiduh Jou. She changed her facial features to look like an average man with an easily forgettable face and then wrapped her scarf halfway around her head, as if it had accidently fallen away.

She took some of Garrick's note paper and a charcoal from the bedside drawer and altered the paper magically, making it heavier and more formal than the mage's stock. Then she turned its colour red and wrote, "By Order of The Namiduh Jou" in a script different from her own. She lay the note on Garrick's body, allowing a little of the dye to stain a corner.

She crept to the front door, returning with her boots, and pulled them on. She opened the window, pushing back the shutters and catching the curtains as they billowed into the room. She stepped outside, barely noting the knifing cold. She let her eyes adjust to the dark and then looked about to confirm where her spies were hidden. Then she let out a scream. When the men looked around, she took off into the night, reaching the woods at the rear of the house in two dozen strides. Once she was out of sight, she formed steps out of hard air, clambered up them to a tree branch twenty feet up in the darkness, then dissolved them behind herself. Just as she was out of view, the three men rushed below her, swords drawn as they pursued the figure they had seen.

Brylee quickly retraced her steps, reverting her clothing and features to their previous state as she ran across the yard and was back through the window in seconds. She took her knife out again, and, wincing, struck herself hard on the side of her head with its handle, drawing blood. There would be a nasty bruise there in no time. She sheathed the blade, then laid down waiting for the household to wake and rush in and hopefully assume she had been attacked and knocked down. As she lay there listening to the people approach, she realised she was still wearing her boots. She kicked them off and threw them behind a chair.

An instant later, the room was full of people. Brylee pretended to be disoriented from the blow but coming around. She was quick to describe the man who had burst in, stabbed Garrick, then fled through the window.

Chapter Sixty-Three

Jyan took Garrick's "assassination" hard even though he had prepared himself for the old man's imminent passing from the heart attack. The invasion of his godfather's home by an assassin, the viciousness of stabbing a defenceless man, and that someone would pay to murder Garrick when waiting a day or two would achieve the same result suggested to the world that something was "off" about a man he had loved his whole life. And Jyan hated anyone thinking Garrick was anything other than what he appeared, a kind and wonderful man who cared about his community. If Brylee could have taken her action back, she would have. It broke her heart to see Jyan suffer so. Telling the truth at that point was an option, but she would only cause more trauma and further jeopardise those in the future she was attempting to save.

Garrick's household staff had sent a man to Harding's immediately, and a manhunt for the assassin had started at dawn. Messengers were sent by horse to all the surrounding settlements, and by evening a sheriff from the nearest town had arrived to inspect the scene and conduct interviews. Anticipating her spy network would reveal they had been hired to look out for strangers, Brylee opted to cover her own part in things by announcing that Mage Garrick had confided in her that an attack was imminent and asked her to hire the watchers on his behalf. Brylee claimed he hadn't shared his reasons and had sworn her to secrecy, in particular not to tell Jyan, and she had reluctantly complied.

Two days after Garrick's death, Jyan and Brylee were in Hop's Head, the nearest town to Harding's, to visit the local representative of the office of the lands. Jyan had a copy of Garrick's documented wishes in hand, which would match the official record the mage had legally registered. Their other business in town had taken longer than expected, so when they arrived at Justice Vee's office, it was lunchtime. Vee was a long-time friend of Jyan and Garrick, having transacted many dealings for them over three decades. He insisted on buying them both lunch before they dealt with their business, so they were sitting in the window seats of the Black Bush Tavern when six dark-cloaked soldiers escorted a black carriage into the town square.

The captain of the escort dismounted, obtained directions from a passing carter, then proceeded up the steps to Justice Vee's office. Brylee had observed this activity while the two men were deep in nostalgic stories about their departed friend and had to interrupt them to draw their attention to the visitors.

"That's the livery of the Council of Magical Law," Vee said through a mouthful of bread covered in clam stew. "I can't imagine what they want, but it would be a big coincidence if their presence here didn't relate to Elijah's passing. I had better go see what they need." Jyan offered to accompany Vee, but the justice declined. On his way out, Brylee heard him tell the barkeep to charge the meal to his account.

Vee was halfway back to his office when the soldier returned to the carriage, so Vee intercepted the man and introduced himself. The carriage door opened, and a tall young man in mage's robes dismounted, then turned and helped an equally tall woman in ostentatious green and gold trappings down the coach's steps. Brylee immediately checked that her shine shadow was optimal. She had not had to worry about it since Levi sent her back in time, as that transfer had left her with just a natural link. As Garrick's gift to her was so much bigger than her bolstered charmer power had been, she had to master a much denser shine shadow than she required during her time back in Rostal.

There was a brief discussion before the justice ushered the strange pair into his chambers. At a signal from the captain, two of his men took up positions on either side of the door, presumably to prevent anyone from joining the group. Twenty minutes passed before the doors opened, and the mage and his party remounted and left the square on the Harding Road, which would take them out to Mage Garrick's manor.

By this time Jyan and Brylee had finished their lunch, so they made their way across to Vee's chambers. They found him flustered and pale as he fumed behind his desk.

"Is everything all right, Jedomire?" Jyan asked, using the justice's given name.

"No, it is not. Not at all, in fact," Vee grumped. "The mage claims to be here at the behest of his council to investigate the circumstances surrounding Elijah's passing."

"That's a good thing, surely," Brylee said, eager to seem to be seeking the assailant and justice.

"Yes, but they've commandeered the official copy of Mage Garrick's wishes as well as the deeds to his lands." Vee shook his head. "In a murder investigation, I would be expected to provide a copy to the investigators, as the documents may provide possible motives, but they insisted on taking the originals and leaving me with nothing."

"That's dreadful," Jyan fumed, upset on his friend's behalf. "Here, take my copy. At least you'll have that. If you can make a second version and return it to me, I would appreciate it. What else can we do?"

"Well," Vee said, returning to his seat and placing the document in a drawer, "you'd better follow them, I suppose. They're looking for you, Jyan. You're the primary beneficiary, and you and the sheriff have handled the investigation to date. I didn't tell them you were seated across the square, as I thought you might like time to prepare."

"That was kind of you, Jedomire," Jyan said, "but I think it's straightforward, no? I'll just explain the circumstances and help as best I can."

"I hope so, Jyan, I really do. But these are not nice people." He pulled his chair tight into his desk, as if taking protection behind it. "They put a scare into me, if I'm honest. The mage was overbearing, disrespectful, and quick to overstep my boundaries. The captain seemed like a brute. But it was the woman who really frightened me. She said little and watched me as if she would devour me, but it was her hands that were truly unsettling."

"Her hands?" Brylee asked. "Why?"

"The woman has a large silver bracelet on her left wrist. It's as thick as a loaf of bread and evidently hollow. From holes along its length, I saw at least two thin snakes slither out to wrap themselves around her fingers like jewellery. One was bright red and the other black. They moved slowly, and several times she raised her hand to her lips and whispered to them, like they were her pets."

"How odd," Jyan said. "That would be unsettling."

"And I could be wrong, but whenever I declined the mage's instruction, I swear the snakes turned to look at me, their tongues flickering my way, as if tasting my resolve. Anyway, between them all, I wilted, I'm afraid, and gave away the original documents."

"Then I will go get them back, Jedomire," Jyan said. "What are their names?"

"They are brother and sister, it seems. He is Mage Alleg Ordel, and she is his sister, Alleph Ordel."

So much for swimming softly, Brylee thought. Alleg was the name Wickham had shared was the Red Assassin's next victim, and Alleph was the woman orchestrating the manhunt and pressuring Wickham to commit his resources to the hunt. All of that would apparently happen in a year and a half's time. *Time will flow in its own way,* she recalled Levi explaining. Brylee was struck with the notion that perhaps it was not that she was doing a poor job of avoiding incidents that might impact the future but rather that she was caught up and sucked into the eddying currents of a whirlpool, to use Levi's analogy. That Alleg would appear on the scene soon after Garrick's death had nothing to do with her actions per se, at least as far as she could see.

By the time Brylee and Jyan caught up with Mage Ordel and his mysterious sister, it was late afternoon. Using a combination of bullying and asserting rights they likely didn't have, the Ordels had gained access to Garrick's house and ransacked his study. The household staff had been sequestered in the living room and were being taken one at a time to the study for questioning.

Jyan stepped out of his carriage and took a moment to compose himself before attempting to brush past the guard at the front door who, being taller and some forty years younger, easily stopped him.

"By whose authority do you block me from my property?" Jyan asked, standing eye to eye with the guard and clearly not in a mood to back down.

"The Office of Magical Law, sir," the guard replied.

"They have no such authority!" Jyan exclaimed, pushing at the guard and trying to step around him. The guard grabbed Jyan's jacket and pushed him firmly but gently up against the door frame while his other hand dropped to the hilt of his dagger. He looked up as a shadow loomed over him. Brylee grabbed his thumbs and twisted. The guard released Jyan and fell to his knees, struggling, but the farm girl from Lanthe easily outmuscled him.

"That might have been a trifle rash, my dear," Jyan said, "but thank you." He stepped around the fallen man and opened the door. Brylee put her foot on the man's chest, released his thumbs, then pushed him onto his back. She checked that her shine shadow was in place and then followed Jyan inside.

The hallway was full of people. The captain of the escort stood at the study door, and two of his men were escorting the cook from the living room to the study for her interview with the Ordels. One of the guards began to draw his sword in response to the intrusion, but the captain waved him back.

"Stop this at once!" Jyan shouted. Brylee admired the man's pluck, but a mage and six soldiers were unlikely to respond well to his bluster. She might surprise them with her magic and the skills Winter had taught her, but she doubted even she would prevail against such a group.

The study door was pulled open wider from inside, and Alleph Ordel stepped out to check on the commotion. The captain was about to confront Jyan, but he deferred to the woman. Before she could say anything, however, Jyan took the initiative.

"I am Jyan Harding. I know you have already acquired the documents outlining Mage Garrick's final wishes—illegally I might add, so you're aware you're on what is now my property and defiling Elijah's home, by the looks of things. Desist at once!" Seeing how the staff were being treated and spying the mess through the study door had thrown Jyan into a rage.

Alleph said nothing, completely unfazed by his outburst. Jyan continued to stare at her, determined to force his will upon the scene. She focussed her attention on him as she approached. She was creepy, Brylee thought, obviously intent on using silence as a weapon. As Alleph neared Jyan, she brought her left hand out from behind her back and made an elaborate gesture. Two small snakes slithered from the bracelet on her wrist and writhed around her long, thin fingers in a mesmerising dance. Moving in slow motion, she reached out as if to affectionately embrace Jyan's cheek.

"If you mean to scare me," Jyan warned with a cold sneer, "farmers routinely dispatch reptiles we find in our house or fields. If you value your . . . pets, you should put them away in their pretty nest."

Brylee was stunned at the amount of malevolence the sweet old man projected. Alleph paused, also taken aback. Then she tried to save face by pulling her hand back and pretending to listen to her brood. She smiled and stepped to the side, revealing her brother glaring from the study doorway.

Brylee had placed herself to Jyan's left, poised on the balls of her feet so if forced to draw her sword, she could quickly bring it into play between Jyan and any attackers. She looked much more relaxed than she felt, as she was frightened. While easing into her fighting stance, she had drawn the attention of the guards, who had clearly decided that if there was a physical threat, it was her, not the old man. Without moving, she engaged her magical sight and inspected the group in front of her. Judging by their links to the source, Alleg had a similar amount of power as Brylee and no doubt more experience at using it. Alleph had an ordinary link, so she was not a magical threat, but Justice Vee was right; there was a sinister evil about her that bled across the room. Surprisingly, the captain's link was a little larger than the norm, and Brylee marked him as a charmer, whether he knew it or not. Alleg showed no reaction to her, which made her suspect that, like most mages, he was unable to see links.

"Everyone take a deep breath," Alleg said, assessing the standoff. "Captain Farborn, please escort the cook back to the kitchen, and release the remaining . . . interviewees. Please have them remain on the estate in case we have questions for them. Have your men wait outside."

As the captain began carrying out the instructions, Mage Alleg pushed the study door open and stepped aside. "Mr. Harding, please come into the . . . into *your* study. We are here on official business, and the sooner we can complete it, the sooner we will leave you to mourn Garrick the Lesser. But we have some questions for you, and if this is Senna Brook, for her as well."

Jyan huffed and brushed past them both. He stopped and took in how the place had been ransacked. A pile of paperwork had been gathered and put to one side on a chair while the rest was strewn about. He stalked over to the chair with the paperwork on it and dragged it around the desk to the far side, then sat beside it on Garrick's big office chair, leaving nowhere for anyone else to sit. He surveyed Alleg across the desk.

Nice power move, Brylee thought, following him in. She stood off to the side by the window, her back away from the door, which Alleph was closing, sealing the four of them into the small space.

"Forget apologising for your rude intrusion," Jyan said as he leaned across the desk. "I doubt it would be sincere. What do you want?"

Alleg shared a look with his sister that Brylee couldn't interpret, then Alleph turned to Jyan. "When a mage of Garrick the Lesser's standing dies in unusual circumstances, the Council of Magical Law dispatches representatives to investigate the circumstances," she said. "We understand you have had no results in your search, and as two days have been wasted, time is now of the essence. Had you been here, we wouldn't have had to force our way past the late mage's uncooperative staff."

"Nonsense," Jyan said, ignoring her baiting. "I assisted Elijah and other mages on several such investigations, and never has it been the norm to remove deeds from a justice's office or ransack the victim's possessions. A search would be conducted with respect." Alleph almost hissed at him for cutting her claims apart so easily. "So, what do you really want?"

Alleg stepped forward "Our authority allows—"

"No, it does not!" Jyan yelled, leaping to his feet. The room fell silent, the tension so great the air was almost sizzling.

The sound of Harding balls clanging together, Brylee thought, chuckling to herself. Facing down a mage and his soldiers took extreme confidence or a bluff to tell tales of later.

Jyan straightened his jacket and eased back an inch but didn't break eye contact with the mage. He huffed away his tension and then sat. "We will see what Maryelle Lockwood has to say about your authority," he said.

"The head of the Office of Trade? Deputy of the Trinity?" Alleph asked. "Why would she have anything to say on the matter?"

"When I witnessed your behaviour at Justice Vee's offices, I immediately wrote to my cousin," Jyan replied. "I'm aware of the Ordels' reputation. I've sat in this very study drinking sherry with Elijah and Maryelle while listening to stories about you."

Alleg and Alleph's jaws hung open at such a similar angle it emphasised their family resemblance.

"But we have questions," Alleph insisted.

"And Senna and I will answer any reasonable ones," Jyan replied, "as soon as you have returned my deeds and anything else you've . . . breached protocol by taking," he added just as the Ordels appeared to relax. Everyone present mentally replaced the phrase "breached protocol" with "stole."

After a protracted silence, Alleg reached into his robes and pulled out the documents taken from Justice Vee.

Within two bells, Brylee and Jyan had laid out what they knew of events, and after a few polite questions to others, the Ordels boarded their carriage and clattered off into the night.

"Did you really send a note to your cousin?" Brylee asked as she and Jyan sat down to a late dinner. "It must have been when I left you with Vee while I fetched our carriage."

Jyan scratched his head and smiled. "Did I say I sent it? Oh my, I guess I got confused. I certainly thought about writing to my *second* cousin . . ."

"Second?" Brylee laughed. "Has she ever been to this house?"

"I wouldn't know." He coughed to cover his embarrassment. "I've never met her."

Chapter Sixty-Four

Garrick the Lesser's sky funeral was not delayed like Inka's had been. It began as a sombre affair, overshadowed by the manner of his death and the intrusion of the Ordels the previous day. The mage's small household staff, some friends from Hardings, and local villagers attended along with Brylee, Jyan, and Justice Vee. Jyan was so upset that Vee had to prompt him to say the Words of Ending for his friend as the fire was lit.

As the wake got underway, it was Brylee and Vee who began telling tales of their experiences with Garrick while Jyan sat quietly off to one side. Others took over the storytelling, and Vee stepped out of his role as civic leader to work the makeshift bar and keep everyone's goblets full. Brylee took a growler of ale over to the bench upon which Jyan had settled and poured them both a refill.

"Why is this jug called a growler?" Brylee asked.

"Because when the two quarts of beer sloshes around it produces gas, and if the cork is a bad fit, the gas escapes, making a growling noise."

"That's why the one-quart jug is a squealer?" she asked. "It's higher pitched?" Jyan nodded and then fell quiet. They sat together for almost a full bell, lost in their own thoughts as they listened to tales of the mage's life.

"You know," Brylee said during a lull in proceedings, "I asked Elijah several times why he was called Garrick the Lesser, but he would just chuckle and wave me away. Do you know, Jyan?"

"I worked for him for over twenty summers," Garrick's chef said, overhearing the question. "He refused to tell a soul." A chorus of agreement whispered around the fire, with some asking for Jyan to share the secret if he knew it, but he just shook his head.

"I badgered the old goat until I was blue in the face," Jyan said, laughing. "He wouldn't say anything about it to me either."

Justice Vee coughed to get everyone's attention, then stood. He stepped unsteadily to stand beside the pyre, slopping his tankard, and in a theatrical and slurry voice announced that he would enlighten them all. He looked as if he was about to lean against the pyre to steady his legs but then thought better of it.

"It's clear to me that the Ordels may also know something about my late friend's secret. They certainly lacked diligence in their investigation, and I doubt they rushed all the way here just to steal the deed to Elijah's manor, as nice as it is." He waved his hands towards the property.

"Then what?" Jyan asked, his curiosity piqued.

"Forty years ago, as you may recall, the town of Hops Head was dirt poor. Hardings had yet to rise in prominence as an ale producer, and unemployment in the region was high. I worked for my papa as a junior clerk and helped draft an agreement that was pivotal to the town's revival. Back then the land the town sits on was rented from a landlord who charged high rents and was driving many in the area to bankruptcy. He lived in Nuulan, and we rarely saw him, so he had no sense of how things were here." Sensing he had the crowd's attention, Vee paused and took a mouthful of ale, looking at each man and woman in turn and letting the tension build.

"When he died," he continued after wiping his mouth on his sleeve, "his nephew was the sole beneficiary and came to inspect his inheritance. The nephew proposed a new agreement for the land rental and asked us to draw up the documents. The charter we drafted was presented for adoption in a private town council meeting. It was about to be signed when the doors burst open and Mage Alloff Ordel, Alleg and Alleph's father, marched in to contest the inheritance." Murmurs of disapproval echoed around the gathering.

"Shame, shame!" someone shouted from the darkness, but Vee waved them to silence.

"But his case was weak," he continued. "Alloff was a third cousin, a more distant relative than the nephew, and not mentioned in the deceased's wishes. But he wrangled and pressured, and some whispered privately of bribes." Everyone sat in rapt attention, and in the dramatic pause Vee allowed, the pyre crackled fiercely as if angered by this history.

"The nephew was also at the meeting but had asked to remain an anonymous benefactor. He was unknown to the Ordels despite the family connection. In his last-ditch attempt to bully those gathered, Ordel demanded to hear the details of the charter, intent on finding a challenge. The charter essentially leased the land to the town at no charge in perpetuity, an arrangement that could only be cancelled by the nephew or his eventual successors.

"Ordel was furious and summoned his magic, which he used to slam objects around and freeze everyone in their seats. I was terrified. We all were. We had heard that the Ordels would go to extreme lengths to acquire land and other assets. We thought we would die there, but then the nephew, who had been quiet up to that point, leapt up, throwing off Ordel's magic and pinning the man to the wall with his own power, which until then he hadn't revealed. He yelled, 'I, sir, am Mage Garrick, the lessor and the deceased's heir. Leave these chambers immediately or forfeit your life.'"

"Elijah anonymously owned the lease to the town all this time? He was the lessor, not the lesser?" Jyan cried, his eyes as big as dinner plates in the firelight.

"Yes, and now you own it, Jyan. Anyway, after the meeting, Elijah moved from Nuulan to the town while we built this manor for him, which was part of the arrangement. Rumours swirled that he was the lease holder, and a few approached him to access his resources. At the next town hall meeting, my papa introduced him as Garrick the Lesser, not Lessor, explaining that there had been some confusion and inferred Elijah's title related to him being the younger, shorter Garrick twin. No one followed up on that ruse, but the title stuck. He's been called Garrick the Lesser ever since and went on to national fame as a healer. Even the Council of Magical Law adopted the term."

It was just the story to raise Jyan's spirits, and he followed Vee's tale with several scandalous toasts and stories of Garrick's life, some of which Brylee had heard after Inka's sky funeral and some she had not.

Later, as the pyre burnt down and people drifted away to their beds, Brylee sat with Jyan, their cloaks pulled around them as the cold pressed its way into the clearing, bringing the sadness back with it. Brylee tried to say something to lighten the moment, but she choked up, hot tears welling up. Jyan noticed and shuffled closer, putting his arm around her shoulders.

"That ache in your chest, that lump in your throat, those tears . . . they are grief, Senna. And grief is just love that has nowhere to go. But a beautiful soul leaves a trail of memories throughout our world, and there are many memories of Elijah in your head and your heart. In time you will learn to redirect that trapped love into those memories instead of into the man." As he spoke, his own trapped tears tumbled out, filling the crags around his eyes before rolling off his cheeks and into his lap. They sat with their thoughts and memories watching the coals turn as grey as their lost friend's beard had been.

"I'll miss the old goat," Jyan said as he stared at the ashes. "Still, at least I have you. I'm so glad you've settled here. I realise you also have a mysterious tale that you will never share, but it won't stop you having us as family if you ever chose to make a home here."

Brylee felt awful. Following her decision to become the Red Assassin, she had determined she must soon leave the estate to prepare for her battle to save Levi. She felt she needed more hands-on experience at healing wounds, and she had to find a way to practise fighting a mage. After replaying the events of the ambush, she had determined that someone, probably Levi's assailant, had used hard air to trap her and make the barrier into which Wickham and Winter had slammed. She thought about telling Jyan her secret but then dismissed the idea. The fewer people who knew about it, the better. The idea had been born out of trying to ease the pain of parting, but deep down, she accepted it wouldn't.

"Jyan," she began, but he raised his hand to silence her.

"Don't worry. I thought you might leave. I've sensed it these last few days. I know you well enough to understand that you can't give me the whole accounting of the night of the assassination, and you must go. Forgive an old man's folly, but I . . . I just wanted you to know that whenever you resolve whatever occupies your mind, there is a place for you here if you want it."

Brylee teared up and reached over to clasp his hand, not trusting herself to speak. After a few minutes, she composed herself, determined not to end the evening on such a sad note.

"Look, you've been experimenting with the beans you brought home from the Green Isle and have a product to take to market. I know you favour selling grou't locally first and expanding from there, but my next stop is Nuulan, the capital. Would you consider opening your first store there? Make a big splash. I think you might be surprised at what a taste they have for it. And we'll see each other for a while longer too."

As Jyan pondered her idea, Brylee saw flickers of light return to his eyes that had nothing to do with the dying flames and everything to do with embracing a new passion.

"What do you say to us calling the first batch 'Senna's Sipper'?" he asked. In truth she thought it a horrible name, not least because it was built on a lie. She cast her mind back to that fateful afternoon, prior to meeting Vekki, where the future Jyan had beamed as he explained the history of his Grinders' business. What was his first product called?

"No, I think you should call it Garrick's Grou't," she said.

Two weeks later, Jyan put a deposit down on his first Grinders location in the capital. Above the shop were two bedrooms, one for him while he oversaw the start-up and the other for Brylee, for as long as she needed it.

Chapter Sixty-Five

Jyan invited Brylee to participate in hiring his team and setting up the store, but he was so absorbed in every aspect that she limited herself to selecting and tasting the menu that would accompany Garrick's Grou't. She used the remainder of her time to progress her agenda, which had two main priorities: to perfect her magical healing and fighting skills and to learn enough about the Ordels to control matters in a way that did not involve killing Alleg. She hoped to concoct a ruse similar to what she had put together for Garrick to avoid staining her soul further. She was becoming certain that the swirling eddies of time righting itself would compel Alleg's death at the hands of the Red Assassin one way or another. She had a feeling akin to riding the dragon, the slooper at the Crow's Nest, that her fate was not hers to direct. Instead, she just had to hold on and ride the horse. Alleg's death was to be the week before midsummer's night in two years' time according to Wickham's briefing. Over the next eighteen moons she hoped to come up with alternatives that wouldn't make her a murderer.

Brylee determined that to achieve her primary goals she needed to move around the city incognito while she improved her fighting and magical skills. Therefore, three days after arriving in Nuulan, she located a seamstress and commissioned a new wardrobe. As her primi skills expanded, she found that she no longer needed the magically reactive dye to change the colour of material. She memorised the attributes for fabric colour and became proficient at altering almost any type of material's hue and, to a lesser degree, its texture. She could loosen or tighten its weave to make it snug or loose. She could also change the sheen, grain, and form. But she was limited by not being able to add or remove material. She had to work with what was there. The four outfits she designed could be adapted magically to resemble any number of general fashions and, if required, transform to the Namiduh Jou uniform. There was even a waterproof pouch sewn into the legs to secrete a vial of red dye made from a supply of bellyberry that Brylee kept in her room.

While her outfits were being created, Brylee explored the areas between the busy market area where Grinders was being constructed and the Ordels' home, which resembled a castle with high walls and fortifications. She was seeking a healing establishment that wasn't operated by the city, with its strict rules and oversight, or by the church. Both would ask questions she couldn't answer.

At the end of the first week of walking the city and not finding a place where she could practise her healing skills without too many questions, Brylee collected her new wardrobe. In the privacy of her room above Grinders, she practised changing each costume's colour, fit, and appearance until she could do so in seconds. In front of a mirror, she also worked on changing her hair and features to create several characters she could assume in moments. She could ad lib on the fly, of course, but creating magical muscle memory around a limited number of personas meant she could rapidly change to something that looked natural rather than a wardrobe disaster.

Once she was comfortable with changing her appearance, Brylee practised in the maze-like alleys and other areas one could walk and be unobserved for a few seconds or more. Using a similar technique to how she had fooled Winter, she worked on becoming proficient at stepping out of sight and emerging seconds later as a different person.

On one such excursion she witnessed an altercation between a street urchin and a wealthy man. The child stepped up behind the noble and deftly cut his purse, but despite his attempt at stealth, he was caught in the act. A flash of a dagger left the robber on his knees without his left ear and blood pouring down his neck while his "victim" strode off into the crowd. From nowhere, the robber's accomplice appeared and supported the injured boy as he staggered away.

"Quick, les' get you t' Ah Lady, Dob," Brylee heard him say. Assuming he was referring to a shady healer who might suit her needs, Brylee trailed the pair from a distance.

Brylee followed them out of the market heading north. With each street they took, she noticed the inhabitants were poorer and poorer and the shops and taverns increasingly unsavoury. As they crossed a bridge over a river she didn't recognise, they passed into a slightly better area, but Brylee pinched her nose at an acrid smell like rotten eggs that hung in the air. She stooped to pick a mint root from a garden, scrunched it up to release its vapours, and placed it in the folds of her scarf, which she strung across her face to fend off the stink. *People live with this smell?*

The injured boy was flagging to the point Brylee considered revealing her presence and helping him when the pair turned off the street into an alley that ran behind a two-storey building. They banged on a door at the rear. It opened, and a short, thin woman in a healer's apron stepped out. Brylee could see no symbols of worship from where she was. The healer examined the boy, then helped him inside, telling his accomplice to return for him in one bell's time. As the boy's companion exited the alley, Brylee stepped out of the shadows and stopped him.

"What goes on in there?" she asked, looking the youth in the eye. Up close, Brylee realised the youth wasn't a boy but a wiry short-haired girl of maybe fourteen years. The girl's eyes widened at being unexpectedly confronted by such a big woman whose clothes marked her as having some means. The girl looked like she was about to bolt, so Brylee grabbed the girl's jerkin. With her other hand she reached into her pocket and pulled out a small coin, holding it just out of reach.

"I'm not here to cause you any trouble," Brylee said. "I'm just curious. Is that a healer? In the basement of the warehouse?" The girl jumped up and snatched the coin, then pocketed it. She relaxed a shade, although she still looked frightened. Brylee pulled out a second coin, which she held up higher. Then she released the girl and took a step back. Brylee's body language was clear: "Run and you get nothing. Talk and you get fed."

"That's Ah Lady . . . a hospital. Looks out for those of us who aren't welcome at other places," the girl said. "She's fixing Dob's ear. Dob's me brother." Brylee thought for a moment, then passed the coin to the girl and pulled a third coin from her pocket.

"You can keep those two. But tell me your name, and when Dob comes out, bring him over to that tavern to see me, and you can have this one too. And I'll give Dob another one to match it."

"What d'ya want with Dob?" the girl asked, her eyes fixed on the coin.

"I'm not with the City Guard if that's a worry," Brylee said. "I just want to look at the healer's work. I might have need of her skills. Come straight to me at the tavern across the street, and I'll throw in a free meal for you both." The girl nodded, mumbled that her name was Moffit, then turned and ran back down the alley. She carried on past the healer's door and vanished around the corner. Brylee circled the building, which appeared to be a warehouse, then took a window seat in the tavern.

Almost exactly one bell after dropping her brother off, Moffit appeared at the healer's door to collect him. Brylee wondered if she would have been as punctual without the hope of a reward. Dob emerged. His skin had been cleaned of blood, but there was still some on his jacket. He looked a little woozy. It took Moffit three attempts to get him to cross the street to the tavern, the first two for him to understand through the haze of the sedative the healer had given him and the third to convince him it wasn't a trap.

Moments later, the pair poked their heads through the tavern door.

"You can come in this time because you're with this lady," the gnarly old woman running the establishment said. "What she wants with you scullions, I have no idea. Here, put these cloths on the seats before you sit your arses on them, or they'll smell for days. My customers won't like it." To Brylee's eyes and nose, the woman's other customers were no cleaner than the youths. The only difference was her customers had coin.

There were four chairs around the small table. Brylee told Dob to sit next to her. He was a year or two older than his sibling, Brylee guessed, but he looked a lot older. *A hard life.* She had arranged the seating so that his injured ear was closest to her. When they were settled, she inspected it both physically and magically. The stitching suggested the efficiency of someone who worked often and quickly but did not have the training of a talented physician. He would have a terrible scar afterwards.

A server brought over two bowls of chicken stew as well as a small loaf with some butter. As she departed, she muttered that she would be checking that all the cutlery remained behind. Dob asked for two mugs of ale—Brylee was impressed he was looking out for his sister—but they got a tankard of water each instead.

"You've looked at his ear or wot's left o' it," Moffit said through a mouthful of food. "You good for the coin you promised us?" Brylee put the agreed payment on the table but held up her hand to stop the girl as she reached over to snatch it up.

"You can take that, and we're done," Brylee said, waving her hand and producing a shiny silver punt, which she held up. "Or you can do me a service, and I'll add this to the pile." The girl agreed at the same moment that Dob asked what the service would be.

"I need you to take a message to the healer for me," Brylee said, amused by the girl's instant lack of fear at the sight of silver.

"A punt seems a lot t' pay for me to walk 'cross t' road and tell someone sumink," Dob said. "What's the message?"

"Well, you're partly the message," Brylee said, pulling out a kerchief that had been white a moment ago but was now a gaudy red. "I want you to ask her to examine your wound once more. And when she does, tell her Scarlet sends her regards, and give her this cloth."

"Look, Miss, she's busy," Dob said. "I was lucky she helped me at all. She might not care to waste her time to check her work twice just because I say so."

"I'm paying you well to make sure she does," Brylee replied.

"I could make him bleed again," Moffit said, brandishing the bread knife.

"Hoy," Dob said, sitting back. "OK, I'll do it."

The deal struck, the youths started eating with a vengeance. When they were done, they readily accepted second helpings. As they ate, Brylee healed the damage to Dob's ear and neck. She worked slowly so he wouldn't feel any itching or heat. When she was done, she transformed the blood that stained his jacket to a light dust that would blow away in a breeze. When she was finished, although his ear was still disfigured, the injury looked moons old, pink but well recovered. Brylee left the stitching in so the healer wouldn't think it was a different boy trying to fool her. The youths were so intent on filling their bellies that Brylee's work went unnoticed, just as she had hoped.

Brylee said goodbye, left the pair to their meal, and went to the latrine at the rear of the building. Seconds later someone looking quite different emerged from the latrine and went to loiter outside the tavern. It didn't take long for the proprietor to hustle Dob and Moffit out, accompanied by a cloud of insults and threats to never return.

Brylee watched Dob cross to the alley and knock for the healer. She was satisfied with the look of astonishment on all their faces when the healer examined Dob's ear. Brylee put her hands in her pockets and walked back to Grinders, whistling a happy tune. As she passed through the warren of alleyways, she reverted to her Senna persona and headed straight to the baths to remove the stink of the healer's neighbourhood and the foul odour of the two young people from her clothing and skin.

Chapter Sixty-Six

Brylee spent the next day researching the healer to which Dob and Moffit had led her. She didn't find anything about the hospital, but the warehouse she had circumnavigated was listed in civic records as the production and distribution facility for Our Lady of Light Spring Water. From what she could glean, several exclusive bathing houses for Nuulan's wealthy purchased the water for their spas because of its supposed healing properties. This explained why Moffit had called the location "Ah Lady," but it told Brylee little else except that due to the smell, the spring had to be close by.

Brylee timed her arrival at the warehouse for just before dusk, this time darkening her skin and altering her features to resemble a Thubian, a nomadic people from the southern deserts. They were not uncommon visitors to the city, and they were well known for living solitary, private lives, rebuffing intrusive questions.

She circled the building again, noting its various entrances and the paths to and from the area by which she might escape if necessary. Once she felt she understood the "operational area," as Winter called such things, she knocked on the door she had seen Dob use the day before. There was no answer for a long time, and she was about to knock again when a panel opened and a young girl's voice asked her business. Brylee had to bend down to be able to peer through the opening, but she couldn't see anyone in the darkness inside.

"I'd like to see the healer," Brylee said, thickening her accent and slowing the pace of her speech. Winter had explained that altering the speed of one's speech was the best way to present a disguised voice.

"Are you injured or sick?" the girl asked.

"Neither," Brylee replied.

"She's busy. Go away." As the speaker went to slam the panel closed to make her point, Brylee held it open with her magic and pressed a bright red kerchief through the slot.

"My name is Scarlet," Brylee said, then she let the slot close.

Feeling vulnerable in the alley, Brylee walked to the alley's entrance and leaned against the wall to wait. After a few minutes the door opened, and a round pink face peered out at her, followed by a skinny hand that beckoned her to come inside. Brylee pulled the door open wide so she could see inside. There was a space where perhaps four people could cram together between the door and a heavy curtain strung across the corridor behind where the only person in sight stood, a girl of perhaps ten summers.

"That's to keep the cold out," the young girl explained. She barely reached Brylee's ribcage. The girl pulled the door closed and slid two bolts in place, plunging the space into darkness. Before Brylee could worry, the youngster stepped around her and pulled the curtain back, revealing a set of steps leading down to a short, dimly lit corridor with a heavy wooden door at the far end. When the girl opened that door, Brylee was amazed by what it revealed.

The warehouse's basement had been converted into a hospital. Roughly a third of it was made up of various treatment stations, including an area with a table upon which surgeries could be performed. Another large portion of the floor contained rows of beds, perhaps twenty-five if Brylee's rough estimate held out, which appeared to contain the sickest patients. A smaller area had about half as many beds containing what Garrick would have called the walking wounded or less severe cases. There were two small offices and another area for food preparation. Thirty neverdark lights supplemented a few oil lanterns, and three evercold devices were being used to offset the heat generated by the fifty or so patients, visitors, and healers who occupied the space.

The young girl led Brylee to one of the offices. The door was closed, but the girl knocked once, then entered without waiting for an answer.

The office was sparse, just a few chairs around a small table and a few cabinets for papers to be stored. The woman sitting at the table wore healer's robes, but she wasn't the person Brylee had seen at the back door the day before. Perhaps forty summers old, she was tall and skeletal with eyes that were pretty despite being framed by dark circles. Her mouth was wide and taut, and her white hair was shaved close at the sides, with a little more on top. She was arresting to look at, and her resemblance to the youth who had shown Brylee to the office was uncanny.

"I know you're busy," Brylee said, "so thank you for seeing me without an appointment. I've never seen a healing facility such as this. Are you in charge?"

"My father started it and passed it to me eight years ago. He was frustrated that the authorities wouldn't provide for the health of the poor neighbourhoods that surround us. We own the Our

Lady water rights and use all the proceeds from that business to fund this place of healing. People pay when and with what they can afford."

"Evercolds, neverdark lamps . . . it must have cost a fortune to build," Brylee said, her voice full of respect.

"They didn't come cheap, but they don't need fuel or maintenance, and they let us see who we are healing as well as making them comfortable while they're here." The woman paused, sizing Brylee up. Brylee didn't feel the tingle she did when Garrick had scanned with his magical sight, and the woman had a normal link to the source, as had everyone she had observed when she walked in. "What can I do for you, Scarlet? We don't get many mages in here. In fact, we don't trust the few who've come. Who do *you* represent?"

Obviously some history here, Brylee thought.

"I represent myself. No one else. May I ask your name, as you know mine?"

The woman paused, one hand worrying at a pocket in her robe. Brylee didn't suspect a weapon was hidden there. It was more of a nervous gesture.

"My name is Aethe Whin. Healer Whin, if we're being formal."

"I'm seeking an opportunity to train as a healer," Brylee said. She pointed to the seats. Aethe nodded, and they both sat, the tension in the room dropping a few degrees. "You're right; I am a mage . . . from overseas. I'm not aligned with the council. I'm here for a year to learn. I have powers and some knowledge, but my practical experience is limited. I don't have time to qualify through an institution before I must leave here."

"Well, we never have enough help," Aethe said. "I can pay, but it isn't much. From what Healer Mary told me about Dob's ear, you have some ability, but you would need to be supervised until we know your skills."

"Of course." Brylee considered turning down the wage but sensed she would be accepted more quickly the more she fit in with the norm. "I'm not here for a salary and will take whatever you think is appropriate."

"I can tell you now, I should pay you more than I can." Aethe smiled. "Tell me about yourself."

Brylee provided the fictitious story she had carefully prepared ahead of time. Brought to Mordeland as a child but now called back to Thubia to look after relatives who were aging. Discovered her magic only recently while working as a farmhand, wanted to prepare to support her village, to contribute as much as possible in her new life. She wanted to keep as near to the truth as she could.

Brylee was nearing the end of her explanation when there was a knock, and the young girl who had brought Brylee in opened the door.

"This is my daughter," Aethe said. "What is it, Kithy?"

"They're bringing Doug the Smithy in on a cart. Some hot metal he was hammering sparked into his face."

"You'll have to excuse me," Aethe said as she stood. "I need to attend to this. Kithy, get me some sleep syrup and bring it to the operating table." Brylee stood and followed Aethe to the door.

"Can I help?" Brylee asked.

"I don't know enough about you yet to answer that, but come and observe at least," Aethe replied. As she walked out of the office, she glanced back over her shoulder. "First come and wash your hands. Kithy will fetch you apprentice robes. Welcome to Our Lady, Scarlet."

As Aethe worked on the smithy, Brylee realised her skills were markedly better than whoever had helped Dob. Brylee was pleased she could be of immediate use, her magical sight being helpful in locating fragments of metal hidden under the skin without requiring Aethe to probe blindly. Even so, the smithy's face and neck were a mess.

"If you wish," Brylee said, "I can do something about the burnt skin. It will scar greatly as it is." Aethe thought for a moment, then nodded and stepped back. Just the two of them bent over the injured man.

"I'm happy to use my magic while I'm here, Healer Whin," Brylee whispered, "but it would suit me to keep my abilities as secret as possible. People don't trust mages, especially around here. Once word spreads, it might attract the wrong sort of attention."

"That would be best, I agree," Aethe replied. "But the other healers will need to know, as will some of the senior helpers. They'll notice anyway."

Over the next moon, Brylee attended Our Lady three days per week, leaving plenty of time for her other priorities. After some initial suspicions, the staff warmed to her work ethic and humble manner. That she was strong enough to lift patients without much help was appreciated too, and when she was on shift, her sheer size prevented many acts of drunken belligerence from escalating into problems. Her fighting skills allowed her to deal quickly with the few exceptions. Brylee's talents increased rapidly, and she enjoyed the friendships that were forming quickly in the tight, hardworking community—at least most of them.

On her third shift she noticed a porter named Ike lifting a coin from a sleeping patient's pocket. She confronted him, and he claimed he was owed the money. He said he had kept the patient company with dice earlier but hadn't been paid his due. On her fifth shift she saw one of the nurses slip a few pills into her pocket. A few days later, she saw a different nurse syphon off some herbs from the small dispensaries store. She said nothing to the thieves but took her findings to Aethe at the end of her next shift.

"You're right to tell me, Scarlet, but we turn a blind eye to most petty pilfering here," Aethe said. "Most of the pilfering stems from staff helping family or others who won't come here to get help. But mention such things to Mary rather than talking to people yourself. She has the relationships and knows people's circumstances the best, and it won't impact your bond with the team that way either. Stealing from patients, though, that we don't abide. The same is true if we think our staff are getting too used to a drug themselves, if you take my meaning."

In her third week, Brylee heard a commotion near the dispensary and saw Ike was reacting badly to Mary giving him a dressing down for presumably stealing from a patient again. She wandered closer, and Ike calmed down, tempered by there being a witness to his behaviour. Once the discussion had ended, Ike walked past Brylee and growled that what he did was none of her business and to keep her nose out. Brylee got the impression she had made an enemy.

Chapter Sixty-Seven

While Brylee spent her first moon in Nuulan working three days each week at Our Lady of Light, she used her remaining time on two other projects: learning and perfecting her magic and building her knowledge of all things Ordel.

Although she had worried about finding resources from which she could learn magic in the aloof, secretive coteries of the mage world, it turned out to be simple. The Council of Magical Law maintained libraries of information on magic, including techniques. They even boasted self-run clubs where like-minded, mostly junior talents could meet to compare experiences and learn from each other. The only qualification for accessing such resources was to be a mage and be sponsored by a mage registered with the council.

Brylee had kept a stock of crested stationery from her time with Mage Garrick and could forge a letter of recommendation, but she needed to be careful about how she crafted her persona for this venture, creating someone whose past would not reveal that she was an imposter. She had never travelled to the Rainbow Archipelago, but Jyan's many tales were rich fodder for her backstory, and she knew it contained hundreds of small isles, many unwelcoming to outsiders. She purported to hail from Berwick Atoll, and she wasn't questioned. A story about doing a service for Mage Garrick the Lesser, travelling to study, and the forged letter earned her an interview with the head of admissions. A short demonstration that she could perform magic, and Scarlet Fisher, her alias, was formally added to the roster of mages and granted a library pass, valid for one year.

The Scarlet Fisher persona had different features and colouring from her own. She was modelled on Fifi, her family's cook. Brylee made herself older, grey haired, and long faced. It was unlikely she would bump into Vekki or others who her future self might encounter, but she wanted to be cautious. She needed to keep track of her Senna of the future, which she referred to as Wickham's Senna. The Senna from the Harding estate differed slightly in looks from the first Senna. There was also Scarlet the Healer and now Scarlet Fisher, the mage. Brylee had decided to use the name Scarlet as often as possible to ease the complexity of remembering the many faces she might wear. She developed her own coded system in a notebook she carried to remind her of the details of each character.

The only place she relaxed as herself was her weekly visit to see Whipcrack at the stable near Grinders. He was happy and well exercised there, but when she could, Brylee, as Senna, took him for a long canter along the riverside. During each visit, Brylee would brush and spoil the horse, telling him about her secret personas and the lives they lived. She also talked about Haxley, Rostal, and Levi. Whipcrack always seemed to understand, and he nuzzled her for more carrots or apples at appropriate moments. Brylee's equine confessions helped her keep her sanity while dealing with so many secrets and lies.

So it was that Scarlet Fisher spent three afternoons and evenings each week poring through the library's voluminous shelves and establishing friendships with other users of the facility.

Brylee spent her remaining time in those early weeks as a different persona observing Castle Ordel, as she called it. Whereas Rostal seemed to have evolved as a tribute to, and example of, what the magic communities could achieve with its impossible architecture, Nuulan's elite district was unimaginative and mundane by comparison, composed of street after street of similar dark brown three-storey buildings laid out in a practical grid, narrow alleys, and wide, smelly cobblestone streets. Only the religious buildings stood out, with the exception of two: the Elect's Palace and Castle Ordel.

Built on the same sized footprint of a typical building, the castle's outer fortifications stood in line with the neighbouring structures' heavily windowed and pillared façades. Inside the perimeter was a partial moat and drawbridge, stables, and a garden. This meant that the manor at the centre of the plot was much smaller than its peers. It had narrow windows and heavy doors and shutters, giving it a foreboding air. Brylee's initial view inside the tall perimeter walls was during a tour of a nearby cathedral, from its spiral staircase's slit windows, as there was little to see from street level. Why the Ordel family sought such protections was unclear, but Brylee was certain that Alleg and Alleph made many enemies.

Brylee spent three mornings disguised in different ways, observing the comings and goings of the castle from the street and nearby vantage points. One significant difference to its neighbours was that for security and due to the manor's small size, many of the castle's staff lived off site. They arrived at the gate each morning to have their passes checked and their bodies searched before being admitted. The other difference was it maintained a sign by the gate advertising various employment positions within the castle. Brylee knew from living with Wickham that most people avoided mages, so getting workers was difficult. No doubt the Ordels had the same challenge, as there were no such signs on nearby buildings.

Brylee reviewed the list of open positions at Castle Ordel. Although she could fulfill most roles, they insisted on attendance seven days per week with only two days off per moon, which her other commitments wouldn't allow. She struck up conversations with current employees as they came and went, asking them what it was like to work there. They said the pay was low and the culture toxic, which didn't surprise her in the least. Only people who couldn't get work elsewhere took such jobs, and most didn't stay long. Over a few days of puzzling how to gain access to the castle, the Ordels' staffing issue inspired an idea. However, it would require more funding than she currently had available.

At the end of the first moon, Brylee went to the bank and withdrew most of her savings from her Hardings salary in the form of two small ingots, one copper and the other silver. She returned to her room at Grinders just in time to help Jyan interview three nearby bakers, each interested in providing food for the menu when the store opened. They had several samples, and Brylee indulged in them all while sipping Garrick Grou't and giving Jyan her opinions. When she retired to her room, instead of the nap she desired, she set about interrogating the two metal ingots to ascertain what attributes made them different from each other.

The ingots were reluctant to reveal their secrets, but by the end of the second week, Brylee had enough of a sense of them to begin to impose the attributes of silver onto the copper bar, but the copper was determined not to change. It would heat, soften, and change colour, but for an age it refused to resemble silver. Its stubbornness almost caused Brylee to give up and seek easier ways to make money. However, with a strong draw on the source of magic and much coaxing and flattery, the copper eventually acquiesced to her will.

Brylee chose a bank in a wealthy neighbourhood and developed a persona that looked like it belonged, but she was quite nervous when she went to exchange her fake silver ingot for twenty copper bars. As much as she tried to convince herself that the silver wasn't fake, that it was now truly silver, she feared being discovered and arrested. But the ingot easily convinced the bank staff, who happily exchanged it.

Using various disguises over the next two weeks, Brylee created several accounts into which she deposited a great deal of silver. To assuage her guilt about stealing, even if she told herself it was to save perhaps the whole world, she took a fifth of her gains and anonymously donated them to Our Lady and various other charities.

With the funds she had raised, Brylee leased a small office three streets away from Castle Ordel. She outfitted it with two desks, some chairs, and filing drawers. She even added some art by local painters to the walls and a bright rug across the floor.

By that point Brylee had been observing the Ordels' staff coming and going for a moon. One older woman stood out as somewhat of a ringleader—but in a positive way. She helped the new faces get through the gruelling gate checks their first few times, and Brylee noted she had useful knowledge that she freely imparted to most of the trades as they waited to enter. She told a new flower girl which blooms made Alleg sneeze. Brylee heard her explain to a seamstress that Alleph liked the cuff of her left hand to be looser than the right to accommodate her snake charms. To all she warned that staying out of sight of Alleph was best, as the woman was evil, a bully, and a tormenter. Intrigued, Brylee followed the woman home several evenings and learnt more about her situation.

The woman, Farriar Monay, Brylee discovered, was skilled and experienced but had difficulty retaining a position. Her romantic partner was also a woman and as employers preferred to provide room and board to avoid higher salaries, this caused Farriar problems. Where same-gender couples were usually discreet in such circumstances, perhaps posing as brothers or sisters to share a room or even a bed, Farriar and Tae were open, proud, and loud about their relationship. It was a huge issue in conservative Nuulan, but it didn't appear to trouble the Ordels, who were desperate for staff. Eavesdropping on Farriar and Tae's post-work conversations at the Linger Longer, their regular tavern, revealed that Farriar hated working for the Ordels, but with Tae employed as a junior accountant to the local market owner, she would put up with it until Tae obtained her guild endorsement and full membership. Then Farriar planned to tell them what she thought of them and leave.

Six weeks into her stay in Nuulan, and now well established at Our Lady and the library, Brylee disguised herself as a young office worker and set out to introduce herself to Farriar. She added a few fashionable touches to her disguise that someone with money might wear before she approached Farriar as she left the Ordels' after her shift.

"Excuse me, Miss," Brylee said. "I know this is forward of me, but I saw you leave Ordels, and I've heard they can be challenging employers. At least that's what someone who left there recently told me."

"Did they now?" Farriar said, her tone cautious.

"They also mentioned you by name and suggested you're one of the best workers at the castle," Brylee said. Farriar glanced over her shoulder at the castle, appearing uncertain.

"This isn't a trick or a trap, if that's what you're thinking," Brylee reassured her. "Let me explain why I've approached you. I have an idea for a new sort of business venture, but I don't have the experience or the time to pull it off. I've been searching for someone with the right experience for some time, and perhaps it might be you."

"Sorry . . . Miss?" Farriar said.

"Call me Scarlet."

"Scarlet," Farriar repeated as if tasting the name to test its trustworthiness. "I'm flattered someone would mention me. Who did you say it was again?"

Brylee smiled. "I didn't. They asked me not to give their name, and the idea I've had relies on people keeping their word and . . . respecting privacy." Brylee let that thought hang, hoping someone in Farriar's romantic situation might appreciate it.

"Well, I'm not sure. What makes you think I'm your person?" Farriar asked.

"I don't. You would be the seventh person I've talked to and perhaps not the last." Brylee stepped back, indicating she wouldn't press Farriar if she wasn't interested. "But if you'd like to be your own boss, run my business for me, and earn three times what I suspect the Ordels pay, I'll buy you dinner, and we can find out together."

Farriar scratched her head as she considered Brylee's offer. Brylee thought the woman had probably never run a business and was intrigued but frightened. Her intuition told her not to press further.

"I'm curious, Scarlet, but I'm supposed to meet my partner for dinner, and I'm never late."

"I like that you're punctual and respect your commitments. Look, it's up to you. I could meet you another time, but, of course, reluctantly, I must keep looking." Brylee forced a disappointed expression on her lips but sensed she had hooked Farriar's interest. "One of the things I was told about you is that your partner is a woman, and that's wonderful if you ask me. In fact, if the person I choose has a partner, I'd like to meet them too. It's a big financial risk for me, and I'd feel better knowing you have both bought into the idea. A new venture means long hours and stress. Why don't I buy you both dinner and she can weigh in on it too? Perhaps even come up with improvements herself."

"You're certainly making it sound too good to be true," Farriar said, grinning. "Let's go see if Tae wants to have dinner with us. I can't promise more than that. My name is Farriar, although I suspect you know that already."

"I do," Brylee replied, smiling. They turned and began the short walk to the Linger Longer, with Brylee letting Farriar lead as if she didn't know the way herself.

"I don't want to give you the wrong impression," Brylee said as they walked. "This could be a great chance for the right person, but as far as I know, it hasn't been done before. I'm happy to carry the financial risk, but you will be doing all the work and solving all the problems. I don't think it will be easy."

"If it's just hard work, I'm not worried," Farriar said.

At the tavern, Farriar made the introductions and asked the server for a quiet booth at the back of the room. They ordered food and drink and then made small talk. Brylee had covertly observed the couple twice, but up close, Tae's wit and warmth was much more tangible. When she made eye contact, Brylee sensed genuine curiosity. She found herself relaxing in the Linger Longer's fun, friendly atmosphere, which reminded her of the Crow's Nest more than anywhere else she had been since leaving Haxley. The memory of her good times with Raegan clenched her chest. To distract herself, she began to explain the bones of her idea. It was the first time she had voiced it out loud, and she felt nervous.

"Until recently I worked with a mage who had trouble hiring domestic help. People are scared of mages, and let's face it, they're often quirky and difficult. They are niche employers, hence an opportunity, perhaps."

Farriar laughed. "That's true," she said, then lowered her voice. "My employers are dreadful."

"The man I worked for died recently," Brylee said, waving away the condolences the couple offered. "He had a fantastic life and was old. He was a truly great man. He even left me some money, but it won't last forever. So I want to make it work for me. That's why I'm creating a company—it already has a small office—that will hire domestic workers on preferential contracts, meaning higher pay. I need someone to vet these workers. That person needs to be experienced at helping people be successful and navigate the challenges of working for a mage."

"Oh, Farriar can do that, alright," Tae said, a proud glow in her eyes.

"So I've heard," Brylee replied, grinning. "The company will also take on other clients who need domestic help but who struggle to attract or retain it. My company will guarantee skilled workers and handle the hassles associated with managing people. Flexibility is important. We will provide people on a full-time or part-time basis, as needed. Our contract will lay out the behaviours that are acceptable. If clients are rude to our workers, we will cancel our contract with them. Tempering employers' behaviour and better pay will help us get the best workers."

"Where would I fit in, exactly?" Farriar asked.

"You would have to vet and manage the workers' problems as well as find and deal with clients. My budget allows for an administrator to manage scheduling, payments, and paperwork. If business expands, so can the team. I want you focussed on client issues and worker quality, not accounting." Brylee was deliberately planting a seed that Tae might be able to work as Farriar's partner once she had her guild stamp.

"I think I have the experience," Farriar said, her mind working at full gallop.

"The obvious problem is cash flow," Tae said, her accounting background showing. "Paying preferential rates to workers will encourage better people to attend some of these clients. And mages have money, even if some hate spending it. But the Ordels could solve their own problem if they were not so miserly. Why would they pay enough to cover the workers' rates?"

"Oh, that's simple," Brylee said. "They won't. Well, not at first anyway. We'll start off charging what they pay today but offer a better, more flexible service with fewer hassles. Once they get used to it, we will gradually raise the rates. I want the business to be self-sustaining, if not slightly profitable, in a year and a half. I'll recoup my investment over the longer term."

"That's a big, high-risk investment," Tae said. Farriar nodded in agreement, her eyebrows wrinkled with worry.

"Yes, but I'm confident in the concept and think the right person can make it fly." Brylee replied. "I budgeted paying your administrator about what you get today and you three times that amount. But if you want some skin in the game, I could pay you two thirds of your retainer in cash and put the remainder into a holding account. When we begin to turn a profit, I'll sell you a fifty percent stake in the company for the amount accrued. I'll take no money out until that point, but then you begin to pay me a percentage of the profits and reinvest a third of your salary until you can buy the other fifty percent."

"Hang on," Tae said. "Farriar would own the entire company?"

"Yes, but she would pay me ten percent of the profit thereafter. That would be in the sales contract. What you did with the other ninety percent would be your business." Brylee stifled a smile. Both women were staring with their mouths agape.

"This is a big city," Brylee continued, "so I might open similar franchises that don't compete with you, if you can show that the model works."

"And all that time you would pay me twice what I make today?" Farriar asked, glancing at Tae. "What will you be doing?"

"Me? Oh, I have other projects to get off the ground. We'll meet once a moon for a progress report, but otherwise you probably won't see much of me, I'm afraid."

"What if we don't get clients or workers for moons?" Farriar asked. "I don't want to risk giving up this role and then—"

"Are you mad?" Tae cut in. "You hate the Ordels. Anyway, you can always get another job if it doesn't work out."

"If you stick at it," Brylee said, "I'll pay you until the end of the year however it goes. I don't want you to worry about your money. I want you to worry about mine."

"I can't see why I wouldn't jump at the chance," Farriar said. "Can we sleep on it, though?" Of course they would want to discuss it without Brylee present.

"There is one other condition," Brylee said. They both looked at her as if they had been expecting a catch. "One of my other projects, which I can't talk too much about, involves extracting people from difficult circumstances and helping them get established on their own. From time to time, I might send you someone and expect you to put them to work. I'll vouch for them, of course, and it will be your decision to keep them on once you've tried them out. They won't be criminals or desperate. They'll be people who were dealt a rough hand or who circumstances conspired against. They'll need a fresh start, free of the baggage of the past." Neither Farriar nor Tae could see anything wrong with the condition, and several rounds of ale were consumed as the three women brainstormed how to get things started.

A moon later, Work Hive—with a logo of a worker bee visiting three houses—had three clients, one of which was the Castle Ordel. Brylee appeared at their office door one morning with a letter from "Scarlet" asking that she be put to work as a flower woman. She claimed to live close to the Ordels. After answering a series of botany and arrangement questions, Farriar gave her a Work Hive pass and sent her to a woman at the market with whom she had contracted for supplies. As Scarlet, Brylee was given a harness that supported several compartments of various sizes containing assorted fresh flowers and greenery. She was a walking flower stand. She was also given a tall trolley with two compartments; one for fresh water, the other for wastewater, so she could travel around the castle refreshing various arrangements without frequent trips to the well.

As Brylee filed through Castle Ordel's gates shortly after, she noted that the new arrangement had already resulted in the Ordels' employing fewer staff to oversee admittance. She would ensure Farriar factored that nugget into future contract negotiations. One security guard was unnecessarily handsy, but Brylee gritted her teeth and didn't react in the moment. Instead, she made a mental promise to visit him in a different persona and impress upon him the error of his ways.

Brylee was escorted from room to room that first visit and left to work on each arrangement before being collected and led to the next location. On subsequent visits she was allowed to move around unescorted. As a part-time flower woman—and with a different face and hairstyle, a wall painter—Brylee was able to learn every inch of Castle Ordel in just a few weeks. She built up her knowledge of household routines as well as security strengths and weaknesses. She saw little of the Ordels, and when she did they treated her as if she was invisible. Alleph and her snakes looked at her longingly from time to time, and Brylee was glad the Work Hive contract protected her from the creepy woman.

Brylee also visited the local justice's office at night when the premises were deserted. She left everything undisturbed, but using her magic, she gained access to every file concerning the Ordels' business holdings. No fraud was documented, but reading between the lines it soon became clear that the tactics they had employed to try to steal Jyan's inheritance had often worked. They had become quite wealthy pressuring people to sell for below market price or stealing property from the rightful owners with various fraudulent practices. As she had been warned, and personally witnessed, these were not nice people. They were dangerous, and Brylee would be careful not to underestimate them.

Farriar and Tae's companionship was so enjoyable that Brylee met them weekly at the Linger Longer. The more she got to know the couple, the more she grew to like them. On their fourth social get-together, she had a thought that if she survived but failed to get back to Levi or Haxley, she might find a place with them in her life as friends in Nuulan. Then she chided herself. *No defeatist thinking!* But the pangs of loneliness gripped her often that year. Never being able to completely let her guard down and be herself wore on her, as did living a lie and deceiving such fine people.

Chapter Sixty-Eight

Winter seemed to stretch on interminably. There were a few cool, sunny days, but there were many more harsh, windy days, often with light, swirling snow that rarely settled for long.

Two moons after arriving in Nuulan, Jyan held the opening event for Grinders. Most businesses would hold evening affairs, but as Grinders was set to capture the morning market, the store opened early to capture the morning crowd as they slogged to work.

Brylee joined Jyan on the pavement outside of the bright new storefront, trying to entice passers-by to step in and try free samples of Garrick's Grou't. They could also try three different pastries, warm bread with a thin coating of cheese, or soft, round biscuits containing chunks of chocolate. The staff played up the fact that grou't would only be available for one week, which would exhaust the supply of beans brought back from the Rainbow Archipelago and those grown in Jyan's limited test planting. "Don't miss this opportunity, and bring your friends back tomorrow," they coaxed. The store would sell tea and Harding's Ales until Jyan harvested and processed his own beans, the first of which would return grou't to Nuulan by midsummer.

There was much interest, especially as the tasters were free, but Brylee was a little disappointed with the initial uptake. Nuulanees were notoriously conservative and shied away from change. As people left, Jyan proudly reminded everyone who partook to be mindful of how clear their heads were for the morning and to return the following day if they felt their spirits were lifted by his morning treat.

Once the morning rush subsided, Brylee congratulated the team on their opening, then left for her shift at Our Lady. As she moved through the market, she changed her clothing and appearance to that of Scarlet the Healer. She arrived at the hospital with a small waterskin of Garrick's Grou't, which her magic had kept piping hot. She gave all the regulars a taste of this "new experience" that she told them she had discovered on her way to work.

Aethe and Mary were preoccupied with a woman who had arrived during the night. The patient was from the Pearl Dragon, a local bawdy house. Her client had been too demanding and forceful, which caused the girl to call for help. One of the establishment's bruisers had burst into the room, panicking the drunken customer, who had lashed out with a shiv he had snuck in. What happened to that man, Aethe wasn't told, but his blood was on the patient, mixed in with hers, which gushed from her right side, just under the armpit.

"We could have used you on this case," Aethe said as she inspected the dressing. "The blade opened a lung and nicked her heart. We've stitched what we could, but this was a wound fit for your skills and interest." Brylee had asked to be included on as many chest puncture wounds as possible, and the staff were only too willing to accept her help.

Brylee inspected the patient magically, using her powers to repair some internal damage.

"If you told us where you live," Mary groused, standing with her arms crossed, "I could have sent for you." Brylee didn't reply. It wasn't the first such jibe from the crotchety healer, but Brylee took no offence. The woman had a good heart and meant well.

Brylee went to the washroom to clean up and noticed her "shadow" had appeared. Kithy, Aethe's daughter, had a crush on her, and had taken to following her everywhere and helping in every way she could. With Aethe's blessing, Brylee taught the youngster much and kept her busy fetching herbs, dressings, and other supplies.

"Did you magic the tramp?" Kithy asked. Brylee's eyes widened as she stifled a laugh.

"She's not a tramp, Kithy. Why would you call her that?"

"I don't know. That's the name Mary used. What does it mean?"

"I'll let your ma answer that, young lady." Brylee dropped to one knee to be closer to the girl. "And remember," she said, keeping her voice low, "we said we would keep my magic our secret, OK?"

"Of course." Kithy laughed and turned to skip away, but Brylee held her arm to bring her in for a hug.

"And that means, Miss Kithy, that you can't run around asking me if I magicked someone even if you don't think other people are around to hear." She tickled the girl, who wriggled and slid down Brylee's body into a heap on the floor.

The next morning was a Work Hive day, so Brylee left her rooms and transformed herself into her flower girl persona in a quiet alley. She arrived at Farriar's office to find that Alleph had sent word that all services were to be cancelled for the day. Brylee wondered what had caused them to keep the trades away and decided to go observe. But before she could leave, Madrid, Farriar's new administrator, stopped her.

"Old Ma Harrington tried to book you for today before the Ordels cancelled. I told her you already had a task assigned, and she was disappointed. Apparently there's a problem with her vines. She'd be pleased if you would drop by now, as you're free. You'll be paid this way too." To avoid attention, Brylee had accepted some shifts at locations other than the castle. The Harringtons had a rooftop garden that the old lady almost lived in. Over the winter there wasn't much in bloom, and she ordered cut flowers and used the help to prune, trim, and set up her garden for the upcoming season. Brylee enjoyed working with the woman, it took her mind back to pleasant times at Plainhand Estate.

"I'll go see her," Brylee promised. On her way to Harrington's, Brylee walked past Castle Ordel, first as the flower girl and then twice in different guises. There was nothing to see, as the gates were closed. She walked to the cathedral and climbed to the belfry, slipping past a dozing guard to gain access. The castle's courtyard was deserted aside from the guards, and the curtains on every window were drawn.

Brylee went to see Mrs. Harrington who, as predicted, was delighted to see the "flower girl."

"Oh, look, dear. See how this vine's leaves have gone much darker than the others?" the old woman said in her deep, vibrant voice, which belied her age. "I hope you can fix it." Brylee inspected the plant. It seemed well apart from the colouring, so she dug into the frozen soil and checked the roots. They were hard, brittle, and had a whitish wash.

"It's got winter blight," Brylee said, shaking her head. "The frost must have penetrated the ground. The root bowl is pretty shallow. The other vines either have deeper roots or are hardier stock."

"Oh dear, I hope you can salvage it," Mrs. Harding said. "They're all from the same stock. In fact, the sick one was the original. Mr. Harrington, may he rest in peace, split the root bowl a few times and grew the others from it."

"It's a long shot, but I have an idea," Brylee said. "Can I take some supplies from your larder?"

Brylee heated a pot of water until it was warm to the touch. In a jug she mixed cold water with some baking soda, vinegar, and a flake of soap. She carried them both to the roof and knelt beside the sick vine. She peeled back the soil, aware that Mrs. Harrington was peering over her shoulder, fascinated.

"First, I use the warm water to wash the soil from the root bowl. Not too warm, mind you," Brylee explained as she worked. "Now we shock the root with the cold water. The vinegar and other items will kill or fend off any infection, at least until the roots settle from the shock and try to take up nutrients from the soil." Before she applied the cold mixture, Brylee sprinkled some manure into the soil surrounding the roots and mixed it in. Then she washed the roots in the freezing water, lowered the bowl back into the ground, and packed it loosely with soil.

"There," Brylee said, sitting back on her heels. "Let's see what that does. I'll pop by in a day or two." As Brylee stood, a few flakes fell from the vine's knotty bark. That was to be expected after such rough treatment, and Brylee explained as much to Mrs. Harrington. What Brylee hadn't anticipated was that the other vines also shed some flakes, as if in sympathy. Brylee wondered if there was a breeze or if somehow the cold water had trickled down the line of plants, but the other vines were uphill from the sick specimen.

Curious, Brylee switched to her magical sight and inspected the vines. There was nothing unexpected, and each plant had a tiny glow in its leaves and roots, a wisp of a link back to the source. She followed the sick vine's link and noticed where it touched the source. It met the wisps coming from the other vines in a protrusion at the connecting point.

"That's interesting," she said, not meaning to say that out loud.

"What is, dear?"

Brylee made up an excuse for her lapse, but her mind was brewing on her discovery. She realised it made sense. If a plant was divided in two, one half would have a link and the other would die, like someone being skriked. But they didn't, so they must have evolved to share the link, hence the stub at the source.

Brylee said her goodbyes and walked back to the flower stall at the market with an idea in her mind. She purchased six different plants and took them back to her room.

Stinkbaum was a small bush that, despite its name, had a pleasant, rosy aroma when its sap was spilt. The smell attracted bees and was part of the plant's propagation strategy. Brylee separated a stinkbaum into two and placed each half at opposite sides of the room. Now if she nicked the bark on one half, both halves of the plant released the fragrant sap into the air. Brylee expanded the experiment, taking a two-inch long cutting from a branch, knowing that the cutting would continue to strive for life for a day or two and succeed if replanted. The smell faded after an hour, but if she cut one of the plants, the cutting also seeped sap, emitting its distinct smell.

The next morning Brylee took half of the stinkbaum to Our Lady. The other half remained in her room, and she shaped a small cutting into a broach that she pinned to her cloak. She explained the idea to Aethe. If they needed her for an emergency, they should cut into the plant's bark. Hopefully, Brylee would smell the reaction and rush to the hospital to assist.

A week later as Brylee sat in the Library of Magical Law reading a dry tome about magically reducing the weight of weapons and armour, the distinctive odour of stinkbaum filled the room. Slightly embarrassed, Brylee hurried out and ran to Our Lady, transforming her persona as she went.

Aethe was surprised to see her dash into the hospital even though she had asked Mary to summon her.

"Over here!" she called, guiding Brylee to the main surgery table. "She collapsed on the street right outside. There are no wounds. I think it's her heart." An elderly woman dressed in rags lay on her side, curled into a ball. She was drenched in sweat, murmuring as she gripped her left arm. Her clothing had been peeled back so she could be examined, but she made no attempt to cover herself.

Brylee did a quick examination, noting the woman's dilated eyes and brown teeth, which were the colour of a tobac smoker, not just decay. She pinched the woman's wrist, counting her heart beats, which were fast and irregular. She switched to her magical sight and did a quick scan of the woman's vital organs, ending with her struggling heart. Her veins were full of fat, some of which had broken free and had lodged in the opening to the main chamber of her heart, obstructing the flow and preventing a steady beat.

"I'll need the curtain," Brylee said as she rolled the woman onto her back. Mary and Aethe tugged at a thin drape that hung from the ceiling next to the pillar, spreading it around the table for privacy. Kithy helped, tying some of the strings that would hold it in place but not taking her eyes off Brylee for a second. Brylee pulled into her mind the general attributes for blood, which her recent experience had helped her commit to memory. She whispered seductively to the woman's blood, which confessed its own composition, and she compared the two. Brylee was discovering that blood fell into different groups, and it wasn't healthy to mix them. It didn't take long to transform the fatty tissue impeding blood flow through the heart into more of the woman's blood type. As the fat melted away, her heart began to beat more steadily until she was lying peacefully asleep.

Brylee spent another hour scouring the woman's blood vessels for fatty build-ups and melting them into blood. As she worked, she wondered for the hundredth time what consequences for the future there would be from the lives she had saved at the hospital. There were days she wished she had the courage to just let nature take its course and not interfere, but it was not in her to be so callous. Over time she realised she had fallen into a pattern of saying a prayer to Ag to protect Levi, her family, and her loved ones from her meddling.

When she was finished, she relaxed her concentration to find Aethe and Mary had moved on to help others, leaving her with Kithy. As soon as she realised Brylee was finished, the girl held up a goblet of water.

"You're always so thirsty when you finish mag—you know!" she lowered her voice to a conspiratorial whisper mid-sentence.

"I am, Kithy, and you're always so considerate. Thank you." Brylee pulled the girl into a quick hug. "Let's go get cleaned up. I'm all sweaty."

They refolded the curtain and handed the woman off to two orderlies who came over when they saw the work was done. Brylee instructed them on the best recovery treatments and herbs and to tell the woman to stop using tobac, or at least to cut back.

As they walked to the kitchen, Brylee noticed a man she had seen before somewhere, holding his side and complaining about severe pain. At first she couldn't place him, but he looked familiar. She scanned his innards but could see nothing amiss. Juli, an experienced healer, seemed to have matters well in hand, so Brylee left her to it.

Chapter Sixty-Nine

Farriar was pleased to see the flower girl; a messenger from Castle Ordel had all but demanded service now that they had reopened their gates. Apparently "the snowbloom was insipid, and the red grass had faded to pink," and Alleph was making everyone's life miserable. Farriar and Madrid thought Brylee's quick impersonation of Alleph, in which she wiggled her fingers like snakes and talked down her nose at them, was hilarious.

An hour later Brylee pushed her empty water trolley into the well-water room at the castle, drew a bucket of fresh water, and added it to the clean side of the pushcart. She shrugged her flower carrier harness into a more comfortable position and then walked out through the kitchen towards the drawing room, which was the first task on the list she had been given at the gate.

The drawing room doors were wide open, and as Brylee approached, she heard voices. Once at the threshold, she saw Alleg, Alleph, and Captain Farborn, who was the leader of the mage's escort during the investigation of Garrick's death.

"Do my study first, will you?" Alleg said to Brylee, striding across to the doors and pulling them closed to shut her out. It wasn't his rudeness that left Brylee with a feeling of shock. It was that she realised Farborn was the man she had seen being treated by Juli at Our Lady the day before. She hadn't recognised him then, as he was wearing nondescript worker's overalls. Whatever had ailed him seemed to be gone now, as he seemed vigorous and animated. She thought about lingering at the door to eavesdrop, but the corridor was too busy with trades coming and going.

Brylee completed her rounds, noting two new guards outside one of the basement's storerooms, which was odd, but she could see no reason why the castle had been closed off the day before. Everything seemed normal, but her mind was occupied as she attempted to discern why Farborn had been at Our Lady with no true ailment as far as she could detect. Whatever the reason, it didn't bode well.

By late afternoon, Brylee had changed into her Scarlet Fisher mage persona and was in the council's library, closing the cover of a tome called *Military equipment weight reduction*. She had to admit the concepts discussed had value, but the author had managed to extract all fun and intrigue from his words, which were so dry Brylee joked to herself that the book's pages should be brittle. She took the book back to the duty librarian and handed it in.

"Mage Fisher," the bright young woman said with a laugh, "I think you might be the most prolific reader here. That's your cap book completed already. Here's your pass."

"Cap book?" Brylee replied, raising an eyebrow.

"Why, yes, didn't they tell you? We call the tenth book drawn and returned the cap book. It goes back to when we had coloured hats to mark a mage's level of achievement. First we got a cap, awarded for reading the Basics of Magic, which were prescribed reading, enshrined in a set of ten volumes. From there you could work through various styles and colours of headwear, but we dropped the whole hat thing a century ago. Except for granting access to the Advanced Magic section, once we gain our 'cap'— well, it's a pass now, not a cap, but you know what I mean." The idea of accessing advanced information set Brylee's heart racing, and she scurried away to dig into the treasure trove.

Following the librarian's directions, Brylee found a plain wooden door behind a row of shelves that contained a collection of poems and fiction written by mages. She opened the door and found a gruff, bored-looking older gent sitting on a stool. He inspected her pass and gave Brylee a once-over. It wasn't a look of flirtation. It was an assessment of whether he thought she belonged in his domain. Whatever his criteria, Brylee seemed to pass. He tapped a sign on the wall that prohibited flames and water and forbade anyone from removing the artefacts from the room. Then he wished her a good day and returned to a book he had been studying.

The room was long and narrow, running the length of the main library. Both sides of the space had floor-to-ceiling shelving crammed with dusty books. In the confined space between the walls sat a series of small, square tables boasting a single chair on each side. They left just enough space to press past each reading station as people made their way down the row to the end of the cramped space.

What struck Brylee was that the two dozen or so people seated or roaming the shelves all wore their long mage robes. Brylee had elected to wear regular street clothes, which she felt was more in line with her guise as an overseas traveller who was not part of Mordeland's registered mage class. In the main library, there had been a mixture of dress styles, and she didn't stand out. Now her outfit made her conspicuous, and she wondered if it was part of why the doorman had studied her for so long.

As she moved down the aisle scanning the shelves to see how they were organised, she noticed people glance at her. Some just did a quick double take, some were more curious and even offered a welcoming smile, and still others stared rudely. Whichever the case, Brylee realised she would be remembered, which was unfortunate.

Brylee found each section fascinating, but two stood out. One was on mage duelling and warcraft. The other was entitled *Magicks of the First People*, which she imagined was primi magic. With so many eyes on her, she thought it prudent to ignore both, so she selected a book on healing and thumbed through it. She was surprised to find it was fairly basic and suffered a ripple of pride when she realised how her skills had flourished under Garrick and at Our Lady.

Brylee had worked her way through several volumes when she realised she was ravenous. She wondered how much time had passed. She returned the book she had been reading to its place and walked to the door. A new doorman was sitting on the stool. She asked him about the hours that section was open and when it was busy or quiet. She was surprised to find it was open continuously, as projects the council needed researched often couldn't wait. However, after twenty-second bell, it rarely had more than one or two visitors.

Brylee bought fruit and bread from the market as she walked to Our Lady and changed into her healer persona in the public latrines in Old Square.

She had been working in the hospital for an hour when she needed some clean bandages, which she sent Kithy to fetch. The eager young girl scampered off but returned empty handed. The dispensary had run out. Brylee asked Aethe about it.

"I asked Ike to replenish it before he left this morning," Aethe said. "I'm busy lancing this boil. Do you think you could bring some down?"

"Gladly," Brylee replied. "Where from?"

"Oh, you've never been up to the main storeroom?" Aethe asked, handing Brylee a key she kept on a chain around her neck.

"I can show her, Ma," Kithy offered, grabbing Brylee's hand.

"OK, but watch those carts up there," Aethe replied. "They could squish you in a heartbeat."

Kithy led Brylee to the rear of the kitchen, through a wide door, and up two long flights of dimly lit stone steps. The sour stink of spring water assaulted Brylee's nose long before they reached the top, where another set of doors led out into the main warehouse. Two dozen people were busy in the production facility. Brylee stood for a few moments trying to understand their process.

A large pool fizzed and bubbled on one side of the room. The floor around it wasn't level, and Brylee realised the warehouse had been built around it a long time ago. A massive waterwheel sat in the pool and turned slowly, driven by a donkey that walked inside it, prompted by a teamster if it slowed. The waterwheel scooped up water in barrels that had been sliced down the middle. They hung on the wheel on swivels, so gravity kept them facing upwards and they retained the water they collected.

As the wheel turned, it carried water up and over itself. As the scoops came down the far side, they struck a bar that flipped them upside down so their contents fell into a trough that spilt down into a holding tank. Carts containing empty barrels pulled up in a line and were filled from the tank before trundling out of the warehouse to deliver the smelly product.

Ingenious, Brylee thought.

"Come on, Scarlet," Kithy said, tugging on her hand. "It's so smelly up here. This way." Brylee let Kithy pull her towards a storeroom at the back of the space.

"Kithy, you're so strong," Brylee said, enjoying the proud giggle she received in return. The storeroom had one wall filled with containers of herbs and other medicinal ingredients and another full of supplies, including the bandages she sought. The third wall was lined with carts full of garbage and dirty linens to be laundered or burnt. She scooped up two boxes of bandages and walked towards the door, anxious to return to the patient she had been helping.

"You have to write it in the book," Kithy said, pointing to an inventory register by the doorway. Brylee leafed through it to the current page and updated it as instructed by the imperious youngster. Brylee closed the book and then pinched Kithy's nose, making her squeal with delight.

As Brylee locked the storeroom door, she noticed the man supervising the donkey watching her. She studied his face, which looked familiar. She realised it was one of Farborn's men. *What's going on?* she wondered. *Time will have its way . . .*

Brylee saw to her patient and then asked Aethe for a private word in her office. When they were alone, Brylee explained what she had seen, but she chose her words carefully, not wanting to reveal her double life.

"There's something strange going on, Aethe," she said. "You know I've always been a bit secretive, yes? Well, I've had some run-ins with some dishonest people. That's partly why I'm so reclusive. Anyway, one of them is working as a teamster up in the loading bay. It could be a coincidence, but then yesterday I saw another one of them. He was being treated down here in the hospital by Juli. I didn't think there was much wrong with him." Aethe nodded as Brylee spoke, as if she knew about them already.

"Do they work for Justice Goath?" Aethe asked. Brylee recognised that name as one of the justices she had covertly visited while researching the Ordels' activities.

"No, why would you say that?" Brylee asked.

"The justice has visited me several times. First, he made a reasonable offer for the water business and the land we own around here. It's worth a lot of money, but its income funds this hospital. I refused, but he has been back since and has become more aggressive. He's threatened to use his contacts to cut off our supply of medicines if we can't come to terms."

Brylee felt a wave of nausea. She didn't know if it was her sensing the eddies of time manipulating events around her or if her head was merely spinning from Aethe's revelation.

"Aethe!" Brylee cried. "Goath is working for Mage Ordel. Do you know him? He's bad people."

"Is he the mage with the sister who has snake fingers?" Aethe replied, her voice an octave higher. No one messed with mages. They always brought bad news. "What can we do?"

"To be honest, I don't know. They're bullies. The person I saw them try to cheat stood up to them and threatened them, so they left him alone."

"I don't think I could stand up to a mage, Scarlet. I really don't." Aethe's shoulders slumped as if she had already been beaten.

"I don't think they would want to be in the spotlight. Could you hire your own justice? Have them challenge Goath in court? Expose their activities?"

"I know a good justice. He helps me with my business and is quite connected. I'll see him today and get rid of the man upstairs too if you tell me what he looks like." Aethe's face warmed a little as she spoke.

Chapter Seventy

Brylee finished her shift late, just after nineteenth bell. She walked over to the Linger Longer, adjusting her disguise on the way. Farriar and Tae were halfway through their meal when she arrived. They happily shuffled around the small table so a third chair could be added. Sliced pork with stewed apple in a long brown bun was the single menu item, but it suited Brylee nicely. She washed it down with a tankard of warm apple cider.

First Farriar and then Tae caught her up on their days, the former recounting Brylee's own flower girl's impersonation of Alleph, with a few minor embellishments and added dramatics. That Farriar thanked her yet again for sending the polite and competent flower girl her way unsettled Brylee. She hated the deceit that underpinned their growing friendship, but there was little she could do about it.

Brylee was back at the Library of the Council of Magical Law by twenty-second bell. Most of the lamps had been extinguished, and the few people who were in the main section were drawn to them like giant moths. A different woman was perched on the stool guarding the door to the Advanced Magic section. She checked Brylee's pass, gave the sign containing the rules a mandatory tap, then handed her a neverdark lantern, a perk reserved for that exclusive area.

Brylee had never seen one before and was fascinated, wondering how it worked after the mage who made it had stopped infusing it with magic. She took it to a table and studied it with her magical senses but couldn't work out its trick. She resolved to look for a book on its design while she had access to the library, but not tonight. Tonight she wanted to browse through the shelves relating to how magic was used to fight.

The mage that Brylee had seen in Sandrick at the ambush had weaponised hard air. Brylee assumed he had other tricks up his sleeve, which she would need to counter. She wished she could practise ahead of her confrontation with the man, but magical combat was strictly forbidden. Even at the border with Backalar, the Elect had dictated magic could only be used for healing and hardening defences and improving weapons. No direct use of magic to fight was permitted, as such a skill was a threat to the non-magical governance of the realm and couldn't be allowed to flourish.

The room was quiet. Two other library users were present, both of them sitting at a table near the door guard and well away from the books on combat at the far end of the long, narrow room. Brylee took her lamp and sauntered down the line of shelves, pretending to browse until she reached the taboo section. She stood reviewing the many titles, taking various books out and leafing through them.

As time went on her disappointment grew. There were books on the history of military magic, on how the laws controlling it had evolved, and on famous duels and duellists, but nothing on the techniques employed to fight.

"You might try *When Iron Fails* by Elyna Stormcrow," a soft female voice said from the darkness nearby. Brylee dropped the book she was holding in surprise. Before it crashed to the floor, a crime that would no doubt bring the door guard running, the book slowed then hovered in the air before rising back up. "Sorry, I didn't mean to startle you, dear," the voice said.

Brylee had spun around to see who was there and initially couldn't see anyone in the darkness outside of the cone illuminated by her lantern. She switched to her magical sight and found an old woman bent over a large book. She had no lantern, but as Brylee watched, the woman turned a page as if she were reading it.

The dropped book was still hovering in front of her, so Brylee took it. As she did, she felt the hard air that the mysterious woman had used to catch it dissipate.

"You're blind," Brylee blurted, then flushed, realising she was being rude. "Sorry, that was crass of me. Let me get my breath." The woman's head swivelled towards Brylee, not as if offended but as if what she said had captured the woman's attention.

"You're not blind, though, are you?" the woman said, raising an eyebrow. "You're a healer. Not many can use magical sight like you can, child."

Brylee recovered enough to nod. She was about to scan the woman's eyes to understand the cause of her blindness when the woman spoke again.

"Then I thank you for not inspecting my eyes. It tingles like crazy. It's polite to ask before probing, don't you think?"

"Er . . . yes," Brylee replied, feeling guilty. The woman reminded her of Mella, who was best handled if she at least attempted to regain some initiative. "What makes you think I would be interested in Stormcrow's works?"

"It's obvious," the woman said. "You're a new face, not wearing mage's robes, so I assume you're a foreigner. You're also here when the library is empty, skulking about, probably embarrassed about being seen researching such a taboo topic. If you were keen to research the history of combat, you would be here at an earlier hour. People would rather be seen looking at the shelf on magically enhancing sex than learning how to fight. Stormcrow is one of the few resources that teaches how to protect yourself from predatory mages, although judging by your magical link, I doubt you have much to worry about."

"Who are you?" Brylee asked, feeling off balance. Aside from herself, Levi was the only person she had met who could see the link to the source and knew of its significance.

The woman paused for a while, then closed her book. "Here, today, I am Mage Reni Bloom. At other times I'm someone else. Which name are you using? I don't care if it's real; you can have your secrets. I would just like to have something to call you."

"I'm Scarlet Fisher," Brylee said. "If I could heal your eyes, would you want me to?" The woman studied her intensely, then Brylee thought she sensed her smile, though expressions were hard to read using magical sight.

"Now that *is* the right question, Scarlet. Well done. You're a perceptive one. I think I'll like you. Take a seat? I have a hip flask with some fine brandy if you care to share with me." Brylee wanted to point out that liquids were not allowed in that area but decided against it. She pulled out the chair opposite Reni and sat, putting the neverdark lantern on the table where it lit up the woman's face. If she was aware of it, Brylee couldn't tell.

Reni Bloom was as short as Brylee was tall and quite old. She would have been beautiful once, Brylee thought, with high, strong cheekbones and a proud forehead. But age hadn't been kind, and neither had whatever had damaged her face, which was scarred, pitted, and flaked as if she had been in the sun too much. Brylee didn't understand the limit of her own healing skills, but the damage was beyond what Garrick could have done for the woman, and he was considered one of the best. Brylee felt rude, being sighted and having the lantern, so she turned it off. The encounter seemed somewhat clandestine, so as the darkness enveloped her, she felt some of her anxiety diminish.

Brylee thought it interesting that Reni had assumed her interest in fighting would be for self-defence, but it made sense, as anything else was forbidden. Technically, so was skriking, but if the predator wasn't obviously thumbing his or her nose at the council, they would probably not be prosecuted.

Reni pulled her flask out of a pocket in her mage robe and took a swig before offering it to Brylee. Brylee didn't think it was a good idea to accept drinks from a stranger, but she was intrigued. She took a sip, and the fiery liquor made her cough as it ripped down her throat.

"Wow! What is this?" Brylee asked, wheezing. "It's tasty, but it could peel paint."

"It's a brandy of my own making. I have my own process that I'm trying to perfect. More?" Brylee shook her head and returned the flask. Reni slipped it into her pocket.

Without warning, a book slid onto the table in front of Brylee. It was the Stormcrow volume that Reni had recommended, plucked from the shelf and delivered to her.

"You have a deft touch with hard air," Brylee said to conceal her surprise. "And you didn't need to look at the bookshelf to find this."

"What would be the point of looking for it with these eyes?" Reni said. "Pointing your eyes at things when using your magical sight is the habit of people who can see. They don't need to; they just do. And I've found since I became physically frail that it is often easier to use hard air rather than my limbs, which often let me down. I shake a lot, if you must know."

"I'm sorry," Brylee said.

"I get by better than most," Reni replied. "Now be quiet and read. I have to finish this, and I want to know what you think of Elyna's work."

Brylee stared at the woman for a few moments. She seemed to have gone back to reading. Then Brylee opened the copy of *When Iron Fails* and became instantly engrossed. It told the tale of Elyna, a blacksmith from decades before who made armour and swords for the current Elect's father. She was renowned and sought out by many, but her projects were chosen for her by the Elect, and for a decade she was happy with that arrangement.

One day Elyna was experimenting with an iron strip that was already mage tempered, trying to make it harder by heating and stretching it under enormous pressure. The strip shattered, firing hot metal shards around the room. The protective visor she had been wearing was blown right off her face, and she was terribly injured. The Elect's personal healer, a mage at the top of his profession, saved her life but not her looks or her sight.

Brylee realised that Elyna and Reni seemed to have similar scarring. *Coincidence?*

She carried on reading. Elyna's loss of sight prevented her from smithing, but the Elect retained her as a mentor for less skilled workers. She found that her students couldn't match her achievements when she left them alone to practise no matter how well they performed when she stood over them. That was when she realised that for her whole career, from her apprenticeship onwards, she had been unknowingly pouring her limited magic into her work. She discovered she was a charmer.

The realisation made Elyna feel vulnerable. Now finding the work unsatisfying, she left the Elect's employ to experiment on ways her limited magic could be used to fight. Brylee came to an index of tactics and techniques that were documented in full later in the book. They were divided into two broad sections: using magic to fight non-mages and fighting mages with or without magic.

As a charmer and removed from the Elect's protection, Elyna was in grave danger from predatory mages. She described several attacks later in life once it became known she was gifted, where her self-taught fighting techniques had saved her life. Having won such battles and not knowing how to skrike, she gained no power from the encounters. Instead, she refined and tweaked the techniques she had come up with, so they were potent with just the power she had.

When Brylee reached the end of the book's history section, she looked up. How long had she been reading? The other visitors had all left. She looked at Reni's link to the source, noting it was far larger than a charmer's but slightly smaller than her own. The deft way she had caught and handled the book Brylee had dropped suggested she had mastered the use of the magic she pulled down.

Unable to escape the feeling Reni was testing her, Brylee decided not to ask the obvious question: were Reni and Elyna Stormcrow the same person? The woman seemed to pride herself in showing sharp insight, yet she talked in riddles, saying, "Today I am Reni," implying that at other times she wasn't. She spent her time sitting in the dark, surprising mages who were sneaking around to read taboo books and guiding them to particular works.

"Elyna has a fascinating history, Reni," Brylee said. "I started life as a charmer and narrowly avoided skriking through the intervention of others." She didn't elaborate, leaving the subject hanging, as Reni often did.

"But you're a full mage, Scarlet. You're the apex predator yourself, unlikely to be hunted by your peers. Are you seeking this knowledge to defeat any charmer who tries to use these techniques to defend themselves from you?" Although Reni appeared to be focussed on her book, Brylee sensed the woman was tense and prepared for anything. If Brylee were a predator who reacted badly to Reni's question and attacked, she was sure it would go badly for her. What was motivating Reni to act as she did?

"You're wondering how I stepped from being a charmer to a mage?" Brylee ventured. "Not at the expense of others, Reni. I am the beneficiary of what I think is called 'the gift' from a beloved friend. No, my path leads me into the company of malevolent and skilled forces, and my history has left me feeling . . . insecure." Brylee thought she saw the corners of Reni's mouth twitch upwards.

"Knowledge is helpful, but experience trumps it," the woman said.

"That's true," Brylee replied, understanding it would be helpful to practise what she had learnt. "But sparring is forbidden."

Reni shrugged. "So is brandy in this room."

"I've heard whispers of illegal groups, some associated through this very library, who meet in private to duel," Brylee said. "Are you recruiting for one of them?"

"That's the first wrong question you've asked, Scarlet," Reni replied, "but it's an understandable presumption, I suppose."

Brylee racked her brains. The woman could just declare her interest, but she seemed to prefer these games. Then Brylee got an idea. "Would it be better if I asked where Elyna Stormcrow is today?"

"That's an excellent question, mostly because you refrained from asking it earlier. But wherever she is, I imagine she misses sparring and teaching worthy warriors."

The two women sat in silence for a few moments. Reni turned a page in her book.

"I wonder what chapters Elyna would think best to read first," Brylee said. Reni carried on reading, but she held up both hands, her right with two fingers up and her left with five.

Chapter Seventy-One

Anticipating Brylee's thoughts, Reni had warned her about attempting to smuggle out the copy of *When Iron Fails,* pointing out that the guard at the door wasn't there solely to check passes. Each book had a copper strip embedded in its spine that the guards had been trained to sense. Forewarned, Brylee could have defeated that measure with her primi magic, but there was no need. Reni explained that Coynes Bookstore on Charter Street would have a copy at a reasonable price.

On the way to Our Lady the next morning, Brylee purchased her own volume of Elyna's work. It had been transcribed identically to the library copy but was crisp and unwrinkled. She also picked up a copy of *Magical Knots: The Key to Making Neverdark Lamps* by Denjrus Cole. She couldn't wait for the end of her shift to delve into the book's secrets. She had arranged to meet Reni back at the library three days hence to discuss her thoughts.

Brylee believed that Reni was, in fact, Elyna, and that she wanted to help people who felt vulnerable to improve their ability to defend themselves. But more than that, Reni was bored. It seemed the old woman still wanted someone to spar with her. Brylee thought this wonderfully outrageous, as the woman had likely seen over eighty summers and relied on two canes to walk and a trained dog to see. Brylee met Lucky, the guide dog, as they left together. Lucky had to wait outside the library kitchen for her mistress but was accomplished at harassing the cook for treats, so she didn't object.

The mysterious woman had refused to confirm any of Brylee's suspicions, perhaps because to do so would leave her open to charges of breaking the prohibition about fighting with magic. Yet another alternative was that Reni worked for the council's law enforcement arm and was in place to trap mages who sought to fight with magic. Either way, Brylee was determined to learn more about Reni before crossing a line with the woman that could lead to complications with the council.

Aethe had achieved both tasks she had set herself. The Ordels' spy was ejected, and her justice sent a cease-and-desist demand to Castle Ordel, ensuring it was copied to the Council of Land's offices. There was nothing illegal about an interest in acquiring Aethe's assets or making persuasive offers, but the demand explained there was nothing for sale, that planting a spy was in bad faith, and any further contact would be referred to the courts. The justice was confident that the note would put the Ordels on sufficient notice and encourage them to focus elsewhere to expand their empire, but Brylee wasn't so sure.

Her shift dragged on through the day. When it finally ended, she almost skipped back to her rooms, grabbing a hot, round flatbread with melted cheese and sliced meat from the baker on Sterling Road. The food was greasy, so she wolfed it down then washed her hands in her bedside bowl before lying down on her bed and opening her book.

By the time her eyes grew too weary to continue to read by lantern light, Brylee had an overview of basic fighting tactics but had yet to dig into the details of each. Mages used variations of three main attacks: using hard air to encase, suffocate, or, if a true master, to puncture; using heat or cold on the surrounding air, surfaces, clothing, or, if powerful enough, directly to a body; or transformation, using techniques such as hardening wood to make ironwood. Working directly on a body and any transformation took a great deal of energy and time for those not blessed with primi powers, so heat and air were the main weapons of choice and were where the book focussed.

To counter these attacks, the book explained various defences, such as applying the opposite energy in the case of heat and cold and hard-air shields to block and deflect hard-air attacks. This seemed obvious to Brylee until she plunged into the details. It was one thing to block a thrust of hard air or break its grip if one was encased within it, as Brylee had been twice, but it was quite another to remove hard air from one's lungs. The latter had to be done while in excruciating pain without shearing the blockage and causing it to puncture something vital, all before suffocating.

It was the nuances such as the lung attack that Stormcrow had developed and documented. They included breaking an encasement of air by using a small shiv of air on the attacker's weak points rather than trying to wrestle the entire trap at once or parrying a spear of air by angling one's defensive shield instead of blocking the thrust, the former of which took much less energy but greater skill.

Brylee realised that the techniques for improving the use of shields, swords, and arrows were being employed by a master in a magical armoury that a mage could conjure if they were sufficiently skilled. The blacksmith had transferred what she knew with great effect. The more she read, the more Brylee confirmed that with a great deal of practice, Stormcrow's techniques enabled someone with little power to compete against a stronger foe. As Brylee wanted every advantage against Levi's assailant—she chose not to call him Levi's murderer, as she was intent on saving the time weaver—she took the lessons to heart. But her mind had already jumped to how she could employ her primi magic to refine her combat style further and develop unique tactics that would defeat such common defences.

Brylee slept well and woke early. Today would see the last of Grinders' grou't sold to the public, but Jyan had kept enough back to see himself and his trusted few through until his new batch was ready. He was quite addicted. Interest in grou't had surged, as Brylee knew it would, and there was already a line at the door when she went downstairs even though the store wouldn't open for another bell. People had brought their friends to get a taste of their find before supplies dried up.

Jyan had a pot made for himself, so Brylee poured herself a cup, then rooted through trays of baked goods, which had just arrived.

"These lemon squares are delicious," he said, his mouth half full. Brylee wished him luck for the day and took a lemon square as well as a cheese scone and a round ginger root biscuit, then went back up to her room to read more of the book.

The next section discussed perhaps the biggest impediment to defending against magic: anticipating the attack. It was difficult because each attack was essentially invisible. A mage could shape air anywhere within their sight. Their opponent could be facing the mage, and the mage might stab them in the back. Brylee found the techniques unsatisfying, though they were better than nothing. The book instructed her to watch her opponent's eyes, learn their favoured attacks ahead of time, and learn to be lightning fast with her defences and counterattacks. Perhaps most helpful was a discussion on how unwieldy most weapons were and how simply moving out of the way shouldn't be ignored. Brylee could attest how heavy hard air could be and how a moving target could be slippery.

When ninth bell struck, Brylee realised she was late for work. She washed up and ran to the Work Hive office. Madrid was snippy with her, which was fair, as Brylee was late. Another man had already been dispatched to Castle Ordel, but as Mrs. Harrington had again requested her, Brylee's persona wouldn't go completely without pay for the day. Brylee played the remorseful flower girl but was secretly glad to skip most of the shift. She decided to cancel her shifts for the next two weeks, claiming the sick aunt who had delayed her that day needed care but confirmed that she would stop by Mrs. Harrington's house.

Her visit to Mrs. Harrington was short. The old lady just wanted to show off the vine, which had recovered, and get Brylee to move some empty hanging baskets and heavy bags of soil to a stand she had set up. The woman would spend the day installing moss, filling each basket, and planting seedlings in preparation for the spring.

"Thank you, dear," Mrs. Harrington said. "With my old joints, lifting these pots and bags is impossible, but I like to do the planting. When I see the shoots emerge and blossom, I know I did something good." Brylee used her magical sight to see if anything other than old age was afflicting the kindly old woman. A quick scan confirmed there wasn't.

Brylee said her goodbyes and then left, planning to return to her room and read more of *When Iron Fails*. As she descended Mrs. Harrington's long, winding staircase, her mind was occupied with the old woman's health. She was also mentally replaying Garrick's techniques for his elderly patients. She had helped him dozens of times as he taught her what he could of his trade. It dawned on her that while she watched him work, she always had a sense of how and where he was applying his magic. It wasn't like she could see it, but she always knew if he was heating, freezing, cutting, applying pressure, or energising tissue to help it regrow and how much power he was applying in each case. *How is healing magic different from fighting magic?* she wondered.

Garrick had always explained everything he was doing as if she couldn't sense it. Most mages couldn't see into bodies or the links back to the magic's source. She had never considered it before, but maybe she could sense the application of magic, yet others could not. If that were true, it would give her an advantage in a duel, but aside from Reni as a sparring partner—which she wasn't ready to commit to yet—she had no way to test her theory. Or did she?

Brylee recalled overhearing a discussion at the library between two young apprentice mages. Neither was allowed into the advanced section, as they hadn't reached the requisite power and skill level. They were bemoaning that, as apprentices, they had to do tasks on behalf of their sponsors. One had been assigned to help build an extension to the Central Meat Market by hardening wood joints once they were laid in place. The market stank, was always freezing, and the work was draining.

The Central Meat Market was on the far side of the city, a three-hour walk. If she set off immediately, Brylee could see if any mages were there and perhaps observe them in action. She set off at once, her mind full of possibilities.

Brylee had never been to that side of the city, but it wasn't much different. Nuulan's architecture wasn't a jewel to draw visitors in the same way Rostal amazed all who saw it. The Central Meat Market's butchery and sales had stopped for the day—it was busy from dawn until just after noon—but construction on the extension was in full swing. The new section was in the form of a wing, at right angles to the old building, but at this point there was little more than a hole in the ground and some framing. A wall had been built around the hole for the safety of the public, but it had viewing windows for passers-by to watch the construction. People all over the world found looking into a hole irresistible.

Brylee had changed her appearance to that of a weary office worker and made her way to stand next to a dozen similarly dressed gawkers at one of the windows. There was no doubt when her route took her downwind of the market, as the smell was nauseating. Brylee always kept mint root in her pocket in case she had to visit Our Lady, and she slipped some into her scarf, which she wound around her face.

Workers below were lifting pre-cut beams from carts and placing them as directed by two foremen who each carried a set of plans that they checked often. Once plumbed and levelled, the beams were nailed into place and then rechecked for alignment. Some beams were much thicker than others, which Brylee assumed meant they were load bearing. Once in place, bricks would be added to match the design of the main building's façade.

Brylee spotted an apprentice mage due to her robes. She was lounging by a food cart. It was almost a full bell before she was called over to harden a series of recently assembled joints. The woman climbed a ladder set against one beam, then shimmied out astride another to reach the first joint. Once there, the apprentice lashed herself to the beam. Brylee assumed this was to prevent her falling once she was fully absorbed in her task.

 The apprentice held her hands on either side of the foot-wide beam, closed her eyes, and began concentrating. There was nothing to see with her regular sight, so Brylee engaged her magical vision. Once again, Brylee could not see anything, but she had the same sense of where and how the apprentice was working. She could also see the woman's link throb and her inner glow dim as she drew large amounts of power through herself before applying it to the wood.

Brylee was fascinated. She could tell transformation magic was being used. First here, then there as the apprentice hardened the wood and then fused the beams together. Yet she couldn't see a shimmer or glow. She just sensed the activity in a way she couldn't describe. Levi had explained that for most magic, a mage linked to something and became the conduit for attributes to flow without truly understanding the mechanics involved. Wickham using the ground to transfer hardness to air was the example she recalled. She focussed on the apprentice, wondering what she used as the source for hardening ironwood. Almost immediately, she sensed magic emanating from the apprentice's satchel, which was beside the chair she had lounged on earlier. Refocussing her magical sight, Brylee saw a large brick of metal inside the bag.

Brylee watched with rapt attention for the remainder of the shift and returned twice over the next two days when she wasn't at Our Lady. Each hour, her sense of the apprentice's use of magic became sharper.

It was with some misgivings that Brylee entered the library to meet Reni two nights later. She had many questions, but she was wary of a trap. She opened the door to the advanced section and showed her pass to the doorwoman.

"The blind lady left you this," the woman said, shoving a letter into Brylee's hand. She opened the note, which contained instructions for Brylee to meet Reni at twenty-second bell and an address in the wealthy section of town, not far from Castle Ordel. She thanked the doorwoman and then left.

Brylee made a looping detour so she could approach the address from the opposite side, using a different persona than Scarlet the mage. She became a beggar woman, shuffling around the neighbourhood, seemingly intent on finding discarded scraps. Meanwhile, she was covertly checking every nook, shadow, and window for danger. Twice Brylee had to shake off a guard who started to follow her, more intent on shooing a tramp away from the area rather than anything nefarious. With half a bell until the meeting time, she reverted to Scarlet and immersed herself in a deep shadow opposite the address on the note where her earlier reconnaissance confirmed she would be invisible yet have a good view of comings and goings.

The address was one of the standard residences, similar to Mrs. Harrington's. Brylee pulled her cloak tightly around herself to fend off the deepening cold and settled in to watch.

With just a few minutes until the appointed time, Brylee heard a noise behind her. It wasn't close yet, but it was coming her way. She sank back into the darkest shadows, crouched to make herself small, and held her breath. The noise resolved itself into an odd series of clicks and clacks. As it grew clearer, Brylee's mind solved the puzzle, recognising Lucky's paws and Reni's canes approaching on the frigid cobblestones.

"There you are, dear," the old woman said as she pulled level with Brylee's hiding place. Her magical sight had easily penetrated the darkness. Brylee chided herself for being so foolish, having met the woman in the dark at the library. That Brylee was now in a completely different persona didn't faze Reni at all. *Does she even notice the difference?*

"Smart of you to be circumspect, Scarlet, but there's no need," Reni said. She shuffled off. "Come get warmed up," she called over her shoulder. "You'll freeze out here."

Reni led Brylee across the street, but instead of climbing the dozen steps to the front door, she slipped down the side of the building and around to the trades entrance at the rear. Brylee followed with every sense she had stretched out, looking for threats. Lucky's tail wagged faster and faster as they approached the door.

"OK, Lucky," Reni said, laughing. "You're off duty now." Brylee heard the lock turn, then the door opened inwards. She assumed someone inside had heard their approach and opened it, but as neither of her forms of sight could detect anyone else, she deduced Reni must have used magic.

"Come in and take a seat. I rent this room from George upstairs. If he knows I'm coming, he lights a fire and banks the coals to keep it warm all night. Be a dear and throw a log on while I feed her majesty here."

Brylee stepped inside and closed the door. It was a single room with a small sink and pantry, sealed off from the main house so it could be rented out. The fireplace was mounted to the left of the door, accessing the common chimney that served all floors. Two oil lamps glowed on side tables at either end of the room. With a distracted wave of her hand, Reni twisted their knobs, which raised the wick in each, and the light increased, revealing the space in more detail. A table sat in the centre surrounded by three tall, padded chairs. There was no other furniture. No bed, dresser, or amenities to wash, other than the sink.

Reni lifted a bowl from a shelf, filled it with dried food, and poured water into a separate bowl, a delay that seemed to annoy the impatient dog, who whined her displeasure.

"Stop it, Lucky," Reni chided. "Does it bother you that I use my magic so casually?" she asked Brylee. "The door, the lights?"

"I don't object in principle," Brylee replied, taking a log from the stack and laying it on the hot coals. It caught before Brylee had walked the short distance to the table. She stood, waiting to be invited to sit. "But it startles me each time you do it. You're so deft and, well, no one . . ." She stopped, not sure how to phrase that people considered it rude without offending Reni.

Reni laughed. "I don't do it around 'normals' or Nuulan's conservative snobs." She put the bowls down and watched Lucky tuck in. "But I find everything in my body hurts these days, and..." She paused as she eased herself into a chair. "Anything that helps avoid moving is a blessing. Now, before you sit down and tell me what you think of the book, could you fetch some wine and cake from the pantry? I'm as hungry as Lucky and barely better mannered. Grab a glass and a plate for yourself if you wish. It's delicious."

Brylee decided to join Reni in the meal, but would let the women eat and drink before she did herself. She was surprised they were drinking from actual glassware. Her mind went back to Niff's wife, Zally, who made the healer's glass eye and all of Judd Brown's bottles. She set the table and then sat down in the light. She realised the lanterns were for her benefit, or perhaps Lucky's, as Reni didn't need them, but she felt exposed sitting so close in the brightness. Reni still hadn't commented on Brylee having the wrong face. She reached out and cut a slice of cake for them both and filled their glasses. Reni tucked into the cake without delay.

"I appreciate you don't trust me yet, but I can assure you I don't poison good cake or wine," Reni said. A wry grin appeared on her scarred face as she continued, "I use the cheap stuff when I poison people. Now, what did you think of the book?"

Brylee took a sip of the wine, which was delicious. "I've never read anything like it." Brylee let her genuine admiration for the book show in her voice. "I've thought of little else all week."

"But . . ." Reni prompted.

"The theory seems excellent, but it would require extensive practice to perfect. Seeing as it's illegal to spar, most charmers facing a powerful mage would die before having the chance to improve their skill."

Reni put her food down and turned her head toward Brylee as if inspecting her with her broken eyes. *An old habit or a compliment at my intuitiveness?* Brylee wondered as Reni sat back in her seat, a serious air about her now.

"And . . ." was all she said, prompting Brylee to continue.

"And . . . Elyna lived a long life, at least long enough to write the book and fend off a few attacks. Maybe she's still alive, but either way, I feel there's some secret she knows that's not revealed in the book. At least not in the parts I've read."

It was probably the hours watching the apprentice's magic being employed that had sharpened Brylee's senses enough to detect Reni drawing her magic to her a moment before she struck, encasing Brylee in hard air. Brylee didn't attempt to move or break Reni's hold on her. The air wasn't harsh as Vekki's had been, and she could breathe easily. Reni released her a moment later, and they both sat in silence.

"You were testing me," Brylee said.

"Yes, but for what?" Reni asked.

"You can see people shaping their magic, can't you? And you wanted to see if I could too." Reni nodded, and the taut, scarred skin on her brow rose with her left eyebrow. "I can't *see* the magic," Brylee continued, "but I can sense it somehow. The book made me realise I perceived it when watching healers, but I hadn't thought much about it. I've been watching more carefully over the past few days since I met you, and I think it's the key. If I can develop that skill, I can beat almost any mage. It would be like they were . . . er, well . . . blind, where I could see, if you'll pardon the phrase."

"Very good," Reni said, tucking into the cake as if nothing much had occurred. "Congratulations. You just leapt from being someone I was considering training to my most advanced student. If you want, we can start tonight." She washed her cake down with a gulp of wine, as if eager to get on with it.

"I guess it's my turn to be crass," Brylee said. "It would be helpful to practise with someone, but how do I know this isn't a trap? The council takes a dim view of such things."

"That's true. But what you already know about me would place me in great danger if the authorities ever became involved. Elyna Stormcrow is wanted for the death of the two mages I listed in my book."

Brylee weighed Reni's admission and then looked at Lucky, who was sleeping. She would take a chance and trust the woman. Not only did she feel it was right, if she wanted to become adept at fighting, she had few options. But it still bothered her that nothing had been said about her face, so she took a chance and changed it from that of Scarlet Fisher to her healer persona.

Reni sat up with a jerk, but Brylee didn't sense her gathering her power. She was just surprised.

"What did you just do?" Reni asked, curious. "It was transformation magic, but nothing seems different."

So, Reni's magical sight has limits, Brylee thought. *She can't see the details of the flesh on my face.* Brylee felt perhaps it was her turn to be cryptic.

"It was, but it was nothing threatening. I'll accept your kind offer to train me, and when I know you better, perhaps I'll share that secret with you in return."

Chapter Seventy-Two

Midsummer came and went in a frenzied routine. Brylee reduced her shifts with Work Hive to one or two every fortnight, which was just enough for her to keep an eye on the Ordels, who appeared to have lost interest in Our Lady. She took four or five morning shifts at the hospital and spent most evenings sparring with Reni. Despite defeat after defeat, Brylee was improving steadily, sensing when and how magic was being used and shaping her own attacks and defence. Reni was becoming a good friend, and they often talked over a meal, well after the lessons ended. The woman didn't have many people in her life and had become lonely of late. She had a few other students, but they didn't progress fast enough to capture Reni's interest, and they treated their training more like a sporadic hobby rather than a passion or a vocation. They found her riddles and tests frustrating, and she preferred Lucky's company.

Jyan left for his estate soon after selling out of grou't and returned with a new batch a moon later. Grinders was thriving, and he was busy scouting three new locations across the city to expand his business. The project seemed to have shaved a decade off the man, giving him a new lease on life since the loss of Garrick. He dined with Brylee every two weeks. She had caught up with him twice since his return, and she relished his updates and company.

Work Hive was flourishing too, and Farriar had already turned a profit, so Brylee sold her a 50 percent stake in the business from the holding account, as promised. Brylee met her and Tae most nights at the Linger Longer, enjoying a meal and company in the hours between Our Lady and Reni's thrashings. The three women had become close. Tae was employed at Work Hive too, having earned her guild stamp, the Accounting Guild's formal endorsement to practise independently.

Tonight's dinner at the Linger Longer was a sad affair. Farriar had broken the news that old Mrs. Harrington had passed away in her sleep. Her steward brought the news that morning. He said it looked like the woman had simply failed to wake, a slight smile on her face, like he remembered from when she and her husband joked with each other. He was certain her husband's ghost had collected her and they were together once more. It was an awkward moment for Brylee, as her flower girl persona knew the old woman, but as far as Farriar and Tae were aware, Scarlet the silent investor had never met Mrs. Harrington.

Brylee left the tavern at dusk, which had started to arrive noticeably earlier. Reni was already in her rooms, and Lucky was asleep in front of the fire. She opened one eye as Brylee let herself in, slapped her tail on the floor several times, then drifted back to sleep.

Brylee greeted Reni as she threw her cloak over the back of a chair and sat down. They each shared about their day, then got on with the lesson. Brylee had progressed to the point that Reni would attack her in two ways at the same time, and tonight the old woman was jabbing at her from various angles with a sharp point of air while simultaneously trying to set her clothing on fire. Most of the time Brylee was able to see each attack forming and deflect, block, or freeze it as required.

Reni increased the speed and ferocity of her attacks to the point it was all Brylee could do to fend her off. Sweat poured from Brylee's brow and into her eyes, reminding her that she was forgetting to blink, so intense was her concentration. Then Brylee sensed a switch in tactics. Reni drew a sharp increase in magic and formed a large block of air over Brylee's head while pouring heat into the metal of her belt. Brylee slapped at the block and stepped out from under it while chilling the metal as it tried to burn her. Just when she felt she had twisted away from the attack, her wine goblet spat its contents into the air, which hardened and flew over and hit her square on the nose.

"Hey, no fair. That's three things!" Brylee said as she patted her face, checking for damage.

Reni laughed. "Well, I thought you were ready for it. I was being too predictable; your real opponents will not be. Come on and take a break. You excelled today."

Brylee sat, feeling her body cooling and her hands shaking. As she caught her breath, she wondered if it was time to ask Reni about some ideas she had. It was a big step in trust that she had agonised over, but if the ideas could work, she needed some way to practise.

After a brief respite, they began again. Brylee stood in the centre of the room, and Reni sat by the table, which had been moved over near the fire. As Brylee readied herself, she decided to try a different tack. She sensed Reni bringing in her power then reaching out to the stone fireplace with it to anchor her hard air. Brylee let the woman form a long air spear, positioned to stab at

Brylee from her left side. Brylee readied her block, knowing that Reni could see that she had done so. Another part of Brylee's mind talked to the wall. *Don't share your secrets with this mage,* she whispered to it, repeating the thought and others like it. In her mind, she imagined a wall between Reni and the fireplace, and she poured her magic into the concept.

"What? How?" Reni cried as her spear dissipated. Brylee was elated and almost missed the old woman shifting her anchor point to the floor beside her chair. Reni had been shocked at the development, but her warrior instincts had kicked in. Brylee intercepted her again, just as a hammerlike block of air formed behind her. It also evaporated. Reni held up her hand, signalling they should stop.

"Now that's a neat trick I've never seen," she said, gasping. "Explain that to me."

Brylee sat and proudly shared part of what Levi had taught her. It seemed so long ago now.

"When we form hard air, we anchor it to something hard. I think we're transferring the hardness from the object, not creating the hardness by ourselves. I'm trying to learn to disrupt the transfer process at the source," Brylee said, feeling strangely shy.

"That's a . . . novel concept," Reni said, deep in thought. "It clearly worked. And it would be terribly effective, of course. Let's practise it some more."

"I'd like that, but . . ." Brylee had been considering another technique, but she was loath to talk about it. It was highly risky.

"Go on, don't clam up now, girl. What else have you come up with?" Reni asked.

"It's dangerous, and I don't see how we could practise it safely, but here it is. We draw our magic from a source, as you know, but what if we could interrupt the other person's access to their power? Then they couldn't fight at all."

"Do you mean skrike them?" Reni asked, shaking her head. "As I say in my book, skriking someone is difficult. Even a mage struggles to skrike a charmer. There are more efficient—"

"No, not skriking," Brylee said. "I'm not suggesting we try to steal their power. Just block it so they can't use it."

Reni thought about it for some time. "I don't know how one could do that. Do you?"

"I have an idea," Brylee said. She wanted to share more but not everything. "My magic seems to be a little different than most people's." It wasn't a lie, but she wasn't going to tell the whole truth either. "I can form hard air without an anchor, for instance." She demonstrated, knowing Reni would sense the air and the lack of it attaching to a solid object. The woman's mouth gaped, but she said nothing.

"I'm not sure how I do it," Brylee lied. "But I think I can do something similar to an attacker's magical connection to their source.

"You can harden their link to stop magic flowing through it and cut them off?" Reni asked, her brow furrowing with concern.

"I've never attempted it," Brylee said. "I'm scared of trying. What if I blocked the link and it broke, or I couldn't unblock it?"

"You would kill your attacker," Reni said.

Brylee nodded. "Which might be OK as a last resort to save my life, but I don't see how to safely test the concept."

They both sat in silence, pondering the problem.

"Leave it with me," Reni said. "It would be an effective weapon. Why don't we practise blocking access to anchors—no, transfer points, as you put it? Perhaps if I can see how you do that, I'll come up with some ideas."

Brylee agreed, thrilled at the older woman's acceptance of her ideas, but before they could begin sparring again, the room was filled with the smell of stinkbaum. It took Brylee a moment to remember it was Aethe's signal for help emanating from the cutting that she always wore as a broach. She stood and grabbed her cloak.

"Sorry, but I have to run," Brylee said, striding towards the door. "I'll be back tomorrow night to practise. Sorry." With that she was gone.

Brylee almost forgot to switch to her healer persona as she ran through the market to Our Lady. It was dark, and she passed many unsavoury characters and drunks who only seemed to come out late at night.

When she reached the hospital door, she banged hard. It took a while for the panel to open, revealing Mary's worried face. The healer opened the door but blocked Brylee from entering.

"I didn't know who else to call," she cried, biting her knuckles. "Aethe is in trouble."

"Just tell me. Is she inside?" Brylee asked. Mary's terror was infectious, causing Brylee to glance nervously up and down the alley.

"She's gone after Ike." Mary gripped Brylee's arms as if it would make her understand. "That spy for the Ordels was here. We threw him out on his ear, but then we couldn't find Kithy. We tore the building apart, then Ike came in with a message. Aethe was to go with him to Castle Ordel, and I mustn't tell the city guard or they would take it out on the lass." Mary's last few words hit empty air as Brylee sprinted out of the alley.

Brylee was gasping for breath as she turned the corner to the Ordels' street just in time to see the castle's heavy door slam shut behind Ike and Aethe. She had to overcome the urge to run to the gate. *Wait in the shadows. Think and plan,* a wise inner voice said.

Brylee was certain the Ordels would use Kithy as leverage to get Aethe to sign away her water rights. If she ran for the justice and the guard, Alleg would have her signature and Aethe's promise of silence by the time they arrived back to intervenc. Perhaps the women would also have disappeared for good. *I have to go in after them, but as who?*

Brylee wondered if she should enter the castle in her healer guise, as a mage, or as someone completely different. It would be a year until the Red Assassin would be accused of killing Alleg, but that persona was also an option. Ike would recognise the healer, and the Ordels might recall her as Senna from their embarrassing moment at the hands of Jyan Harding at Garrick's manor. Time was wasting, so Brylee chose her library persona, Scarlet Fisher. She changed her appearance as she raced through the shadows of the dark, empty street.

There was a large tree near the north corner of the castle that in her many reconnaissance visits had struck Brylee as a vulnerable security point to someone with her talents. She conjured some hard air steps to reach the lower branches, dissolving them once she was climbing through the limbs above. When she was parallel with the top of the wall, she formed a bridge of air, colouring it grey so she could see it, then ran across and sat in the dark on top of the brickwork.

After ensuring the courtyard below was empty and the castle's shutters closed, Brylee conjured a series of grey air steps down to the shadows at the side of the manor below. It was the part of the yard where the moat didn't extend, enabling her to keep her creation close to the wall. She climbed down, made the steps and the bridge transparent, then tied off the effect of the magic using the trick she had practised from Denjrus Cole's textbook. The escape route would remain undetected unless someone happened to bump into it. This would be her main exit option with Aethe and Kithy, but she was also prepared to destroy the gate if she didn't have time for subtleties.

Brylee crept along the wall to the corner and risked a glance around to the front of the building. Two guards were standing inside the barred gate looking her way. She reversed her course and snuck around to the rear of the manor. Using her magic, she released the firewood shed's shutter and window latch and slunk inside, where the pungent smell of sap and decaying bark assailed her nostrils. The room had a connecting door into a corridor that separated the kitchen and the well-water room. She felt her way through the pitch-black space, remembering how the logs and kindling were laid out. When she reached the interior door, she paused to listen, extending her magical sense to confirm the corridor beyond was empty. Then she opened the door and gained access to the manor proper.

Brylee crept along the corridor, noting the well-water room was dark but that the kitchen door was open, spilling light into the corridor. She clung to the deep shadows and listened to the voices of several guards eating a late meal, making jokes at a chambermaid's expense. She crept past the kitchen door and crouched in the doorway to the well-water room, from which she could peer into the lobby that led through to the main part of the manor.

Brylee didn't hear a sound that alerted her to the soldier behind her, but an urgent sixth sense made her drop as he launched himself at her back from the darkness by the well while thrusting a dagger at her throat. The blade nicked her ear, triggering reflexes from moons of sparring with Reni. Brylee pivoted and drove her own hard air dagger up into the man's brain through the soft spot just beneath his chin. As she realised what she was doing, she tried to halt her action, but fear and reflex had already done their worst, and the man was crumpling. She caught him before he made a noise and laid his corpse on its back. Her hands rose to stifle her cry of shame. She knew that at some point on her journey back to Levi she might have to take a life, but this was so sudden and unexpected.

A wave of shock overtook her. Her hands trembled and tears welled up, blurring her vision. Brylee took several deep breaths, determined to block out her rising emotions until she had Kithy safe. She looked down at the corpse, recognising it as Captain Farborn. His uniform was awry, the top of his trousers gaping. It appeared he had been too lazy to visit the privy, choosing instead to warm the wastewater chute in the well-water room. He must have seen her creep into the doorway and chose to attack rather than challenge her. Jumpiness due to being party to Kithy's abduction had cost him his life and bloodied Brylee's conscience.

Farborn's size gave Brylee an idea, but for it to work, she knew that no one could find his body. She tugged him around so his face was in the light and examined its every contour, mark, and line while morphing her own face to match. She had to shed most of her hair to approximate his close crop, making it lighter and bristlier. It took much longer than she felt she had time for, but the ruse she planned would allow her to move freely around the castle. She pulled the man's outer clothing off and put it on, relaxing the tightness of its weave to fit her slightly larger frame.

Brylee's strength enabled her to pull Farborn across the floor and onto the lip of the wastewater chute. She summoned her transformation magic and linked it to the water in the well. *Give me your secrets,* she whispered to it as she extracted the attributes of liquidity, which she pressed into Farborn's skin and bone. It didn't work exactly as she had imagined, but the soldier began to dissolve anyway, his remains slopping down the chute. Brylee gagged, unprepared for the smell of his innards.

"Ag, Farborn, what did you eat?" a disgusted voice from the kitchen asked, accompanied by several other complaints and much laughter. "The waste is for peeing in. Go to the privy if you have to shit a dead animal."

Brylee made some adjustments to her magic, speeding up the process, and was relieved when the last of his body vanished into the darkness. She kept her eyes glued to the door throughout, not wanting to see what she was doing to the captain as much as keeping a lookout.

Now in a rough Farborn persona, Brylee straightened herself out and walked into the corridor. She strode across the lobby to the main part of the house, which was dark and quiet. She checked each room, finding them deserted. In the living room mirror she examined her Farborn persona, making a few adjustments to her face and the fit of the uniform.

As she climbed the steps to the upper floor, Brylee heard voices. She followed them along the hallway that led to the west wing where Alleg's study was located. Rounding the corner, she found four heavily armed men guarding the study door. She was about to duck back, but then they saw her. They stood straighter, reminding Brylee whom she was emulating. She supposed Aethe was in the room behind the men, but was Kithy there too? She extended her magical sight, attempting to see through the wall. She could only see silhouettes. One was a figure on her knees before a man, and another behind the man was clearly a child. In addition, four adults were present. *I need to create chaos and try to smuggle Aethe and Kithy away.*

"You men," she said in what she hoped was a reasonable facsimile of Farborn's voice, "I just saw an intruder in the yard from the window at the top of the stairs, dressed in assassin's black. Go rouse the men from the kitchen. Post a man at each outer door while the rest of you search the grounds. Go!" The men hurried out and didn't look back.

Brylee went to the study door and listened. Alleg's voice was loud but unintelligible, the door's thick wood muffling his words. She would have only minutes before the guards sent back a report, so she took a deep breath and checked her shine shadow, then opened the door and barged in.

"Sir, an assassin, inside the perimeter. I've sent the guards to deal with him!" she yelled, glancing at the room, then turning and looking back through the door in a defensive position as she imagined Farborn would have done, a move that also hid her face. From her quick survey, Alleg was towering over Aethe, a man she believed to be Justice Goath was at the desk with some documents, and Ike was standing next to Alleph, who was terrorising Kithy with her finger snakes, causing the girl to sob. Brylee had hoped the mage would rush straight out to lend his power to the hunt, but he strode to the windows instead, peeking through the closed shutters' slats.

"There are two men dead and one injured, sir. It might be best if you use your magic to support us," Brylee prompted.

Alleg looked scared, but then he looked at the faces in the room, all hoping he would act. He didn't want to be seen as a coward, so he gulped down his terror and put on a face of bravado that he clearly didn't feel. "Must I do everything?" Alleg snarled, striding across the room. "Farborn, guard my study. We're far from done here. Alleph, give Ike one of your daggers. He's coming with me."

Brylee slammed the door behind the mage and his henchman. If her plan was to work, she would have to move fast. Using her magic, she banged on the window, causing all heads to turn that way, then she ripped the window open, as if someone were forcing their way inside. There was a ledge there, which she knew from her previous visits. With everyone riveted by the distraction, Brylee struck Goath and Alleph in the side of the head with hard air, knocking them unconscious. Kithy ran to her mother, who scooped her up and cowered behind the desk.

"Don't worry," Brylee said in her Farborn voice. "I'm here to rescue you. I'm working with Scarlet, your mage."

"Is she here?" Aethe cried, glancing about.

"Nearby, lending her magic. Quickly, onto the ledge. We've no time." Brylee's idea was to create an air bridge across to the top of the wall, then descend on the far side. But looking down, she saw several men milling about, and the chances were good they would be spotted if she pursued that plan. Instead, she created grey steps that spiralled up onto the rooftop and urged Aethe ahead. Aethe just stared at her, and Brylee realised it was because the healer couldn't comprehend how Farborn was doing magic.

"Scarlet has a friend helping us too. They're watching from the cathedral spire and creating what we need to escape. Now, go up. I'll be right there." Aethe picked up Kithy, tested the steps with her foot, then worked her way up to the roof as her confidence in the unnatural staircase grew. Brylee pulled the windows closed behind her and pushed the shutters back into place. A close inspection would show the truth, but she hoped that anyone bursting into the study would assume Farborn and the women had left via the study door. She charged up the steps, dissolving them once she completed her ascent.

The roof was made of cold tiles that were slick with algae, but the slope was shallow. It wasn't difficult to pick a path over to the far side of the building where Brylee had left the stairs in place to get across to the tree. Looking down, she could see the guards scurrying about, checking each window and doorway. They had taken the time to collect crossbows, she noted. She heard Alleg yelling orders. His voice appeared to be coming from the far side of the manor.

The side of the building where she was and the wall where her air steps stood were in darkness at ground level, but up higher the moonlight was unobstructed. Brylee thought they had a better chance if they avoided an air bridge to reach the top of the wall. She created steps that zigzagged to the courtyard and led the way down.

Staying low, they crept across the gap to the outer wall. Brylee undid the magical knot that kept the steps in place and changed them from transparent to grey. She heard voices coming closer and realised she would need another diversion.

"Go up here," Brylee instructed in her Farborn voice. "At the top, Scarlet left a bridge across to a tree. Climb down it. You will have to drop the last part, but it isn't too high. Don't go home. Go through the butcher's market, then down Sterling Road. Keep going past the Blue Goose until you come to a new store called Grinders. Scarlet's friend, Senna, has a room there that we can use. Tell Senna or Jyan you've escaped from the Ordels, but don't mention my name. The name 'Farborn' isn't in favour with them. Here, Scarlet gave me this key. It will let you inside Senna's room," Brylee pulled her key from her pocket and pressed it into Aethe's hand.

"Aren't you coming?" Aethe asked, still terrified.

"No, Scarlet will meet you soon. I'm to stay here and confuse the search," Brylee replied. Then she pushed Aethe towards the stairs. The woman took off and disappeared over the wall just as two soldiers appeared around the corner. They were checking the house, not looking into the corner. Brylee dissolved the stairs but left the bridge in place, then stepped out into the light and ran up to the searchers.

"No luck?" she asked, checking behind with her magical sight. She sensed Aethe was halfway down the tree, helping Kithy navigate the branches. Brylee let the bridge go, and it faded to nothing.

"Ain't seen no one," one of the men whispered, his tone indicating that he hoped he wouldn't. "But the firewood window's been opened. There are damp footprints inside the room. Mage told us two to keep circling the perimeter and sent everyone else inside to search."

"Carry on, and stay alert," Brylee commanded. "I'll go inside too." She had no intention of doing so, but the courtyard flared with mage's light, which steadied and left no place to hide. She heard Alleg order a guard to each corner of the building where they could see every part of the courtyard. Alleg stepped around the corner and spotted Brylee immediately.

"Why are you out here, Farborn?" he snarled. "I left you to guard our . . . guests."

"Thank Ag I found you, sir. The assassin broke in through the study window and knocked us out. When I woke, the captives were gone. Your sister is out cold but breathing well."

Alleg ran towards Brylee, who at first worried he was attacking, but then she realised he had to pass her to reach the nearest entrance to the building, the firewood room behind her.

"Well, they haven't had time to climb the wall, and no one's been out through the gate. They're inside somewhere. Come with me, Farborn." Brylee hated to go back inside, but she didn't see any option. She had to play the part of Farborn a little longer, then make her escape. She told the men to keep searching outside, then fell in beside Alleg as he jogged past.

The mage used his magic to open the firewood room doors. They walked into the corridor by the well-water room and the kitchen and then the mage stopped. Brylee thought he had paused to listen, to determine which way to go, until she found herself flung hard onto the floor, Alleg looming above her.

The massive weight of hard air that Alleg pinned her with was crushing, but that wasn't Brylee's worst realisation. Her lungs and throat were also full of the stuff. She was choking and gagging. The mage was also pouring heat into her face.

"You're not Farborn. Who are you?" Alleg yelled. A fleck of his spittle landed near Brylee's eye. He eased his attack slightly, assuming he had the imposter immobilised and terrified. That small reprieve allowed Brylee to summon her own magic, and she inserted a layer of her own air between the floor and Alleg's, which took away some of the pressure. Next, she countered the heat in her face with cold energy. A shocked look gripped Alleg's face as he realised he was locked in battle with a mage. But he didn't hesitate, asserting the full power of his attack.

Reni's training might have allowed Brylee to defeat the surprise attack except for the pressure in her lungs. That was something they couldn't practise for fear of doing permanent damage, and the choking panic it induced was overpowering. Brylee said a quick prayer that Alleg's fear had caused him to focus on doubling down on the heat and pressure rather than ripping Brylee apart from the inside, but she knew he would think of that in moments.

Brylee formed an air spear behind Alleg's head, but it struck a barrier he had erected. She didn't have time to press her way through the barrier, as she was beginning to black out. She fought to relax and locate the anchor points Alleg was using to harden his air. He was using several at once. She whispered to them, but they didn't find her words convincing in her weakened state, and they refused to cut Alleg off from sharing their properties.

Part of Brylee's mind realised Reni's sparring had the slowness of an old woman, which allowed her time to solve problems and defeat the attack. Her defences weren't instinctive enough to avoid becoming overwhelmed. She didn't want to die but sensed she was moments from it. *Ride the horse, Brylee,* she heard her old instructor say. *Focus.* Perhaps she could distract him or make him curious enough to pause, giving her an opening. She changed her face to match the sweaty, straining mage's own as he pressed down on her, even mimicking the look of shock that her trick evoked. She realised her mistake immediately, as the mage panicked, which added power to his attack. She felt her lungs stretching to their limit.

Was he more powerful than her? Using her magical sight, she compared his link to the source with her own. They were similar, so skriking wouldn't be an option.

Brylee's eyes closed as her body began to shut down, but she kept her magical sense fixed on Alleg's link. She imagined compressing the link and poured her power into that idea. As her own energy ran out, she felt a small amount of relief from Alleg's attack. She refocussed her attention on where Alleg's link touched the source. She had always thought links looked rawer there and hoped that meant softer. She gripped his link with her mind and pulled. It didn't break, but it did pinch together, slowing Alleg's magic even further.

Brylee intuited that with her current inability to focus fully, her power wasn't enough to sever Alleg's connection to the source. She had one last idea. Could she use his own power against him? She remembered Mrs. Harrington's vines, and how they shared a stub. She pictured a variation of that, where Alleg's link split, funnelling part of his power to her link, and put everything she had left into that idea. There was a trembling, then the link she imagined formed just as she pictured it. Immediately, Brylee's power increased by the amount Alleg's lessened. This gave her increased leverage, which increased the effect. Moments later, the combination ripped Alleg's link away from the source, and Brylee could breathe again.

When someone was skriked, there was normally a few moments of lingering life while the victim survived on the small amount of power retained in their body. Alleg was pouring everything he had into his attack, however, so he was drained instantaneously. His eyes rolled up, and he dropped like a sack of potatoes on top of his pile of hard air, which dissolved as the magic sustaining it faded. He slid into Brylee's much thinner defensive layer and hung there. Brylee felt instant relief, which allowed her exhaustion to catch up to her. She passed out, and as her own defence evaporated, Alleg settled on top of her like human blanket.

Brylee came to a few moments later, wondering if she had skriked the mage. *No, I didn't take his link,* she told herself, *I just snapped it.* Her chest was so sore she could barely move. Each breath was agony. She rolled over, depositing the dead mage onto the floor, then dragged herself onto her knees. She had been woken up by approaching voices. She called on her magic and forced her face back into the persona of Captain Farborn. Three men, all with crossbows, ran up to her. She pointed to the firewood door.

"He just left . . . the assassin." Two men reluctantly ran after the assailant, not keen to chase someone who had downed a mage and their captain. The other hovered, making a show of helping his captain to his feet.

"Go with them, you coward," Brylee croaked. "I think he was injured by Alleg," she added, trying to instil confidence in the man. He ran off after his peers.

Brylee took stock. Alleg was dead, a full year ahead of Wickham's investigation had concluded. What implications would that have for the future? Brylee didn't know, but it seemed as if time wanted it that way.

Eddies and currents . . .

She scanned Alleg's body. She found no link and no glow. He couldn't be brought back even with her primi ability. Her own link looked unchanged. She hadn't skriked Alleg, just destroyed his link.

The mage had been killed by an assassin, and a search had begun. That much aligned with the history she had been told. But some things were missing. She took Alleg's dagger, not wanting to sully her own, and plunged it into his chest, then withdrew it. With his heart dead, little blood emerged, which didn't seem authentic. Brylee used her magic to draw some of his blood out, spattering it on the floor and higher up on the wall as she imagined it should be. Then she cleaned the dagger and replaced it in the sheath at his side. From her trousers she withdrew the small vial of dye she had made from the bellyberry and threw the contents into Alleg's face, ashamed of the satisfaction it gave her.

Brylee wanted to run, but she knew that Farborn's disappearance would raise suspicion. She pulled herself to her feet, staggering into the well-water room to wash her face, and barely made it to the waste shoot before vomiting. When she recalled what she had put down there perhaps fifteen minutes earlier, she gagged until she was empty, then slipped down onto the floor, exhausted.

Alleph's voice rose above the melee outside, so Brylee hauled herself to her feet and staggered out to the lobby. Alleph was distraught, looking for her brother.

"He's here, ma'am!" Brylee cried, making her voice sound as authentic as possible in terms of tone, shock, and sadness. Alleph raced past her and threw herself down on her dead brother. Brylee left her there and made herself busy organising a proper search of the premises.

Once she confirmed Aethe had made it away safely, she searched the surrounding streets. She even sent Ike to check for Aethe at Our Lady, hoping the woman had followed Brylee's instructions and was now at Grinders. She discovered later that Ike hadn't gone near Our Lady, instead choosing to abscond into the night.

The city watch was called, and soon thereafter, the Council of Magical Law sent investigators. They linked the red dye and Captain Farborn's description of the clothing worn by the assassin with the Namiduh Jou. Brylee had to answer a few other questions as a witness, but Alleph vouched for Farborn as a long-term retainer, so Brylee's main role was to ensure each of the guards shared their testimony. As each guard waited to give their statement, Brylee talked to them at length, frequently describing what she saw, and was pleased that some of the men embellished their own stories with her observations.

Brylee stayed for three hours until friends and family arrived to console Alleph, including her father, who was high up in the council and flanked by several mages as guards. Deciding not to press her luck with such a force, Brylee slipped away. Farborn's departure would be seen as suspicious, but it couldn't be helped. Before she left, she mentioned to several people how worried she was due to being the only person who saw the assassin up close. A few days later, placing wreaths around the castle as the flower girl, Brylee learnt that her piece of misdirection had worked. Investigators believed Farborn had been killed by the assassin or fled for his safety. Either way, no one expected to hear from him again.

Chapter Seventy-Three

Brylee arrived at Grinders in her Senna persona, claiming she had attended an overnight party and the hangover was beginning to kick in. She managed to act surprised to find Aethe and Kithy in her rooms but readily accepted their situation as she owed Scarlet the healer a debt she was pleased to repay. She told the pair to stay as long as they needed and then left to "stay with a friend" after accepting a hangover cure from Aethe as a thank-you. Later that day, Scarlet the healer arrived and explained she would cover Aethe's shifts for the week while matters with the Ordels settled down. She shared that somehow the mage had died, Captain Farborn was missing, and investigations were intense.

Brylee took a room at the Linger Longer in her Work Hive persona, telling Farriar and Tae her own rooms were being painted. They offered her their guest room, which she politely declined, as her comings and goings might be difficult to explain. Her Nuulan life had been complicated from day one, and recent events had made it even more so.

The day after Alleg's death, Brylee created a letter from the Red Assassin to Alleph and arranged to have it delivered to the gate by a street urchin in return for a warm meal. The note had a formal tone and informed Alleph that if she didn't want to meet the same fate as her brother, all interest in taking over the property of Our Lady and investigating the Namiduh Jou must stop immediately. If Aethe or Kithy so much as stubbed their toe, Alleph would be paid a visit by the Red Assassin. It was signed, somewhat dramatically, in red ink.

Later in the week, Brylee broke into Justice Goath's office at midnight. She was pleased to note he had marked the Our Lady files as "Case Closed" and filed them with other completed records.

The next day, Senna returned to Grinders and informed Aethe that Scarlet was confident it was safe for her and Kithy to return to their normal lives. Brylee wasn't surprised that Jyan had taken a shine to the healer and her daughter, but she hadn't expected him to accept a tour of Our Lady. She found out later that he had become a silent supporter of the hospital, making regular donations, He also wined and dined Aethe with intent but no success. She kept him politely at arm's length, her life devoted to her good works.

Alleg's death nearly a full year ahead of schedule terrified Brylee. Had her and Levi's interactions with the timeline shifted events to the point the world would end, perhaps earlier or by different means, or had time adapted? Would Levi need to visit at all? That thought made her chest ache, reminding her how much she had fallen for the man and how strange that was given they had known each other for only a week. Was this the synchronisation Levi had tried to explain? If she couldn't find him in the future, would he be trapped there and die alone? Or worse, would he end up with another woman? That notion brought a pang of jealousy that was sharp and unexpected, but as much as anything else, it drove her to action. Brylee realised she couldn't sit back idly and see how things developed. She needed to seek out answers and influence events as needed.

Over the following week, all her personas made excuses, explaining they had to travel for an unspecified time but hoped to return soon. She sold her remaining shares in Work Hive to Farriar and arranged to have the ongoing dividend sent anonymously to Aethe, not for Our Lady but to pay for Kithy to have whatever education she chose.

Reni was as perceptive as ever and sensed the change in Brylee before being told. She even mentioned Alleg's assassination, fishing for information. Brylee didn't confirm or deny the connection, but she did hint that recently she had cause to use Reni's teachings for real and declared she would require additional lessons to perfect her craft when she returned.

It surprised Brylee how painful she found all the goodbyes with each of her personas' communities. It would have been difficult with only one life to leave, but she found that each parting built on another, and she was terribly sad as she carried her travel bags to the stables near Grinders and saddled Whipcrack. She was surprised to find Jyan waiting for her, despite her leaving at the crack of dawn to avoid another teary farewell. He pressed a small bag of Garrick's Grou't into her hands, kissed her forehead, then left without a word, the sound of his cane clicking on the cobblestones receding in the distance.

"You've been patient, Whipcrack," she whispered to her mount as it nuzzled her shoulder. "Let's go have an adventure together, eh?" Brylee walked him out, said goodbye to the grooms and thanked them for taking care of her horse, then mounted Whipcrack and trotted off towards the west.

As they left the boundaries of Nuulan, Brylee reviewed her plans. She wanted to visit Haxley and Rostal to see if she could detect any changes to events as she recalled them. She also wanted to track the stranger who had attacked Levi. He had left Sandrick with a caravan, headed for Troll Lake. She would start there, as her route to Haxley passed close by.

As she stopped to let Whipcrack drink at a stream, Brylee reviewed the maps she had purchased earlier in the week. Nuulan was in eastern Yarrow, so she would soon cross the border into Quartt. A well-travelled route across the northern part of that region avoided the mountainous spine that ran north to south. Once past the spine, the trade route turned south before entering Lanthe, but Brylee would continue due west to follow a quiet road that would take her to Troll Lake.

Brylee could have reached the lake with four days of hard riding, but she chose to take her time instead. She was exhausted, and even more so, she wanted to clear her head of her Nuulan responsibilities and recall as much about her old life as she could. Over eight nights staying at inns along the route, Brylee made copious notes from her memory about events, people, and notable conversations. She also wrestled with her long-standing dilemma: should she warn Levi of the attack? Perhaps there was a different way to prevent the Unravelling. She yearned for her old, impulsive self who wouldn't have to endure watching her friends die. The old Brylee would have told Levi for sure, but her instincts were warning her to let history repeat itself in this instance. *Instincts suck!*

Then there was Vekki. Brylee's memory of the Red Assassin remained vivid. It was understandable she hadn't recognised herself given the shock and the assassin's face covering. Now that she knew the assassin was her, it was easy to see the similarities in build and movement. The assassin version of Brylee had skewered and then skriked Wickham's apprentice. She would need to learn more about the woman who could act so ruthlessly, because right now she couldn't see herself being so cold blooded.

At Troll Lake, Brylee stabled Whipcrack at an inn in the village named after the large body of water nearby. Some discreet inquiries confirmed that the van Hyke estate was not far to the south. She learned that the town had mourned for several weeks following the announcement of the old man's passing. Ostryd had been a quiet benefactor to many, a fact that only emerged after his death. The estate retained his name, but had passed to a distant relative, or so they understood. They never saw much of the new owner.

Brylee spent almost a week posing as a bird watcher, walking the hillsides with a notepad and spyglass and pretending to catalogue the local wildlife. Much of that time was actually spent on a hill overlooking the van Hyke estate. She caught a few glimpses of the assailant, whom she recognised instantly. She could even sense his link suffering the turbulent tremor of the future time crisis. He spent most of his days in a small outbuilding that Brylee determined might be a library, judging by the shelves of books she could see through the windows.

The other face she recognised was Lu, Wickham's hired escort. That the pair had been in cahoots for so long galled her, especially considering how Brylee had warmed to the woman. How could she have been taken in so easily? Lu seemed to be living near the main building, but when visible, she had little contact with the assailant. It was clear they knew each other, but they seemed more like colleagues than lovers or family.

Lu spent several hours each day training with weapons or doing complex fighting exercises. Sometimes she did it alone, and other times she trained with several others. One evening just as Brylee was gathering her belongings to return to the inn, a large cat and two cubs detached themselves from the shadows in the bushes below and stalked towards Lu as she trained. Brylee froze and checked the wind direction. She was downwind, which explained why the cat didn't appear to notice her presence—or if it did, it didn't care.

Lu sensed the cats approaching and ran to meet them. The cubs were tiny. One hung back with its mother, but the other was more curious and bounded close to Lu before stopping and sniffing. Lu dropped to her knees and held out her hand. The cub approached, circling the woman twice before nuzzling her hand. The mother had stopped to watch the greeting but now leapt forward in what Brylee at first thought was an attack but soon realised was a greeting of old friends. *Lu is Mobi'dern*, Brylee realised. That explained her fighting abilities.

With the cat in the area, Brylee chose to suspend her surveillance. She had been lucky so far but would surely be detected if she persisted.

The next morning she set off for Rostal, this time pushing Whipcrack hard so she made it to the city's east gate by nightfall of the second day. She rode Whipcrack through the underground pathways to a stable near Wickham's manor and took a room at an inn nearby. She visited the baths, soaking away the aches of the last twenty days of riding and lying in fields, spying.

Brylee spent six weeks in the city. She watched Wickham's manor with caution, knowing Winter's senses were as sharp as a Mobi'dern blade. It was gutting to think the man was dead or would be soon. He seemed indestructible. But mostly she trailed Vekki. Seeing the woman caused potent emotions in Brylee, from terror to pity. The more she learnt about the apprentice, however, the more her overriding reaction changed to disgust. Around Wickham, Vekki was smart enough to hide her true self, which was a moral vacuum. When not at Wickham's manor or doing his errands, Vekki lived at a residence near the Creative.

A few nights of surveillance in various personas revealed Vekki made a great deal of money working for a man called Slater, who was based in the Sour Witch Tavern. Over the course of three weeks, Brylee witnessed Vekki terrify women into working in the brothel above the tavern, act as muscle when Slater took over another man's street-corner drug business, and kill a man in a gruesome fashion as an example to others when he couldn't pay a petty debt.

It pained Brylee that she couldn't intercede in these dealings, but she was pleased to have done at least one good act. A young woman entered the Sour Witch with her boyfriend. That she was a charmer was evident immediately; her aura was denser than the norm and her shine shadow was badly constructed. The way Vekki's head spun towards the girl, the sickeningly familiar look of delight, and the quiet whisper of "Hello, little rabbit" that Brylee heard drip from the apprentice's lips almost made her gag.

Brylee watched Vekki insinuate herself into the couple's company with sweet words and a few drinks before inviting them to dine with her at an establishment across the alley, behind the tavern. The girl wanted to go, but the boy held back, then eventually conceded. Brylee followed the threesome through the back door and into the darkness.

Vekki wasted no time at all. The boy was unconscious, and the girl pinned to the wall with Vekki drooling, her face pressed close. Brylee recalled the apprentice's exact expression, the terror it had evoked in herself in the theatre box and in her dreams ever since. It was all she could do to knock Vekki out rather than kill her right then. Brylee used her healing power to revive the boy and watched the girl help him walk away after Brylee had made her promise to seek help with her shine shadow and never to return to that neighbourhood.

Brylee knelt over the unconscious apprentice for a long time, considering ending her ahead of schedule. How many people would suffer before Brylee killed this monster in the theatre? To walk away, leaving the woman breathing, was one of the hardest things Brylee had ever done. But she did it, after spitting on Vekki's prone body.

If Brylee had found Vekki difficult to observe, she found Haxley and Plainhand Estate hard in a different way. She saw her mother and father taking the air but couldn't let herself do anything about the mass she could see growing in the man's chest. She saw the cook, Fifi, sitting alone and looking forlorn within the protective ring of bushes, as if she hadn't moved since their last meeting, which had yet to happen. Brylee had never noticed the woman was sad, and now she felt guilty at not having a better relationship with her.

She saw Raegan in her abusive marriage to Gunnar. She stood outside and watched her best friend in the world carrying lunch into the Barrow Building, about to discover her husband in the act of sexual blackmail. Brylee didn't dare follow her inside, as she couldn't guarantee she wouldn't beat the man to a pulp. It was only because Brylee knew the outcome would ultimately be positive for Raegan that she could turn and walk away.

She went to her brother's grave and sat for hours, telling him about her adventures and listening for a reply. She cried throughout, not caring about the looks from passers-by. She also spent time sitting in the gallery and observing two council meetings, admiring Mella and hating Judd.

Brylee rode out of Haxley on Whipcrack, feeling empty and alone. As far as she could recall, life was progressing just as it had. If the timeline had changed, she saw no sign of it. The one bright spot in the past weeks was observing the younger version of herself, a headstrong, naïve woman who looked a full decade younger than Brylee would look now if she returned her face to its natural state. It had only been three years since Levi saved her by sending her back in time and four years since she had blithely thrown Gunnar down the slooper, but time had not been kind to her features. Seeing the woman she had been and knowing who she could become was reassuring and lifted her spirits.

Brylee was determined to return to Nuulan for the remainder of the time before she had to be in the theatre in Rostal. She decided to buy the Linger Longer, creating as much silver as it took to convince its current owners to part with it. Perhaps she would offer it to Raegan as part of an expansion to the Crow's Nest. She would live above the tavern to avoid Jyan. She didn't want to run into him again until events were settled. She would help Aethe but focus on sparring with Reni and find someone else to help her sharpen her physical combat skills. If she had to fight Lu and could not rely on her magic, she needed to be much better than she was.

Brylee's first task as she arrived in Nuulan two weeks later was to send Alleph another missive from the Red Assassin, warning her not to investigate her brother's death. "If the search for me continues beyond the first day of the mages' conference in Matalon, you will die." As the messenger took the note, Brylee felt the currents of time strengthen. She knew the note would prompt Alleph to beg her father to pressure Wickham into using his network of spies to track down the Red Assassin.

Chapter Seventy-Four

Brylee returned to Haxley in time to watch herself leave town with Judd and his money-laden guards. She joined the caravan that followed them and was present when the younger Brylee and Judd were discovered injured in the flaming shack after the ambush. She trailed herself to Rostal and watched Vekki's sham fight with Buck, her fake drunken husband. All the happenings affirmed that events were unfolding as she remembered them. The fact that time seemed to be back on track contributed to Brylee's ruthlessness, as she feared any new disruption to events.

From behind the curtain in the theatre's box, Brylee, in the Red Assassin persona, watched Vekki summon her magic and envelop her younger self in hard air. She was not sure if she could kill the woman in cold blood. Her hands trembled as her decisions and morals threatened to rip her apart from the inside. But when she heard the words "my little rabbit" slither out of Vekki's mouth in that sick, seductive voice and saw the rapture on her face, the shame and guilt that had swirled around her like crows worrying a marauding eagle evaporated, and Brylee's blade slid through the apprentice with a life of its own. Although she had relief in that moment, the stain that act imprinted on her soul would forever leap out at her when least expected, making her breathless with panic.

Brylee didn't enjoy skriking Vekki, and she wasn't sure why she had, but it was what her earlier self witnessed and had dreamt about since the attack. The older Brylee was fascinated to see if her assassin persona had to prompt her earlier self to run. Her memory didn't contain that act, but her dreams did. Her earlier self stood frozen to the spot until she gave the command.

Brylee kept an eye on events after the attack at the theatre. She intercepted Jobb, the drunk she had talked to and later impersonated, as he left the jail. He confirmed, for some coin, that he had talked to a charmer in the cell across from his. Brylee watched Wickham lead her younger self back to his manor, and later she observed some of her training sessions with Winter.

Brylee was also present when "Senna" fooled Winter with her cloth colour-change trick, and soon after had watched Winter's killer catch sight of her younger self for the first time. She hadn't seen the man who would ambush them since spying on him and Lu at Troll Lake.

Her heart almost burst when she saw Levi talking to her younger self in the market. It was their first meeting. She recalled every word, and she watched magic form and swirl around them, unnoticed. It was the spirit mating, she assumed, though she wasn't sure. If they survived, she would ask Levi.

Brylee rode ahead of Wickham's party as they struck out for Matalon. She stayed out of sight at each stop, bribing strangers to confirm when the group checked into their inns. She did all this to verify that the timeline remained consistent, propelling them towards their fate. She covertly observed the link to her earlier self's magic begin a final intensification of its vibration as each hoofbeat carried her towards Levi's desperate act of calling his own magic to save her life.

While she dug out her hiding spot in the bushes near the archway on the edge of the Harding estate, Brylee reflected on everything that had occurred over the past four years. The previous night she had crept into Jyan's stables and left Whipcrack in a stall. She hoped to collect him later, but if not, she knew he would be well looked after. She put a few valuables and some food in a small bag and walked out to the ambush site. She chose a spot across from the arch where the attacker would create hard air to kill Wickham and Winter and then dug a hole she would cover with branches and leaves.

It was dawn on the day of the attack. Brylee magically heated some stones lining her hiding spot for warmth and settled in to watch events unfold. Her plan was to stay hidden until her other self was cast back in time, then emerge to save Levi. If she could also save Wickham, Winter, and Rosemary, she would, but Levi was her priority. She would dearly love to defeat and capture the attacker as well, but if that was not possible, she would settle for saving lives. After four years, she still hadn't figured out the reason for the attack, nor did she know if she would be able to resist interfering with his plans. If she acted too early, would she ruin her chances of being able to circle back to this moment and save the man whom she loved? She fought her impulse, but it was hard to contain.

Brylee had chosen her Work Hive persona, which no one there would recognise. Having two Sennas in the same clearing wouldn't be helpful, but she would reform herself to look exactly like the Senna whom Levi threw back in time if he managed to do so, assuming the world didn't end.

*

Gideon had chosen the location for his ambush from memory, having passed that way several times in recent years. The hill and the lake formed a natural funnel, and the archway was easy to block and a natural distraction as riders gawked at the unusual feature. When he arrived just after the tenth bell and confirmed the benefits of the spot in person, he was pleased, but Tuli was not.

Tuli had been quiet for some time, but now that the ambush was imminent, she had returned with a vengeance, full of questions. *Why this spot? Why now? Do you have enough men? Why not wait for a better time and location?*

Gideon's retort was just as harsh. *You have nagged and belittled me for years, sister. I have been patient and at last have a clear path to the past so I can prevent your death. Enough of your prattling.* He dismissed her after that, forcing her presence to the back of his mind.

Gideon went over the various scenarios he could imagine unfolding. Mostly, they revolved around the order in which the riders arrived, which would dictate where he would deploy hard air and where his crossbow men should stand. He was only worried about two threats: Wickham and the time weaver. The remainder of the party would be easy to defeat. Gideon didn't know what abilities a time weaver possessed, but he decided the time weaver must die quickly too. Incapacitating him wouldn't suffice. Once Levi realised his amulet was missing, he would rush to the cavern in the south to retrieve it. Gideon would have liked to draw on the man's experiences to learn how he could shape the world to be a better place. He regretted that Levi's death was necessary. In fact, he regretted all the deaths.

Skrike the charmer, Tuli demanded. *The more power, the more good we can do.*

No! Gideon snarled in disgust at his inner voice, his face set in a determined rictus. How his sister's ghost had become so bloodthirsty, he couldn't fathom. Yes, Wickham and the time weaver had to die; that was unfortunate but necessary. Charmers were the social caste he felt committed to elevate, not slay. He shook his head, banishing Tuli to the back of his mind once more.

Gideon briefed his men on what the targets looked like, whom they should shoot first, and under what circumstances. He stressed that nothing was to happen until the mage collided with his hard-air trap, which he would erect just as Wickham rode up to it. Then Gideon sent each man into hiding, checking their concealment from every angle. Once he was certain they were out of sight, he hid behind the archway to wait. If Wickham's party had left on time, they would arrive within the hour. He went over his objective. Ostryd's library inferred there were two amulets. One worn by the weaver to gain access to the cavern. The other hidden in the cavern and allowed the wearer to travel back and forth through time far more than the minute or two a slipper could achieve. He still had to figure out how to activate either of the pieces. *If only I could drug Levi as Tuli did Ostryd and extract the information*, he thought.

Gideon's men had been settled for about ten minutes when a mountain cat cub wandered into the clearing, stalking one of the hidden bandits. It was a playful game, not a determined kill.

What's Shanna's brat doing there? Tuli's voice snarled. Gideon had assumed Lu would take Shanna with her on the wild goose chase. He hadn't accounted for the cats in his plans. *Kill all three of them quickly,* Tuli barked. *Otherwise they'll ruin everything.*

Gideon considered Tuli's demands. They had merit in the context of the ambush, but Lu was the only person who had shown him any loyalty since he had left the HAC, and she loved her pets. If he could avoid killing them, he would, but he wouldn't let them spoil things.

He reached out and magically lifted the cub high into the air. Shanna crashed out of the bushes with death in her eyes, heading straight for the mage. Gideon erected a barrier between them, wanting the big cat to back away.

"Kill me, and your cub will fall!" Gideon shouted while readying an air spear. He had tried communicating with Shanna on several occasions, with mixed results. Lu had explained that the cat didn't understand much of their language but could relay the sounds to her to translate. He wasn't sure over what distance that could occur and would reluctantly slay the beast if it came much closer. Shanna slid to a snarling halt, a crossbow bolt thudding into the ground just in front her.

"Hold your fire!" Gideon yelled to his men. Then he addressed Lu, through Shanna. "Your prida is interrupting my business here, and I can't allow it. If I sense them around again, I will drop the cub. If they go, you have my word the cub will be safe. I realise this looks strange, but I can explain." Gideon realised his relationship with Lu was probably beyond salvaging; he was surprised how sad he felt about that. He didn't want to accede to Tuli's constant pressure to kill the Mobi'dern. He was glad she was a day's ride away. Life would certainly be simpler once Tuli was saved and out of his head. She would be his companion, and he and Lu could never become as close.

Seconds went by with Shanna prowling along the invisible barrier, testing its limits and growling at the mage. Eventually, she turned and ran off the way she had come. Gideon moved the cub through air to near a tall tree some 200 yards distant and out of sight of the clearing. He tied off his magic so that the cub was suspended, anchored to the tree but not close enough for Shanna to reach if she climbed up to rescue her. Gideon picked up the stray crossbow bolt and returned it to the man who fired it. Once everyone was back in hiding, they settled in to wait.

*

Hours before the ever-curious Tak had snuck away from her mother to join the game she thought the men were playing, Shanna had shared visions with Lu of Gideon gathering his men and talking about setting up his ambush. It didn't take her long to deduce that he had created her mission to find replacement mercenaries as a ruse. She realised she was being decoyed away while Gideon attacked Wickham's party. Shocked and sickened, she shared the news with Sirius, and they turned to gallop back to prevent the slaughter.

As they rode, Lu considered her allegiances. She had helped Gideon out of loyalty to Tuli. She also felt partly responsible for the mage's situation because Shanna had killed Lord Arkly. She had ensured his escape but stayed with him over recent years more out of convenience to herself. He paid her well for seemingly straightforward work, and his estate was a peaceful place, well away from the world of the Mobi'dern. Shanna had disliked the man from the start, although in truth, she disliked most men. Lu had grown increasingly impatient with Gideon's behaviour and many times had considered parting company. In contrast, spending time with genuine and talented people like Senna, Wickham, Rosemary, and Sirius in particular had reminded her of the world she was missing while hiding in Gideon's shadow.

Lu and Sirius retraced their steps and made the turn back onto the road that led out to the Harding estate and the ambush site just as Shanna rushed to her cub's defence. Lu held the cat back with great effort, her will versus Shanna's instincts. Eventually, she convinced Shanna to take Smak a short distance away to safety. Now the cat was watching events from a nearby bluff.

Later, Shanna shared a panicked image of Wickham's party, several hundred yards from the ambush. Shanna was disturbed because she recognised Levi as the apparition from the clearing overlooking the HAC. *It's the man who wasn't there.* Lu realised she had never shared Levi's image with Shanna. She liked Levi, but Shanna's vision showed he was unnatural.

Lu estimated they were only two or three miles behind Wickham as they neared Gideon's ambush. She didn't know what she would do once she arrived at the scene, but reached back into her pack and drew her Mobi'dern blade. One way or another, she would have her answers.

*

Gideon's heart raced as he watched Wickham's party trot around the corner 200 yards distant. He noted the order they rode and confirmed his attack plan. But then they stopped and dismounted. He watched, tapping the rock he was hiding behind in frustration as the group pulled out their waterskins, drank, and stretched. The charmer, Senna, strolled over to a stream and refilled her waterskin.

Calm yourself, Tuli whispered. Gideon tried. He took a moment to confirm the cub was still his hostage and there was no sign of the big cat, although he imagined she wasn't far away. His men remained well hidden, waiting for him to spring his trap. Gideon licked his lips although they were not dry. He found such actions disturbing, attributing them to Tuli manifesting within him, more eager to skrike than to snatch the amulet.

Senna found something, rushing it over to Wickham and the time weaver. A brief discussion followed, and they remounted and set off. At the last moment there was some jostling, and Wickham and Winter moved to the front of the pack, changing the order in which Gideon must trigger his ambush. He rehearsed the new sequence in his mind. He would throw up the barrier moments before the mage rode through the arch. That would take care of Wickham and Winter, but if not, his crossbowmen would finish them off. The time weaver and the charmer were next in line. Gideon would encase them in hard air and use it to drag them off their mounts if they hadn't fallen already. Then he would kill the time weaver with his sword. A thrust through the heart would be quickest. He reminded himself he could slip back and adjust if his plans went awry.

He would hold the charmer trapped while he took the amulet, then he would rush back behind the barrier that was blocking the arch. He would tie off that barrier and leave it in place to prevent pursuit while he escaped on his horse, which was hobbled on the far side of the hill.

Just as the party cantered up to the arch, gazing at its beauty, Gideon flung a wall of hard air in their path.

*

Brylee couldn't see the party enter the clearing from her hiding spot, but she heard them pausing for water. She could see the ambush site and part of the attacker's face as he hid behind the arch. His link to the source was huge and highly turbulent. Whatever means he had used to suppress his link's tremoring had been forgotten in his excitement and bloodlust. His face had taken on a hideous, determined grin of concentration, which increased her urge to leap out and prevent the attack. Instead, she readied her magic. As soon as her other self disappeared, she would reach out and begin healing Levi.

Brylee watched the mage summon his magic and sensed the barrier forming over the archway. She almost squealed a warning, but instead some instinctual part of her snapped up an air wall of her own just in front of the other but much softer in nature.

Sensing something unnatural, Wickham and Winter's horses plunged their front hooves into the earth, catapulting their riders into her cushioning wall. There was still an almighty crunch, and it looked like Winter got the worst of it judging by the way his neck was wrenched around.

As both men lay still, the attacker leapt over them and drew his sword. Brylee let her cushioning air go, as she would need all her power to heal Levi. She closed her eyes and turned her head, not wanting to watch the thrust, praying to a god she didn't believe in that she was making the right choice.

When Brylee dared look again mere seconds later, the assailant was standing over her younger self, who was trapped on all fours. Her magical sight revealed the brief struggle for her younger self's link, which his massive power snatched away in moments. He discarded her dying husk, which survived on the dwindling amount of residual energy left inside. He looked manic for a moment, then his features softened to confusion, pity, and then... regret?

The man took a few gasps of air and then turned back to finish off Levi. The sight of herself being slain and the callousness of the act made her want to vomit, but she choked it down and readied an attack on the assailant if he tried to harm Levi further. Using her magical sight, she realised that Levi's heart and one lung were already wrecked. He was dying. She reached across the gap with her mind, holding the remains of Levi's heart together and forcing it to continue beating. Some of the blood leaked into his collapsed lung, but there was little more she could do but focus on keeping Levi from fading completely.

*

Gideon's vision blurred, and upon its return, he found himself standing over the charmer's discarded, dying body. He was stunned. What had happened?

You were too cowardly and pitiful to take the power we need, so I did.

It took a moment to process, but Gideon realised Tuli had wrenched control, as she had in Sandrick to kill Ostryd. Should he slip back in time and stop her? Would she let him?

Taking a few steadying breaths, Gideon turned and dug under Levi's cloak and found the amulet's chain. He tried to snap it, but whatever it was made from wouldn't yield, so he pulled the dead man's head forward and undid the clasp, then yanked the jewel and chain out from where it was tangled in Levi's clothing.

Four strides later, he was through the archway. As he resealed and tied off his magical wall, he felt lightheaded. As he steadied himself against the wall, he knew nothing could stop him now.

Moments later he was galloping away. Tears rolled down his cheeks, and they had nothing to do with the wind in his face.

I've done it, Tuli, I'm coming back for you, you murderer!

Chapter Seventy-Five

Lu urged her horse to go faster, standing in the saddle so far forward she could have whispered into his swept-back ears as he strained to please her. Sirius was only a stride behind, full of questions about the unexplained race back to catch his master. Lu was pleased he had stopped asking questions and just concentrated on keeping up. She felt he trusted her lead, and that made her feel good. She promised herself she would reveal everything to him when there was time, perhaps even her feelings for him.

Shanna, on the other hand, had sent urgent, desperate thoughts continuously, though they weren't useful images, being mostly about Tak's danger. Although the cub could fall to its death, from the visions Lu received from her cat, Tak didn't seem worried. She was fascinated by a hawk at the top of the nearby tree and tantalised by how the points of the branches whipped in the light breeze. Through Shanna's eyes, Lu saw Gideon galloping away just as the ambush site raced into view from her own vantage point above her steed.

Track Gideon? Lu asked her cat.

No, save Tak! was Shanna's abrupt response.

I will retrieve Tak from the sky, Lu said, *but if I can't, we will need the mage. Follow? Trust!* She felt Shanna's indecision, so Lu offered some reassurance. *If Gideon wanted your babies dead, they would be dead already. Don't kill him! I need to understand why he acted so.* Lu breathed a sigh of relief when she sensed Shanna command Smak to wait under a bush before taking off after the fleeing mage. Smak seemed happy to wait. The excitement was draining. Perhaps he would nap.

As she bore down on the archway, Lu saw three men on foot with crossbows encircling Wickham's maid and the one remaining guard, who were still mounted. Two of the men turned, hearing their approach. Lu raised her sword, ready to deflect any shot. Sirius forced his horse forward, attempting to shield Lu from the danger. *Unnecessary, but sweet,* she thought.

As Lu shielded herself behind her mount's head for protection, she saw Rosemary spur her own horse forward, crashing into one of the ambushers. Then she leapt from her horse onto another attacker. *Feisty,* Lu thought with respect. In the moment of distraction, Lu blew past the last man, his neck left bloody from her sword. She heard Sirius reining in behind her and trusted him to defeat any further attack from the ambushers.

She slowed her horse, leaping off before it stopped and landing in a defensive stance. Wickham and Winter were down, and Senna was scrambling across to Levi, who appeared to be mortally wounded. She circled the group, her sword held defensively above her as she scanned for more threats. Sensing none, she ran to check on the downed men.

Brylee had watched her younger self disappear. She had been dying, rolling from all fours onto her side. Then the space she occupied pulsed green and swelled outwards and she was gone. There was a *whoosh* and a *crack* as air snapped into the space her body had vacated. She changed to resemble her younger self as she jumped out of her hiding spot and ran to Levi's side.

Up close, Brylee deepened her vision and determined that his injured lung could wait. She examined Levi's heart, assessing the actions she would need to repair its damaged parts while at the same time pressing her lips to his, forcing good air into his remaining lung.

"He's gone," she heard Lu say, her voice full of sadness.

"I'm not a maid!" Brylee cried between gasps. "I'm a . . . a magical healer." There was a pause as Lu processed her revelation.

"Maybe so, but he's too far gone. Help me with Wickham. He's still breathing."

Brylee ignored Lu while she stabilised Levi. Her years of practice at Our Lady proved priceless, and in a short time she had Levi's heart back to the point where it could beat on its own if she held it together. She continued pouring vast amounts of her magic into Levi's body until it was more of a straightforward regeneration of tissue than a messy puzzle. Only then did her mind have the capacity to look up and scan Wickham and Winter. The latter's spine was snapped, which she could repair, but she had never worked on repairing the nerves that run through it. She doubted there was anything she could do for him.

Wickham had a broken shoulder, and his brain had a burst blood vessel. It would kill him if she didn't act soon. Brylee repaired it in moments. However, she could do nothing about the brain's subsequent swelling. It was a hard choice, but she left the mage to his fate.

"I think Wickham will make it," Brylee said to Lu. "Pull Winter's head and neck straight. Take it slow and gentle. I don't think I can help him, but I will try as soon as I stabilise Levi."

Brylee didn't watch to see if Lu complied. Instead, she focussed her attention on Levi until he took his first unaided breath. It was horribly laboured with one useless lung, but she helped him take a few more until his body found its rhythm.

Once she was relieved of having to breathe for Levi, and his heart was a little stronger, she turned her attention to Winter. She had never worked on multiple people at once, and she felt drained. She focussed on the damaged nerves in his spine. *How can I fix you?* she asked. *What do you need?* There was no response.

Brylee widened her magical view. Winter's glow had faded completely, and his link had detached, shrivelling before her senses. He was gone. She told Lu as much and then switched her attention back to Wickham, slowly relieving the swelling in his head. She couldn't mend his shoulder in the position he was in, so that would have to wait. She returned her focus to Levi, willing his body back together.

From the corner of her eye, Lu had watched Sirius, his guard, and Rosemary defeat the two bandits who remained. They were bound against a tree, with the guard standing over them. Sirius had learned they were recently hired by a man called Arkly. *A false name, but I see why Gideon chose it,* Lu thought.

She didn't want to reveal her association with Gideon at that point, but she did confide to Sirius and Senna that she was ex-Mobi'dern and that Shanna, who was pursuing their attacker, was bombarding her with pleas to save Tak.

"Do we know why they attacked?" Sirius asked. Now it was Brylee's turn to feel guilt over her secrets. She saw the assailant had taken something from Levi but had not realised it was his amulet until she examined him. Levi would take a long time to heal to the point where he could be moved, but she could relax her efforts for a few moments.

"Where's the cub?" she asked Lu, who pointed to the animal hanging precariously in the air. Brylee examined the assailant's work. When she felt she understood his technique, she wrapped her own layer of air around his and severed the knot that held his trap together. The cub dropped several inches before settling into Brylee's air. Brylee lowered Tak to the ground and then released her. The relieved cub bounded over to Lu and rolled onto her back for a belly rub as if nothing had happened.

Can I kill Gideon now? Shanna asked when Lu informed her that her cub was safe.

"Shanna is within striking distance of the fleeing bandit," Lu reported. Her thoughts whirled at Gideon's unprovoked attack. She needed time to process them before admitting she knew him, realising she would be implicated by association. "She wants to kill him, but I'm holding her off." As betrayed as she felt, Shanna killing Lord Arkly in a fit of revenge had started this all, and besides, Lu wanted some answers from Gideon. She wished she hadn't posed the thought of unleashing Shanna to Senna.

"The man is an incredibly powerful mage," Brylee explained, unsure of how much Lu knew of him, as he had apparently duped her in regard to some things. "If she misses, not only will you lose your friend, we'll also lose our tracker."

To Lu's relief, they agreed to let Gideon think he was safe until they could catch up to him.

Brylee dismantled the hard air wall that Gideon had created in the arch and then sent Rosemary up to Harding estate, briefing her on what to say.

"I'm well known there as Senna, and I know Jyan will help. Explain that we were ambushed, and we need a wagon for Levi, Winter, and Wickham as well as the sheriff for the outlaws."

Wickham woke just as Rosemary returned, riding the wagon with Jyan next to her. He had been at home and was bursting to see Senna. Six men followed the wagon. If Jyan noticed that Brylee looked years younger than the last time he had set eyes on her, he didn't mention it. They loaded both injured men and Winter's body into the wagon, and Brylee climbed in beside them. She was exhausted, and she knew she would collapse into sleep shortly, but she would not do so until she was sure that Levi was stable.

"Mr. Harding," Lu said, "do you have a small shed or lockable stall in a barn I could use?" She explained about the cubs and needing a place for them to wait for their mother's return. Jyan agreed immediately, and Lu loped off with Tak to find Smak. They would follow on foot, and Jyan would ensure his foreman provided for her animals.

By the time the wagon reached the manor, Brylee's continued efforts had Levi's lung reinflated and drained of blood. His heart was also stable, though it still bore significant damage. Wickham and others were impatient for explanations, which they felt Senna could provide, but she refused to respond. She did fuse the bones in the mage's shoulder, however, which he grumped was some compensation for her silence.

Once they transferred Levi to a bed, she lay next to him. Barrow, Jyan's healer, had been called immediately after Rosemary arrived asking for help. He fussed over them both. Brylee obtained a promise he would wake her if Levi's condition changed, even a little, then let herself drift into a deep sleep. Her last observation was of the links of all people in the room. They all had the tremor of turbulence, worse than she had ever seen. She had saved Levi from the ambush, but their problems were far from over.

Chapter Seventy-Six

Brylee stirred six hours later—just after the third bell—drifting up from dreamless darkness, drawn by Levi's musky scent and the warmth from his body. Her wits returned to her just as she was about to nuzzle into him. She opened her eyes wide in shock, pushing the deluge of memories aside. Using her mind, she checked the health of her most precious patient.

Levi's breathing was ragged, but he was sleeping soundly. A vein near his heart had failed, causing a slow internal bleed. Barrow watched Brylee sit up and get to work, smothering a curse before it reached her voice. She was unreasonably annoyed with the man, even though she realised he didn't have her magical ability to see what she could see so plainly.

Barrow broke away at some point and returned with food for Brylee, which she downed while she worked on her weaver—she flushed realising it was the first time she had thought of him as "her weaver". She didn't come up for air until she was sure he would recover without her magic. As she relaxed her concentration, she was surprised to see the healer had left, and Wickham and Jyan were perched in chairs watching her. She stood and stretched, and with a last look at Levi, she waved at them to follow her out of the room so they could talk without disturbing his sleep.

"I think you owe us an explanation," Wickham said once they were seated in the living room. Brylee appreciated how strange things probably seemed from his perspective. Lu had been sent for and joined them from the stall in which she had slept with Tak and Smak. She smelled of straw. She had introduced the cats to Jason, a ten-year-old stable hand, who would feed the cubs if she had to pursue Gideon, although that had yet to be determined. He was Tak's best friend already, and even Smak grudgingly liked the boy.

Brylee felt unsure about speaking openly in front of Lu and Sirius, who were there at Wickham's insistence. She wrestled with her choices as she sipped hot grou't while breakfast was laid out for the others. The thought that their aid in chasing the amulet might make all the difference swayed her, but it was her desire for openness, after four years of deceit, that convinced her to include them. As soon as she made the choice, she felt so much lighter.

"I do, Gil, more than you know. But I must limit it to the essentials for now, as it's vital that I head south at dawn in pursuit of Winter's killer," Brylee began.

"His name is Gideon Strangelore," Lu said. She had decided to throw in her lot with Sirius, come what may. She outlined the circumstances that threw her together with Gideon and how she occasionally helped him using her Mobi'dern talents. Her shame at spying on the party was authentic. She never imagined Gideon's intent was to stage an attack. Wickham was livid and voiced his anger, no doubt devastated by the death of his long-time friend.

"I'm so sorry," Lu replied following his outburst. "I had assumed the favour related to some charity endeavour, as he does much good work, but as each day passed and I got to know you all, things felt wrong. I was relieved when Gideon told me to hire replacement guards and that he was returning to Troll Lake." Seeing Sirius look her way, she made eye contact with him. "I told him I would stay behind in the area to see if Smak would find a mate and . . ." Her internal voice said that she hoped to find a mate in Sirius, but her mouth clammed up and she blushed bright red.

"Anyway," Brylee said, knowing time was against them, "Lu's race back here likely saved Rosemary and the rest of us." She explained what she had seen during the battle. In half a bell she summarised everything else, including meeting Jyan for the first time at Grinders and nearly being skriked by Vekki on the same day. She also told them about Wickham's support of her parents in return for her help with the Red Assassin. That she was the Red Assassin stunned everyone. She explained Levi's mission and blushed as she admitted they had fallen for each other so completely. She explained how Levi taught her the rudiments of primi magic and how he threw her back through time, causing the very calamity he was attempting to identify and fix. Brylee finished recounting her last four years by describing her actions at the ambush scene.

She blushed with pride at her successes at Our Lady, Reni, and the Work Hive. She wept when describing losing Garrick. Her eyes glittered with tears of remorse as she recounted the deaths of Farborn, Alleg Ordel, and Vekki, even though all of them were justified.

She apologised to Jyan for deceiving him all these years and confessed her real name to those who didn't know it. Jyan reached across the table and took her hand. Brylee knew she was forgiven in the way a parent would forgive their child.

Brylee waved off questions that she thought were motivated merely by unhelpful curiosity, but she interrupted her tale to answer those that helped focus on tracking Gideon before he could get to the time amulet and wreak further havoc. When she told the group that she could see the turbulence in their links and that it was stronger than hers was before being sent back in time, everyone fell silent.

"The question is, how do we find Gideon?" Brylee asked, breaking the spell. "He has a half day's head start. We know he must head south to the border at some point to search for the cave, but I don't know where it is."

"He's heading south already," Lu said. "I know where he is. Shanna can't give me the names of roads or villages, but she told me that Gideon met a man just after dusk outside of a village south of here. I've seen the man before. He met with Gideon the day before the ambush, and I overheard them talking about a cavern. I would guess the man is leading Gideon to it."

"Then we must leave at dawn," Sirius said. "Jyan, do you have men to draw on for a posse?"

Brylee cut him off. "No, you only saw a fraction of Gideon's power at the ambush, and the fact he knows enough about Levi to steal his amulet means he has knowledge and power we don't understand. Perhaps he's a primi too. Armed fighters will not help us. What we need is speed and stealth."

"I must go," Lu said. "You will need me to communicate with Shanna."

"I was hoping you would offer," Brylee said with a respectful nod. "You know the man the best, you're stealthy, and you're a one-woman army. The Mobi'dern are legendary warriors and trackers, and he thinks I'm dead. The two of us should have surprise on our side at least."

Sirius opened his mouth to volunteer at the same moment Wickham did, but Brylee shut them both down. It would be a posse of two, aided by an angry cat.

"I'm going to check on Levi," Brylee said, standing. "Could you provide us with a spare set of fast horses so we can trade off to rest our own? And supplies, anything Lu or anyone suggests. Jyan?" He seemed almost offended that she had asked, explaining nothing had changed just because her name had. He told her everything he owned was hers as he led Lu and Sirius outside to make the arrangements.

Levi appeared to be sleeping soundly under Barrow's watchful eye. Brylee told the healer to take a short break while she checked Levi one more time and said farewell to his sleeping form. Brylee leaned over the time weaver, stroked his hair, and kissed his cheek. His eyes opened slowly, and his right hand rose to cradle the back of her head.

"You're awake," Brylee said, surprised.

"And you found your way back," Levi replied, pulling her down and kissing her lips. It was a long, deep kiss that Brylee didn't want to end, but eventually she sat back.

"Your heart is still weak, Levi, so go easy," she said, smiling. Then her face turned serious. "Ostryd is dead, I'm afraid. I think he told a man called Gideon about you, and he was the one who ambushed us. He has your amulet." Levi's other hand wandered to his neck. Finding nothing there, his eyes went vacant. For a heartbeat she panicked and checked his wound, assuming a relapse, before realising he was just accessing his magical sight.

"Well, me sending you back with my native magic didn't end the world, it seems. And your last four years splashing about in the past doesn't appear to have harmed the timeline too much either. But the turbulence has changed in nature and amplitude."

Brylee shook her head. "I don't understand."

"I think me sending you back was the very crisis I came to prevent, but it was occluding a greater crisis caused by this man using the time-travel amulet. He will kill us all if he's not stopped. I'm sure of that now. I sense the Unravelling beginning, where a thick source of magic comes apart into billions of strands."

"I'm leaving now with Lu to stop him," Brylee said. Levi tried to sit up, which ignited sharp pains throughout his chest.

"Your heart was all but destroyed, and you lost a lung," Brylee explained. "You wouldn't make it to the porch. I've done what I can for now, but you need rest before I can do more. Lie back. You would be a liability, not a help." Levi settled back, nodding in acceptance, his face twisted in agony. The small action had tired him to the point that he struggled to stay awake.

"Sleep, love," Brylee whispered, kissing Levi's forehead.

Levi squeezed her hand and closed his eyes. Then reached out with his mind for the Galei stones and found them not around her neck but in a small pack near the door. He smiled inwardly, finding them full of primi magic. Drawing on the stones, he planted information in Brylee's mind about the doorway to the cavern. If she didn't catch Gideon in time and he made it through, she might be able to work out how to follow him. It was the best he could offer before darkness took him.

When Levi woke six hours later, his mind was occupied with Ostryd as he pondered his connection to Gideon. It was then he realised Brylee was probably pursuing a slipper, and he hadn't warned her how lethal they could be. He couldn't even recall mentioning that such a skill existed.

*

Brylee rode Whipcrack, and Lu had a fresh horse. They each led another gelding who would share their load so they could move fast. Lu would dismount often and lead her horses at a run, relying on her loping gait to keep up. Running also helped release some of her anger. They carried only the necessary supplies but had plenty of money. They would trade for replacement horses along their route, and Lu was adept at living off the land if vendors were not available. Lu wore her Mobi'dern sword openly. As she ran, replaying every part of her life with Gideon, she wondered for the first time if he had anything to do with Ostryd and Brightstone's deaths.

*

For six days and nights, Gideon and his guide rode hard. The climate became warm and then hot as they descended into the desert region. Their guide had arranged for fresh mounts at waystations and had organised food, lighter clothing, and places to sleep as they sped south. At two different locations, Gideon paid for men to watch for and delay any pursuers. Gideon had no knowledge of who might be pursuing them, so he couldn't give a firm description. His traps were easy for Shanna, Lu, and Brylee to detect and avoid.

On the seventh day of heading south, Gideon neared the border and turned west towards a range of mountains that rose up out of the flat, arid waste he had sweated across for some time. It was then that he felt the first discomfort due to the presence of the aggar's cavern. His guide had warned him of its impacts and whined that it would get a great deal worse as they neared their destination, which was another half day's ride.

Brylee and Lu reached the border two hours behind Gideon, having made up time. The next morning they passed Gideon's guide, who had turned back after giving Gideon final directions to the cavern's mouth, claiming he was unable to face the discomfort a second time. Lu recognised him from Shanna's imagery. They considered interrogating the man, but they chose not to as time was pressing. It was just a bell later when Shanna shared that Gideon had dismounted, tied his horse to a gnarled tree, and entered the cavern. She could also see Lu and Brylee on the horizon approaching his location. They were too late.

Chapter Seventy-Seven

Gideon had ridden at a walking pace since mid-afternoon when his guide had turned back. Then he dismounted and led his horse on foot. His head hurt, and his horse was jumpy and reluctant to proceed. He wondered what had happened to Shanna's cub, left high in the treetops. His horse might be skittish because of the cave, but it was how the animal would act if there was a predator abroad too. He could see no sign of Shanna, but his hackles were up. If he could be certain the cavern was where he had been told, it would have been easier to have left the beast under one of the rare trees. As much as his horse, and even his own body, were telling him to turn back, his heart was excited to press forward.

Ostryd's notes had few mentions of the cavern, and what he had unearthed were only snippets the historian had written down from his conversations with the time weaver. A massive space. Species the aggar treasured, preserved for eternity. A barrier. An amulet to gain access and a time amulet hidden somewhere inside. Gideon was excited yet full of concerns that he would have liked to discuss with Tuli, but she had faded into a petulant silence. It was a relief, but her insights might have helped him. What if the amulet needed to be activated to allow him through the barrier? Where in the vast cavern should he look for the other amulet? How did one use the time amulet to navigate to the correct location and time? These thoughts pressed on him as he struggled towards his goal.

Gideon's guide had described a canyon between two small peaks. One had a steep overhang resembling the prow of a boat, and the other was sheer, distinct from its neighbours' gentler slopes. The canyon's entrance was almost blocked by higgledy-piggledy square boulders, the guide said, comparing the blocks to a drunken dice game of the gods. Gideon had disparaged the man's thoughts and his directions until he walked over a small rise and saw the formations for himself. He gathered his confidence, sped up, and in a short time had picked his way through the obstructions to find the cavern hidden deep in the shadows beyond.

His horse looked anxious as Gideon tethered it to the thick scrub in the shadow of the boulders. It grieved him that the horse would have to take its chances with whatever predators roamed there, but he doubted he could take it inside. He cursed himself for not forcing his guide to endure the last few miles so he could guard the animal he would surely need to return to civilisation if he ran out of food before locating the time amulet. The guide was eager for money, which Gideon had no end of, but his constant whining and fears were a distraction from Gideon's other problems.

Gideon had loaded large paniers of water on his mount, which he now decanted into a waterskin for himself and into a bowl, which he put down for the horse along with some grain. Then he hefted his saddlebags over one shoulder and approached the cavern entrance. He pulled Levi's amulet from his pocket, opened its clasp, and fastened it around his neck. He didn't know if it was required to be worn to function, but wearing it also kept his hands free in case he needed them. As the weight settled onto his chest, he felt every inch of his body quiver and his arm hair stand up straight, as if someone had walked over his grave. A moment later he felt like himself again, but something had changed. By way of experiment, he removed then refastened the clasp, feeling the same sensation ripple through him again.

He shifted the pack on his shoulder and peered in through the cavern's entrance. Beyond the first few feet, he could see nothing but blackness. He walked back to the scrub and picked up a stout, dry branch. Using oil and cloth from his pack, he fashioned a torch. A few sparks from his flint, and it was alight.

Gideon advanced toward the cavern entrance, one hand out in front, the other holding the torch high. He probed for a barrier but felt nothing. Step by step he crossed the threshold, poised to run back to the daylight at any moment. Once he was inside, the blackness gave way to a bluish light that came from nowhere yet lit everything. His mouth hung open, and the torch fell from his hand. Stretched out in front of him as far as he could see was a panorama containing every natural feature he had ever seen and more, all organised in large square parcels of land, almost like fields of crops, except that analogy was too limiting. He stood rooted to the spot, a sense of vertigo tugging at him.

Gideon realised that the oppressive pressure he had felt approaching the cavern had vanished as soon as he crossed the threshold. If anything, he felt energised and refreshed. *I'm in a cavern full of magic,* he realised. *Magic is life and I'm standing in a large pool of it.*

Gideon didn't know how long he stood there, fascinated, but part of him realised he needed a plan if he were ever to find the time amulet. Should he follow his instincts and wander until he found it, or would a grid search pattern be best? He looked up at the cavern's roof, noting it curved up in a smooth arch to a distant point, what he imagined was the centre of the cavern, which dropped down in a massive, jagged stalactite. He could start there and spiral outwards. It dawned on him how easy it would be to get disoriented and lost. There were not enough features on the stalactite to use as a reference point, so he determined he would orient himself by counting gridlines at the perimeter.

Trained as a scientist and a healer, he decided to be deliberate and organised in his search. He would walk across one end of the cavern to determine its width and then backtrack to the centre. From there he would walk across the cavern, bisecting it. If he found no clue to inform his strategy upon reaching the far side, he would search each quarter in turn. His mind made up, he marched off, whistling a happy tune.

*

Brylee and Lu were harder on their mounts than Gideon, and their animals were lathered and dehydrated. Lu worried they were pushing too hard to sustain the chase.

There is water here, Shanna said, sensing her thoughts, including an image of water trickling down the side of the cliff into a small pool that was perhaps two feet square. *Drink only from where the water runs fast, as the pool below smells foul.*

Brylee had learned basic hand signals from the Mobi'dern guards employed to protect her crops, so Lu switched to them as she realised Shanna was close by and their voices might carry to Gideon. They led their horses through a cleft between some boulders and saw the large cat in the shadow of a rock. Behind her was the waterfall. They also found a tethered horse that they assumed was Gideon's.

Whipcrack reared slightly, skittish at the sight of the predator. Brylee and Lu dismounted and secured their mounts next to Gideon's, a short distance away from Shanna and the pool, then fetched water for all three animals.

The man entered the cavern some time ago, Shanna sent. *The entrance is blocked. My face and paws strike a door that isn't there.* Lu relayed this to Brylee, confirming what Levi had told them.

Brylee approached the barrier and reached out to touch it. It buzzed under her fingers, reminding her of the cell she had been locked in at the Rostal jail. Wickham had charmer-proofed that door and the prisoner bindings. She wished now that she had taken the time to understand his method. Gritting her teeth, she probed around the entryway to confirm it was blocked completely and that there were no gaps. She was relieved when at last she withdrew her hand. Levi had said the barrier was to keep out all people, not just mages. She had Lu touch it. To her it felt solid, though not like it was filled with angry bees, as it did for Brylee.

Brylee stepped back and used her magical sight to examine the barrier and the surrounding rock. She found the barrier extended under the rock and the ground as far as she could sense. This negated her and Lu's idea of bypassing the barrier by tunnelling around it.

For half a bell, Lu pried and hammered on the barrier with rocks, sword point, and anything else she could think of, all to no effect. At the same time, Brylee pummelled the barrier with hard air, heat, cold, and various transformations. She coaxed, begged, and commanded the barrier to give up its secrets, with no more success than Lu's physical attack. Exhausted, they retreated to the waterfall to drink, receiving pitying looks from Shanna, who thought all the exertion pointless.

A memory tugged at Brylee. It took some effort to bring it into focus, and she didn't understand it at first. It was akin to how she looked deeply into an object to understand its attributes, though somewhat different. It wasn't about the properties of a thing; it was about how they influenced its structure. The memory was of zooming into the tiniest detail, going further and further until the subject was lost all around her, so big compared to the minute parts now visible. She had no idea when she had ever looked at something that closely, but she was astounded at the complexity of all the tiny parts, each facing in a million different directions. Why had that memory come to her?

Brylee picked up a rock and looked into it. It looked like a rock. She held it close to her face and tried to see its smallest detail. *Now it looks like a big rock,* she thought, throwing it away. She grunted in frustration, which made the horses snicker. Time was slipping away from them. She returned to the memory. Its strangeness and lack of context among her other thoughts compelled her to think of it as a clue. After reviewing it several times, she realised the memory was from the perspective of magical sight, not physical. Yet it was unfamiliar, as if she were seeing things through someone else's perspective. The image of a mostly naked Winter washing in the stream surfaced unbidden. *This is Levi's memory,* Brylee realised.

She kept his memory in the forefront of her mind and focussed on a spiky cactus growing out of the rock face beside her. Switching to her magical sight, she imagined overlaying Levi's memory with what she could see of the plant, including its stems and spikes and its minute glow of magic. As Levi's memory zoomed in, she tried to force her view to follow, and it did to a point. Between the glow and the plant's substance was a fabric that formed the plant's various components. The skin of the cactus was made up of layers of the fabric, and each layer had small parts that made what it needed to be. The memory continued to zoom in, but her senses stalled. She pushed and pushed and then stopped in frustration.

"Where did you go?" Lu asked, her voice full of concern. "It's like you were in a trance." As Brylee gulped some water, she explained what she was attempting.

"It all sounds so crazy to me," Lu said, shaking her head. "Looking into a plant and looking deep inside a body. You amaze me, Brylee."

"It is like looking inside a body," Brylee said, laughing. Then she realised she hadn't been using that part of her brain or doing what Levi had told her: using all her senses, not just sight.

Trying again, she tunnelled into the plant, going deeper and deeper with multiple attempts. Each time she attempted to match the technique, she saw farther and it seemed easier. It was dark when she finally reached the point where she could see the tiniest elements, which faced in myriad directions. She rocked her head back and sighed. *Yay for me, but how does this help, Levi?*

Brylee knew Levi planted the memory in her for a reason, so after much puzzling, she stood and walked back to the barrier and applied the same technique. It was harder as the barrier was invisible, so there was little to focus on, just a shimmer of moonlight. Then something came into focus, a myriad of elements aligned in neat rows, parallel to the ground. She put her finger on the barrier, gritting her teeth against the buzz, and tried to see her finger and the barrier at the same depth. But it buzzed so hard she couldn't concentrate, and she let the vision go.

"No good?" Lu asked, feeling helpless that she couldn't contribute.

"My magic reacts with the barrier, and the discomfort it gives me breaks my concentration," Brylee said. "I want to study the barrier and my finger side by side."

"Use my finger," Lu said, standing up and approaching the entrance.

Brylee slapped her own forehead and laughed. "Of course! Thank you!"

This time Brylee could focus on both the barrier and Lu's finger, which was pressing against it. The barrier's elements were aligned and symmetrical, but the fingers were spread in a chaotic cloud.

Do this, another memory instructed. Without thinking, Brylee's brain straightened all the elements in Lu's fingertip to align with the barrier, and the finger slipped inside the cavern. Lu whipped her hand back in surprise, breaking Brylee's concentration.

"I'm sorry; it just happened," Brylee said. She grabbed Lu's hand, ready to heal whatever damage she had caused.

"No . . . wait," Lu said. "It doesn't hurt. I was just shocked." Lu was embarrassed she had acted in such a non-warrior-like manner. "It wasn't just my finger; it was as if a nerve had been struck in my elbow, only it was all over my body. Let me touch the barrier again."

Lu reached for the barrier, but it wasn't there. Or at least if it was, she passed right through it. Taking a tentative step, she passed into the cavern and vanished. A moment later she reappeared, her face split in an enormous grin and her eyes wide with amazement.

"You should see this!" she exclaimed. "It's incredible." Then she frowned, recalling that Brylee couldn't follow her.

Brylee felt an urgent nudge on her thigh and looked down to see Shanna.

"She wants to follow me. She senses I'm going after Gideon," Lu said, walking over to where she had left her sword. "Do your vision thing to her, she says."

Now that she knew what to do, Brylee aligned Shanna with the barrier. The transformation caused the cat to roar in surprise, slink back, then rush at the barrier. She barrelled inside, not knowing what to do with herself.

"She's alright," Lu said, receiving a thought from the breathless cat moments later.

Brylee tried to align herself to the barrier using the same trick but found it didn't work. She held her hand close to it and zoomed in. She discovered she had aligned her elements perfectly, but they were jiggling around, catching and banging against the barrier's elements. *This movement is my magic, and the way it scrapes on the barrier causes the bees,* she realised. Though she tried several times, she was unable to still her elements. The act of aligning her particles took magic, and using magic made her particles jiggle.

"Can you move the barrier to match your movement?" Lu asked when Brylee explained her frustration. "Some of our fighting styles require us to use small strikes to force our opponent to open up, then we exploit the gap with a larger attack."

After several attempts, it worked. Ten minutes later, Brylee was standing beside Lu and Shanna inside the cavern, marvelling at its scale and beauty.

There's nothing to hunt here, Shanna said, turning up her nose after sniffing around the edge of the first two blocks of vegetation. *The man went this way, but his scent has faded, like he passed this way moons ago.*

"Shanna says Gideon followed the path that runs along this wall but that his scent is faint," Lu said. "She isn't confident in tracking him."

Brylee had been attempting some tracking of her own. She had thought that she might be able to spot Gideon's massive link to the source across the cavern and follow it to his location. Not only did she fail to see his, neither Lu, Shanna, herself, or any of the bounteous plants had any sign of a link either. And yet she felt alive with power. She tried to conjure a block of hard air, but nothing happened. She tried several other things before giving up and drawing her sword.

"My magic doesn't work here, Lu," Brylee warned.

"That's to our benefit, isn't it?" Lu replied, her mind seizing upon the tactical advantage. "Assuming the same is true for Gideon, he's outnumbered. His sword skills are pretty good, but he's not at your level. Shanna and I will make mincemeat of him, unless he has a crossbow. Even then he'll only get one of us if he's lucky."

"Let's go get him then," Brylee said, setting off after the cat, a grin warming her tired face.

*

Gideon had also realised he had no magic. He had tried to slip. Initially, he wasn't sure if it worked, as everything in the cavern was so still. Then he had the idea of breaking the stem of a plant, then slipping back and seeing if it was whole, which it was. He didn't understand why slipping worked but magic did not, but he gained some comfort that he wasn't completely vulnerable.

After two hours of walking, Gideon reached a junction in the grid from which he could see up to the top of the stalactite in the distance. It was the fiftieth turning, which reinforced his suspicion he was halfway across the cavern. The grid pattern suggested the aggar was a structured being and a one-hundred-by-one-hundred-foot lattice seemed fitting. He changed his strategy and turned, heading towards the centre of the space. After ten minutes he doubted his decision. Some of the blocks he had passed were different lengths. Forests took up more ground than wheat. He reminded himself he was safe from pursuit now that he was inside the cavern, even if someone had somehow tracked him from the ambush site. He had all the time in the world—literally. He backtracked and continued along the wall in the direction he had originally chosen.

Two parcels later he came to an orchard with several different types of fruit trees. He stepped off the pathway and examined them, noting every fruit was attached to a twig, and there were no windfalls. He tried an apple and then a plum. They were delicious. He wondered about pollination, as he had seen no insects, birds, or animals, before recalling that everything there had been created by the aggar rather than grown. He took a drink from his waterskin and then settled down to rest.

Gideon dozed, but a distant sound pulled him back to his senses. He pressed himself down behind the tree and listened. He couldn't hear anything, but the hairs on his neck were standing tall, yelling a warning. He rolled onto his belly and crawled to the pathway. Looking back the way he had come, he saw two figures stalking behind him with swords in their hands. He recognised Lu, which was confirmed as Shanna emerged from the pathway sniffing the ground, presumably tracking his scent. His hand dropped to his sword, but he didn't draw it in case the noise drew their attention.

*

"Shanna is struggling with the scent," Lu whispered to Brylee. "The plants all smell strange, which confuses her. She thinks Gideon walked one way, then doubled back, but which way he is headed now, she isn't sure."

"That he's wandering implies he hasn't found the amulet yet," Brylee said. "If he had and is now exploring out of curiosity, there's nothing here that would tempt him to backtrack, is there?"

Lu shrugged. Brylee's intuition suggested they would find the amulet under the stalactite in the distance. If it wasn't by the door, that was the natural place to put it, or so it seemed to her. Perhaps there are multiple entrances to the cavern. If so, leaving it at the centre would make sense. *It's what Levi would do,* she thought.

"Let's go that way," Brylee said, pointing at the stalactite and feeling a little more confident. "If it's not there, I'll wait there in hiding while you search with Shanna. It seems like Gideon would go there sooner rather than later."

Lu nodded. "I agree. That sounds more effective."

Lu signalled for Shanna to lead the way, then the three set off towards the centre of the cavern.

*

Gideon was terrified, but he breathed a quiet sigh of relief as he saw his pursuers head off in the wrong direction. He couldn't fathom how they could be there. He figured Shanna must have trailed him somehow, but Brylee was supposedly dead. He had watched her link merge with his own as he rode away from the ambush. He was sure the time weaver was dead too. His sword had struck true. And how did they penetrate the barrier? Didn't he have the only amulet? None of this made any sense, nor did it matter now.

Feeling vulnerable without his magic, he fought the urge to slide away into the bushes and hide. Instead, he took a swig of water and tried to think. The last thing he needed was to lose sight of the enemy and stumble into them later. He gathered his courage, crept out of hiding, and slunk back along the pathway to where the women had turned, considering his options. He could set up an ambush at the entrance, but what if there was another way out? He could ride back to the nearest settlement for reinforcements and ambush them along the trail somewhere. At least he would have his magic to fight them if he found them. While his mind raced, Gideon followed his pursuers, keeping just off the pathway and out of sight.

After a while, Lu and Brylee stopped, letting Shanna work on the scent. He estimated they were where he had changed his mind and reversed course. Shanna was intent on following her nose, but her head snapped up, and she made eye contact with Gideon and snarled. The women spun around, their swords raised.

Gideon pulled his head in, but it was too late. Or was it? He slipped back in time a few moments and made sure he was out of sight. He counted to ten before peeking out and was relieved to see the women had chosen to continue along the trail. Twice more in the next hour Gideon had to slip to avoid being spotted by the cat. He was avoiding detection, but he still had no plan to overcome a Mobi'dern, her cat, and the charmer, who had mysteriously been resurrected.

Any suggestions? he asked Tuli, but all he received in reply was a cold silence.

As he neared the stalactite, Gideon saw a similar but much smaller collection of rocks reaching up from the ground to meet it. It was surrounded by boulders that had steps carved in their sides so one could easily climb the short distance to the top, where a table-like altar stood. Gideon was convinced he would find the amulet up there.

Lu was already skipping up the steps. When she reached the top, she put her blade on the altar and lifted the amulet by its chain. Gideon's experience with the barrier's amulet suggested he would have to put the amulet around his neck to activate it. He would have to figure out how to navigate to the chosen place and time, but if it would take him anywhere away from there, he could escape.

Gideon considered creeping back to the entrance and setting up an ambush. He could steal their horses and trap them. Then he remembered Lu could run for days with little sustenance. Gideon felt tired. He had come this far, made few friends, and done things that disgusted him. He had always wanted to help people, not harm or take advantage of them. He believed in his dream of using his longevity for the betterment of all, especially the poor, but events seemed to force him back to actions that he was ashamed of. *No, if the fates want me to live like this for the good of many, they can prove it.* He would make his stand there, using his slipping ability against their combat skills.

*

Lu and Brylee exchanged hand signals, agreeing that Lu would remain atop the mound, watching for Gideon's approach. Brylee would stay at ground level, watching the direction they had come from while Shanna would scour the wider area.

Range, Lu said to Shanna.

Hunt! The cat replied.

Lu had agreed to Brylee's demand that if they secured the amulet before Gideon, and they could capture Gideon without risk to themselves, they would. Lu wasn't sure she agreed with that plan, and she sensed Shanna would be completely against it, but she impressed the command to range on her prida, unsure if she welcomed the Mobi'dern discipline she was enforcing.

Gideon watched the big cat lope into the parcel of bamboo-like bushes on the far side of the stones. There would be no better time, he realised. As he stalked the women, they had passed through a grid containing a strange fruit that looked like a member of the melon family. Each was perhaps twice as large as his fist but hard and much heavier than the species he knew. He had picked up two and held one ready to throw as he crept through the last few rows of thick coniferous trees concealing his approach.

He hadn't imagined he would get so close without detection, and Gideon was pleased when he stepped out onto the path not fifteen feet from Brylee. He waited until she turned to look along the path in the opposite direction. Then he threw the first fruit with all his strength, aiming for the back of Brylee's head. His first attempt was a glancing blow to her shoulder, which only served to alert the large woman. He slipped back and threw again, and on his fifth attempt, the melon struck her temple, which Gideon's medical training told him would incapacitate and perhaps kill her. Either way, she crumpled to the floor, out of the fight.

Gideon allowed himself a moment to celebrate, which almost cost him his life. Shanna burst out of the trees he had just left and launched herself at his neck. Gideon was so panicked he almost forgot to slip, and the cat's claws were penetrating his skin before he flicked back two seconds. This time he was prepared and whipped his dagger out of its sheath, sidestepping the attack. Straight away he realised he had been too eager. The cat was mid-launch but had enough contact with the ground to adjust, angling to crush Gideon with her weight. He slipped again, waited a heartbeat, then sidestepped and plunged his knife into the cat's flank as it overshot, Shanna's momentum carving a large gash down her side as Gideon held his blade tight.

Lu couldn't believe her eyes as she witnessed the attack. Her heart was in her mouth, her head filled with Shanna's agony as the cat lay panting but otherwise still, blood pooling under her belly. To her eyes, Gideon seemed to move with more precision and skill than ever before.

She let go of the amulet and three steps and a somersault later, Lu dropped to the ground in a fighter's stance, ten feet from Gideon.

"I've no quarrel with you, Lu," he said, trembling but not cowed. "I need the amulet to save Tuli. You know it was my fault she died. I have to go back and fix it."

Lu shook her head. "No. The time weaver believes that doing so will destroy this world—you'll kill us all," she said in a measured voice, but inside she was desperate to end the fight quickly and help Shanna. She shuffled two steps forward and shifted her blade over her head.

"Lu, don't be silly. I get the amulet, and you can help them."

"No, I can't," Lu said. She looked at Shanna, her fortitude waning in the face of her partner's blood spilling out.

"Lu," Gideon said, trying to inject calmness into his voice as he lowered his blade, "we have plenty of time. Give me the amulet. I'll save Tuli, then I'll come straight back and save your damn cat. I'm a powerful healing mage, for Ag's sake. Work with me. We can save both of them."

Lu was wavering. She hated herself for doing so, but she felt her resolve to stop Gideon shifting. Shanna meant that much to her. She looked at Brylee, perhaps dead on the ground. She thought of Ostryd, Brightstone, and Winter. Dead. Wickham would have been dead too if Brylee hadn't been there.

Gideon felt he had reached through the madness and made Lu see sense. He could see her resolve crumbling as she looked from the cat to the charmer. But then her eyes hardened. He barely had time to raise his dagger before she attacked.

She was halfway across the gap that separated them, her sword a blur, before it registered that she had moved. He slipped back, but she was still too close for him to react, so he slipped again. He moved towards her to cut under her stroke, knowing where she would step. He determined he would cut through the large vein in her leg no matter how many times he had to slip. Not confident in his position, he sought a better way to make his strike count. He slipped again, willing himself to move faster than ever before. *Almost,* he thought. *One more slip and I have her.*

Lu had been sure her attack would be fatal, but Gideon seemed to anticipate it so completely, he was moving through the perfect counter, a thigh strike. She tilted her hips an inch and dropped her shoulder so her blade arced lower, slicing through the muscles of Gideon's wrist and causing the knife to fly from his hand.

Gideon tried to slip, but he couldn't. Time had slowed to a crawl and would not reverse as he commanded. He watched in terror as his thrust registered on the warrior's face, and she began to counter.

Why can't I slip? he wondered. *What's wrong?*

Tuli's voice dripped with venom inside his head. *I won't let you kill her, Gideon.*

Why not? Was Lu really that much of a friend? Gideon was frozen in confusion as Lu's blade sliced into his wrist.

No! Tuli's voice cried. *You want to go back and save* her, *and if you save her, then I won't exist. And I want to live.*

The faulty logic of the bizarre, unhinged statement clarified everything for Gideon in an instant, even as Lu reversed her blade and swept it up towards his face. Tuli's rantings were merely his own worst nature, toxically grasping any excuse in a cowardly attempt to avoid grieving for his sister. His mind had manifested her presence to fill the moral vacuum that enabled his obsessive, egotistical behaviour—both before and during his altercation with Lord Arkly—to lead to her death. And now this loathsome fragment of himself wanted to live on rather than travelling back to repair his mistake and face his sister with his shame. He let go of his sword.

An instant before Lu plunged her blade through his eye and lodged it deep inside his brain, silencing all thoughts, Gideon asked Tuli—the real Tuli—for forgiveness.

Before Gideon's corpse hit the cavern floor, Lu was at Shanna's side, examining her wound. The cat had lost a lot of blood, but the gash was beginning to congeal and the flow was reduced.

"Hold on, Shanna," Lu whispered as she turned to Brylee, who was still out cold. Lu knew that the only way to help the cat was for Brylee to use her magic, which she wouldn't be able to do inside the cavern even when she recovered from the blow to her head. Lu considered her options. With a last look at Shanna, she took a deep breath, removed the amulet from around Gideon's neck, and fastened it to her own, then sprinted toward the cavern entrance.

Lu was surprised to see the sun had set. The moonless sky was ablaze with stars as the amulet let her out of the cavern. Wasting no time, Lu mounted Whipcrack, the largest horse, and guided it towards the cavern's entrance. She said a small prayer that the amulet would allow them both to enter, and when it did, she let out a long breath she hadn't realised she had been holding.

On the way through the cavern, Lu stopped and cut four sturdy branches from a copse of pine-like trees to fashion a stretcher. She tied them into a bundle using a strap from her waist, hauled them up, and balanced them across Whipcrack's rump, then set off toward the centre of the cavern. She was completely unprepared for the sight that greeted her. Gideon's body was gone, replaced by three men.

Levi was crouched over Brylee, who was sitting up and holding her head in her hands, looking dazed. He was pale and moved carefully, but clearly his healing had advanced dramatically. The couple held each other tightly, each glad to see the other alive.

The second man was sitting apart, perched on a low boulder. His unusual posture struck Lu as familiar. When he looked up at the sound of Whipcrack clattering into the clearing she recognised him instantly.

"Ostryd?" Lu leapt down from Whipcrack's saddle, letting the branches she carried fall where they may. As she ran over to kneel next to Shanna she called to him "How are you alive? What about Brightstone?"

Ostryd shook his head, casting an imploring glance at Levi, who was helping Brylee to her feet.

"I'm sorry," Levi said. "I could only help Ostryd because . . ."

"Tell me later," cut in Lu. She pressed her hands over the cat's wound expecting a roar of pain but there was no reaction. She was aghast at how shallow Shanna's breathing had become. "Help me tie these branches into a stretcher so we can pull Shanna outside where one of you mages can save her." Brylee and Levi both moved to help but the third man stepped in their way, and gently pushed Lu aside so he could kneel to examine the cat.

"I think we can dispense with the stretcher," he said. In his hand was the amulet from the top of the steps, its chain glowed with a soft green light as he worked on Shanna's wounds.

"How are you accessing naether in the cavern, Garalon?" asked Levi.

"A master weaver has a few tricks up his sleeve, young one," replied the man. Everyone held their breath as Garalon worked, tutting and whispering to himself occasionally. Ostryd walked over and squatted next to Lu, his curiosity distracting him. Lu saw how tight with sadness his features were and glanced up at Levi.

"I was only able to save Ostryd because we are linked in the future," said Levi. "Saving Brightstone and Winter is impossible. Winter's end came at the moment I made the timeline unravel. It's too unstable to interfere then, I'm sorry." As he spoke, Lu noticed his eyes flick toward Garalon. "As for Brightstone, well, it's against the code. Ask *him*."

"Levinial has already broken the code and done too much, for which he will suffer repercussions," said Garalon in a curt tone without looking up. Brylee and Lu looked to Levi for an explanation.

"When you killed Gideon, the timeline became more unstable, not less," Levi said. "It turns out there were three separate temporal calamities obscuring each other. The turmoil I created sending Brylee back in time was one, and the havoc Gideon would have created had you not stopped him, another. They were resolved by his death and Brylee navigating back to the moment from which I sent her back. But in their absence, the rift caused by Ostryd's death while linked to me through the future became the predominant temporal catastrophe." When everyone looked at Levi in bafflement, he looked to Garalon to pick up the story.

"The aggar," he began in a raspy voice, "summoned me to prevent this world's destruction as he recognised Levinial had failed." Garalon gave Levi a look of disappointment, which made Brylee bristle with annoyance. "At first the aggar could not recall the time-riding amulet. I suspect that was because it was too embroiled in Gideon's actions, until you killed him, at which point it was released from whatever gripped it and responded to the summons.

"Using the amulet, I found Levinial recovering in his bed. His magic is now fully synchronised to this world due to your extensive healing and er . . . other interactions, he was able to progress the rejuvenation of his own body. We rode the amulet to this place some moments ago and found Gideon dead and the timeline breaching elsewhere, due to the combination of his and Ostryd's deaths.

"Levinial had a brilliant idea, which somewhat atones for his dereliction of duty. His talents as a weaver will be missed. We located Ostryd by traveling to the new breach and observed the attack on him. Once we understood what was transpiring, we then transported Gideon's corpse to the moment before Ostryd was killed and froze time for those present. We adjusted Gideon's corpse to resemble Ostryd and substituted the bodies a moment before the knife sliced through Ostryd's throat."

Levi took over the tale. "Gideon's corpse is in the past now, and Ostryd is here and whole. We have assessed the situation, and time is restoring itself completely. The crisis is over."

"And my work here has concluded," Garalon said, running his hand down Shanna's flank and patting her shoulder as the cat turned her head to look up at him. "I abhor needless harm to these beautiful creatures."

Without another word, Garalon opened a doorway to the beginning of time, nodded to Levi, then stepped through the portal with the amulet and vanished.

Epilogue

The Mucky Trough was the seediest bar in Haxley and one of the few that Gunnar was allowed to frequent. After arranging for Brylee to be skriked in Rostal and spreading the news that she was a filthy charmer, he enjoyed a moon of terrorising Raegan at the Crow's Nest before "they" visited him. He didn't know who the visitors worked for, nor did Judd, who received similar attention. The hard men were criminals judging by their demeanour, but they took no money from him. However, they banned him and Judd from most places not directly related to their employment upon pain of severe beatings or death.

It could have been worse, Gunnar thought, feeling good about having seduced Dabby Chandler, who kept his bed warm most nights. She was a pretty lass, younger and more willing than Raegan had been and more easily cowed with a backhand. Part of him wished she had more fight in her, having agreed to marry him perhaps too quickly. His betrothal to Dabby didn't stop him from having fun on the side, though. The skank at the table with him now had fallen for his lines and joined him for a drink. He would make sure the money he spent on her led to sex. The woman had a bit more spark in her eyes, and he would enjoy dominating her until she knew her place. Perhaps she would be a better bet than Dabby, but time would tell.

"Ain't you with that lass, Dabby?" the skank asked. "I don't eat from another's fruit bowl." He wanted a spark, but this was the sort of pushback he wanted to knock out of his women.

"I didn't say I wanted to bed you," Gunnar said. "Do you think me the cheating type?"

"Cheatin' don't start with sex, Gunnar. It starts with sneaky talking, dunnit? And that's what you been doin' for ten minutes."

Gunnar was about to grab the woman's forearm—he knew a bit of pressure was a good way to underscore whatever barb he was about to come up with—only to realise he couldn't move. Something hard and rough had wrapped itself around his body, even clamping his mouth closed. He could breathe, but barely.

The woman's face began to change right in front of him. It became fleshier, her chin stronger and her lips redder. Her hair shortened and changed colour. He knew the new face from somewhere, but in his terror he couldn't place it. Then he did. He hadn't spoken to Vekki personally, at Judd's insistence, but he had seen her from afar. What did a mage's apprentice want with him?

"This was the last face you expected Brylee Plainhand to see when you arranged for her to be skriked," Vekki said. "Vekki trapped Brylee just like you are now and tried to suck the life out of her."

Gunnar felt a tugging on his soul for a few moments, and then it stopped. *Tried?*

Vekki's face changed again. Gunnar couldn't move, but he felt his bladder release and his lap get warm.

"You told everyone here I was a charmer," the woman said, now wearing Brylee's face. "You put me and my family at risk."

Gunnar wanted to shake his head and deny it, say he didn't, but he was powerless. Whatever held him squeezed and heated up. It felt like every thud of his heart would break it out of his chest. His body trembled in terror within her relentless grip.

"But you had it wrong," Brylee continued. "I'm not a charmer; I'm a full mage. I'm back, and there isn't room for both of us in this town. If I were you, Gunnar, I wouldn't be here in two hours' time. I'd leave Dabby and everything you can't pack on your sorry horse and go somewhere else. But you won't be done with me even then. My magic will track you wherever you go. I could be anyone..." She changed her face to mirror his. "And I mean *anyone* you try to mess with." She made him repeat her expectations and the consequences of non-compliance, released him, then sent him running from the tavern.

Brylee had visited Judd at his estate on the way to town and given him a similar ultimatum. Judd had a moon to wrap up his more complex interests, but he couldn't come to Haxley during that time or breathe a word of her visit if he wished to see another summer.

Brylee had visited her parents earlier that day. She sent a messenger just ahead of her arrival, warning them that she was alive and coming home. When she had disappeared in Rostal and news broke she was a charmer, everyone assumed she had been skriked. Brylee felt it was cruel to let those close to her believe she was dead, but she thought she could never return, and their searching for her would put them at risk.

When she walked through her parents' front door, they greeted her with tears in their eyes. She didn't try to sneak through the kitchen this time as she was so excited to see them. Brylee checked her father's health and was pleased with the work Wickham's healer associate had done.

She spent two hours with them, eating a special meal that Fifi had prepared. As they ate, she shared a story that she, Levi, and Wickham had concocted. She also listened to what they had done with Wispy Weed and the business in her absence. Brylee was impressed with their accomplishments. They had even landed some contracts she had been pursuing for years. Her father's revived health and his feeling of loss over Brylee's disappearance and presumed death had filled him with more vigour than she would have guessed. Brylee teared up. This was the father she had loved without reservation, restored to her by circumstances and healing. She wouldn't forget this version of him so readily now. The following day she would introduce them to Jyan—who was visiting with Mella today—and see if they wanted to follow through on the notion of growing and distributing grou't.

Jig and Jag had been manning the door at the Barrow Building and had wrapped her in bear hugs until she made them put her down. Jig insisted on leaving his post and riding the elevator up to the tavern at her side. Raegan was crouched behind the bar putting the takings in a safe as Brylee stepped out onto the rooftop. Stacii Willow was about to call out, but Brylee held a finger to her lips as she crept over to sit on a barstool.

When Raegan stood, Brylee complained about the speed of the service and then watched a series of emotions ripple across her best friend's face: offence, recognition, disbelief, and then joy.

"You cow!" Raegan squealed. "You're alive?"

Both women raced around the bar into a hug filled with tears.

Modwyn heard the commotion and left her office to see what was going on. She joined in once she saw who was back from the dead.

Levi, Lu, and Ostryd had arrived at the bar moments ahead of Brylee and were introduced over drinks. They all chipped in as Brylee shared the highlights of her adventures. As Lu explained how she had almost lost to a man she thought was a much lower skill level than herself, Brylee added that she now felt safe to return and tell people she wasn't dead. No mage would touch her, and there was no Red Assassin.

"But what happened to Shanna?" Raegan gripped Lu's hand, ready to console her.

Lu laughed. "She's fine. She's a tough old lady. Smak found a mate near Hardings and stayed there. Shanna and Tak are roaming Plainhand Estate as we speak."

"You didn't seem this upset when you thought I was dead," Brylee replied, laughing. They shared a look and then swallowed hard, affirming her joke was far from true.

Raegan stood and hugged her friend once more, afraid it was all a dream. Stacii brought over more drinks, and Brylee shared what she had done to Gunnar and Judd.

"I still don't understand why you couldn't save Brightstone and Winter," Modwyn said, casting a compassionate look towards Ostryd.

"Garalon had the amulet, and it was his decision," Levi explained. "That is our way. And I agree with him about Winter. Strictly speaking, our code mandates Brightstone's situation also remain unchanged. With my new emotional attachment to you all and this world, I might have saved her, were it within my power. But to Garalon, who sets the rules and is a stickler for them, it was unacceptable. And as sad as that is, I understand it."

"I'm so sorry about your daughter," said Lu, putting her hand on top of Ostryd's, expecting him to recoil from her touch to avoid her germs, but he just sat unmoving. After a while, looking at no one in particular he broke the silence that settled around them.

"In four thousand years I've lost many loved ones. Some to age, some to illness, and a few to violence. I grieve them all, and you never get used to it." He stopped talking but the table remained quiet, sensing he was trying to release another thought from the depth of his trauma. "Gideon's betrayal is devastating, but that night, when his drugs rendered me frozen and unable to hold my secrets, he was changed. His voice was different, his pattern of speech . . . Even as he told me he had drugged Brightstone and neither of us would see the sun again, I felt it wasn't him talking. I lie at night wondering." He wiped several tears off his cheeks. "What sort of party is this?" he said, pulling his hand from Lu and waving the attention away from himself.

"Now you're trapped here, in our time, with this old hag," Raegan said to Levi, as she elbowed her friend in an attempt to lighten the mood. Levi put his arm around Brylee's shoulders.

"I think I can bear it," he said, a smirk creeping across his face.

"If it's not too personal a question," Modwyn said, "are you still a time weaver?"

Levi's smile didn't falter, but his eyes softened. "I still have the mind and the memory that I brought to this world. Garalon took the time amulet back to the aggar, so I'm in this 'now' for the remainder of my life." Levi tightened his arm around Brylee before he continued. "This body ages just like yours does."

"So, are you back for good? Taking over Plainhand again?" Raegan asked Brylee.

"No, I think it's in good hands at the moment," Brylee replied. "I'm excited to see if Father and Jyan can make grou't grow here, but I have other dreams now. I bought you some grou't, Raegan. If you like, you could be the first outlet in Haxley. Levi seems to have transitioned almost fully from his source of magic to ours and has the mind of a primi. He wants to start a college teaching primi magic as part of the Council of Magical Law to anyone who is capable. That will depend on discussions with them, of course, but if it goes ahead, we'll want to spend part of the year in Nuulan. Lu is interested in meeting Reni and talking about a fighting academy with Sirius. That will be in Nuulan and Rostal as well, perhaps."

"But what will you do?" Raegan asked. "I've just got you back."

"Oh, you'll see a lot of me. I'm going to invite Farriar here to help me start up a new franchise of Work Hive. Domestic work and farm and transportation services. And I purchased the Linger Longer. It's got great potential, and I was hoping you would help me hire the right people to make it as good as the Crow's Nest."

As the conversation broadened to expand on everyone's dreams for the future, Brylee felt a twinge deep in her tummy. She looked into her body with her magical sight and was delighted at what she saw.

She met Levi's eye. He had sensed her discomfort, and he glanced down and used his own magical sight. Then his face lit up in a silly grin. They clasped each other's hands and silently agreed it was too early to tell their friends that some of their plans might have to wait until after the baby was born.

What's next?

If you enjoyed *Strands of Time and Magic*, please consider leaving a review (even if it's just a few lines) on Amazon, Goodreads, or whichever platform you prefer. Reviews help other readers find books they enjoy and are much appreciated by the author.

For more information about the Weavers of Destiny series, and to receive updates on new and upcoming books, exclusive offers, and behind-the-scenes content, visit my website at:
www.andrewplatten.com.

As a thank you for subscribing to my newsletter, you'll receive a free copy of *Bonds of Ascension*. This novella is a shorter read that explores Lu's coming of age in the fierce Mobi'dern clan before the events of *Strands of Time and Magic*.

Acknowledgements

Darielle, my fun and patient wife, encouraged me to write this novel and worked hard with me on almost every aspect. I may have created the initial story and characters but our (too) frequent trips to the pub to debate (bicker), brainstorm, and agonise brought the manuscript to life. She has been my inspiration and coach, and together we are plumbing the mysteries of editing, marketing, and the dozens of other things that go into getting Brylee and friends into your hands. Thank you, Darielle, the novel would not exist without you.

I want to express my gratitude to Zenia, my daughter, who is the author of our family. Witnessing her bring her own novels to life has been truly inspiring. Despite juggling two jobs, she found time to offer an invaluable peer review. However, it was her patience in answering countless spontaneous questions about character flaws, eliminating adverbs, and delving into the technical minutiae that newbies like me must learn about our craft that truly made a remarkable difference in my writing journey.

Darren Bold collects rare books and knows so much about the craft and industry it makes me wonder when we will see him publish one of his own. Darren was the first beta reader to give me feedback, at a time I was too close to the project to know if my draft had potential. Thank you for instilling the confidence in me to press on, and your insights into Ostryd, especially.

Nicole Bertram (owner of the very cool *Spool Sewing Studio* in the Comox Valley) was so insightful about my character and world building and suggested several key improvements. Thank you, Nicole, for your detailed insights, but also for teaching me to sew, in case I need a fallback career.

Roxanne Hopkins spotted several embarrassing plot holes and raised great questions about how I had approached a character's mental state. Getting this right was critical to the grand finale. Thank you, Roxanne, for your keen attention to detail.

When I accepted that Roxanne (mentioned above) had a valid point, I found myself fortunate to have recently crossed paths with Cheryl Lynn Lim, M.C., C.C.C., Registered Clinical Counsellor,

Clinical Supervisor, and Owner of Walk Along Side Counselling. Cheryl's expertise in mental health, combined with her shared love for fantasy literature, proved invaluable in providing feedback that ensured the authenticity and compelling nature of a crucial character's emotional struggles. Cheryl, I am immensely grateful for your assistance in allowing me to exercise my artistic license while maintaining believability. Thank you.

Anita Kuehnel-Atar, thank you for donating so much of your time helping me understand writing structure and grammar, as well as providing me endless moral support.

And, last but not least, thank you Kevin Miller, award-winning author and filmmaker, who professionally evaluated the draft manuscript, encouraged me to move forward to publishing and later diligently edited it. Are you sure I can't keep at least some of those adverbs, Kevin?

About the Author

Born in England, I emigrated to Canada with my two children and now live in the Comox Valley on Vancouver Island.

My initial career was in technology; a realm akin to magic with its ability to make lives better (and worse). It has mystery, a language few can master, and often fails us just when we need it most. It's no surprise to me that many who revel in fantasy are drawn from the ranks of technology.

I am a view junkie and am drawn to places where I can imagine being an explorer discovering them for the first time. It's why I became a pilot. People-watching is also one of my favourite hobbies. I try to understand how our minds, perceptions, and emotions work. The hundreds of hours of podcasts and papers I devour don't make me a psychology expert, but they have helped me develop the characters that act out the book's plot.

Oh, and I am tormented by cheese. I love cheese.

Learn more about me, my work, events, and access bonus content at www.andrewplatten.com

Printed in Great Britain
by Amazon

53586578R00263